"Nash?"

He opened his eyes to find Regan staring up at him, surprise, fear, and fascination written across her face. "Your eyes," she said. "They're glowing red."

"A trick of the light." He leaned closer, close enough to nibble at her full lower lip.

"But—"

He sucked at her lip. "Kiss me back," he murmured against her mouth, and felt her shudder. "Kiss me," he said again, his words demanding. "You want me. Almost as much as I want you. I'm going to make you moan," he promised. "I'm going to make you beg."

Regan uttered a sobbing sigh as he licked and kissed her, lingering at the hollow of her throat, sucking, tasting, feeling the thrum of her heartbeat under his tongue. She stifled a small scream, biting down hard on her lip.

Blood. The scent filled his head, feeding his darkest desires. With a choked growl, he lunged for her throat.

ALSO BY CATHERINE MULVANY

Shadows All Around Her

Run No More

I'll Be Home for Christmas
A Short Story Anthology

Something
Wicked

CATHERINE
MULVANY

Pocket Star Books
New York   London   Toronto   Sydney

An Original Publication of POCKET STAR BOOKS

Pocket Star Books
A Division of Simon & Schuster, Inc.
1230 Avenue of the Americas
New York, NY 10020

Copyright © 2007 by Catherine Mulvany

First Pocket Star Books paperback edition August 2007

POCKET STAR BOOKS and colophon are registered trademarks of Simon & Schuster, Inc.

For information regarding special discounts for bulk purchases, please contact Simon & Schuster Special Sales at 1-800-456-6798 or business@simonandschuster.com.

Cover design by Min Choi
Cover art by Craig White

Manufactured in the United States of America

10 9 8 7 6 5 4 3 2 1

ISBN-13: 978-1-4165-2557-8
ISBN-10:   1-4165-2557-2

By the pricking of my thumbs,
Something wicked this way comes.

—William Shakespeare,
Macbeth, act IV, scene I

ONE

The late-afternoon sun beat down like a curse. A hundred and two in the shade. Not that there was any shade. "Go to hell, Ms. Cluny," reclusive philanthropist Charles Cunningham Nash had said the last time Regan had pestered him for an interview. And here she freaking was.

A clever woman would have realized fate was conspiring against her when mechanical difficulties delayed her flight from JFK to Reno. A clever woman would have taken the hint when her favorite Louis Vuitton bag vanished into luggage limbo. A clever woman would have said, "Screw this," when her rental car's air conditioner gasped its last shortly after she crossed the California border.

But Regan had persevered.

Huge mistake.

The only thing playing on the radio now was static, the gas gauge was flirting with empty, and Juniper Basin was nowhere to be seen, even though according to the MapQuest directions she'd taped to the Corolla's dash, she should have been there already. She must have made a wrong turn somewhere.

Right. Like the second she'd decided to pursue this story so doggedly. After all, those tabloid photos had been obvious fakes. Alien cities buried deep beneath the Modoc Plateau? No way. But her instincts had told her to follow her nose, and damn it, Nash's lame-assed explanation of what he and his team of archaeologists were really doing out here in the middle of nowhere stank to high heaven. After all, why would anyone invest millions to excavate a nondescript Paleo-Indian village unlikely to yield anything more exciting than Clovis points and grinding stones?

Still, was tracking down the truth worth a detour through hell?

The molten sun was riding the rimrocks by the time Regan reached the next outpost of civilization, a blink-your-eyes-and-miss-it town named Chisel Rock.

She pulled up to the pumps in front of the Oasis Truck Stop, where neon palm trees decorated one windowless side wall of the cinder-block building housing the restaurant and minimart. A shabby twelve-unit motel edged the back of the property, and to the west stood a row of Lombardy poplar skeletons, their elongated shadows stretching across the parking lot like bony fingers. Two dusty pickup trucks, a PT Cruiser, and half a dozen cherried-out Harleys huddled in the meager shade.

Wasn't exactly the Big Apple, but Regan figured someone inside could tell her how to find the dig at Juniper Basin. She unbuckled her seat belt and stepped out of the car.

A bowlegged mutt with a scruffy patchwork coat suddenly bounced out from between two big rigs parked along the shoulder on the opposite side of the highway. The dog crossed the road at a trot, then made a wide detour around her before pausing to christen both rear tires of the Corolla.

"Amen, buddy." Smiling in grim amusement, Regan filled her tank, then headed inside to pay.

The Oasis's interior reeked of stale grease. An old-fashioned jukebox blared eighties tunes at a deafening decibel level. Worse yet, the moment Regan crossed the threshold, six badass biker types glanced up from the pool table in the corner to focus their X-ray vision on the front of her cami. None of which carried any weight when balanced against the blessing of air-conditioning.

"Pump two." She handed a twenty to the middle-aged brunette at the cash register. "What's the best way to get to Juniper Basin?"

The cashier rang up the gas and counted back the change. "Never heard of the place, but then, I'm from Reno. Haven't lived here long. Josh!" she called to a lanky teenager who was busing tables on the far side of the room.

"Yeah?" The kid stuffed a tip in the pocket of his Wranglers.

"Lady here's looking for directions to Juniper Basin."

The kid ambled across the dining room to Regan's side. "You looking for Mr. Nash, too?"

"Too?" she said.

"His dig site's become a regular tourist attraction since it got all that media attention." He shot her a puzzled look, probably thinking she didn't fit the profile. Most tourists weren't stupid enough to set off across the desert in silk suits and stilettos.

"Charles Cunningham Nash and I have business to discuss," she said. "He gave me directions to Juniper Basin"—which was a lie of the big fat you're-going-to-hell variety—"but I got turned around. Could you help me, Josh? I'd really appreciate it." She gave him her best pleading, doe-eyed look.

He turned three shades of pink and shot her a shy smile. "Yes, ma'am," he said.

Ma'am? Since when did thirty-three qualify a woman for ma'amhood?

"Take the first gravel road to the left just past the church and follow it to hell and gone," he said, "until you come to Calliope Rock, a formation that looks like a big pipe organ. Little dirt track there cuts off to the right along the riverbank. The dig's about a mile in. Can't miss it. Just look for all the tents lined up along the edge of the basin."

Lightbulb moment. Juniper Basin wasn't a town. It was an actual basin.

So much for MapQuest.

"Be careful if you're headed out that way, though. Road's full of ruts and potholes. Easy to get high-centered. You don't want to end up buzzard bait." A faint frown drove a line between his eyebrows. "In fact, if I were you, I'd stay overnight here in Chisel Rock and head for the dig site in the morning."

"Don't tell me. Your parents own the motel."

"Well, yeah, but—"

"How long a drive are we talking about?" she asked.

"Half an hour. Forty-five minutes tops, only—"

"Thanks. You've been a big help." She treated him to fluttery eyelashes and a sultry smile. *Ma'am that, cowboy.*

Regan moved her car around the side of the building, parking under the neon palm trees. Then she headed inside again where she lingered over a Coke, reluctant to go back out into the heat. Twenty minutes ticked by. Finally, grabbing a six-pack of bottled water—buzzard bait was so *not* a good look on her—she settled her bill.

She emerged from the air-conditioned interior to find that the sun had dropped behind the mountains, leaving the town swathed in gray twilight. She'd assumed she had a couple hours of daylight left to find Nash's camp, but she hadn't factored in the brevity of the desert dusk.

She brushed past the bikers, who, having abandoned the pool table, now loitered under the awning that shaded the front of the building. Ignoring their lewd suggestions and mocking laughter, she hurried to her car. The directions, which had sounded relatively straightforward in daylight, now seemed a lot trickier. Would she be able to find her way in the dark? Maybe Josh's suggestion about staying the night here in Chisel Rock wasn't such a bad one after all.

Juggling her water and purse in one hand, she fumbled for the car keys.

A breeze stirred the rapidly cooling air, carrying with it a musky male scent.

Regan spun around to find that one of the bikers had followed her. He crowded close, backing her against the Toyota. Taller than average and muscular, with dark eyes, dark hair, heavy beard stubble, and an all-too-lifelike snake tattoo coiled around one arm, he was dressed in fatigues and a grubby wifebeater. "Need some help, blondie?"

"No, thanks," she said, feigning a calm she was far from feeling. "I'm fine."

He grinned. "Yeah. Yeah, you are." He grabbed her chin and tilted her face up to his. Their gazes locked. His grin faded, and the color leached from his face. "Katie?"

Katie?

He released her chin. His hand was trembling. "How?" he demanded, his voice husky with emotion. "I don't understand."

Neither did Regan. "Look, I—"

"You're dead."

Despite the heat, gooseflesh rose along her arms.

What can you earn?

Grooms can start at around £12,500 a year
Experienced grooms can earn around £16,000
Head lads/girls in a racing yard can earn £20,000 or more.
Some employers provide accommodation, food, free stabling for your own horse and riding lessons.

Entry requirements

You must be at least 16, and there may be weight restrictions for some jobs. Although you may not need qualifications, employers may prefer you to have experience, and some may ask for a nationally-recognised qualification such as:

- BTEC Level 2 Certificate and Diploma in Horse Care
- BTEC Level 3 Diploma in Horse Management
- British Horse Society (BHS) Stage 1 in Horse Knowledge and Care
- Association of British Riding Schools (ABRS) Preliminary Horse Care and Riding Certificate.

BHS or ABRS qualifications you must be at least 16, and would usually experience of handling and riding horses. Visit the BHS and ABRS s for details.

d get practical experience as a volunteer, for example helping out at a . This could give you an advantage when looking for paid work.

n in race-horse care at the British Racing School in Newmarket hern Racing College in Doncaster. You will not need riding start, as there is a non-rider option up to NVQ level 2. rainees do ride. sted in the horse breeding industry, you can train at the n Newmarket or at other training centres. See the ders' Association website for details.

t into this job through an Apprenticeship scheme. The s available in your area will depend on the local jobs

---

More information

National Gamekeepers Organisation
www.nationalgamekeepers.org.uk

Scottish Gamekeepers Association
www.scottishgamekeepers.co.uk

GROUNDS PERSON OR GREEN KEEPER

The nature of the work

Your main responsibility would be to manage the soil and grass to make sure the turf is always in top condition. Your duties would typically include:

- preparing land for turf laying
- applying nutrients
- rolling and mowing the turf
- identifying and controlling weeds
- setting out and marking lines on surfaces
- installing and maintaining equipment like nets, posts and protective covers
- ensuring irrigation and drainage systems are maintained
- looking after surrounding areas - decorative displays, concrete or tarmac
- operating equipment like hedge cutters, strimmers and ride-on mowers
- painting, removing rubbish and carrying out general duties
- maintaining good communication with your customers

Your tasks would vary according to the season and weather conditions.

What can you earn?

Salary scales for this work can be:
Groundsperson: £14,985 to £18,310 a year
Skilled groundsperson: £18,700 to £22,850
Head groundsperson: £24,445 to £31,795.

There may be bonuses and payment for overtime, and accommodation is sometimes provided.

Entry requirements

If you have experience in horticulture, you could find work as an unskilled groundsperson without relevant qualifications. You may then be able to progress to skilled level by gaining experience and working towards qualifications.

Alternatively, you could start by doing a course that would help you develop the skills needed for the job. Relevant courses include:

- Certificate/Diploma in Horticulture at levels 2 and 3
- Certificate/Diploma in Sports and Amenity Turf Maintenance at Level 2.
- Entry requirements for courses vary, so you should check directly with colleges.
- A driving licence will be useful for some jobs.
- You may be able to get into this job through an Apprenticeship scheme. The range of Apprenticeships available in your area will depend on the local jobs market and the types of skills employers need from their workers.

More information

Lantra
Lantra House
Stoneleigh Park
Nr Coventry
Warwickshire
CV8 2LG
Tel: 0845 707 8007
www.lantra.co.uk

Institute of Groundsmanship (IOG)
28 Stratford Office Village
Wolverton Mill East
Milton Keynes

MK12 5TW
Tel: 01908 312511
www.iog.org

British and International Golf Greenkeepers Association Limited (BIGGA)
BIGGA HOUSE
Aldwark
Alne
York
YO61 1UF
Tel:+44(0)1347 833800
Fax:+44(0)1347 833801
Email:info@bigga.co.uk
www.bigga.org.uk

HORSE GROOM

The nature of the work

As a groom, you would:

- provide food and water for horses
- replace bedding
- clean equipment such as saddles and bridl
- clean, brush and sometimes clip, horses
- muck out stables
- check for changes in the conditio
- treat minor wounds, change dr
- follow instructions from ver

You may also be responsible fo
If you work with show ju
events, and may accompa
with stallions, mares a
schools you may greet ch
on horseback.

market and the types of skills employers need from their workers. To find out more, visit the Apprenticeships website.

Visit the British Horse Racing Board careers website for full details of careers in horse-racing and breeding.

More information
Lantra
Lantra House
Stoneleigh Park
Nr Coventry
Warwickshire
CV8 2LG
Tel: 0845 707 8007
www.lantra.co.uk

British Racing School (BRS)
Snailwell Road
Newmarket
Suffolk
CB8 7NU
Tel: 01638 665103
www.brs.org.uk

Northern Racing College (NRC)
The Stables
Rossington Hall
Great North Road
Doncaster
South Yorkshire
DN11 0HN
Tel: 01302 861000
www.northernracingcollege.co.uk

Association of British Riding Schools (ABRS)
Queens Chambers
38-40 Queen Street
Penzance

Cornwall
TR18 4BH
Tel: 01736 369440
www.abrs-info.org

British Horseracing Authority
www.britishhorseracing.com

British Horse Society (BHS)
Stoneleigh Deer Park
Kenilworth
Warwickshire
CV8 2XZ
Tel: 0844 848 1666
www.bhs.co.uk

HORTICULTURAL MANAGER

The nature of the work

As a horticultural manager you would oversee the development and growth of plants for one of the following purposes:

- Production / commercial horticulture - producing food crops and ornamental plants for sale to wholesalers, retailers, nurseries, garden centres and the public
- garden centres - producing plants for sale to the public along with products such as tools and garden furniture
- Parks and Gardens - designing, constructing, managing and maintaining areas such as parks, gardens (historic or botanic) and public green spaces.

Your day-to-day tasks would vary depending on your particular job, but could include:

- managing, and possibly helping with, all aspects of cultivation
- preparing and modifying operational and business plans

- keeping records and handling budgets and accounts
- analysing procurement costs
- developing new products and markets and negotiating with suppliers
- designing layouts and developing planting programmes
- scheduling the planting and harvesting of crops
- managing the implementation of health and safety regulations and procedures
- recruiting and managing staff
- maintaining a skilled and trained workforce

What can you earn?

Horticultural managers can earn from around £16,000 to over £30,000 a year.
Senior managers can earn around £40,000.
Figures are intended as a guideline only.

Entry requirements

You may be able to work your way up to management by starting in a more basic position and gaining experience and qualifications.

To start directly as a manager, you would usually need a higher education qualification and practical experience. Relevant qualifications include:

- degrees in subjects such as horticulture and commercial horticulture
- BTEC HNCs/HNDs and foundation degrees in subjects like horticulture, horticultural management and professional horticulture.

You should check with colleges and universities for their exact entry requirements as these can vary.
You can also complete Royal Horticultural Society (RHS) qualifications:
See the RHS website for details of qualifications and a list of course providers.

Examples of the ways you can gain practical experience include:

- work placements
- RHS voluntary internships

- Management Development Services graduate training – a paid programme of job placements and formal training for the food and produce industry.

See the Management Development Service website for details of their graduate training.

If you have not gained experience before, during or after a course you may need to begin at a more basic level before being considered for a management position. You could move into horticultural management if you have appropriate experience in a related area, such as farming, forestry, retailing or marketing.

More information
Management Development Services Ltd
www.mds-ltd.co.uk

National Trust
www.nationaltrust.org.uk

Royal Horticultural Society (RHS)
www.rhs.org.uk

Lantra
Lantra House
Stoneleigh Park
Nr Coventry
Warwickshire
CV8 2LG
Tel: 0845 707 8007
www.lantra.co.uk

Grow Careers
www.growcareers.info

Institute of Horticulture
www.horticulture.org.uk
hs.org.uk

10. THE HEALTH SERVICE

The health sector is a large and diverse area. the job opportunities are very varied and are within the private and public sectors, mainly the NHS. In this section we cover mainly NHS opportunities as follows:

- Adult Nurse
- Ambulance Paramedic
- Anesthetist
- Clinical Support Worker
- Health Visitor
- Health Service manager
- Hospital Doctor
- Hospital Porter
- Mental Health Nurse
- Occupational Therapist
- Pharmacist
- Physiotherapist
- School Nurse
- Speech and Language Therapy Assistant
- Radiographer
- Surgeon
- Psychiatrist

For further details about the wide variety of jobs in the health sector (NHS) you should go to:

NHS Careers
PO Box 2311
Bristol
BS2 2ZX
Tel: 0345 60 60 655
www.nhscareers.nhs.uk

ADULT NURSE

The nature of the work

Adult nurses check patients' progress and decide with doctors what care to give. They may also advise and support patients and their relatives.

As an adult nurse, the practical care you give could include:

- checking temperatures
- measuring blood pressure and breathing rates
- helping doctors with physical examinations
- giving drugs and injections
- cleaning and dressing wounds
- giving blood transfusions
- using high technology (high-tech) medical equipment.

You could specialise in an area such as accident and emergency, cardiac rehabilitation, outpatients, neonatal nursing, and operating theatre work. As well as hospitals, you could also work in the community, health centres, clinics or prisons.

What can you earn?

Nurses can earn between £21,176 and £27,534 a year. Nurse team leaders and managers can earn around £30,460 to £40,157 a year. Nurse consultants can earn up to £55,945 a year. Extra allowances may be paid to those living in or around London.

Entry requirements

To work as an adult nurse, you need a Nursing and Midwifery Council (NMC)-approved degree or Diploma of Higher Education in Nursing (adult branch). Please note: The final opportunity to start the nursing diploma will be Spring 2013. From September 2013, students will only be able to qualify as a nurse by studying for a degree.

To do an approved course, you need:

- proof of your English and maths skills, good health and good character

138

- evidence of recent successful study (especially if you have been out of education for a number of years)
- Criminal Records Bureau (CRB) clearance.

Course providers can also set their own academic entry requirements, which can include:

- for a nursing diploma – five GCSEs (A-C) preferably in English, maths and/or a science-based subject
- for a nursing degree – the same GCSEs as the diploma, plus two or three A levels, possibly including a biological science or an equivalent qualification.

Some course providers offer Advanced Diplomas in Adult Nursing. This qualification and the entry requirements lie between diploma and degree level.

Check with universities for exact entry requirements, as other qualifications, such as an Access to Higher Education course, may also be accepted. For a list of degree and diploma course providers and application advice, visit the Universities and Colleges Admissions Service (UCAS) website.

You may be able to become an adult nurse through an Apprenticeship scheme. You will need to check which schemes are available in your area.

Professional registration

As a qualified nurse you must renew your professional registration with the NMC every three years. To renew, you need to have worked a minimum of 450 hours and completed at least five study days of professional development every three years. Check with the NMC for details.

Return to practice

If you are a former registered nurse wanting to return to the profession, you can take a return-to-practice course. Contact your local NHS Trust for details.

More information

Nursing and Midwifery Council (NMC)
23 Portland Place
London
W1B 1PZ
Tel: 020 7333 9333
www.nmc-uk.org

Queens University of Belfast
School of Nursing and Midwifery
Medical Biology Centre
97 Lisburn Road
Belfast
BT9 7BL
Tel: 028 9097 2233
www.qub.ac.uk

University of Ulster at Jordanstown
School of Nursing
Shore Road
Newtownabbey
Co Antrim
BT37 0QB
Tel: 08700 400 700
www.ulster.ac.uk

Health Learning and Skills Advice Line
Tel: 08000 150850

National Leadership and Innovation Agency for Healthcare
Innovation House
Bridgend Road
Llanharan
CF72 9RP
Tel: 01443 233 333
www.nliah.wales.nhs.uk/

NHS Careers
PO Box 2311
Bristol

BS2 2ZX
Tel: 0345 60 60 655
www.nhscareers.nhs.uk

Skills for Health
Goldsmiths House
Broad Plain
Bristol
BS2 0JP
Tel: 0117 922 1155
www.skillsforhealth.org.uk

AMBULANCE PARAMEDIC

The nature of the work

As a paramedic, you could deal with a range of situations, from minor wounds to serious injuries caused by a major road or rail accident. Your job would be to provide immediate care or treatment.

When responding to a call, you would check a patient's condition and decide what action to take. Your work may also include:

- making quick decisions about moving the patient
- using advanced life support techniques, such as electric shocks, to resuscitate patients
- carrying out surgical procedures, such as inserting a breathing tube
- using advanced devices to keep people breathing
- providing drug and fluid therapy
- giving medicines and injections
- putting on dressings for wounds and supports for broken bones.

Daily tasks include keeping accurate records and checking equipment.

You could work on a traditional ambulance or alone using a car, motorbike or bicycle. With experience you could work in a helicopter ambulance team.

What can you earn?

Student paramedics may be paid around £15,500 to £18,600 a year.

Qualified paramedics can earn around £21,200 to £27,500 a year.

Emergency care practitioners (ECPs) and team leaders can earn up to £34,200 a year, and area managers may earn around £40,200 a year.

Additional allowances may be paid to staff in certain parts of the country and to those working on standby or in shift patterns.

Entry requirements

You need to be registered with the Health Professions Council before you can work unsupervised as a paramedic. To join the register, you need to complete a Health Professions Council (HPC) approved qualification that includes clinical placements with an ambulance service and various other health providers.

There are two ways that you can work towards HPC registration:

- by taking a Foundation Degree, Diploma of Higher Education (DipHE), or degree in paramedic emergency care (other subject titles may also be used)
- by getting a student paramedic job with an Ambulance Trust and studying whilst learning on the job (see the NHS Jobs website for vacancies).

To do a course, you will usually need five GCSEs (A-C) including English, maths and science, and between one and three A levels, often including a science. Check with course providers for exact requirements as other qualifications, such as an Access to Higher Education course, may also be accepted. Course providers are listed on the HPC website.

For a student paramedic job, requirements can vary but in general you will need:

- four or five GCSEs (A-C) including English, maths and science
- **or** around 12 months' experience as an ambulance care assistant, technician or emergency care assistant, plus evidence that you can study at higher education level. Some employers prefer those with Open University 'Openings' course credits, which cover research and study skills.

For further advice, contact your local ambulance service. These are listed on the NHS Choices website.

More information

Health Professions Council
Park House
184 Kennington Park Road
London
SE11 4BU
Tel: 020 7582 0866
www.hpc-uk.org

NHS Careers
PO Box 2311
Bristol
BS2 2ZX
Tel: 0345 60 60 655
www.nhscareers.nhs.uk

College of Paramedics
The Exchange
Express Park
Bristol Road
Bridgewater
TA6 4RR
Tel: 01278 420 014
www.collegeofparamedics.co.uk

Health Learning and Skills Advice Line
Tel: 08000 150850

ANESTHETIST

The nature of the work
Anesthetists are qualified medical doctors who specialise in pain management, anesthesia for surgery and intensive care. They often deal with emergency situations by providing advanced life support, the ability to breathe and resuscitation to the heart and lungs.

- As an anesthetist, your work could include:

- preparing patients for surgery and giving anesthesia
- relieving pain during childbirth
- easing pain after an operation
- managing acute and chronic pain
- helping psychiatric patients receiving electric shock therapy
- providing sedation and anesthesia to patients having radiology and radio-therapy.

You would use a range of techniques, including local anesthetics such as epidurals and other nerve blocks. During an operation, you would observe your patient, monitor their progress and respond to any changes. You would work closely with other healthcare professionals to provide the most appropriate and complete treatment plan for your patients.

You could work in areas ranging from high dependency units to cardiac arrest teams. As a senior doctor, you could lead a team and train junior doctors, undergraduate medical students, nurses and paramedics.

What can you earn?
Foundation house officers (junior doctors) can earn between £33,300 and £41,300 a year.

Doctors in specialist training can earn up to £69,400, and consultants can earn between £74,500 and £180,000 a year.

The salaries given for doctors in training include an additional amount based on average hours of overtime worked, time spent covering unsocial hours and workload.

Consultants working in private hospitals may be paid higher fees.

Entry requirements

To become a doctor specialising in anesthetics you will need to complete:

- a degree in medicine, recognised by the General Medical Council (GMC)
- a two-year foundation programme of general training
- three years of core training, including acute care
- higher specialty training in anesthesia, intensive care medicine and pain management.

To do a five-year degree in medicine you will usually need at least five GCSEs (A-C) including English, maths and science, plus three A levels at grades AAB in subjects such as chemistry, biology and either physics or maths. See the GMC website for details of recognised courses.

If you do not have qualifications in science, you may be able to do a six-year degree course in medicine that includes a one-year pre-medical or foundation course. You will need to check with individual universities.

If you already have an honours degree in a science subject (minimum 2:1) you may be able to join a four-year graduate entry programme to medicine. Some universities will also accept non-science graduates. See the Medical Schools Council website for details of course providers.

When you apply for a degree in medicine, you may be asked to take the UK Clinical Aptitude Test (UKCAT). Universities use this test to help them select students with the personal qualities and mental abilities needed for a career in medicine. Your university will tell you if you need to take the test.

If you trained as a doctor overseas, contact the GMC for details about registering and practising in the UK.

More information

Royal College of Anesthetists (RCA)
Churchill House
35 Red Lion Square
London
WC1R 4SG
Tel: 020 7092 1500
www.rcoa.ac.uk

UKCAT (UK Clinical Aptitude Test)
www.ukcat.ac.uk

British Medical Association (BMA)
Tavistock Square
London
WC1H 9JP
Tel: 020 7387 4499
www.bma.org.uk

General Medical Council (GMC)
Regent's Place
350 Euston Road
London
NW1 3JN
Tel: 0845 357 3456
www.gmc-uk.org

CLINICAL SUPPORT WORKER

The nature of the work

As a clinical support worker, your duties could include a range of lab skills such as:

- labelling, sorting and storing specimens
- assisting with the analysis of tissue and fluid samples
- putting together chemical solutions
- loading and operating machines
- using a computer to input and analyse data
- disposing of hazardous waste
- sterilising equipment
- maintaining stock levels.

Part of your work may also include responding to telephone enquiries as well as the keeping and filing of records.

You could work closely with scientists in a range of areas:

- biochemistry: studying chemical reactions in the body like kidney failure
- histopathology: examining the structure of diseased tissue
- virology: analysing viruses, the diseases they cause, and vaccines
- cytology: studying the structure and function of cells, and screening for cancers
- haematology: analysing diseases of the blood and blood forming tissues
- immunology: examining how the immune system works, for example with allergies

- transfusion science: transferring blood and blood products from one person to another.

You could combine your role with working in a closely related area of work such as phlebotomy.

Please see the phlebotomy job profile for more information.

What can you earn?
Clinical support workers can earn around £13,600 to £16,700 a year. With experience this can rise to around £18,500.

Entry requirements

You may not need any qualifications to start as a clinical support worker. Some employers will prefer you to have GCSEs (A-C) including English, maths and science, and basic IT and word processing skills. It would be an advantage to have experience in the NHS (especially in a lab setting) and an understanding of medical terminology.

You could contact the personnel or biomedical sciences department at your local hospital for further information on their specific entry requirements. See the NHS Choices website for details of local NHS Trusts.

Joining a professional body, such as the Association of Medical Laboratory Assistants (AMLA), could also be useful in giving you access to education and training opportunities and helping you keep your skills up to date.

More information

NHS Careers
PO Box 2311
Bristol
BS2 2ZX
Tel: 0345 60 60 655
www.nhscareers.nhs.uk

Institute of Biomedical Science
12 Coldbath Square
London
EC1R 5HL

Tel: 020 7713 0214
www.ibms.org

Health Learning and Skills Advice Line
Tel: 08000 150850

HEALTH VISITOR

The nature of the work

As a health visitor you would provide information, practical care and support to help your clients cope with any difficulties they are experiencing. You would work with a broad section of people in the community and your duties would often include:

- advising older people on health related issues
- giving advice to new mothers about their baby – for example hygiene, safety, feeding and sleeping
- counselling people on issues such as post-natal depression, bereavement or being diagnosed HIV positive
- coordinating child immunisation programmes
- organising special clinics or drop-in centres.

You would work closely with other agencies such as social services and local housing departments.

What can you earn?

Health visitors can earn between £24,800 and £33,500 a year. Team managers can earn up to £39,300.

Extra allowances may be given for additional responsibilities, location and length of service.

Entry requirements

You will usually need around two years' experience as a qualified midwife or nurse (any branch) before you can begin an approved health visitor training programme and work as a health visitor.

To qualify as a registered nurse or midwife you will need to complete a Nursing and Midwifery Council (NMC) approved degree or Diploma of Higher Education.

More information

Nursing and Midwifery Council (NMC)
23 Portland Place
London
W1B 1PZ
Tel: 020 7333 9333
www.nmc-uk.org

Queens University of Belfast
School of Nursing and Midwifery
Medical Biology Centre
97 Lisburn Road
Belfast
BT9 7BL
Tel: 028 9097 2233
www.qub.ac.uk

University of Ulster at Jordanstown
School of Nursing
Shore Road
Newtownabbey
Co Antrim
BT37 0QB
Tel: 08700 400 700
www.ulster.ac.uk

NHS Careers
PO Box 2311
Bristol
BS2 2ZX
Tel: 0345 60 60 655
www.nhscareers.nhs.uk

Community Practitioners' and Health Visitors' Association
33-37 Moreland Street

London
EC1V 8HA
Tel: 020 7505 3000
www.amicustheunion.org/cphva

Health Learning and Skills Advice Line
Tel: 08000 150850

National Leadership and Innovation Agency for Healthcare
Innovation House
Bridgend Road
Llanharan
CF72 9RP
Tel: 01443 233 333
www.nliah.wales.nhs.uk

HEALTH SERVICE MANAGER

The nature of the work
As a health service manager, your duties could include:

- supervising staff and taking responsibility for the work they do
- dealing with day-to-day operational matters
- using statistical information to monitor performance and help with long term planning
- setting and maintaining budgets
- creating and carrying out the company objectives
- implementing the policies of the board, making sure government guidelines are followed
- working with clinical staff and other professionals
- managing contracts.

Your role could range from chief executive of a large hospital to manager of a GP surgery. You could also be a manager within the ambulance service, community health service (Primary Care Trust) or a strategic health authority (local NHS headquarters, monitoring service and performance of local NHS Trusts). Alternatively, you could specialise in an area such as personnel and finance, or clinical, therapeutic or technical support.

What can you earn?

On completion of a graduate scheme, you can earn between £27,000 to £37,000 a year. Directors and chief executives can earn between £90,000 and £100,000.

Entry requirements

There are a number of ways you could get into health service management. The most direct route is through one of the NHS Graduate Management Training Schemes. To get on to a scheme, you will need a degree (minimum grade 2:2) or an equivalent qualification in a health or management related subject. Check the training and development section below for more information.

Alternative routes into health service management include:

working your way up from an administrative post by taking in-service training courses such as those run by the Institute of Healthcare Management (IHM) – to start as an administrator you are likely to need four or five GCSEs (grade A-C) and possibly A levels

- applying directly to the NHS for a junior management position – for this you will usually need a degree plus management experience
- taking an in-service training programme leading to a Certificate or Diploma in Managing Health and Social Care – for this you will usually need to be working within the NHS in a clinical role (or a profession related to health).

You can also check the IHM and NHS Careers websites for more details of schemes, training programmes and alternative entry qualifications.

More information

NHS Graduate Training Schemes
www.nhsgraduates.co.uk/About-the-NHS

NHS Careers
PO Box 2311
Bristol
BS2 2ZX

Tel: 0345 60 60 655
www.nhscareers.nhs.uk

Health Learning and Skills Advice Line
Tel: 08000 150850

Institute of Healthcare Management (IHM)
21 Morley Street
London
SE1 7QZ
Tel: 020 7620 1030
www.ihm.org.uk

HOSPITAL DOCTOR

The nature of the work

If you're interested in science and want a career in medicine, this job could be ideal for you. Hospital doctors treat illness, disease and infection in patients admitted to hospital.

To become a hospital doctor you will need a degree in medicine. And you'll also need to complete a two-year foundation programme of general training.

As a hospital doctor, you would examine and treat patients referred to you by GPs and other health professionals. You could work in one of about 60 specialist fields within four main categories: medicine, surgery, pathology and psychiatry.

Medicine – general medical conditions, emergencies, and specialisms like paediatrics, cardiology, dermatology, ophthalmology, geriatrics and neurology.

Surgery – caring for patients before, during and after an operation. You could work within one of nine areas including cardiothoracic, neurosurgery or plastic surgery.

Pathology – investigating the cause of disease and the effect on patients. You could specialise in subjects such as histopathology (diagnosing disease from changes in tissue structure), chemical pathology (examining biochemical changes relating to medical conditions) or molecular genetics (identifying abnormalities in DNA and chromosomes).

Psychiatry – working with patients experiencing mental health problems, ranging from depression and anxiety to personality disorders and addictions. Your work could include psychotherapy, counselling, psychiatric tests and prescribing medication.

You could also work in areas such as anaesthetics, obstetrics, gynaecology, radiology and oncology.

Please see the anaesthetist job profile for more information.

Your duties may include leading a team or managing a department, and teaching and supervising trainee doctors. You would keep accurate and up to date patient records, write reports, go to meetings or conferences, and keep GPs informed about the diagnosis and care of their patients.

What can you earn?
Junior hospital doctors can earn between £33,300 and £41,300 a year.

Hospital doctors in specialist training can earn up to £69,400 a year, and consultants can earn between £74,500 and £176,300 a year.

The salaries given for hospital doctors in training include an additional amount based on the average overtime worked, cover during unsocial hours and workload.

Consultants working in private hospitals may negotiate higher fees.

Entry requirements

To become a hospital doctor you need to complete:

- a degree in medicine, recognised by the General Medical Council (GMC)
- a two-year foundation programme of general training (see training and development section below)
- specialist training in your chosen area of medicine (see section below).

To do a five-year degree in medicine you will usually need at least five GCSEs (A-C) including English, maths and science, plus three A levels at grades AAB in subjects such as chemistry, biology and either physics or maths. Check the GMC website for a list of degree courses.

If you do not have qualifications in science, you may be able to join a six-year degree course in medicine. This includes a one-year pre-medical or founda tion year. If you already have a degree in a science subject (minimum 2:1) you could take a four-year graduate entry programme into medicine. Some universities will also accept non-science graduates. See the British Medical Association (BMA) website for details.

When you apply for a course, you may be asked to take the UK Clinical Aptitude Test to check your suitability for a career in medicine. This tests your mental abilities and behaviour characteristics, rather than your academic achievements. If you trained as a doctor overseas, contact the GMC for details about registering and practising in the UK.

It could be an advantage to have some relevant paid or voluntary experience, for example as a care assistant in a hospital, nursing or residential home. For paid opportunities, you could approach care homes directly or check the NHS jobs website. For voluntary work, or to arrange time watching a doctor at work, contact the voluntary services coordinator or manager at your local NHS Trust.

More information

NHS Careers
PO Box 2311
Bristol
BS2 2ZX
Tel: 0345 60 60 655
www.nhscareers.nhs.uk

Royal College of Surgeons of England
35-43 Lincoln's Inn Fields
London
WC2A 3PE
Tel: 020 7405 3474
www.rcseng.ac.uk

British Medical Association (BMA)
Tavistock Square
London
WC1H 9JP
Tel: 020 7387 4499
www.bma.org.uk

General Medical Council (GMC)
Regent's Place
350 Euston Road
London
NW1 3JN
Tel: 0845 357 3456
www.gmc-uk.org

Health Learning and Skills Advice Line
Tel: 08000 150850

HOSPITAL PORTER

The nature of the work

As a hospital porter your work could take you anywhere on the hospital site. In some hospitals you would help with security, which could involve working on the reception desk.

You could also carry out other duties such as:

- taking meals to patients
- transferring clean linen to wards from the laundry
- moving furniture and vital equipment safely
- disposing of waste, which may be hazardous
- delivering post, files and specimens, such as blood samples, to different parts of the hospital.

What can you earn?

Starting salaries can be around £13,600 a year. With experience this can rise to around £16,700 a year. Senior porters or team leaders can earn around £18,500 a year.

There are additional payments for working overtime and shifts. Salaries in private hospitals are based on those in the NHS.

Entry requirements

You do not usually need any qualifications to become a hospital porter, however you will need good written and spoken communication skills. It could help you if you have a manual handling, or health and safety qualification.

Some employers will test your physical fitness when you apply for a job, which may include a medical check. Larger hospitals or NHS Trusts may prefer you to have a driving licence so that you can work at a number of different sites during a working day.

Experience of working with the public, especially in a caring role, would be particularly helpful. If you do not have relevant experience, you could learn about this role by volunteering in a hospital, helping the porter with duties. Contact the voluntary services coordinator or manager at your local NHS Trust for further advice.

You could go on to work towards NVQ Level 2 in Support Services in Health Care.

More information

NHS Careers
PO Box 2311
Bristol
BS2 2ZX
Tel: 0345 60 60 655
www.nhscareers.nhs.uk

Health Learning and Skills Advice Line
Tel: 08000 150850

MENTAL HEALTH NURSE

The nature of the work
As a mental health nurse, you would support people who have conditions such as:

- anxiety
- depression
- stress-related illnesses
- personality disorders
- eating disorders
- drug and alcohol addiction.

You could work with a variety of clients, or specialise and work with a particular group, like adolescents or offenders. Your duties could involve:

- assessing and supporting patients
- encouraging patients to take part in role play, art, drama and discussion as therapies
- physical care, if the patient is too old or ill to look after themselves
- giving medication to patients.

You would work closely with support workers, psychiatrists, clinical psychologists and health visitors. You may also help clients if they need to deal with social workers, the police, relevant charities, local government and housing officials.

What can you earn?

Nurses can earn between £21,176 and £27,534 a year.

Team leaders and managers can earn between £30,460 and £40,157 a year, and nurse consultants can earn up to £55,945 a year.

Extra allowances may be paid to those living in or around London.

Entry requirements

To work as a mental health nurse, you will need to complete a Nursing and Midwifery Council (NMC) approved degree, or a Diploma of Higher Education in Nursing (mental health branch).

Please note: from September 2013, students will only be able to qualify as a nurse by doing a degree. Until this date, you could complete either a diploma or a degree, however the final chance to start the nursing diploma is Spring 2013.

To do an approved course, you will need:

- proof of your English and maths skills, good health and good character
- evidence of recent successful study experience (especially if you have been out of education for some time).

You must also agree to a Criminal Records Bureau (CRB) check.

You will probably need to have previous experience (paid or voluntary) of working with people. This could include those who use mental health services. If you want to gain experience like this, contact the voluntary services coordinator or manager at your local NHS Trust for details of opportunities.

Course providers can set their own academic entry requirements, which can include:

- for a nursing diploma – five GCSEs (A-C) preferably in English, maths and/or a science-based subject
- for an Advanced Diploma in Mental Health Nursing – this qualification and the entry requirements for it are between diploma and degree level
- for a nursing degree – usually the same GCSEs as the diploma, plus two or three A levels, possibly including a biological science.

Check with universities for exact entry details as other qualifications, such as an Access to Higher Education diploma, may be accepted. For a list of degree and diploma course providers and application advice, see the Universities and Colleges Admissions Service (UCAS) website.

If you are interested in social work as well, you could take a degree in, for example Mental Health Studies (Nursing and Social Work) accredited by the NMC and the General Social Care Council. After gaining your degree, you could do a variety of jobs including mental health nurse, and social worker specialising in an area such as child and adolescent mental health or substance misuse.

Funding

Nursing students starting to study in 2011 on the nursing diploma and degree courses may get non-repayable bursaries to cover living expenses. Those

158

starting their studies on an approved nursing course from September 2012 will receive a non means-tested grant of £1,000, an additional means tested bursary of £4,395 per year (£5,460 for students in London) and a reduced rate non-means tested loan.

For more information on NHS student bursaries and for eligibility, see the NHS Business Services Authority website.

Other entry routes

You could prepare for a nursing course by doing a two-year Cadet Scheme or Apprenticeship. Schemes vary between NHS Trusts, but will usually include clinical placements and working towards a QCF/ NVQ Level 3 in Health. To find out more about Apprenticeships, visit the Apprenticeships website. Contact your local NHS Trust for details of Apprenticeships and cadet scheme opportunities.

If you are a healthcare assistant with an NVQ or QCF qualification at Level 3 in Health and you have financial support from your employer, you may be able to complete part-time nurse training by applying for a secondment. You would receive a salary while you study. Once you qualify, you may need to commit to working with the NHS Trust that funded you for a minimum period.

If you have a first or second class honours degree in a subject related to health or nursing, you could qualify as a nurse by taking an accelerated programme for graduates. You can search for courses on the NHS Careers Course Finder facility.

If you are a nurse who trained outside the UK and European Economic Area (EEA), you may need to complete the Overseas Nurses Programme before you begin work. Occasionally, EEA trained nurses may be required to take an aptitude test (or similar) in order to prove professional competence. See the NMC website for details.

More information

Nursing and Midwifery Council (NMC)
23 Portland Place
London

W1B 1PZ
Tel: 020 7333 9333
www.nmc-uk.org

Queens University of Belfast
School of Nursing and Midwifery
Medical Biology Centre
97 Lisburn Road
Belfast
BT9 7BL
Tel: 028 9097 2233
www.qub.ac.uk

University of Ulster at Jordanstown
School of Nursing
Shore Road
Newtownabbey
Co Antrim
BT37 0QB
Tel: 08700 400 700
www.ulster.ac.uk

Health Learning and Skills Advice Line
Tel: 08000 150850

National Leadership and Innovation Agency for Healthcare
Innovation House
Bridgend Road
Llanharan
CF72 9RP
Tel: 01443 233 333
www.nliah.wales.nhs.uk/

NHS Careers
PO Box 2311
Bristol
BS2 2ZX
Tel: 0345 60 60 655
www.nhscareers.nhs.uk

Skills for Health
Goldsmiths House
Broad Plain
Bristol
BS2 0JP
Tel: 0117 922 1155
www.skillsforhealth.org.uk

OCCUPATIONAL THERAPIST

The nature of the work
As an occupational therapist, you would often work with clients on a one-to-one basis and adapt treatment programmes to suit each person's needs and lifestyle. Your work could include things like:

- teaching an older patient recovering from a stroke how to dress themselves
- encouraging someone suffering with depression to take up a hobby or activity
- suggesting ways to adapt an office so that an employee injured in a car accident can return to work
- helping clients adjust to permanent disabilities.

You would also keep notes about clients' progress, and advise and support clients and their families and carers.

Some patients may have conditions such as motor neurone disease or multiple sclerosis, which means that they gradually become less mobile and more disabled. You would work with these clients to encourage a positive attitude, which can help them keep active for as long as possible.

With experience, you could specialise in an area such as:

- burns or plastic surgery
- cardiac or stroke rehabilitation
- paediatrics
- orthopaedics (spinal injury)
- community disability services
- mental health.

You could work with patients for several months or just for a few sessions. You would often work as part of a team of professionals, including physiotherapists, nurses and social workers.

What can you earn?
Starting salaries can be between £21,200 and £27,500 a year. With experience and extra responsibilities, this can rise to around £40,000 a year.

Entry requirements

To become a registered occupational therapist you will need to have a degree, or have completed a postgraduate course, in occupational therapy that is approved by the Health Professions Council (HPC). See the HPC website for approved courses and course providers.

Before you apply for a course, it is a good idea to gain some relevant experience or knowledge of the profession. You could contact the occupational therapy unit at your local hospital, nursing home or other health centre where therapists practice, to ask how you could get involved.

To do a degree in occupational therapy, you will usually need:

- five GCSEs (A-C)
- three A levels, often including at least one science subject (biology may be preferred).

Check with individual universities for exact entry details as other qualifications, such as an Access to Higher Education course, may be accepted.

To do a postgraduate course you will usually need an honours degree in a related area plus previous healthcare experience. Course providers will be able to tell you which degree subjects they accept.

You can join the British Association of Occupational Therapists (BAOT) and the World Federation of Occupational Therapists (WFOT) as a student or graduate. The BAOT website also includes details of course providers.

Another option is to start as occupational therapy support worker. With backing from your employer, you could work towards qualifying as an occupational therapist by completing a four-year in-service course leading to state registration.

You will need to agree to a Criminal Records Bureau check when you apply for a course and before you can register with the HPC. See the Criminal Records Bureau for details.

More information

Health Professions Council
Park House
184 Kennington Park Road
London
SE11 4BU
Tel: 020 7582 0866
www.hpc-uk.org

NHS Careers
PO Box 2311
Bristol
BS2 2ZX
Tel: 0345 60 60 655
www.nhscareers.nhs.uk

British Association of Occupational Therapists
106-114 Borough High Street
Southwark
London
SE1 1LB
Tel: 020 7450 2332 (Careers Info)
www.cot.co.uk

Health Learning and Skills Advice Line
Tel: 08000 150850

PHARMACIST

The nature of the work
Pharmacists provide expert advice on the use and supply of drugs and medicines. This could include checking prescriptions and making sure that laws controlling medicines are followed.

You would usually be based at a retail location (where you would be known as a community pharmacist) or at a hospital pharmacy.

As a community pharmacist in a retail location your work could include:
- giving healthcare advice and help to the public
- delivering medication to people who are unable to leave home
- visiting care homes to advise on the use and storage of medication
- preparing medicines bought at the counter
- giving advice on how to use medicines correctly, including the amount to use (dosage) and any risks selling a range of products
- ordering and controlling stock
- running or helping to run a business, including supervising and training staff.

In a hospital setting, your duties could include:

- giving advice on dosage and the most suitable form of medicine (such as a tablet, inhaler or injection)
- producing medicines (for example, creating a treatment or solution when ready made ones are not available)
- visiting wards, giving advice about medicines to colleagues and providing them with current information
- buying, quality testing and distributing medicines throughout the hospital
- supervising trainees and junior pharmacists.

Another option is to work as a pharmacist with a local primary care trust. This could involve giving advice to GPs on prescribing, running clinics at a GP practice and training local prescribers on issues related to managing and prescribing medicines.

You could also work in education or in industry, carrying out research into new medicines and running clinical trials.

What can you earn?

Pharmacists can earn between around £22,000 and £34,200 a year.

Pharmacy consultants or team managers can earn between £45,300 and £80,810 a year.

Entry requirements

Before you can work as a pharmacist, you need to complete:

- a four-year Master of Pharmacy (MPharm) degree
- a one-year pre-registration training course in a pharmacy
- a registration exam.

Your degree and training must be approved by the Royal Pharmaceutical Society of Great Britain (RPSGB), the professional body for pharmacists. See the RPSGB's Careers in Pharmacy website pages for links to a list of approved degree courses.

To do a degree, you will usually need five GCSEs (A-C) including maths and English, plus three A levels, usually in chemistry and two other science-based subjects such as biology, maths or physics. Check with course providers for exact entry requirements as other qualifications may be accepted.

When you have finished your degree, you can apply for the one-year pre-registration programme. This includes spending at least six months in a community or hospital pharmacy, and leads to a final registration exam. For details of pre-registration training vacancies, check the NHS Hospital Pharmacy Pre-registration Training website.

Once you have completed all three stages of training you can apply for state registration and membership of the RPSGB.

Pharmacy regulation

The General Pharmaceutical Council (GPhC) is the regulator for pharmacists, pharmacy technicians and pharmacy premises. For more information, see the GPhC website.

More information

General Pharmaceutical Council
129 Lambeth Rd
London
SE1 7BT

Tel: 020 3365 3400
www.pharmacyregulation.org

Pharmaceutical Society of Northern Ireland
73 University Street
Belfast
BT7 1HL
Tel: 028 9032 6927
http://www.psni.org.uk/

Royal Pharmaceutical Society of Great Britain
1 Lambeth High Street
London
SE1 7JN
Tel: 020 7735 9141
www.rpsgb.org.uk

NHS Careers
PO Box 2311
Bristol
BS2 2ZX
Tel: 0345 60 60 655
www.nhscareers.nhs.uk

Association of the British Pharmaceutical Industry (ABPI) Careers
12 Whitehall London
SW1A 2DY
Tel: 020 7930 3477
http://careers.abpi.org.uk

Health Learning and Skills Advice Line
Tel: 08000 150850

PHYSIOTHERAPIST

The nature of the work

As a physiotherapist your work could include:

- helping patients with spine and joint problems, especially after an operation

- helping patients recovering from accidents, sports injuries and strokes
- working with children who have mental or physical disabilities
- helping older people with physical problems become more mobile.

You could work in various areas and departments, such as paediatrics, outpatients, intensive care, women's health and occupational health. You could use a variety of treatments and techniques including:

- physical manipulation
- massage
- therapeutic exercise
- electrotherapy
- ultrasound
- acupuncture
- hydrotherapy.

You would keep accurate records of patients' treatment and progress, and you would often work closely with other health professionals. These could be occupational therapists, health visitors and social workers.

What can you earn?

Starting salaries for physiotherapists in the NHS are between £21,200 and £27,500 a year. Specialist physiotherapists can earn around £34,200 a year. Team managers and advanced physiotherapists can earn up to £40,200 a year.

Salaries in the private sector are usually similar to those in the NHS.

Entry requirements

To become a chartered (qualified) physiotherapist you need a physiotherapy degree approved by the Health Professions Council (HPC). This will make you eligible for state registration and membership of the Chartered Society of Physiotherapy (CSP). Check the HPC and CSP websites for a list of course providers.

To do a degree in physiotherapy, you will usually need:

- at least five GCSEs (A-C) including maths, English and a range of science subjects
- four AS levels at grade B or above (including a biological science)

- three A2 level subjects at grade C or above (including a biological science).

Check with universities for exact entry requirements as other qualifications, such as an Access to Higher Education course, may also be accepted.

It would help you if you also had some relevant experience, for example as a volunteer. Contact the voluntary services coordinator or manager at your local NHS Trust for details.

When you apply for a course you will have a Criminal Records Bureau (CRB) check, however a criminal conviction does not automatically prevent you from working in the NHS. The admissions tutor for your course can give you details.

Alternative entry routes

Cadet or apprenticeship scheme

You may be able to prepare for a career in physiotherapy through a two-year Cadet/Apprenticeship Scheme. This involves clinical placements and working towards a qualification such as an NVQ Level 3 in Health, and may meet the entry requirements for a physiotherapy degree. Check with your local NHS Trust or NHS Careers for details.

Physiotherapy assistant

As an assistant you may be able to take a part-time degree in physiotherapy whilst you are working. The CSP website has details of part-time, work-based degree course providers. The HPC website also includes a list of approved courses.

Accelerated postgraduate courses

If you have a first class or upper second class honours degree in a relevant subject (such as a biological science, psychology or sports science) you could qualify as a physiotherapist by taking a fast-track postgraduate course. Contact the CSP for details.

More information

Health Professions Council
Park House
184 Kennington Park Road
London
SE11 4BU
Tel: 020 7582 0866

NHS Careers
PO Box 2311
Bristol
BS2 2ZX
Tel: 0345 60 60 655

Chartered Society of Physiotherapy
14 Bedford Row
London
WC1R 4ED
Tel: 020 7306 6666

Health Learning and Skills Advice Line
Tel: 08000 150850

SCHOOL NURSE

The nature of the work
School nurses work with pupils, teachers and parents to promote good health and wellbeing in school age children.

As a school nurse, your duties could include:

- raising awareness of issues that can have a negative effect on student health (such as smoking and drug abuse)
- promoting healthy living, including safe-sex education
- administering immunisations and vaccinations
- carrying out developmental screening
- contributing to social education and citizenship classes
- supporting children with medical needs such as asthma, diabetes, epilepsy or mental health problems.

169

You may also give training to teachers about the health care needs of individual children.

You could work for a single school or cover a number of schools. If your role involves visiting a range of schools, you will probably be based at a GP practice or health centre.

You could also work in a private boarding school, which may involve living on school premises and being on 24-hour call (in case of emergency).

What can you earn?

Nurses can earn between £20,700 and £26,800 a year. Nurse specialists, such as school nurses, may earn around £33,500. With experience and managerial responsibilities, this can rise to around £39,300.

Extra allowances may be paid to those living in or around London.

Entry requirements

You will usually need around two years' professional experience as a qualified nurse (any branch) before you can begin training or working as a school nurse.

To qualify as a nurse you need a Nursing and Midwifery Council (NMC) approved degree or Diploma of Higher Education. For more information about becoming a nurse, check the relevant Nurse job profiles.

You could start work as a school nurse without further training or qualifications, especially if you have relevant experience. However, some employers will prefer you to have completed a (shortened) degree or postgraduate course leading to registration as a Specialist Community Public Health Nurse (School Nursing).

Courses are available on a one-year full-time or two-year part-time basis. You could fund yourself or you may be able to find a vacancy, for example on the NHS Jobs website, that includes working under supervision and studying for the specialist qualification. Check the NMC website for details of course providers.

You could have an advantage (when looking for work or applying for a course) if you have experience in health promotion or working with children in the community. Knowledge of child protection and an understanding of family planning issues and the health needs of school children would also be helpful.

You are likely to need a driving licence for this job.

More information

Nursing and Midwifery Council (NMC)
23 Portland Place
London
W1B 1PZ
Tel: 020 7333 9333
www.nmc-uk.org

Queens University of Belfast
School of Nursing and Midwifery
Medical Biology Centre
97 Lisburn Road
Belfast
BT9 7BL
Tel: 028 9097 2233
www.qub.ac.uk

University of Ulster at Jordanstown
School of Nursing
Shore Road
Newtownabbey
Co Antrim
BT37 0QB
Tel: 08700 400 700
www.ulster.ac.u

NHS Careers
PO Box 2311
Bristol
BS2 2ZX
Tel: 0345 60 60 655
www.nhscareers.nhs.uk

Community Practitioners and Health Visitors Association
33-37 Moreland Street

London
EC1V 8HA
Tel: 020 7505 3000
www.amicustheunion.org/cphva

Health Learning and Skills Advice Line
Tel: 08000 150850

National Leadership and Innovation Agency for Healthcare
Innovation House
Bridgend Road
Llanharan
CF72 9RP
Tel: 01443 233 333
www.nliah.wales.nhs.uk/

SPEECH AND LANGUAGE THERAPY ASSISTANT

The nature of the work

If you are interested in communication problems and you want to help others, this job could be ideal for you.

As a speech and language therapy assistant, you would support registered speech and language therapists during their assessment and treatment of people with communication, eating, drinking and swallowing problems.

You could work with a range of client groups, including:

- children
- adults with physical disabilities, mental health issues or learning difficulties
- people recovering from medical conditions, such as a stroke
- older people.

Your duties would usually involve:

- working with clients on a one-to-one basis
- liaising with the therapist about adjustments to a client's therapy
- group work and activities
- preparing therapy rooms and equipment

- supporting clients with any personal needs, for example, mobility issues.

You may also carry out general administrative tasks.

What can you earn?

Speech and language therapy assistants can earn between £13,600 and £18,500 a year. With experience and relevant qualifications, this could rise to around £21,800.

Entry requirements

Each employer can set their own entry requirements – some NHS Trusts may not ask for any academic qualifications whereas others will prefer a good standard of general education (possibly including four or five GCSEs grades A-C). For some jobs it may be desirable, possibly essential, to have the ability to speak a second community-based language, knowledge of British Sign Language and an awareness of other cultures.

Qualifications in childcare (such as the Council for Awards in Care, Health and Education (CACHE) Certificate/Diploma in Child Care and Education) or an NVQ Level 2 in Health or Health and Social Care would be useful, though not essential.

It could be an advantage to have paid or unpaid experience of working with older people, children or people with physical disabilities, mental health problems or learning difficulties. Contact the voluntary services coordinator or manager at your local NHS Trust for further advice.

Another way to get experience would be through a Cadet Scheme or Apprenticeship (in many parts of the country, cadet schemes have been replaced with Apprenticeships). Schemes vary between NHS Trusts, but will usually include clinical placements and working towards a qualification such as the new Level 3 Diploma in Clinical Healthcare Support (title subject to change). To find out more, visit the Apprenticeships website.

You could also contact your local NHS Trust for details of both Cadet and Apprenticeship schemes in your area.

More information

Royal College of Speech and Language Therapists
2 White Hart Yard
London
SE1 1NX
Tel: 020 7378 1200
www.rcslt.org

NHS Careers
PO Box 2311
Bristol
BS2 2ZX
Tel: 0345 60 60 655
www.nhscareers.nhs.uk

Health Learning and Skills Advice Line
Tel: 08000 150850

RADIOGRAPHER

The nature of the work

There are two types of radiography – diagnostic and therapeutic.

As a diagnostic radiographer, your work would involve:

- producing and interpreting high quality images of the body to identify and diagnose injury and disease
- screening for abnormalities
- taking part in surgical procedures, such as biopsies (examining tissues to find the cause of disease).

As a therapeutic radiographer, your duties would include:

- planning and delivering treatment using x-rays and other radioactive sources
- working closely with medical specialists to plan and treat malignant tumours or tissue defects
- assessing and monitoring patients throughout treatment and follow up.

Both areas of radiography involve working as part of a team alongside radiologists, clinical oncologists, physicists, radiology nurses and other health care professionals.

You would usually wear a uniform, and if you specialise in diagnostic radiography, you would sometimes wear protective clothing. This work can be physically and emotionally demanding.

What can you earn?

Newly qualified radiographers can earn between £21,200 and £27,500 a year. With experience, this can rise to about £34,200 a year.

Senior radiographers or team leaders can earn about £40,200 a year, and consultant radiographers can earn up to about £67,200 a year.

Entry requirements

To work as a radiographer you will need a degree approved by the Health Professions Council (HPC). Before you apply, you will need to decide whether you want to work in diagnostic radiography or therapeutic radiography. Visiting a radiography department or radiotherapy centre may help you decide. You will need to contact your local NHS Trust to arrange this.

To do a degree in diagnostic or therapeutic radiography you will usually need five GCSEs (A-C), plus three A levels, including a science. Check exact entry requirements with course providers as other qualifications, such as an Access to Higher Education course, may be accepted.

If you are a health professional or a graduate with a relevant first degree, you may be able to qualify in radiography by completing a pre-registration postgraduate diploma or Masters qualification. See the Health Professions Council website for details of all approved courses.

Most places on approved courses are funded by the NHS. Check the NHS Business Services Authority website for details.

Another route into radiography is to start as a radiography assistant and work your way up to assistant practitioner. At practitioner level, your employer may give you the opportunity to work and study part-time for a degree and professional qualification as a radiographer.

Once you are on a radiography degree, you will combine theoretical study with clinical placements in local hospitals and therapy/diagnostic units. Courses usually take three years full-time or the part-time equivalent.

More information

NHS Careers
PO Box 2311
Bristol
BS2 2ZX
Tel: 0345 60 60 655
www.nhscareers.nhs.uk

Society and College of Radiographers
207 Providence Square
Mill Street
London
SE1 2EW
Tel: 020 7740 7200
www.sor.org

Health Learning and Skills Advice Line
Tel: 08000 150850

Health Professions Council
Park House
184 Kennington Park Road
London
SE11 4BU
Tel: 020 7582 0866
www.hpc-uk.org

SURGEON

The nature of the work
To become a surgeon, you will need to complete a degree in medicine, recognised by the General Medical Council. You will also have to do further training that would last another ten years.

A surgeon needs to put people at their ease and inspire trust and confidence. They also need to work under pressure and make quick, accurate decisions.

Surgeons specialise in caring for patients who may need an operation. This could be, for example, if the patient has been injured, has a disease or has a condition that is getting worse.

As a surgeon you would use your in-depth knowledge of physiology, biochemistry, pathology and anatomy to work in one of nine surgical specialities. These are: cardiothoracic surgery; general surgery; plastic surgery; ENT; paediatric surgery; trauma and orthopaedic surgery; urology; neurosurgery; and oral and maxillofacial surgery.

Patients would be referred to you by other hospital doctors and GPs, and through admission to accident and emergency. Your key duties would involve:

- making a diagnosis
- deciding on the most appropriate course of action
- operating on patients
- monitoring patients after an operation.

You would also be responsible for training and supervising junior doctors and other healthcare professionals in the hospital. In addition, you may carry out research and write papers for publication.

As a senior or consultant surgeon, you would see patients in outpatient clinics, lead a team during surgery, and see patients on wards before and after an operation. You would keep patient records and write to GPs about their patients' condition and treatment.

What can you earn?

Foundation house officers (junior doctors) can earn between £33,300 and £41,300 a year. Doctors in specialist training can earn up to £69,400 a year, and consultants can earn between £74,500 and £180,000 a year.

Salaries for doctors in training include an additional amount based on the average hours of overtime worked, time spent covering unsocial hours, and workload.

Surgeons working in private sector hospitals may obtain higher fees.

Entry requirements

To become a surgeon, you will need to complete:

- a degree in medicine, recognised by the General Medical Council (five years)
- a foundation programme of general training (two years)
- core training (two years)
- specialty training (five to six years).

Each medical school has an individual approach, so it is important that you research each one and choose a course that will best prepare you for a career in surgery. See the Royal College of Surgeons of England website for advice, and check the General Medical Council (GMC) website for a list of degree courses.

To do a degree in medicine, you will usually need:

- at least five GCSEs (A-C) including English, maths and science
- plus three A levels at grades AAB in subjects such as chemistry, biology and either physics or maths.

If you do not have qualifications in science, you may be able to do a six-year degree course in medicine that includes a one-year pre-medical or foundation year. You will need to check with individual universities.

If you already have an honours degree in a science subject (minimum 2:1) you may be able to get on to a four-year graduate entry course. Some universities will accept non-science graduates. See the Medical Schools Council website for details of course providers.

When you apply for a course in medicine, you may be asked to take the UK Clinical Aptitude Test (UKCAT). This is used to check your suitability for a career in medicine by testing your mental abilities and behavioural characteristics, rather than your academic achievements. For details see the UKCAT website.

If you trained as a doctor overseas, you will need to contact the GMC to find out about registering and practising in the UK.

When you are awarded the CCT, you will be eligible to join the General Medical Council (GMC) Specialist Register and apply for a licence to practise. For more information on licensing and a new system of revalidation, check the GMC website.

This is the most direct route through surgical training and covers most specialties. For help with choosing your specialism, see the NHS Medical Careers website. Throughout your career you will be expected to continue learning and developing your surgical skills. The Royal College of Surgeons' website has information on all aspects of training and continuing medical education for practising surgeons.

More information

Royal College of Surgeons of England
35-43 Lincoln's Inn Fields
London
WC2A 3PE
Tel: 020 7405 3474
www.rcseng.ac.uk

UKCAT, UK Clinical Aptitude Test
www.ukcat.ac.uk

Health Learning and Skills Advice Line
Tel: 08000 150850

British Medical Association (BMA)
Tavistock Square
London
WC1H 9JP
Tel: 020 7387 4499
www.bma.org.uk

General Medical Council(GMC)
Regent's Place
350 Euston Road
London
NW1 3JN
Tel: 0845 357 3456
www.gmc-uk.org

PSYCHOLGIST

The nature of the work

If you are interested in how people behave and in helping them to deal with challenges, this career could be perfect for you.

Psychologists study people's behaviour, motivations, thoughts and feelings and help them overcome or control their problems.

Psychologists usually specialise in one of the following areas. They may be referred to by their specialism or as a chartered or practitioner psychologist.

- educational psychology – helping children and young people to overcome difficulties and further their educational and psychological development
- occupational psychology (also known as organisational psychology) – helping businesses improve their performance and increase employees' job satisfaction
- health psychology – promoting healthy attitudes and behaviour, and helping patients and their families to cope with illness
- counselling psychology – helping people resolve their problems and make decisions, particularly at stressful times in their lives
- neuropsychology – helping patients with brain injuries and neuropsychological diseases to recover or improve their quality of life
- forensic or criminological psychology – using psychological theory to help investigate crimes, rehabilitate offenders and support prison staff
- clinical psychology
- sports psychology.

Some areas of psychology have no direct training route. For example, to become a child psychologist you might first train as a clinical or counselling psychologist and then specialise in working with children. Or you could train in educational psychology and work with children in education.

What can you earn?

Assistant psychologists can earn around £15,000 to £23,000 a year. With experience, this can rise to between £30,000 and £40,000 a year.

Managers and consultants can earn up to around £80,000.

Entry requirements

To work as a chartered or practitioner psychologist, you need to complete training in psychology approved by the Health Professions Council (HPC).

Your training would begin with a British Psychological Society (BPS) accredited degree in psychology leading to the Graduate Basis for Chartered Membership (GBC). To undertake a degree course you will usually need five GCSEs (A-C), plus three A levels. Check with course providers for exact entry requirements.

If you already have a degree in a subject other than psychology, you may be able to achieve GBC by completing a BPS-approved conversion course.

Once you have completed your BPS-accredited course/exam and are eligible for registration with the HPC, you will need to achieve the following depending on your specialism:

- educational psychology - a Doctorate in Educational Psychology (in England, Northern Ireland and Wales)
- occupational psychology - the BPS Qualification in Occupational Psychology, which usually consists of an accredited MSc in Occupational Psychology plus two years' supervised practice
- health psychology - an MSc in Health Psychology and two years' supervised experience
- counselling psychology - the BPS Qualification in Counselling Psychology or a BPS accredited Doctorate in Counselling Psychology
- neuropsychology - training in either clinical or educational

- psychology, plus two years' supervised practice and an accredited course in neuropsychology
- forensic psychology - an MSc in Forensic Psychology plus two years' supervised practical experience.
- clinical psychology - a three-year, full time, NHS funded Doctorate in Clinical Psychology.
- sport and exercise psychology - an accredited MSc in Sport and Exercise Psychology plus two years' supervised work experience.

Competition for postgraduate training is strong. Entry requirements will often include a first or upper second class honours degree, evidence of your research skills, plus relevant work experience. Whichever specialist area you want to go in to, it is important to check that your postgraduate programme is approved by the HPC. See the Register of Approved Programmes page on the HPC website.

More information

NHS Careers
PO Box 2311
Bristol
BS2 2ZX
Tel: 0345 60 60 655
www.nhscareers.nhs.uk

British Psychological Society
St Andrew's House
48 Princess Road East
Leicester
LE1 7DR
Tel: 0116 254 9568
www.bps.org.uk

11. INFORMATION TECHNOLOGY

The world of information technology is now very broad, having expanded over the years to cover many roles. In this chapter we look at the following:

- Computer service and repair technician
- Database administrator
- software developer
- Systems analyst
- Web content manager
- Web designer

For more details of careers in information technology go to:

Skills Framework for the Information Age

www.sfia.

org.uk

COMPUTER SERVICE AND REPAIR TECHNICIAN

The nature of the work

As a computer service and repair technician you would install, maintain and repair computer systems and equipment.

You could work as a member of an IT support team in a large organisation, on commercial contracts for an IT servicing company, or as a field technician for a computer manufacturer. You might also run your own PC repair and upgrade business.

Your day-to-day tasks would include:

- installing new IT systems
- upgrading existing hardware and software
- visiting home users to set up their PCs or fix faulty equipment
- testing systems to make sure that they are working properly

- servicing printers, scanners and other office equipment (known as peripherals)
- preparing cost estimates for new installations
- carrying out routine administration, like organising staff rotas.

In a larger organisation, you may also be responsible for training staff to use equipment correctly and safely.

What can you earn?

Starting salaries are between £14,000 and £17,000 a year.

Experienced staff can earn between £18,000 and £25,000 a year, and senior staff with management responsibility can earn up to £30,000 a year.

Entry requirements

You could start without formal qualifications if you have a good enough working knowledge of computer systems and software. However, you may improve your chances of finding work by taking a computer maintenance qualification at college, for example:

- BTEC National Certificate and Diploma for IT Practitioners (Systems Support) Level 3
- City & Guilds IT Practitioners Diploma Level 2
- OCR Certificate and Diploma for IT Practitioners levels 1 and 2
- CompTIA A+ Certification.

You may be able to start this job through an apprenticeship scheme with an IT company or a technical support team in a larger company. You will need to check which schemes are available in your area. For more information, visit the Apprenticeships website.

For more information about careers and qualifications in IT, see the e-skills UK website.

More information

Microsoft UK
www.microsoft.com/uk

Skills Framework for the Information Age (SFIA)
www.sfia.org.uk

UK Resource Centre for Women in Science, Engineering and Technology
(UKRC)
Listerhills Park of Science and Commerce
40-42 Campus Road
Bradford
BD7 1HR
Tel: 01274 436485
www.theukrc.org

DATABASE ADMINISTRATOR

The nature of the work

As a DBA you could work on a variety of databases, from banks' customer account networks to hospital patient record systems. Your tasks could range from upgrading an existing database to creating a completely new system.

On a new system, you would work with an organisation to:

- establish what the database is for, who will use it and what other systems it will link to (for example telephony)
- plan the structure of the database, working out how to organise, find and display the data
- build a test version and check the results to iron out any technical problems (bugs)
- fill (populate) the database with new information or transfer existing data into it

185

- plan how to update information, create back-up copies and report errors
- put in security measures.

You may have extra duties, like supervising technical support staff, training users and producing performance reports for IT managers.

Increasingly, you could be working with web-based technologies and would need to understand how databases fit in with these systems. Database security is another area of growing importance.

In a senior position you would normally be responsible for strategic planning, information policy, budgets and managing client relationships.

You would work on projects with other IT professionals, such as analysts, programmers and IT project managers.

What can you earn?

Starting salaries are between £18,000 and £22,000 a year.

Experienced staff can earn between £23,000 and £35,000 a year, and senior DBAs can earn over £45,000 a year.

Rates for short and medium-term contract jobs may be significantly higher than those listed above, particularly at senior levels.

Entry requirements

For most database administrator jobs, you would need to know how to use structured query language (SQL) and database management systems (DBMS), which include:

- DBMS (relational database management systems)
- OODBMS (object-oriented database management systems)
- XML database management systems.

Employers often look for previous experience in computing such as IT support, programming or web development.

You could study for a qualification such as a BTEC HNC/HND or degree, then join a company's graduate training scheme straight from college or university. Relevant subjects include:

If you do not have an IT-related degree, you may still be able to get a place on a graduate training scheme, as larger employers tend to accept graduates from any discipline. You could study for a postgraduate IT conversion qualification, although this is not essential.

More information

Skills Framework for the Information Age (SFIA)
www.sfia.org.uk

e-skills UK
1 Castle Lane
London
SW1E 6DR
020 7963 8920
www.e-skills.com

BCS – the Chartered Institute for IT
Block D
North Star House
North Star Avenue
Swindon
Wiltshire
SN2 1FA
www.bcs.org.uk

Institute for the Management of Information Systems
5 Kingfisher House
New Mill Road
Orpington

Kent

BR5 3QG

Tel: 0700 002 3456

www.imis.org.uk

Computer Technology Industry Association (CompTIA)

www.comptia.org

e-skills UK

1 Castle Lane

London

SW1E 6DR

0207 963 8920

www.e-skills.com

SOFTWARE DEVELOPER

The nature of the work

Software developers (also known as programmers) design and build computer programs that help organisations and equipment work effectively.

As a software developer, your work could involve:

- designing computer controls for industrial and manufacturing machinery
- building administrative and financial databases
- developing software for home entertainment equipment (known as embedded controls).

You would work closely with senior programmers and business analysts, and create technical plans to meet the needs of the client.

You may write computer programs from the beginning, or amend existing programs to meet the needs of the project.

You could work with a range of web-based technologies, and you would need to understand how databases integrate with these systems.

What can you earn?

Starting salaries for graduates can be between £20,000 and £26,000 a year.

Experienced developers can earn between £28,000 and £40,000, and software developers with management responsibilities can earn over £50,000 a year.

Entry requirements

You will normally need a degree, foundation degree or BTEC HNC/HND to become a software developer. You could choose from a variety of subjects, including:

- computer science/studies
- information technology
- software development
- software engineering
- business information systems.

If you do not have an IT-related degree, you may still be able to find a place on a graduate trainee scheme, as larger employers often accept graduates in any subject. You could study for a postgraduate IT conversion qualification, although this is not essential.

Several universities are now offering the Information Technology Management for Business (ITMB) degree. The degree, which was developed by e-skills UK and major employers, combines both IT and business skills, such as project management and business thinking.

Experience in IT or a related area can be useful. You can gain experience through work placements, internships or a year in industry.

You will also need a working knowledge of the main programming languages and operating systems used, for example:

- SQL, Java, C++, XML, Smalltalk and Visual Basic
- Oracle, UML (Unified Modelling Language), Linux and Delphi
- .NET frameworks (such as C# (C-sharp), ASP and VB).

Visit the developer.com website for information and links to resources relating to programming languages.

More information

Skills Framework for the Information Age (SFIA)
www.sfia.org.uk

e-skills UK
1 Castle Lane
London
SW1E 6DR
0207 963 8920
www.e-skills.com

British Computer Society
Block D
North Star House
North Star Avenue
Swindon
Wiltshire
SN2 1FA
www.bcs.org.uk

Institution of Analysts and Programmers
Charles House
36 Culmington Road
London
W13 9NH
Tel: 020 8567 2118
www.iap.org.uk

Institute for the Management of Information Systems
5 Kingfisher House
New Mill Road
Orpington
Kent

BR5 3QG
Tel: 0700 002 3456
www.imis.org.uk

National Skills Academy for IT
www.itskillsacademy.ac.uk/

SYSTEMS ANALYST

The nature of the work

Your work could range from integrating the telephone and computer networks in a call centre, to re-structuring a bank's customer account databases to make them more secure.

Your work would involve:

- identifying the client organisation's needs
- drawing up plans for a modified or replacement IT system
- carrying out feasibility studies of proposals and making recommendations
- working closely with programmers and software developers to build the system
- overseeing installation and testing correcting problems ('bugs') before the final version is released
- providing staff training and instruction manuals for the new or upgraded system.

An important part of your job would be to make sure that your designs are flexible enough to adapt as the organisation or business grows (known as 'future-proofing'). You would use various computer assisted software engineering (CASE) tools and programming methods in your job.

What can you earn?

Salaries can range from around £20,000 and £45,000 a year depending on experience. Senior analysts can earn significantly more.

Entry requirements

To work as a systems analyst you normally need a BTEC HNC/HND or degree, backed up with industry experience. Relevant subjects include:

- computer science/studies
- information management systems
- business information systems
- maths and operational research.

Alternatively, you could take the Information Technology Management for Business (ITMB) degree. The degree has been developed by e-skills and employers to meet specific industry skills shortages, for example in project management and business awareness. For more details, see the e-skills UK website.

If you have a non-IT related degree, you could take a postgraduate IT 'conversion' course, although companies may still ask for relevant work experience. Employers recommend that you look for a course which focuses on business skills as well as technical knowledge.

You would be expected to have a working knowledge of programming skills and analysis methods. Some of the most common are:

- SQL
- Visual Basic, C++ and Java
- Unified Modelling Language (UML)
- SAP business software applications.

See the websites for e-skills UK, British Computer Society (BCS), the Institute for the Management of Information Systems (IMIS) and the Institution of Analysts and Programmers (IAP) for more details about careers in this field.

For more information about professional development options, see the Skills Framework for the Information Age (SFIA) website. This website has been developed by professional bodies and employers and allows you to identify your current skills and work out career development options.

More information

Institute for the Management of Information Systems
5 Kingfisher House
New Mill Road
Orpington
Kent
BR5 3QG
Tel: 0700 002 3456
www.imis.org.uk

Institute of Analysts and Programmers
Charles House
36 Culmington Road
London
W13 9NH
Tel: 020 8567 2118
www.iap.org.uk

Skills Framework for the Information Age (SFIA)
www.sfia.org.uk

British Computer Society
Block D
North Star House
North Star Avenue
Swindon
Wiltshire
SN2 1FA
www.bcs.org.uk

e-skills UK
1 Castle Lane
London

WEB CONTENT MANAGER

The nature of the work

As a web content manager, you could work on sites that are open to the public on the world wide web, or sites for staff use only on a company's intranet.

Your duties could include:

- taking a lead role in maintenance and development of the site
- meeting with editing, marketing and design teams to plan and develop site content, style and appearance
- using web content management systems to analyse website usage statistics
- writing reports for senior managers, clients and partnership organisations
- setting permissions for site users
- promoting information about the website to target customers and partners
- carrying out quality assurance checks on content
- reporting technical problems to IT support staff
- dealing with legal issues, such as copyright and data protection.

In larger companies, you may manage an editorial team who research and produce material – text, images and multimedia – for publication on the website. In smaller organisations, you might have a more 'hands on' role in content production and writing.

What can you earn?

Web content managers' salaries fall between £24,000 and £50,000 a year, depending on the level of experience.

Entry requirements

There is no set entry route into this career. You may have a background in journalism, marketing or IT, or you might move into the role after gaining experience in another area of a business.

194

Whatever your background, you would normally need previous experience of writing content in some form, although not necessarily online. A useful way to show employers your skills is to build up a collection of your published work.

You could take a course that would teach you some of the skills needed for producing web content. Relevant subjects include journalism, publishing, media, and communications, PR and marketing. Contact your local colleges for course details and entry requirements.

You do not need specific IT skills for a management position, although knowledge of web design, desktop publishing and photo imaging would broaden your options, as many jobs combine management with writing or web design.

An understanding of web content management systems and how they work could be useful, but you would be given training in specific packages once you start working.

More information

Society for Editors and Proofreaders (SfEP)
Apsley House
176 Upper Richmond Road
Putney
London
SW15 2SH
Tel: 020 8785 6155
www.sfep.org.uk

National Union of Journalists (NUJ)
www.nuj.org.uk

SW1E 6DR
0207 963 8920
www.e-skills.com

BCS Professional Certification
http://certifications.bcs.org

National Skills Academy for IT
www.itskillsacademy.ac.uk

WEB DESIGNER

The nature of the work

As a web designer, you could work on any kind of website, from an interactive education site to one offering online shopping. Your main tasks would include:

- meeting clients to discuss what they want their site to do and who will use it
- preparing a design plan, showing the site structure and how the different parts link together
- deciding which text, colours and backgrounds to use
- laying out pages and positioning buttons, links and pictures using design software
- adding multimedia features like sound, animation and video
- testing and improving the design and site until everything works as planned
- uploading the site to a server for publication online.

Depending on the project, you could also be asked to manage your client's website once it is up and running.

What can you earn?

Starting salaries can be between £15,000 and £22,000 a year. The average salary is £30,000. Experienced designers can earn up to £37,500 a year, and senior designers and those with specialist skills can earn over £40,000 a year.

Self-employed web designers set their own rates.

Entry requirements

You do not usually need qualifications to become a web designer. However, most designers have experience in other types of design, or have done training in web design, either through college or by teaching themselves.

You will need to show evidence of your creative and technical skills, usually in the form of a CD, DVD or 'live' websites you have worked on. You could gain this evidence from college, paid work or volunteering.

You will need a good working knowledge of HTML, and experience of writing web pages in a combination of codes. It could be useful if you a working knowledge of the following programs:

- Dreamweaver
- Photoshop
- Flash and Fireworks
- CSS
- Javascript
- .Net

Colleges offer courses on these programs. You can also find many online tutorials, which are often free to use.

You could take one of the following qualifications, which provide good basic training in web design, interactivity and internet technology:

- BTEC Interactive use of Media levels 1 to 3
- OCR ITQ levels 1 to 3
- OCR Creative iMedia levels 1 to 3
- City & Guilds E-Quals IT Users awards (7266) – Level 2 (Diploma) and Level 3 (Advanced Diploma).

You could also take a higher level course, such as a foundation degree, BTEC HNC/HND, or degree in a design or multimedia subject. Relevant subjects include:

- web design and development
- multimedia design

- digital media development
- interactive computing.

To search for colleges and universities offering foundation degrees, HNC/HNDs and degrees, visit the Universities and Colleges Admissions Service (UCAS) website.

To find out more about careers in web design, visit the E-skills UK, British Computer Society and Big Ambition websites.

More information

UK Web Design Association
www.ukwda.org

World Wide Web Consortium (W3C)
www.w3.org

Big Ambition
www.bigambition.co.uk

British Computer Society
Block D
North Star House
North Star Avenue
Swindon
Wiltshire
SN2 1FA
www.bcs.org.uk

Certified Internet Web Professional (CIW)
www.ciwcertified.com

12. JOURNALISM AND PRINTING

The world of journalism offers many exciting opportunities. However, like ever other career, you need to gain a toehold. There are a number of ways to enter this profession. Printing is also a fascinating career choice and there are a number of opportunities available. In this section, we cover:

- Newspaper journalism
- Magazine Journalism
- Advertising copywriting
- Proof reading
- Sub-editing
- Bookbinding and print finisher
- Printing administrator
- Machine printing

For details of all career opportunities in these fields go to:

National Council for the Training of Journalists
The New Granary
Station Road
Saffron Walden
Essex
CB11 3PL
Tel: 01799 544014
www.nctj.com

British Printing Industries Federation (BPIF)
Farringdon Point
29/35 Farringdon Road
London
EC1M 3JF
www.britishprint.com

NEWPAPER JOURNALIST

The nature of the work

Newspaper journalists cover any event of interest to their specific audience, ranging from reporting on council meetings and school fetes for a local paper, to general elections and world events for the national press.

As a newspaper journalist, your work would typically include:

- investigating a story as soon as it breaks
- following up potential leads
- developing new contacts
- interviewing people, both face-to-face and over the phone
- attending press conferences
- recording meetings and interviews using recording equipment or shorthand
- coming up with ideas for new stories and features
- writing up articles in a style that will appeal to the intended audience.

You could choose to specialise in a specific subject such as sport, politics or entertainment. Because most newspapers have an online edition, you may also write stories for the web. Newspaper journalists sometimes work as sub-editors, preparing reporters' writing ('copy') for printing.

What can you earn?

Trainees earn around £15,000 a year on local newspapers
Experienced journalists can earn from £15,000 a year to over £40,000
The highest paid journalists and national newspaper editors can earn up to £100,000.
Freelance journalists negotiate a set fee for each piece of work they do. Fees can be negotiated individually or from guidance provided by the NUJ.

Entry requirements

You can become a newspaper journalist by training at college or university (known as pre-entry) or by joining a local or regional newspaper and training on the job (known as direct entry).

For both types of entry you will be at an advantage if you have relevant experience. To build up your experience you can:

- volunteer for student and community newspapers
- submit articles to websites or keep an online journal or blog
- work for local or student radio stations
- submit articles and reviews to local, free or specialist papers.

It is a good idea to keep cuttings and printouts of your published work to show to potential employers, especially if these include your name (known as a 'byline').

Training before starting work

This is the most common way to enter journalism. It involves completing a journalism course, then finding work as a trainee.

It is advisable to choose a course that is accredited by the National Council for the Training of Journalists (NCTJ). Some courses accept five GCSEs (including English) and two A levels, or similar qualifications, whilst others will expect you to have a degree. If you have a degree, you may be able to do an 18-20 week Fast Track course. See the NCTJ website for details of courses and training providers.

As part of any journalism course, you will take the NCTJ preliminary exams, which you need to pass before being taken on as a trainee.

You may be able do the NCTJ self-study programme, and enter yourself for the preliminary exams. To follow this route you would need to arrange work experience so that you can practise your skills. See the NCTJ website for details.

On-the-job training

To become a journalist by direct entry you need to apply to the editors of local and regional newspapers to be taken on as a trainee. You can find contact details on the Newspaper Society website.

You will need a minimum of five GCSEs (A-C), including English, or equivalent qualifications. However, it is increasingly rare for applicants to be accepted at this level. More than 60% of recruits have degrees, and most others have at least two A levels or the equivalent.

You can find advice and information on starting or developing your career in journalism on the NCTJ and National Union of Journalists (NUJ) websites.

More information

NUJ Training
www.nujtraining.org.uk

Creative Skillset
Focus Point
21 Caledonian Road
London
N1 9GB
www.creativeskillset.org

Creative Skillset Careers
Tel: 08080 300 900 (England and Northern Ireland)
Tel: 0845 850 2502(Scotland)
Tel: 08000 121 815 (Wales)
www.creativeskillset.org/careers

National Council for the Training of Journalists
The New Granary
Station Road
Saffron Walden
Essex
CB11 3PL
Tel: 01799 544014
www.nctj.com
National Union of Journalists (NUJ)
www.nuj.org.uk

Newspaper Society
www.newspapersoc.org.uk

MAGAZINE JOURNALIST

The nature of the work
Types of magazine include:
- consumer magazines – for the general public
- specialist consumer magazines – for people with interests in a particular subject, such as travel, arts and crafts, or cars
- professional magazines – for those working in a particular career such as human resources or management
- business and trade magazines
- in-house (internal) company magazines.

You would usually have specialist knowledge of the subject covered by the publication you write for.

As a magazine journalist, your work would vary depending on the type of magazine you are writing for, but would normally include:

- going to meetings to plan the content of the magazine
- suggesting ideas for articles that would interest the magazine's readers
- interviewing and researching to collect information for articles
- writing articles to suit the magazine's style
- keeping up to date with developments and trends in the magazine's subject area.

You might also produce versions of your articles for the magazine's website.

As a freelance (self-employed) journalist, you could write for both magazines and newspapers.

What can you earn?
Starting salaries can be between £18,000 and around £25,000 a year. With experience earnings can be up to £35,000 or more a year.

203

Entry requirements

There are no set qualifications for becoming a magazine journalist, although most people applying for this role have a degree.

A common starting point is to work as an editorial assistant for a magazine publishing house. This allows you to develop your skills and make contacts in the industry. Making contacts is important, as many journalist vacancies are not advertised.

You could gain a journalism qualification or degree before looking for work. Although this is not essential, doing this would help you learn about the magazine industry and develop the skills you would need as a journalist. Qualifications that are recognised by the industry are accredited by:
Periodicals Training Council - courses are delivered by the Professional Publishers Association (PPA)
National Council for the Training of Journalists (NCTJ)

See the PPA and NCTJ websites for details.

The NCTJ also runs distance learning courses, including Writing for the Periodical Press, which gives a basic understanding of the magazine industry.

Whether or not you have journalism qualifications, you will have to be proactive and persistent in order to start in magazine journalism. The key to getting into the industry is to gain practical experience and build up examples of your published work. Ways to do this include:

- contacting magazines to ask about opportunities for unpaid work experience
- contacting editors with ideas for articles relevant to their magazine
- writing reviews of films, plays or products
- volunteering to work on newsletters run by not-for-profit organisations.

Visit the PPA website for advice on finding work experience and applying for jobs.

Competition for jobs is strong, especially with the better-known magazines. It may be easier to get started on a specialist, trade or business publication, especially if you have knowledge of the area it covers. The more specialist the magazine, the more likely you are to need appropriate knowledge or experience.

More information
NUJ Training
www.nujtraining.org.uk

Newspaper Society
www.newspapersoc.org.uk

Periodicals Publishers Association (PPA)
Queens House
28 Kingsway
London
WC2B 6JR
Tel: 020 7404 4166
www.ppa.co.uk

Creative Skillset Careers
Tel: 08080 300 900 (England and Northern Ireland)
Tel: 0845 850 2502(Scotland)
Tel: 08000 121 815 (Wales)
www.creativeskillset.org/careers

Creative Skillset
Focus Point
21 Caledonian Road
London
N1 9GB
www.creativeskillset.org

National Union of Journalists (NUJ)
www.nuj.org.uk

Broadcast Journalism Training Council
18 Miller's Close
Rippingale
near Bourne
Lincolnshire
PE10 0TH
Tel: 01778 440025
www.bjtc.org.uk

Association of British Science Writers
www.absw.org.uk

European Medical Writers Association
www.emwa.org

National Council for the Training of Journalists (NCTJ)
The New Granary
Station Road
Saffron Walden
Essex
CB11 3PL
Tel: 01799 544014
www.nctj.com

ADVERTISING COPYWRITER

The nature of the work

As a copywriter, you would work as a team with an art director, who would provide the visual images to go with your words. Your job would begin with a briefing about the client, their product, the target audience and the advertising message to be put across. Your work could then involve:

- creating original ideas that fit the brief (working closely with the art director)
- presenting ideas to the agency's creative director and account team
- helping to present ideas to the client

- making any changes that the client asks for
- writing clear and persuasive copy
- making sure that ads meet the codes of advertising practice
- proofreading copy to check spelling, grammar and facts
- casting actors for TV and radio advertisements
- liaising with photographers, designers, production companies and printers.

What can you earn?

Starting salaries can be around £18,000 to £25,000 a year. With experience this rises to between £25,000 and £50,000 a year. Senior creatives in leading agencies can earn up to £100,000 or more.

Entry requirements

Employers will usually be more interested in your creativity, writing skills and business sense than your formal qualifications.

However, advertising is a very competitive industry to join, so you may have an advantage with a qualification that includes some copywriting, such as:

- a foundation degree, BTEC HND or degree in advertising
- Communication, Advertising and Marketing Education Foundation (CAM) Diploma in Marketing Communications.
- Other useful courses include BTEC HNDs or degrees in journalism, English, media studies and marketing.

Most people get their first copywriting job as a result of work experience. This can give you the chance to make industry contacts and impress potential employers.

You could contact agencies directly to ask about placements, and make industry contacts through relevant groups on social networking sites. See the Work Experience section of the Institute of Practitioners in Advertising (IPA) website for more information and a list of member agencies. The IPA also runs a Graduate Recruitment Agency, and D&AD runs a Graduate Placement Scheme.

When looking for jobs, you will need to show a portfolio of your work (known as a 'book') to potential employers, as you will be employed on the strength of your creative ideas, versatility and writing ability.

It's a good idea to team up with a would-be art director and work together on campaign ideas for your portfolio, as this can help prove your ability to fulfil a client's 'brief'. See D&AD's website for details of their advertising workshops, aimed at helping people build a portfolio and make contacts in the advertising industry.

If you join the IPA, you can also showcase the best of your portfolio online on their All Our Best Work website.

Visit the Diagonal Thinking website to find out if you have what it takes for a career in advertising.

More information

D&AD
9 Graphite Square
Vauxhall Walk
London
SE11 5EE
Tel: 020 7840 1111
www.dandad.org

Institute of Practitioners in Advertising (IPA)
44 Belgrave Square
London
SW1X 8QS
Tel: 020 7235 7020
www.ipa.co.uk

Communication Advertising and Marketing Education Foundation Limited (CAM)
Tel: 01628 427120
www.camfoundation.com

Creative Skillset
Focus Point
21 Caledonian Road
London
N1 9GB
www.creativeskillset.org

Creative Skillset Careers
Tel: 08080 300 900 (England and Northern Ireland)
Tel: 0845 850 2502(Scotland)
Tel: 08000 121 815 (Wales)
www.creativeskillset.org/careers

PROOFREADER

The nature of the work

As a proofreader, you would carefully check the 'proofs' (which show how the final pages will be laid out), using either a printed ('hard') copy or an on-screen version. Your main tasks would include making sure that:

- there are no errors such as letters in the wrong order
- all the material is included and is in the right place
- page numbers are in the right order
- the document follows the 'house style'
- chapter titles match the list of contents
- there are no confusing word, column or page breaks
- illustrations have the right captions and relate to the text
- the layout is logical and attractive.

You would mark any necessary changes using British Standards Institution symbols, which are internationally recognised. When working directly on computer, you may use specialist software to mark up the document. If necessary, you would also produce a separate list of any queries which need to be resolved.

Before marking any changes that could result in unacceptable costs or delay, you would discuss them with your client.

What can you earn?

Freelance proofreaders are usually paid by the page or the hour. The minimum rate suggested by the Society for Editors and Proofreaders (SfEP) from March 2012 is £20.75 an hour. Visit the SfEP website for the latest figures.

Rates of pay depend on experience, with new proofreaders often being paid a lower rate.

Entry requirements

You do not need any particular qualifications to be a proofreader. Employers will usually be more interested in your experience than your qualifications, and many proofreaders have worked in publishing, journalism or other related areas.

However, proofreaders are often graduates, so it could be an advantage if you have a degree, perhaps in English or in a subject which could become your specialist area for proofreading. For example, a science degree would be useful for proofreading scientific textbooks or manuals.

You can gain proofreading skills by completing short courses through the Society for Editors and Proofreaders (SfEP) and the Publishing Training Centre. Courses are also offered by private training providers. You can study the Publishing Training Centre Basic Proofreading course by distance learning. When you have completed the SfEP courses, you can get support in establishing your career by joining the SfEP mentoring scheme.

See the SfEP and the Publishing Training Centre websites for more details.

More information

Creative Skillset Careers
Tel: 08080 300 900 (England and Northern Ireland)

Tel: 0845 850 2502(Scotland)
Tel: 08000 121 815 (Wales)
www.creativeskillset.org/careers

Society for Editors and Proofreaders (SfEP)
Apsley House
176 Upper Richmond Road
Putney
London
SW15 2SH
Tel: 020 8785 6155
www.sfep.org.uk

Women in Publishing
www.wipub.org.uk

Publishers Association
29b Montague Street
London
WC1B 5BW
Tel: 020 7691 9191
www.publishers.org.uk

Publishing Training Centre at Book House
45 East Hill
Wandsworth
London
SW18 2QZ
Tel: 020 8874 2718
www.train4publishing.co.uk Job profiles

SUB EDITOR

The nature of the work
As a sub-editor, your work would typically include:

- making sure articles are accurate and do not break laws such as libel and copyright
- checking any queries with the reporter or journalist
- re-writing articles if necessary to make them clearer or shorter
- making sure articles follow the publication's house style
- writing headlines, captions, short paragraphs (known as 'standfirsts') which lead in to articles, and 'panels' which break up the text
- making sure articles are in the right place on each page
- using page layout and image editing software like Quark Express, InDesign and Photoshop
- sending completed pages to the printers.

You would work closely with reporters, editors, designers, production staff and printers.

What can you earn?

Starting salaries can range from £15,000 to £23,000 a year, depending on the type of publication. Experienced and senior sub-editors can earn from £25,000 a year to over £40,000.

Entry requirements

For newspaper sub-editing you would need a journalism qualification or experience. Industry-recognised qualifications are accredited by the National Council for the Training of Journalists (NCTJ).

It is common to move into sub-editing after gaining experience as a reporter. However, you can train specifically in sub-editing by completing a 12-week Diploma in Production Journalism at Brighton Journalist Works in Brighton – at present this is the only NCTJ-accredited sub-editing course available.

There are also several NCTJ-accredited newspaper courses which offer an additional certificate in sub-editing, which involves completing a subbing exam at the end of the course, as well as the reporters' exam. See the NCTJ website for details.

There are no set qualifications for becoming a magazine journalist, although most people applying for this sort of work have a degree. A common starting point is to work as an editorial assistant for a magazine publishing house. This route allows you to develop your skills and make contacts in the industry, which is important as many vacancies are not advertised.

Alternatively, you could prepare for a magazine sub-editing job by:
- completing the Diploma in Production Journalism mentioned above
- completing an industry-recognised journalism qualification accredited by the NCTJ or the Periodical Publishers Association (PPA).

See the NCTJ and PPA websites for full details of journalism careers and qualifications.

The NCTJ distance learning course, Basics of Sub-Editing, will help you to develop sub-editing skills, but does not lead to a qualification.

For many sub-editing jobs you will need to be able to use QuarkXpress. InDesign and Photoshop skills could also be useful. Courses in these are available at many colleges and private training providers.

More information

Creative Skillset Careers
Tel: 08080 300 900 (England and Northern Ireland)
Tel: 0845 850 2502(Scotland)
Tel: 08000 121 815 (Wales)
www.creativeskillset.org/careers

Society for Editors and Proofreaders (SfEP)
Apsley House
176 Upper Richmond Road
Putney
London
SW15 2SH
Tel: 020 8785 6155
www.sfep.org.uk

Creative Skillset
Focus Point

21 Caledonian Road
London
N1 9GB
www.creativeskillset.org

National Council for the Training of Journalists (NCTJ)
The New Granary
Station Road
Saffron Walden
Essex
CB11 3PL
Tel: 01799 544014
www.nctj.com

Periodicals Publishers Association (PPA)
Queens House
28 Kingsway
London
WC2B 6JR
Tel: 020 7404 4166
www.ppa.co.uk

Creative Skillset
Focus Point
21 Caledonian Road
London
N1 9GB
www.creativeskillset.org

BOOKBINDER OR PRINT FINISHER

The nature of the work
As a print finisher or machine bookbinder, your tasks would include:

- setting up machinery
- feeding the machinery with paper
- reporting machine breakdowns

- taking away and stacking the finished products.

As a craft or hand bookbinder, you would work on a much smaller scale. Your tasks would typically include:

- hand binding small numbers of books, such as family histories or books for libraries and museums
- using specialist hand tools to make bindings for books and to sew pages
- adding decoration such as gold lettering and edging, or marbled end-papers.

You could also restore and repair antique books, cleaning discoloured pages or using leathers and papers to match those originally used.

What can you earn?

Starting salaries can be around £14,000 a year.
Experienced binders and finishers can earn between £16,000 and £35,000.
Earnings for self-employed craft bookbinders vary widely depending on the amount of work they have.

Entry requirements

You may not need formal qualifications to be a print finisher or machine bookbinder and you would usually receive on-the-job training. However, some employers may prefer you to have GCSEs or equivalent qualifications, including English and maths.

You may be able to get into this type of work through an Apprenticeship scheme. The range of Apprenticeships available in your area will depend on the local jobs market and the types of skills employers need. To find out more, visit the Apprenticeships website.

To be a craft bookbinder, you would need to gain skills before starting work. You can attend part-time or short courses in bookbinding at many colleges. You can also complete higher education courses, including BTEC HNCs/HNDs and degrees in craft bookbinding at specialist colleges. Visit the Society of Bookbinders (SoB) website for details of courses.

The Designer Bookbinders (DB) website also lists courses offered by colleges and private providers, as well as joint SOB/DB courses and DB lectures.

More information
Proskills UK
www.proskills.co.uk

Society of Bookbinders
www.societyofbookbinders.com

Designer Bookbinders
www.designerbookbinders.org.uk

British Printing Industries Federation (BPIF)
Farringdon Point
29/35 Farringdon Road
London
EC1M 3JF
www.britishprint.com

City & Guilds
London
EC1A 9DD
Tel: 0844 543 0000
www.cityandguilds.com

PRINTING ADMINISTRATOR
The nature of the work

You could be involved in various areas of print production, such as planning, estimating, buying, sales and overall management. Your duties would include:

- supervising print orders through the pre-press, printing and finishing stages
- coordinating different print runs by planning the most efficient way to use machinery and staff

- solving problems in the production process
- using software packages to help put together quotations for jobs
- negotiating with suppliers, stocktaking and purchasing materials
- developing new business opportunities and looking after existing clients.

If you manage a print workshop or department, you would organise workloads, supervise staff and plan schedules. You would also meet with customers and take overall responsibility for making sure print runs are cost-effective, meet deadlines and achieve quality standards.

What can you earn?

Starting salaries range from £14,000 to £17,000 a year. Experienced print administrators earn between £18,000 and £25,000. Senior administrators with management responsibilities can earn around £30,000 a year.
There are additional payments for overtime and shiftwork.

Entry requirements

You would usually need previous experience in the industry to work as a print administrator. Supervisory, management or sales experience gained from other industries would also give you an advantage when looking for work. Employers may ask for GCSE or A level passes in maths, English, art and IT, or equivalent qualifications.

Alternatively, you could complete a print-related qualification before looking for work, such as:

- City & Guilds Certificate in Printing and Graphic Communications levels 2 and 3
- BTEC Certificate, Diploma and Award in Graphics levels 1, 2 and 3
- ABC Diploma in Digital Origination at Level 3.
- Higher level options include a foundation degree, BTEC HNC/HND or degree in print media, digital media, graphics or graphic design. See the Universities and Colleges Admissions Service (UCAS) website for colleges and universities offering these qualifications.

217

Alternatively, you may be able to get into this career through a printing Apprenticeship, working your way up to an administration role. The range of Apprenticeships available in your area will depend on the local jobs market and the types of skills employers need from their workers. To find out more, visit the Apprenticeships website.

See the British Printing Industry Federation (BPIF) and the PrintIT! websites for more details on printing careers and training providers.

More information

PrintIT!
www.printit.org.uk

Proskills UK
www.proskills.co.uk

British Printing Industries Federation (BPIF)
Farringdon Point
29/35 Farringdon Road
London
EC1M 3JF
www.britishprint.com

Institute of Paper, Printing and Publishing
www.ip3.org.uk

MACHINE PRINTERS
The nature of the work

Machine printers, also known as print minders, operate and maintain printing presses. Their work involves taking instructions from the pre-press operator and setting up the press with the right materials for the production run.

As a machine printer, your work would involve:

- matching colours to the pre-press proofs
- restocking ink levels
- feeding the print materials into the presses
- putting job data into computerised control units
- carrying out quality checks during the print run
- identifying problems and fixing faults
- cleaning presses after a print run has finished (either by hand or using automatic cleaning systems)
- carrying out basic machine maintenance.

You would usually work on a particular type of press, but you would train in a variety of printing techniques. These could include:

- flexigraphic (relief process) – commonly used to print onto items like shopping bags and food packaging
- screen printing (stencilling) – for printing onto clothing, posters or display signs
- gravure (intaglio process) – used for high quality work on catalogues, fabrics and wallpapers
- digital printing – using inkjet and laser printing methods
- lithographic (planographic process) – the most widely used method and often used for large print runs such as catalogues, newspapers and magazines.

On large presses, you might work in a team, but on smaller ones you could be responsible for all the tasks on the print run.

What can you earn?

Starting salaries for qualified printers are between £16,000 and £19,000 a year. Experienced machine printers can earn up to £40,000 a year. Additional payments are made for shift allowances, specific responsibilities and overtime.

Entry requirements

Most employers expect a good standard of general education, such as GCSEs in English and maths, science subjects and IT. You would also be expected to have good colour vision.

You may be able to get into this career through an Apprenticeship scheme with a printing company. To get on to a scheme, you are likely to need four or five GCSEs (A-C) including maths and English, or equivalent qualifications. The range of Apprenticeships available in your area will depend on the local jobs market and the types of skills employers need from their workers. To find out more, visit the Apprenticeships website.

You could learn some of the skills needed for this job by taking a college printing course, such as:

- ABC Diploma in Print Media at Level 3 covers various processes including digital printing and print finishing
- City & Guilds (5261) Certificate in Printing and Graphic Communications – covers all the main print processes.

General art and design courses may offer you options in techniques like screen printing. Contact your local colleges to find out what is available.

For more details about careers in printing and training providers, visit the British Printing Industries Federation (BPIF) website and the PrintIT! website.

More information

Proskills UK
www.proskills.co.uk

PrintIT!
www.printit.org.uk

British Printing Industries Federation (BPIF)
Farringdon Point
29/35 Farringdon Road
London
EC1M 3JF
www.britishprint.com

City & Guilds
London
EC1A 9DD
Tel: 0844 543 0000
www.cityandguilds.com

****

13. THE LEGAL PROFESSION

The legal profession is very diverse and can be a very rewarding career. the training is long and arduous and not always that glamorous. However, for the right person the rewards can be many. In this chapter we cover:

- Solicitor
- Barrister
- Barristers clerk
- Legal secretary
- Licensed conveyancer

For details of other roles in the legal profession you should go to:

Law Careers
www.lawcareers.net

All About Law - The Law Careers Website
www.allaboutlaw.co.uk

SOLICITOR

The nature of the work
You could work as a solicitor in a range of settings, including:

- private practice - providing legal services such as conveyancing, probate, civil and family law, litigation, personal injury and criminal law
- commercial practice - advising and acting for businesses in areas including contract law, tax, employment law and company sales and mergers
- in-house legal advice for companies, the government or local authorities

- Crown Prosecution Service - examining evidence to decide whether to bring cases to court.
- You would often choose to specialise in a particular area of law.

Your duties would vary according to the setting you worked in, but might typically include:

- advising clients about legal matters
- representing clients in court, or instructing barristers or advocates to act for your clients
- drafting letters, contracts and documents
- researching similar cases to guide your current work
- keeping financial records
- attending meetings and negotiations
- preparing papers for court.

What can you earn?

The minimum salary for trainee solicitors is £18,590 a year in London, and £16,650 in the rest of England and Wales.

Once qualified, salaries can rise to between £25,000 and £70,000 a year, depending on experience and the type of employer. Salaries for partners in large firms or heads of in-house legal departments can reach £100,000 a year or more.

Entry requirements

To become a solicitor, you must first meet certain academic standards, and then you must complete vocational training.

In England and Wales, you can meet the academic standards in one of the following three ways:

- by gaining a qualifying law degree

- by gaining a degree in any other subject, then taking a postgraduate law conversion course – either the Common Professional Examination (CPE) or Graduate Diploma in Law (GDL)
- by qualifying as a Fellow of the Institute of Legal Executives (ILEX)

To do a law degree, you will generally need at least five GCSEs (A-C) and two A levels with good grades, or alternatives such as an Access to Higher Education qualification. Some universities may ask you to pass the National Admissions Test for Law (LNAT) before accepting you for a law degree. You should check exact entry requirements with course providers.

You can find lists of qualifying law degrees and postgraduate law conversion courses at the Solicitors' Regulation Authority (SRA) website.

In Northern Ireland, you can meet the academic stage by either:

- gaining an approved law degree, or having a degree in another subject and proving that you have a satisfactory level of legal knowledge
- having substantial experience of relevant legal work.

After this you must complete an apprenticeship of between two and four years with a solicitor. This will include a year's study at the Institute of Professional Legal Studies in Belfast or the University of Ulster in Londonderry. Contact the Law Society of Northern Ireland for more details.

More information

Law Society
113 Chancery Lane
London
WC2A 1PL
Tel: 0870 606 2555
www.lawsociety.org.uk

Law Society of Northern Ireland
Law Society House

40 Linenhall Street
Belfast
BT2 8BA
Tel: 028 9023 1614
www.lawsoc-ni.org

National Admissions Test for Law (LNAT)
www.lnat.ac.uk

Law Careers
www.lawcareers.net

All About Law - The Law Careers Website
www.allaboutlaw.co.uk

BARRISTER

The nature of the work

If you are interested in a career in law and want to specialise, this could be perfect for you.

Barristers give specialist legal advice to professional and non-professional clients, and represent individuals and organisations in court, at tribunals and at public enquiries.

As a barrister, your work could include:

- taking on cases (known as briefs)
- advising on the law and how strong your client's legal case is
- researching points of law from previous similar cases
- providing written legal opinions to advise on cases
- having meetings with clients to discuss their case and offer legal advice
- getting cases ready for court by reading witness statements and reports, and preparing legal arguments
- representing clients in court – presenting the case to the judge and jury, cross-examining witnesses and summing up

- negotiating settlements for clients.

You would specialise in one particular area of law, which would determine the amount of time you spend in court. For example, as a criminal law specialist working in private practice or for the Crown Prosecution Service, you would spend most of your time preparing for cases and presenting in court.

In other areas of law, such as civil law (family law, property and tort) or chancery law (company law, tax, wills, trusts, and estates), you would mainly do office-based advisory work.

What can you earn?

Salaries during pupillage are at least £12,000 a year (pupillage is the final stage of training to be a barrister). In the first few years of practice, earnings can be anywhere between £25,000 and £200,000 a year, depending on specialism and reputation.

Salaries in the Crown Prosecution Service are between £28,000 and £60,000 a year.

Top earnings in private practice can reach £750,000 a year or more.

Entry requirements

To become a barrister, you must first complete an academic stage of training, followed by a vocational stage and a practical pupillage.

You can complete the academic stage by gaining:

- either an approved law degree (known as a qualifying law degree) at class 2:2 or above
- or a degree at 2:2 or above in any other subject, followed by a postgraduate Common Professional Examination (CPE) or Graduate Diploma in Law (GDL).

Many Chambers require that applicants for pupillage have a minimum 2:1 degree, and the proportion accepted with a lower second class degree is very low.

See the Education and Training section of the Bar Standards Board website for details of qualifying law degrees and postgraduate law courses.

To do a qualifying law degree, you normally need three A levels with good grades, plus at least five GCSEs (A-C). Other qualifications, such as an Access to Higher Education course, may be accepted. At some universities, you may also need to pass the National Admissions Test for Law (LNAT). Check exact entry requirements with individual course providers.

Most barristers begin vocational training straight after getting their law degree or postgraduate law qualification, but this is not essential. Others work for a number of years in related fields first, and some transfer from other professions. For information about the vocational stage and pupillage, see the Training and Development section below.

Competition is extremely strong for all stages of barrister training, so any relevant work experience can improve your chances. In particular, you should try to undertake at least three mini pupillages - a short period of work experience shadowing a barrister in Chambers. Information on mini pupillages and how to apply is available on individual Chambers' websites.

BARRISTERS CLERK

The nature of the work
Your day-to-day duties could include:

- preparing papers and taking books, documents and robes to and from court
- messenger work (collecting and delivering documents by hand)
- photocopying, filing and dealing with letters, e-mails and phone calls
- handling accounts, invoices and petty cash

- collecting fees
- organising the law library
- managing each barrister's daily diary and keeping their case information up to date
- liaising between solicitors, clients and their barristers=
- reorganising barristers' schedules when necessary.

With experience, you might become a senior barristers' clerk (which may also be known as chambers director or practice manager). In this key role you would also be responsible for:

- recruiting, training and supervising junior clerks
- bringing business into chambers
- allocating cases to barristers
- negotiating fees
- financial management of the chambers.

What can you earn?

Entry requirements

Most chambers will expect you to have at least four GCSEs (A-C), including maths and English, although many barristers' clerks have higher qualifications such as A levels or degrees.

It would be useful to have some experience in court administration, legal secretarial work, accounts or management.

Some chambers offer work experience to potential applicants, which may give you an advantage when applying for jobs.

More information

Institute of Barristers' Clerks (IBC)
289-293 High Holborn
London
WC1 7HZ

Tel: 020 7831 7144
www.ibc.org.uk

LEGAL SECRETARY

The nature of the work

As a legal secretary, you would provide administrative support for lawyers and legal executives, and help with the day-to-day tasks involved in running a legal firm.

Your tasks would be varied and depending on what department you work in your duties could include:

If you worked in a small local law firm, you would develop experience in a wide range of legal matters, whilst in larger firms you would tend to specialise in a particular area of law.

What can you earn?

Starting salaries can be between £12,000 and £20,000 a year depending on your location. This can rise with experience.

Entry requirements

Employers will expect a good standard of literacy, and you may have an advantage with a GCSE (A-C) in English, or a similar level of qualification.

You will usually need experience of office work, plus accurate typing skills. You would also have an advantage if you had audio transcription skills. Temporary office work (known as 'temping') is a good way of getting relevant experience. Full- and part-time courses in computer and secretarial skills are widely available at local colleges and through training companies.

You may find it useful to take a recognised legal secretarial course before you look for work. However, this is not always essential if you have good general administrative skills and a knowledge of law.

You may be able to get into secretarial work through an Apprenticeship scheme. The range of Apprenticeships available in your area will depend on the local jobs market and the types of skills employers need from their workers. For more information, visit the Apprenticeships website.

More information

Chartered Institute of Legal Executives
Kempston Manor
Kempston
Bedfordshire
MK42 7AB 01234 841000
www.ilex.org.uk

Institute of Legal Secretaries and PAs
308 Canterbury Court
Kennington Business Park
1-3 Brixton Road
London
Tel: 0845 643 4974 / 0207 1009210
Fax: 0203 384 4976
e-mail: info@institutelegalsecretaries.com
www.institutelegalsecretaries.com

City & Guilds
1 Giltspur Street
London
EC1A 9DD
Tel: 0844 543 0000
www.cityandguilds.com

LICENSED CONVEYANCER

The nature of the work

Conveyancing is the legal process of transferring a house or flat, commercial property or piece of land from one owner to another. Licensed or qualified conveyancers are specialist property lawyers who deal with the paperwork and finances involved in buying and selling property in England and Wales.

As a conveyancer, your main duties would include:

- advising clients on the buying and selling process
- researching who legally owns the property being bought
- conducting 'searches' – asking local authorities about any plans that might affect the property in the future
- drafting contracts with details of the sale
- liaising with mortgage lenders, estate agents and solicitors
- paying taxes such as stamp duty
- preparing leases and transfer documents
- keeping records of payments
- checking that contracts are signed and exchanged.

What can you earn?

Starting salaries can be between £14,000 and £20,000 a year. After qualifying, earnings can be between £20,000 and £50,000

Entry requirements

To become a licensed conveyancer you must pass the Council for Licensed Conveyancers (CLC) exams. To begin CLC training, you will usually need at least four GCSEs (A-C) including English, or equivalent qualifications. However, if you have relevant work experience from a solicitor's or licensed conveyancer's office, you may be accepted without the minimum qualifications. Contact CLC for advice. In practice, people often start with higher qualifications, for example law degrees, LPC or Institute of Legal Executives (ILEX) qualifications. You do not need to be working in the legal profession to start studying for the CLC exams.

Some solicitors specialise in conveyancing. If you are already a qualified solicitor, you don't need to pass any further exams but you must apply to the CLC for a licence to practise as a conveyancer.

More information

Council for Licenced Conveyancers
16 Glebe Road
Chelmsford
Essex
CM1 1QG
Tel: 01245 349599
www.clc-uk.org

****

14. MARKETING

Marketing is a very important field of work, and calls for creative dynamic people. The rewards can be significant for the right candidates. In this section we cover key jobs in the field:

- Marketing Executive
- Marketing manager
- Marketing Research Data Analyst
- Market research Interviewer

For further details of careers in the field of marketing go to:

Chartered Institute of Marketing (CIM)
Moor Hall
Cookham
Maidenhead
Berkshire
SL6 9QH
Tel: 01628 427120
www.cim.co.uk

MARKETING EXECUTIVE

The nature of the work
Your work would involve:
- researching the market, consumer attitudes and competitors
- coming up with ideas for marketing campaigns
- arranging for advertisements to go into newspapers, magazines, the trade press, TV or radio
- organising the production of posters, flyers and brochures
- writing and distributing press releases and mailshots
- maintaining a database of customers
- arranging sponsorship

233

- organising and attending events and exhibitions
- making sure that all parts of a campaign run smoothly
- reporting on the campaign's progress to managers
- networking with clients, suppliers and the media.

In some jobs you may be known as a marketing officer, brand executive or account executive.

What can you earn?

Starting salaries can be between £18,000 and £22,000 a year
With experience, this can rise to between £25,000 and £40,000
Marketing directors can earn £50,000 a year or more.

Entry requirements

You could get into marketing with various levels of experience, but generally the more experience and skills you have, the higher up the career ladder you can start.

Many marketing executives have a degree or BTEC HNC/HND in marketing or another business-related subject. With a degree, you could join one of the graduate training schemes that larger employers often run for new recruits. Most degree subjects are acceptable, but you may have an advantage with one of the following:

- marketing (especially if the course included work placements)
- communications
- advertising
- business and management
- psychology.

A degree is not always essential if you have business and marketing skills gained from previous jobs such as sales, customer service or public relations work. You could also join a company's marketing department as an administrator or assistant (perhaps as a temp), and work your way up to marketing executive with experience.

Taking a professional qualification from the Chartered Institute of Marketing (CIM) could help your promotion prospects or increase your chances of finding your first marketing job. Some CIM qualifications are suitable if you don't already have a marketing-related degree or relevant work experience:

- Introductory Certificate in Marketing – an entry-level qualification open to anybody
- Professional Certificate in Marketing – for anyone educated to A level standard, or with a little marketing experience.

CIM qualifications are available full- or part-time at many colleges, and by distance learning – see the Training and Qualifications section of the CIM website for more information.

More information

Chartered Institute of Marketing (CIM)
Moor Hall
Cookham
Maidenhead
Berkshire
SL6 9QH
Tel: 01628 427120
www.cim.co.uk

Institute of Direct and Digital Marketing (IDM)
1 Park Road
Teddington
Middlesex
TW11 0AR
Tel: 020 8614 0277
www.urthebrand.co.uk
www.theidm.com

Communication Advertising and Marketing Education Foundation Limited (CAM)
Tel: 01628 427120
www.camfoundation.com

Arts Marketing Association
Tel: 01223 578078
www.a-m-a.co.uk

Focus Point
21 Caledonian Road
London
N1 9GB
www.creativeskillset.org

Creative Skillset Careers
Tel: 08080 300 900 (England and Northern Ireland)
Tel: 0845 850 2502(Scotland)
Tel: 08000 121 815 (Wales)
www.creativeskillset.org/careers

MARKETING MANAGER

The nature of the work

You would use various marketing strategies (such as media advertising, direct mail, websites and promotional events) to communicate with customers. Your typical tasks would include:

- researching and analysing market trends
- identifying target markets and how best to reach them
- coming up with marketing strategies
- planning campaigns and managing budgets
- organising the production of posters, brochures and websites
- attending trade shows, conferences and sales meetings
- making sure that campaigns run to deadline and on budget
- monitoring and reporting on the effectiveness of strategies and campaigns
- managing a team of marketing executives and assistants.

You would often specialise in certain types of product or market, such as fashion, fast moving consumer goods (FMCG) or financial services. In some companies you might be known as a brand or account manager.

What can you earn?

- Management salaries are usually between £25,000 and £40,000 a year.
- Senior managers and marketing directors can earn £50,000 a year or more.

Entry requirements

You will usually need solid experience as a marketing executive before you progress into management.

For jobs at management level, employers are likely to be more interested in your skills, track record and industry knowledge than your formal qualifications.

If an employer does ask for qualifications, they will generally prefer you to have a marketing or business-related degree, or a professional marketing qualification such as:

- Chartered Institute of Marketing (CIM) Professional Diploma in Marketing
- Institute of Direct and Digital Marketing (IDM) Diploma in Direct and Interactive Marketing.

You could also move into marketing management if you have a strong background in a related area such as sales management or public relations.

More information

Chartered Institute of Marketing (CIM)
Moor Hall
Cookham
Maidenhead

Berkshire
SL6 9QH
Tel: 01628 427120
www.cim.co.uk

Communication Advertising and Marketing Education Foundation Limited (CAM)
Tel: 01628 427120
www.camfoundation.com

Institute of Direct and Digital Marketing (IDM)
1 Park Road
Teddington
Middlesex
TW11 0AR theidm.com

Arts Marketing Association
Tel: 01223 578078
www.a-m-a.co.uk

MARKETING RESEARCH DATA ANALYST

The nature of the work

As a market research analyst, it would be your job to analyse statistics that have been collected through market research surveys. This could be consumer, industrial or social and political research commissioned by all types of client in industry, business and government.

Your work would involve:

- writing proposals describing how you will carry out the research
- advising researchers about survey methodology and design
- checking that the data that has been collected
- analysing the data using statistical software programmes and techniques

- presenting the findings through talks, written reports, graphs and tables
- explaining the results to research executives (who may not have specialist mathematical or statistical knowledge)
- helping research executives present the findings in a way that the client can understand and use.

Job titles can vary, for example you might be known as a data analyst, statistician or insight professional.

What can you earn?

Graduate starting salaries are around £22,000 a year. With experience, earnings can rise to between £25,000 and £35,000. Salaries for senior posts can range from £40,000 to £55,000.

Entry requirements

You will need a degree in statistics or a related subject that involves statistics, such as maths, business studies or economics. The most useful courses focus on the practical applications of statistics. To get onto a statistics degree you will usually need at least five GCSEs (A-C) plus three A levels including a good grade in maths, or equivalent qualifications. You should contact universities to find out about their exact entry requirements.

Many market research data analysts also have a Masters degree (MSc) or PhD in statistics or applied statistics. You may find it particularly useful to take an MSc if you want to specialise in an area like medical or social science statistics. See the Education and Qualifications section of the Royal Statistical Society (RSS) website for a list of degrees and Masters degrees that they accredit.

You will find it useful to have work experience in research, advertising, data analysis, or as a market research interviewer.

When looking for your first graduate job, you could start as a junior statistician/analyst, perhaps on a structured graduate training scheme offered by some of the larger companies. Alternatively you could start as a research assistant, and move into statistical work after gaining more experience.

More information

Market Research Society (MRS)
15 Northburgh Street
London
EC1V 0JR
Tel: 020 7490 4911
www.mrs.org.uk

Royal Statistical Society (RSS)
12 Errol Street
London
EC1Y 8LX
Tel: 020 7638 8998
www.rss.org.uk

Association for Qualitative Research (AQR)
Davey House
31 St Neots Road
Eaton Ford
St Neots
Cambridgeshire
PE19 7BA
Tel: 01480 407227
www.aqr.org.uk

MARKET RESEARCH INTERVIEWER

The nature of the work

As a market research interviewer, you would gather information on people's attitudes and opinions by asking them questions from pre-prepared surveys. The research that you carried out could be commissioned by a wide range of organisations, including:

- advertising agencies

- businesses of all kinds
- government
- opinion polls
- charities.

The market research process starts when the commissioning organisation briefs a research agency about what they want to find out. The agency then prepares questionnaires to use with the target audience, and recruits interviewers to carry out the surveys.

As part of a market research interviewing team, you would:

- attend an agency briefing about the research project
- approach interviewees in the street, phone them or call on them at home
- explain about the research and how it will be used
- ask a series of scripted questions from the questionnaire
- record people's answers on paper forms, a hand-held computer or video
- carry out a set number of interviews to meet a quota
- collate the results and pass them back to the market research organisation.

What can you earn?

- Earnings are usually £50 to £65 a day or £5.75 to £8.50 an hour, plus expenses.
- This is the equivalent of around £11,000 to £16,000 a year in a permanent full-time job.
- Field supervisors or research assistants can earn £18,000 to £22,000 a year.

Entry requirements

You don't need any qualifications to become a market research interviewer. Employers will be more interested in your personality, enthusiasm and communication skills.

You will find it useful to have experience of dealing with the public, in any kind of customer service job.

Employers may prefer you to have a driving licence and your own transport.

More information

Market Research Society
15 Northburgh Street
London
EC1V 0JR
Tel: 020 7490 4911
www.mrs.org.uk

Association for Qualitative Research (AQR)
Davey House
31 St Neots Road
Eaton Ford
St Neots
Cambridgeshire
PE19 7BA
Tel: 01480 407227
www.aqr.org.uk

****

15. MUSIC RADIO AND TV

Without a doubt, this is one of the most competitive and difficult areas of work to gain a foothold in. However, for those who persist the rewards are great. This chapter covers a cross section of jobs, as follows:

- Pop Musician
- Roadie
- Studio Sound Engineer
- Radio Broadcast Engineer
- Screen Writer
- TV or Film Assistant Director
- TV or Film Camera Operator
- TV or Film Director
- TV or Film producer
- TV or Film production Assistant
- TV or Film Sound Technician
- Wardrobe Assistant
- Make Up Artist

As can be appreciated the number of opportunities in these areas are numerous. For more details you should go to the various websites listed below each job.

POP MUSICIAN

The nature of the work
If you've got musical talent and you enjoy performing in front of an audience, being a pop musician might be ideal for you.

You would spend your time:

- practising and rehearsing
- playing in front of an audience

- composing songs and music to perform (or learning 'covers' of other artists' music)
- taking part in recording sessions (as an individual performer, with your own band or by providing backing or vocals at recording sessions)
- promoting your act in various ways, such as contacting agents and record companies, setting up a website and making 'demos'
- arranging gigs and tours (or dealing with a manager or agent who arranges this for you).

You would often combine music with other types of work, particularly at the start of your career.

What can you earn?

Your annual income would vary according to how successful you were and how much work you could get.

See the Musicians' Union, Equity (the performers' union) and the Incorporated Society of Musicians (ISM) websites for recommended rates of pay for session musicians and live performers.

Entry requirements

You will need a good level of musical ability as a singer or on your chosen instrument. It's not essential that you know how to read music, but it can be an advantage, especially if you want to work as a session musician.

Many musicians start learning an instrument from an early age, and you can take part-time classes at many colleges, adult education centres, private music teachers and performing arts schools. Some of these may offer qualifications such as Rockschool popular music graded exams in:

- guitar
- bass
- drums
- popular piano
- vocals.

You could take a college or university course in popular music or music technology, although this is not essential. Relevant qualifications include BTEC National Certificates/Diplomas, or foundation, undergraduate and postgraduate degrees. Check with colleges for exact entry requirements, as you may need to pass an audition to get onto some courses.

The most important thing, however, is to gain plenty of practical experience by performing and doing gigs. Many record companies send Artists and Repertoire (A&R) staff to small clubs, pubs and other venues to scout for emerging talent.

When trying to break into the music business, you can approach record companies with a 'demo' CD or MP3 of your music. Companies receive thousands of demos so yours will need to stand out immediately: if it does not attract the listeners attention after 30 seconds or so, they are likely to discard it. See the BPI and Showcase websites for record company contact details.

It is common for bands and solo artists to showcase their music on networking websites. You could also get yourself noticed by entering talent competitions.

More information

Creative and Cultural Skills
Lafone House
The Leathermarket
Weston Street
London
SE1 3HN
www.creative-choices.co.uk

Incorporated Society of Musicians (ISM)
10 Stratford Place
London
W1C 1AA
Tel: 020 7629 4413
www.ism.org

BPI - The British Recorded Music Industry
Riverside Building
County Hall
Westminster Bridge Road
London
SE1 7JA
Tel: 020 7803 1300
www.bpi.co.uk

Rockschool
Evergreen House
2-4 King Street
Twickenham
Middlesex
TW1 3RZ
Tel: 0845 460 4747
www.rockschool.co.uk

Equity
Guild House
Upper St Martin's Lane
London
WC2H 9EG
Tel: 020 7379 6000
www.equity.org.uk

Musicians Union
Tel: 020 7582 5566
www.musiciansunion.org.uk

RADIO BROADCAST ASSISTANT

The nature of the work
Broadcast assistants (often known in the radio industry as 'BAs') support producers and presenters in making radio programmes. As a broadcast assistant, it would be your job to handle the administration, help to plan

programmes and provide technical support in the studio. Becoming a BA is a common starting point for a career in radio.

The work can vary widely from one station to the next and even from one programme to the next. The main differences are between speech and music radio, and between live and pre-recorded radio. However, your administrative duties would generally include:

- typing scripts
- keeping track of costs
- researching programmes
- booking guests, preparing their contracts and arranging payment
- producing programme logs and running orders
- archiving programme material
- arranging and sending out competition prizes
- booking studio time and equipment
- updating the programme or station website.
- Studio production work can include:
- managing phone lines for phone-ins and competitions
- timing shows
- operating recording, editing and mixing equipment on pre-recorded or live programmes (often known as 'driving the desk')
- recording and editing programme trailers
- offering creative input, such as writing links or devising quiz questions.

With experience, you may also take on some of the more high-profile tasks, such as contributing programme ideas, interviewing guests or presenting part of a programme. In speech or news radio, you would often be asked to go out and collect short interviews (known as 'vox pops') from the general public.

What can you earn?

Starting salaries are often between £13,000 and £18,000 a year
With experience, this could rise to around £25,000 a year.
If you work freelance, you will usually negotiate a fee for each contract. Rates can vary, and there may be gaps between contracts.

Figures are intended as a guideline only.

Entry requirements
The key to becoming a broadcast assistant is to get plenty of practical experience in radio (paid or unpaid), and to prove your initiative, enthusiasm and flexibility to employers.

You can gain useful experience through:

- community, hospital or student radio – see the Community Media Association website for a list of local stations, and the Hospital Broadcasting Association for a list of hospital stations
- work placements – for details of possible opportunities, see BBC Work Experience Placements or the RadioCentre (for commercial radio).

As your experience grows, it's a good idea to develop a 'demo' or 'showreel' CD or MP3 of productions you have worked on to send to potential employers.

You may also find it helpful to take a course in radio or media production. Look for courses that include practical skills training and work placements. Several colleges, community media schemes and universities offer relevant full-time, part-time and short courses including:

- ABC Level 3 Awards in Broadcast Media (Talk Radio Broadcast Skills and Radio Production Skills)
- NCFE Certificates and Diplomas in Radio Production at levels 1 and 2
- City & Guilds (7501) Diploma in Media Techniques (will be the Level 1, 2 and 3 Award, Certificate and Diploma in Media Techniques (7601) from September 2010)
- BTEC National Certificate/Diploma in Media Production (BTEC Level 3 Certificate/Diploma in Creative Media Production from September 2010)
- BTEC HNDs, Foundation Degrees, degrees and postgraduate courses in radio or media production.

Check with course providers for entry requirements.

For news-based and factual radio, you may have an advantage with a background in journalism or research.

More information
Creative Skillset
Focus Point
21 Caledonian Road
London
N1 9GB
www.creativeskillset.org

Creative Skillset Careers
Tel: 08080 300 900 (England and Northern Ireland)
Tel: 0845 850 2502(Scotland)
Tel: 08000 121 815 (Wales)
www.creativeskillset.org/careers

The RadioCentre
4th Floor
5 Golden Square
London
W1F 9BS
Tel: 020 3206 7800
www.radiocentre.org

Radio Academy
2nd Floor
5 Golden Square
London
W1F 9BS
Tel: 020 3174 1180
www.radioacademy.org

Broadcast Journalism Training Council
18 Miller's Close
Rippingale

near Bourne
Lincolnshire
PE10 0TH
Tel: 01778 440025
www.bjtc.org.uk

Community Media Association
15 Paternoster Row
Sheffield
S1 2BX
Tel: 0114 279 5219
www.commedia.org.uk

Hospital Broadcasting Association
www.hbauk.com

ROADIE

The nature of the work

Roadies, sometimes called technical support staff or crew, help to stage music concerts and other events. You would set up before a gig, look after the instruments during the show, and pack away afterwards.

You might work alone or as part of large crew, doing some or all of the following duties:

- lifting and carrying equipment and sets
- driving, loading and unloading vans, trailers and buses
- acting as security for equipment and band members
- setting up and looking after sound equipment
- setting up video equipment and screens
- rigging up wiring and lighting
- setting up pyrotechnics (fireworks) and laser displays
- tuning the instruments during the show.

You could also be responsible for other tour management duties like booking travel and caterers or issuing backstage passes.

What can you earn?

Unskilled roadies working full-time can earn around £12,000 a year. With technical skills, earnings could be £20,000 to £30,000 a year or more. You may also be paid living expenses when on tour.

Entry requirements

You would often start by working for free for local bands – many people get their first job through making contacts in this way. You can also get relevant experience through things like:

- working backstage in college or amateur theatre productions
- casual work at local concert venues and gigs
- working for equipment hire and supply companies.

It would be helpful to have a driving licence. You may have an advantage if you have a Large Goods Vehicle (LGV) licence or Passenger Carrying Vehicle (PCV) licence, which would allow you to drive tour buses and lorries.

You don't need formal qualifications to work as a roadie, but you may have an advantage with experience and qualifications in electronics, electrical work, sound production, music technology or lighting. The more skills you have, the more employable you will be. See the related profiles for more information on these jobs.

More information

Roadie
www.roadie.net

Association of British Theatre Technicians
55 Farringdon Road
London
EC1M 3JB
Tel: 020 7242 9200
www.abtt.org.uk

Production Services Association
PO Box 2709
Bath
BA1 3YS
Tel:01225 332668
www.psa.org.uk

Broadcasting Entertainment Cinematograph and Theatre Union (BECTU)
373-377 Clapham Road
London
SW9 9BT
Tel: 0845 850 2502
www.bectu.org.uk

SCREENWRITER

The nature of the work

Screenwriters create ideas and bring stories to life in scripts for feature films, TV comedy and drama, animation, children's programmes and computer games.

As a screenwriter, you might develop your own original ideas and sell them to producers. Alternatively, producers may commission you to create a screenplay from an idea or true story, or to adapt an existing piece such as a novel, play or comic book.

Your work would typically involve:

- coming up with themes and ideas
- researching background material
- developing believable plots and characters
- laying out the screenplay to an agreed format
- preparing short summaries of your ideas and selling (known as 'pitching') them to producers or development executives
- getting feedback about the first draft of your work from producers or script editors

- rewriting the script if necessary (you may need to do this several times before arriving at the final agreed version).

You might also spend time networking with agents and producers, and handling your own tax and accounts. You would often combine writing with other work such as teaching, lecturing or editing.

What can you earn?

As a freelance writer, you or your agent would negotiate a fee for each piece of work. You might be partly paid in advance. Depending on your contract, you might also receive a percentage of the profits from a feature film.

See the Writers' Guild of Great Britain website for recommended minimum pay rates for writers in film, TV and theatre.

Entry requirements

You will need imagination, writing talent and creativity rather than formal qualifications. However, when starting out you may find it useful to take a course that helps you develop your skills and understand dramatic structure.

Courses in creative writing and scriptwriting for all levels from beginner to advanced are widely available at colleges, adult education centres and universities.

Some screenwriters have degrees or postgraduate qualifications in creative writing, English or journalism, but this is not essential. You may have an advantage if you have writing and storytelling experience from another field such as journalism, advertising copywriting or acting.

You would normally start by coming up with your own screenplays and ideas, and trying to sell them to agents and producers. Once you have had some work accepted and started to build a professional reputation, producers might then commission you to produce scripts for them.

As a new writer, you could get yourself noticed by entering screenwriting competitions, which broadcasters and regional screen agencies sometimes hold to discover new talent. Contact Creative Skillset Careers for more information. You can also find advice about submitting your work to the BBC at the BBC Writers' Room website.

More information

Creative Skillset
Focus Point
21 Caledonian Road
London
N1 9GB
www.creativeskillset.org

Creative Skillset Careers
Tel: 08080 300 900 (England and Northern Ireland)
Tel: 0845 850 2502(Scotland)
Tel: 08000 121 815 (Wales)
www.creativeskillset.org/careers

The Script Factory
Welbeck House
66/67 Wells Street
London
W1T 3PY
Tel: 020 7323 1414
www.scriptfactory.co.uk

Writers Guild of Great Britain
49 Roseberry Avenue
London
EC1R 4RX
Tel: 020 7833 0777
www.writersguild.org.uk

BBC Writers Room
www.bbc.co.uk/writersroom

STUDIO SOUND ENGINEER

The nature of the work

As a sound engineer in a recording studio, you would make high quality recordings of music, speech and sound effects for use in different media, from music recordings to commercials.

In this job you would need good hearing. You would also need a good appreciation of pitch, timing and rhythm.

You would use complex electronic equipment to record sound for many different uses, such as:

- commercial music recordings
- radio, TV, film and commercials
- corporate videos
- websites
- computer games and other types of interactive media.

Your work would involve:

- planning recording sessions with producers and artists
- setting up microphones and equipment in the studio
- setting the right sound levels and dynamics
- operating equipment for recording, mixing, mastering, sequencing and sampling
- recording each instrument or item onto a separate track
- monitoring and balancing sound levels
- mixing tracks to produce a final 'master' track
- logging tapes and other details of the session in the studio archive.

With experience, you might also act as studio manager.

What can you earn?

Starting salaries can be from £13,000 a year full-time equivalent. With experience, salaries can rise to between £20,000 and £40,000. Freelance earnings can be higher or lower, depending on reputation and how much work is available.

Entry requirements

You will need a good knowledge of music and recording technology, and you'll also find it useful to understand physics and electronics. Many sound engineers start by taking a music technology course at college or university, to develop skills before looking for work in a studio.

Music technology courses are available at various levels, such as:

- City & Guilds Level 1, 2 and 3 Award, Certificate and Diploma in Sound and Music Techniques (7603)
- BTEC National Certificate/Diploma in Music Technology
- foundation degrees, BTEC HNCs/HNDs or degrees in sound engineering, audio technology, music technology or music production.

Check with colleges or universities for course entry requirements. See the Association of Professional Recording Services (APRS) JAMES website for information on industry-approved courses.

Alternatively, instead of taking a music technology course before looking for work, you could start as an assistant or 'runner' in a recording studio. Here you would carry out basic routine jobs, but you would also get the chance to learn how to use studio equipment and assist on sessions.

When looking for your first job, you'll find it helpful to have practical experience of using studio equipment. Taking a music technology course can help with this, and you could also build up your experience through:

- community music or DJ projects
- hospital or community radio
- mixing and recording music in a home studio.

Customer service experience and good 'people skills' such as teamwork and communication are also important, as you would often be working in close contact with clients and artists.

More information

Creative Skillset Careers
Tel: 08080 300 900 (England and Northern Ireland)
Tel: 0845 850 2502(Scotland)
Tel: 08000 121 815 (Wales)
www.creativeskillset.org/careers

PLASA
Redoubt House
1 Edward Road
Eastbourne
BN23 8AS
Tel: 01323 524120
www.plasa.org

Association of Professional Recording Services
PO Box 22
Totnes
Devon
TQ9 7YZ
Tel: 01803 868600
www.aprs.co.uk

BPI - The British Recorded Music Industry
Riverside Building
County Hall
Westminster Bridge Road
London
SE1 7JA
Tel: 020 7803 1300
www.bpi.co.uk
Institute of Sound and Communications Engineers
PO Box 7966
Reading

RG6 7BP
www.isce.org.uk
Tomorrow's Engineers 🖵
www.tomorrowsengineers.org.uk

TV or FILM ASSISTANT DIRECTOR

The nature of the work

Assistant directors (known in the industry as 'ADs') support film directors by organising and planning everything on set. Most productions use a team of assistant directors, with a 1st AD, at least one 2nd AD and possibly one or more 3rd ADs, each with different tasks.

1st ADs have the most important supporting role to the director. In this job you would do much of the planning before production begins, and you would manage the set during filming to leave the director free to concentrate on the creative side. Your responsibilities would include:

- working with the director to break the script down into a shot-by-shot 'storyboard' and decide the order of shooting
- planning a filming schedule, taking into account the director's ideas and the available budget
- overseeing the hire of locations, props and equipment
- recruiting the cast and crew
- making sure that filming stays on schedule
- supervising a team of 2nd and 3rd ADs and runners
- motivating the cast and crew
- responsible for health and safety on set.

2nd ADs support the 1st AD and make sure that their orders are carried out on set. As a 2nd AD you would:

- produce each day's 'call sheet' (a list of timings and logistics for the following day's shoot)
- be the link between the set and the production office

- distribute call sheets, so that the cast and crew know exactly when they are needed on set
- deal with paperwork
- organise transport and hotels
- make sure that cast members are in make-up, wardrobe or on set at the right time
- find and supervise extras on productions where there is no 3rd AD.

3rd ADs assist 2nd ADs, 1st ADs and location managers on set. As a 3rd AD your main job would be to make sure any extras were on set at the right time and place. You would brief the extras and give them their cues, and you might direct the action in background crowd scenes. You would also act as a messenger on set.

What can you earn?

Freelance assistant directors are usually paid a fee for each individual contract or project. Rates can vary widely, and may be based on the budget available and your track record.

Contact the Broadcasting Entertainment Cinematograph and Theatre Union (BECTU) for current pay guidelines.

People working on films may agree to work for little or no pay on the understanding that they will share in any profit that the film makes. You should check the exact terms before going ahead with this type of contract or agreement.

Entry requirements

The key to becoming an assistant director is to get practical experience of the production process, and also to develop a network of contacts in the industry. Employers are usually more interested in your experience and your enthusiasm and initiative than your formal qualifications.

You would often start as runner or production assistant on set, and work your way up to 3rd or 2nd AD and beyond. To get a job as a runner, you will need to show your commitment by finding work experience and being involved in activities like student or community film or TV. It can take several years to move from Runner through to First AD.

It is not essential to have studied film, video or media production before you look for work, although it can be helpful as the most useful courses include practical skills and work placements. Several colleges and universities offer relevant courses, including:

- City & Guilds (7501) Diploma in Media Techniques (will be Level 1, 2 and 3 Award, Certificate and Diploma in Media Techniques (7601) from September 2010)
- BTEC National Certificate/Diploma in Media Production (will be BTEC Level 3 Certificates and Diplomas in Creative Media Production from September 2010)
- BTEC HNDs, degrees and postgraduate courses.

Check with course providers for entry requirements, and see Creative Skillset's website for details of industry-endorsed Film and TV production courses.

More information

Creative Skillset Careers
Tel: 08080 300 900 (England and Northern Ireland)
Tel: 0845 850 2502(Scotland)
Tel: 08000 121 815 (Wales)
www.creativeskillset.org/careers

Creative Skillset
Focus Point
21 Caledonian Road
London
N1 9GB
www.creativeskillset.org

Broadcasting Entertainment Cinematograph and Theatre Union (BECTU)
373-377 Clapham Road
London

SW9 9BT
Tel: 0845 850 2502
www.bectu.org.uk

TV or FILM CAMERA OPERATOR

The nature of the work

As a camera operator, it would be your job to record moving images for film, television, commercials, music videos or corporate productions. You would operate film, videotape or digital video cameras, usually under instructions from the Director or Director of Photography.

Your work could involve:

- setting up and positioning camera equipment
- planning and rehearsing shots
- following a camera script and taking cues from the director or floor manager (in TV studio recording)
- choosing the most suitable lenses and camera angles
- solving practical or technical problems such as lighting
- working closely with other technical departments such as lighting and sound.

You may be the only camera operator and use a portable single camera, or you could be part of a TV studio camera team. On feature films and TV drama productions you may be part of a large crew with a specific role, such as:

- second assistant camera (clapper loader) – loading and unloading film, counting the takes and helping the camera crew
- first assistant camera (focus puller) – judging and adjusting the focus on each shot
- grip – building and operating any cranes and pulleys needed to move a camera during shooting.

You would usually specialise in either film or television work, as the equipment and techniques can differ, however with the advent of digital cameras and HD technology, camera professionals are finding it easier to work across all sectors ensuring more stable employment.

What can you earn?

Freelance camera operators are usually paid a fee for each contract.

Rates can vary widely. You could negotiate fees based on the type of production and your own track record. Contact BECTU for current pay guidelines.

Entry requirements

Employers will be more interested in your technical skills and practical experience than your formal qualifications. In practice, many camera operators take a college or university course to develop the necessary skills before looking for work. Relevant courses include:

- City & Guilds Diploma (7501) in Media Techniques (Level 1, 2 and 3 Award, Certificate and Diploma in Media Techniques (7601) from September 2010)
- BTEC National Certificate or Diploma in Media Production
- BTEC HNC/HND in Media (Moving Image)
- degrees in media production, media technology or photography
- trainee courses run by the GBCT (camera guild).

The most useful courses offer practical experience and may include work placements. Please check with colleges or universities for exact entry requirements.

As well as gaining technical skills, you should also build practical experience and make contacts in the industry. Courses can help you with this, but you can also get useful experience from:

- getting involved in community film projects
- working for a camera equipment hire company
- finding work experience as a runner or camera assistant with a production company.

You may also find it useful to have skills in stills photography and basic electronics.

You should also make a 'showreel' DVD of productions that you have worked on, to demonstrate your skills to employers when you are looking for work.

More information

Creative Skillset
Focus Point
21 Caledonian Road
London
N1 9GB
www.creativeskillset.org

Creative Skillset Careers
Tel: 08080 300 900 (England and Northern Ireland)
Tel: 0845 850 2502 (Scotland)
Tel: 08000 121 815 (Wales)
www.creativeskillset.org/careers

Creative Skillset Craft and Technical Skills Academy
Easling, Hammersmith and West London College
The Green
Ealing
London
W5 5EW
info@craftandtech.org
www.craftandtech.org

Guild of Television Cameramen
www.gtc.org.uk

Guild of British Camera Technicians
c/o Panavision UK
Metropolitan Centre
Bristol Road
Greenford

Middlesex
UB6 8GD
Tel: 020 8813 1999
www.gbct.org

TV or FILM DIRECTOR

The nature of the work

Directors have overall responsibility for the way films or television programmes are made. As a director, you would use your creativity, organisational skills and technical knowledge to manage the whole production process.

You might lead a small team or a large cast and crew, to direct full-length feature films, short films, live or recorded television programmes, commercials, music videos or corporate videos. Your main purpose would be to make the creative decisions that guide the rest of the crew.

Your work could include:

- meeting producers
- commissioning a script or an idea for a documentary
- interpreting scripts and developing storyboards
- deciding on how the production should look and where it should be filmed
- planning the shooting schedule and logistics
- hiring the cast and crew
- guiding the technical crew
- directing the actors (or the contributors to a documentary)
- supervising the editing to produce the final 'cut'.

In some cases you might write your own scripts and raise finance for projects. On some productions you might also operate camera or sound equipment – this is particularly common with documentaries or productions with a small budget.

What can you earn?

Freelance directors are usually paid a fee for each individual contract or project. Rates can vary widely, and may be based on the budget available and your track record.

Contact the Broadcasting Entertainment Cinematograph and Theatre Union (BECTU) for current pay guidelines.

People working on films may agree to work for little or no pay on the understanding that they will share in any profit that the film makes. You should check the exact terms before going ahead with this type of contract or agreement.

Entry requirements

You could take various routes to becoming a director. The most important requirements are to have substantial experience in TV or film, in-depth understanding of the production process, and a network of contacts in the industry.

Many successful directors start as runners and work their way up through other jobs like 3rd and 2nd assistant director or floor manager. Others move into directing after experience in camera work or acting.

To get a job as a runner, you will need to show your commitment to working in the media. You could do this through taking part in activities like student or community film or TV, and finding work experience placements.

You may find it helpful to take a filmmaking or media production course that helps you to build practical skills and make contacts. Several universities and colleges offer relevant BTEC HNDs, degrees and postgraduate courses, and some private film schools offer intensive directing and filmmaking courses. See Creative Skillset's website for details of industry-endorsed courses.

Another way of breaking into film directing is to make your own short films (known as 'shorts'), which you could market to agents or enter into film festivals and competitions such as those run by the BBC and Channel 4. To make your own films, you will need access to equipment, crew and actors. Getting involved in community film projects can help you with this.

More information

Creative Skillset
Focus Point
21 Caledonian Road
London
N1 9GB
www.creativeskillset.org

Creative Skillset Careers
Tel: 08080 300 900 (England and Northern Ireland)
Tel: 0845 850 2502(Scotland)
Tel: 08000 121 815 (Wales)
www.creativeskillset.org/careers

Broadcasting Entertainment Cinematograph and Theatre Union (BECTU)
373-377 Clapham Road
London
SW9 9BT
Tel: 0845 850 2502
www.bectu.org.uk

Directors Guild of Great Britain
4 Windmill Street
London
W1T 2HZ
Tel: 020 7580 9131
www.dggb.org

Shooting People 🖵
www.shootingpeople.org

TV or FILM PRODUCER

The nature of the work

Producers play an important role in the film, television and video industries. As a producer, your main purpose would be to deal with the practical and business side of a project, so that the director and crew could concentrate on the creative side. Film Producers are instrumental in obtaining funding for a film while in TV, programmes are usually (but not always) commissioned and therefore funding is not a major part of the job.

You would manage the production process from start to finish, organising all the resources needed and often coming up with the initial idea for a project. Your work might include:

- deciding which projects to produce, or creating programme ideas yourself
- reading scripts
- securing the rights for books or screenplays, or getting writers to produce new screenplays
- raising finance for projects
- pitching to television broadcasters to commission your programme
- identifying sources of film funding and pitching projects to investors
- assessing what resources will be needed
- planning the schedule
- hiring all the necessary technical resources and support services
- recruiting key production staff and crew, and being involved with casting performers
- editing scripts
- managing cash flow
- making sure that the entire production stays on schedule and within budget
- overall responsibility for the quality of the production.

On feature film and large-scale TV productions, you would be part of a team of producers and may be responsible for just some of these duties. On a smaller production such as a documentary, you would often do all of these tasks and may also direct the project.

267

What can you earn?

Freelance producers are usually paid a fee for each individual contract or project.

Rates can vary widely and you could negotiate fees based on the type of production, the budget available and your track record. Contact the Broadcasting Entertainment Cinematograph and Theatre Union (BECTU) for current pay guidelines.

Depending on your contract, you may also receive a percentage of the profits from a feature film.

Entry requirements

You will need substantial experience in both the creative and business sides of film or programme making. You will also need an in-depth understanding of the production process, and a network of contacts in the industry.

You could work your way up through the industry in various ways. In TV, you could start as a runner or production assistant. Producers of factual programmes often start as programme researchers or journalists. Alternatively, you could progress through production office roles, from production secretary to assistant production coordinator and beyond.

In film, you would usually start as a runner. You could then work your way up to production coordinator, line producer and production manager, or alternatively progress through the roles of 3rd, 2nd and 1st assistant director.

Before finding an entry-level job in film or TV, you will be expected to build as much practical experience as you can. You can do this through activities like student film/TV, work experience placements, or hospital or community radio. It is not essential to have studied film, video or media production before you look for work. However, you may find it helpful to take a course that includes practical skills, work placements and the chance to make contacts. Many colleges and universities offer relevant courses. See Creative Skillset's website for details of industry-endorsed courses.

More information

Creative Skillset
Focus Point
21 Caledonian Road
London
N1 9GB
www.creativeskillset.org

Creative Skillset Careers
Tel: 08080 300 900 (England and Northern Ireland)
Tel: 0845 850 2502(Scotland)
Tel: 08000 121 815 (Wales)
www.creativeskillset.org/careers

Production Guild
Tel: 01753 651767
www.productionguild.com

Broadcasting Entertainment Cinematograph and Theatre Union (BECTU)
373-377 Clapham Road
London
SW9 9BT
Tel: 0845 850 2502
www.bectu.org.uk

Indie Training Fund (ITF)
www.indietrainingfund.com

TV or FILM PRODUCTION ASSISTANT

The nature of the work

As a production assistant, you would give practical support to the director and production team during the making of films and television programmes. It would be your job to handle administrative and organisational tasks so that the production ran smoothly and on time.

You would be involved in a wide range of tasks before, during and after filming, which would often include:

- hiring studio facilities and equipment
- booking hotels and making travel arrangements
- attending production meetings
- copying and distributing scripts
- typing and distributing schedules ('call sheets') and daily reports
- getting permission to use copyrighted music or film clips
- dealing with accounts and expenses.

In television, you might also carry out production duties such as:

- timing the show in the studio gallery
- calling camera shots
- cueing pre-recorded material
- keeping records (known as 'logging') of shots taken
- keeping continuity.

You would work as part of a wider production team, including producers, researchers, and technical staff like camera crew and editors.

What can you earn?

Freelance production assistants are usually paid a fee for each contract.

Freelance rates can vary widely, and may be negotiated based on the type of production and your track record. Contact the Broadcasting Entertainment Cinematograph and Theatre Union (BECTU) for current pay guidelines.

Entry requirements

You will need good office IT skills and plenty of initiative, enthusiasm and common sense. You should also build as much practical experience as you can. Although many production assistants are graduates, this is not essential as most employers will be more interested in your experience and personal qualities than your qualifications.

You can build useful experience through activities such as:

- student or community film/TV projects
- community or student radio
- work experience placements (often unpaid).

Creative Skillset Careers offers advice on finding work experience – visit their website to find out more.

It isn't essential to have studied film, video or media production, although you might find it helpful to take a course that includes practical skills, work placements and the chance to make contacts. Several colleges and universities offer relevant courses, including:

- Level 1, 2 and 3 Award, Certificate and Diploma in Media Techniques (7601)
- BTEC Level 3 Certificates and Diplomas in Creative Media Production
- BTEC HNDs, degrees and postgraduate courses.

Check with course providers for entry requirements, and see Creative Skillset's website for details of industry-endorsed courses.

Your first paid job would often be as a runner or a junior assistant or secretary in the production office, and you would work your way up the production ladder as you gained experience.

More information

Creative Skillset
Focus Point
21 Caledonian Road
London
N1 9GB
www.creativeskillset.org

Creative Skillset Careers
Tel: 08080 300 900 (England and Northern Ireland)

Tel: 0845 850 2502(Scotland)
Tel: 08000 121 815 (Wales)
www.creativeskillset.org/careers

Broadcasting Entertainment Cinematograph and Theatre Union (BECTU)
373-377 Clapham Road
London
SW9 9BT
Tel: 0845 850 2502
www.bectu.org.uk

TV or FILM SOUND TECHNICIAN

The nature of the work

As a sound technician, you would record, mix and check the sound for live and recorded film and television productions. You would use microphones, recording equipment and editing software to record sound and produce a clear, high-quality soundtrack. You could specialise in one of the following:

- production sound – recording sound on set or location
- post-production – putting the final soundtrack together in an editing studio.
- On a production sound team you could work as sound recordist (also known as production mixer), a boom operator or a sound assistant. Depending on your job role, your duties may include:
- setting up equipment to suit the acoustics and the sound designer's instructions
- selecting and placing fixed microphones
- operating the boom (positioning the moving microphones around the performers for the best sound)
- monitoring sound quality
- recording onto digital audio tape
- servicing and repairing equipment
- playing music or sound effects into a live programme.

- Post-production teams can include a re-recording (dubbing) mixer, dialogue editor/mixer, foley artist and foley editor. Post-production sound work can involve:
- following a sound designer or sound supervisor's instructions
- mixing and balancing speech, effects and background music
- editing speech to fit the action on screen
- creating extra sound effects and adding them into the soundtrack (known as the 'foley').

What can you earn?

Starting salaries can be around £18,000 to £25,000 a year for ongoing full-time work (although it is common to work for less at the start of your career). Experienced freelance rates can be between £800 and £1600 a week (before tax). Freelance rates can vary widely. You could negotiate fees based on the type of production and your own track record. Contact BECTU for current pay guidelines.

Entry requirements

You will need a good knowledge of sound technology and equipment, and you will find it useful to understand basic electronics and the physics of sound.

You may increase your chances of getting into the industry by taking a relevant course to develop your knowledge and skills before you look for work. Courses include:

- City & Guilds 7503 Certificate/Diploma in Sound and Music Technology (will be the City & Guilds Award, Certificate and Diploma in Sound and Music Techniques (7603) at levels 1-3 from September 2010)
- BTEC National Certificate/Diploma in Media Production (Sound Recording) or Music Technology (BTEC Level 3 Certificates and Diplomas in Creative Media Production (Sound Recording) or Music Technology (Production) from September 2010)

- BTEC HNC/HND in Media (Audio) (will become BTEC Level 4 and 5 HND Diplomas in Creative Media Production or Music (Production) from September 2010)
- foundation degrees or degrees in sound engineering, music technology, media technology or technical theatre.
- Check with colleges or universities for entry requirements.

When looking for your first job, you will find it useful to have practical experience of using sound equipment. Taking a relevant course can help with this, and you can also build experience in the following ways:

- working on student or community film or radio projects
- setting up ('rigging') sound equipment for amateur theatre or local bands
- working for a sound equipment manufacturer or hire company
- assisting in a recording or editing studio.

Contact Creative Skillset Careers for more advice about finding work experience.

More information

Creative Skillset
Focus Point
21 Caledonian Road
London
N1 9GB
www.creativeskillset.org

Creative Skillset Careers
Tel: 08080 300 900 (England and Northern Ireland)
Tel: 0845 850 2502(Scotland)
Tel: 08000 121 815 (Wales)
www.creativeskillset.org/careers

Association of Professional Recording Services
PO Box 22

Totnes
Devon
TQ9 7YZ
Tel: 01803 868600
www.aprs.co.uk

Broadcasting Entertainment Cinematograph and Theatre Union (BECTU)
373-377 Clapham Road
London
SW9 9BT
Tel: 0845 850 2502
www.bectu.org.uk

WARDROBE ASSISTANT

The nature of the work
Wardrobe assistants help to make, find and look after the clothing and costumes used in theatre, film and television productions. In this job you will need to have good sewing skills. You will also need to have an eye for design and style.

As a wardrobe assistant, you would work under the direction of a costume supervisor or wardrobe master/mistress. Your work might include:

- helping to buy and hire costume items
- looking after the costumes between takes or scenes
- mending and altering items
- packing and unpacking costumes and accessories
- cleaning and ironing
- helping to make pieces and put costumes together
- fitting the performers
- making sure that all items are available when needed
- keeping an accurate record of all items needed
- storing costumes and returning hired items (known as 'breaking down' costumes).

In theatre, you might also act as a 'dresser', helping performers with costume changes during the show.

What can you earn?

Wardrobe assistants tend to work on a freelance basis. Freelance rates can vary widely. You could negotiate your fees based on the type of production and your own track record. Contact BECTU for current pay guidelines for film and TV.

Entry requirements

You will need practical skills in hand and machine sewing, pattern cutting and dressmaking. You don't always need formal qualifications, but you could build useful skills on college courses such as:

- City & Guilds Certificates and Diplomas at levels 1, 2 and 3 in Creative Techniques – part-time courses, with options including for theatre costume and pattern cutting.
- BTEC Level 2 Certificate/Diploma in Fashion and Clothing or Level 3 Certificate/Diploma in Production Arts (Costume) – courses may be full-time or part-time.
- You may have an advantage with a BTEC HND, degree or postgraduate qualification in costume design, fashion or textiles, especially if you want to eventually become a costume designer. You should check entry requirements with course providers.

The key to finding paid work is to get practical experience, which you can get from:

- student theatre and film productions
- amateur or community theatre
- dressmaking
- work for a theatrical costume hire company
- casual work as a costume 'daily' (temporary helper) on film and TV sets.

Contact Creative Skillset Careers for advice about work experience in film and television.

More information

Creative and Cultural Skills
Lafone House
The Leathermarket
Weston Street
London
SE1 3HN
www.creative-choices.co.uk

Creative Skillset
Focus Point
21 Caledonian Road
London
N1 9GB
www.creativeskillset.org

Creative Skillset Careers
Tel: 08080 300 900 (England and Northern Ireland)
Tel: 0845 850 2502(Scotland)
Tel: 08000 121 815 (Wales)
www.creativeskillset.org/careers

Get Into Theatre
www.getintotheatre.org

Association of British Theatre Technicians
55 Farringdon Road
London
EC1M 3JB
Tel: 020 7242 9200
www.abtt.org.uk

Broadcasting Entertainment Cinematograph and Theatre Union (BECTU)
373-377 Clapham Road
London
SW9 9BT

Tel: 0845 850 2502
www.bectu.org.uk

The Costume Society
www.costumesociety.org.uk

MAKE UP ARTIST

The nature of the work
Make-up artists apply make-up and style hair for anyone appearing in front of a camera or a live audience. They can work in film, television, theatre, concerts, photographic sessions or fashion shows.
Most make-up artists start by taking a specialist course in make-up or beauty therapy and building up their practical experience.

As a make-up artist, you might create anything from a straightforward natural look to one using historical wigs and make-up. You could also create special effects such as scars and artificial pieces (prosthetics).

You could work alone, as an assistant to a senior colleague, or as part of a larger hair and make-up design team. Depending on the job, your tasks might include:

- researching and designing make-up and hairstyles to suit the job
- working to detailed notes or to general design instructions
- hair tidying and styling
- fitting wigs, hairpieces and bald caps
- applying prosthetic make-up to completely change someone's look
- making notes and taking photographs as reference so that you can recreate the look easily (continuity)
- standing by on set to redo make-up and hair
- keeping work areas and equipment clean and tidy.

You would work closely with production designers, costume designers, camera and lighting crew, and performers. See the Creative Choices website to read a theatre make-up artist's story.

What can you earn?

Freelance make-up artists are usually paid a fee for each contract. Rates can vary a lot and will usually depend on the type of production and the work you have done in the past. The Broadcasting Entertainment Cinematograph and Theatre Union (BECTU) publishes recommended pay rates on its website. For example, it recommends a rate of around £200 for a 10-hour day in TV or film. It also recommends that trainees are paid at least the minimum wage (or the London living wage, if in London).

Entry requirements

Most make-up artists start by taking a specialist course in make-up or beauty therapy and building up their practical experience.

There is a wide range of specialist courses available. College courses include Awards, Certificates and Diplomas at level 3 (and sometimes level 2) in fashion and photography make-up, and media make-up. Some universities offer foundation degrees and degrees in media make-up. You may need a level 2 qualification in hair and beauty to do some of these courses. Check entry requirements with course providers.

Courses in media make-up training are also run privately.

As well as taking a relevant make-up course, you should also try to gain practical experience, build a portfolio of your work to show to employers and get to know people in the industry (networking).

You could get useful experience in various ways, such as:

- amateur theatre
- student film, theatre and photography projects
- charity or student fashion shows
- with established make-up artists and photographers.

Once you have built up some experience and made some contacts, your first paid work in film or TV may be as a trainee or assistant to the make-up team.

You might also find casual work doing make-up and hair for extras in crowd scenes.

More information

Creative Skillset
Focus Point
21 Caledonian Road
London
N1 9GB
www.creativeskillset.org

Skillset Craft and Technical Skills Academy
Ealing, Hammersmith and West London College
The Green
Ealing
London
W5 5EW
info@craftandtech.org
www.craftandtech.org

Creative Skillset Careers
Tel: 08080 300 900 (England and Northern Ireland)
Tel: 0845 850 2502(Scotland)
Tel: 08000 121 815 (Wales)
www.creativeskillset.org/careers

National Association of Screen Makeup and Hair Artists (NASMAH)
68 Sarsfield Road
Perivale
Middlesex
UB6 7AG
www.nasmah.co.uk

Vocational Training Charitable Trust (VTCT)
3rd Floor
Eastleigh House
Upper Market Street

Eastleigh
Hampshire
SO50 9FD
Tel: 023 8068 4500
www.vtct.org.uk

International Therapy Examination Council
4 Heathfield Terrace
Chiswick
London
W4 4JE
Tel: 020 8994 4141
www.itecworld.co.uk

Get Into Theatre
www.getintotheatre.org

Hairdressing and Beauty Industry Authority (HABIA)
www.habia.org

Broadcasting Entertainment Cinematograph and Theatre Union (BECTU)
Tel: 0845 850 2502
ww.bectu.org.uk

****

281

16. THE POLICE FORCE

Jobs in the police force can be very rewarding indeed. However, you will need to be a certain type of person to fulfill what are demanding roles. There are a number of opportunities within the police force. In this chapter we cover:

- Police officer
- Police community support officer
- Forensic computer analyst

For the many other roles within the police service you should contact:

Police Recruitment Service

www.policerecruitment.homeoffice.uk
www. npia.police.uk

POLICE OFFICER

The nature of the work

You could work as a uniformed officer on foot or in a patrol car (known as on the beat), or at a police station. You would carry out a range of tasks, which could include:

- responding to calls for help from the public
- investigating crimes and offences, and making arrests
- interviewing witnesses and suspects, preparing crime reports and taking statements
- searching for missing people
- giving evidence in court
- going out to accidents and fires
- duties relating to custody
- working at the station reception desk dealing with the public
- two-way contact with officers on the beat from the communications room

- policing large public events, concerts and demonstrations
- visiting schools to give talks.

You would need to complete a trial (probationary) period as an officer. After that you could specialise in a specific branch such as the Criminal Investigation Department (CID), the drug squad or the traffic police.

What can you earn?

Salaries can vary between police forces. The starting salary is generally between £20,000 and £23,000 a year. With several years' experience, earnings can reach around £36,500 a year. A sergeant can earn around £40,000 a year and inspectors can earn around £50,000. There may be extra pay for working overtime. Police officers working in the London area may receive an additional cost of living payment.

Entry requirements

Police officer recruitment is handled by individual police forces, and their requirements can vary. In general you will need to:

- be a British citizen, a citizen of the Commonwealth, European Union (EU) or other European Economic Area (EEA) country, or a foreign national allowed to stay in the UK for an unlimited time.
- be at least 18 years old.
- pass background and security checks, and give details of any previous convictions.
- have above average physical fitness, and good vision and colour vision (with or without glasses or contact lenses).

In most cases, you will also need to have been resident in the UK for the three years before applying.

As well as meeting the standards above, you will also need to pass a series of tests before being accepted as a trainee police officer. These are in areas like working with numbers, communication, reading and writing skills, handling information, making decisions and making judgements. You will also have a physical fitness test and a health check.

As a probationer (trainee) or serving officer, you may be able to join the High Potential Development Scheme (HPDS). The scheme develops those with the potential to become future police leaders, and leads to a Masters qualification. Check the Police Service Recruitment website , or the National Policing Improvement Agency (NPIA) website for details.

More information

Police Recruitment Service
www.policerecruitment.homeoffice.uk
www. npia.police.uk

Scottish Police Forces
www.scottish.police.uk

Skills for Justice
Centre Court
Atlas Way
Sheffield
S4 7QQ
www.skillsforjustice.com

Police Service of Northern Ireland (PSNI)
http://www.joinpsni.co.uk/

Police Service Recruitment
www.policecouldyou.co.uk

POLICE COMMUNITY SUPPORT OFFICER

The nature of the work
Your duties would vary (depending on the needs of the police force and your local community), but they are likely to include:

- dealing with incidents of nuisance and anti-social behaviour, such as truants, vandalism and litter
- directing traffic and having vehicles removed
- guarding crime scenes
- offering advice on crime prevention
- issuing fixed penalty notices for anti-social behaviour
- detaining someone until a police officer arrives
- providing support at large public gatherings, such as sports events and public demonstrations
- other work relating to Neighbourhood Policing Teams and work around Anti-Social Behaviour
- work in partnership with other agencies.

You could work alone, in pairs or small teams, under the direction of the police commander in your area.

What can you earn?

Starting salaries can be around £16,000 a year. With experience, this can rise to around £19,000, plus a shift allowance. In some geographical areas PCSO salaries can be up to £25,000 a year.

Entry requirements

You will be selected for the role of PCSO based on your application and interview. You can apply if you have a permanent right to remain without restriction in the UK. Full security and reference checks will also be made.

Local police forces set their own entry requirements so the following is intended as a general guideline.

You will not usually need formal qualifications, but you will need good spoken and written communication skills. You need to be fit enough to carry out foot patrols, so you may be asked to take a fitness test.

A qualification in public service may give you an advantage when looking for work as a PCSO. Relevant qualifications include:

- NVQ Level 2 in Public Services
- BTEC First Diploma or National Diploma in Public Services
- BTEC National Certificate or Diploma in Uniformed Public Services
- foundation degree in Public Service.

Some police forces will also want you to have experience of working within the community (paid or voluntary), and it may be helpful if you have a driving licence.

Vetting of applicants is undertaken in line with HMG Personnel Security Controls. You can find local force contact details on the Police.uk site.

FORENSIC COMPUTER ANALYST

The nature of the work

As a forensic computer analyst, you could be involved in a range of investigations, such as:

- hacking, online scams and fraud
- political, industrial and commercial espionage
- terrorist communications
- possession of illegal pornography

You could work for the police or security services, a bank, or for an IT firm that specialises in computer security. You might also work in a broader security role, for example, testing the security of a company's information systems.

What can you earn?

Trainee forensic computer analysts can earn around £20,000 a year. Salaries for analysts with 12 months' experience can be between £25,000 and £35,000 a year. With four to five years' experience, this can rise to between £40,000 and £60,000 a year.

Entry requirements

To work as a forensic computer analyst you will need a background in IT. Employers may also ask for a degree, a postgraduate qualification or industry certification. For more details, see the Training and Development section.

You could start in this career by working for a company, for example as a network engineer or developer. By taking professional development courses and applying for opportunities as they come up, you may eventually be able to move into a more specialised security or analyst role.

You can find further information about this career on the Forums section of the Computer Forensics World website.

To get an idea of some of the technical skills you would need to apply, analysts suggest looking at the way different operating systems work and how they can be taken advantage of. You could download and practice on a free open-source system like Linux.

More information

Skills Framework for the Information Age (SFIA)
www.sfia.org.uk

UK Resource Centre for Women in Science, Engineering and Technology (UKRC)
Listerhills Park of Science and Commerce
40-42 Campus Road
Bradford
BD7 1HR
Tel: 01274 436485
www.theukrc.org

Skills for Justice
Centre Court

Atlas Way
Sheffield
S4 7QQ
www.skillsforjustice.com

e-skills UK
1 Castle Lane
London
SW1E 6DR
Tel: 020 7963 8920
www.e-skills.com

MI5 Careers
www.mi5careers.gov.uk

National Skills Academy for IT
www.itskillsacademy.ac.uk

****

17. RETAIL

The retail sector encompasses many and varied jobs. The work is challenging and can be exciting and the right candidates can forge a lively career in this area. Jobs vary from shop assistant to store managers and many more besides. in this section we look at:

- Retail Manager
- Sales Assistant
- Shopkeeper
- Store Demonstrator
- Post Office Customer Service Assistant
- Check Out operator
- Customer Service Assistant
- Customer Service Manager

For details of the numerous other opportunities in the area of retail you should go to:

Skillsmart Retail
Fourth Floor
93 Newman Street
London W1T 3EZ
Tel: 0800 093 5001
www.skillsmartretail.com

RETAIL MANAGER

The nature of the work

A retail manager is responsible for the day-to-day management of a store/retail outlet in line with overall company policy. The main focus of any retail manager's job is to improve the commercial performance of the store by increasing its turnover and maximising profitability. The major parts of the job on a day-to-day basis include managing and motivating staff, finding new ways to improve sales, and meeting customer demand.

Depending on the type of store and its opening times, unsociable hours are usually expected from weekends to late nights and early mornings. Managers are often in early to prepare for the day, and stay after closing to make sure systems and premises are closed down and secured properly. Some of your duties would depend on what the store sells and whether it is part of a chain, but your typical tasks would include:

- managing and motivating a team to increase sales including recruiting, training, day-to-day managing, appraisals, disciplining, dismissing, promotions and team building
- responsibility for maintaining the premises and displays
- organising stock checking and re-ordering as necessary, through computerised or manual systems
- organising sales and promotions
- dealing with queries, complaints and comments from customers
- analysing and interpreting consumer trends
- taking responsibility for seeing all security, health and safety and legal procedures
- analysing sales figures and forecasting future sales volumes to maximise profits
- ensuring standards for quality, customer service and health and safety are met
- regularly 'walking the sales floor' talking to colleagues and customers, and identifying or resolving urgent issues
- maintaining awareness of market trends in the retail industry, understanding forthcoming customer initiatives, and monitoring what local competitors are doing
- monitoring budgets and controlling expenditure
- dealing with takings and banking/security banking couriers
- serving customers when required.

What can you earn?

- Starting salaries start at around £20,000 a year

- With experience, typical earnings can rise to around £31,000
- Some senior store managers earn £47,000 a year.

You may also earn extra bonuses and commission for meeting sales targets.

Entry requirements

Entry requirements vary from company to company. Entrants may possess A levels/Highers or a degree or equivalent qualification. Experience of working with customers, especially in a retail environment, is very important and much more important in many cases than formal qualifications.

Entry is also possible through promotion – this is the most common entry method for store managers, entering as a retail sales assistant and through training and development gaining sufficient experience through the career path of sales assistant, supervisor, department manager, deputy store manager, store manager.

Apprenticeships and retail management schemes are also popular entry points for individuals with some retail experience who want to fast track their retail management career – individuals undertaking this path normally enter a store manager position after developing experience as a department manager and deputy store manager during their training.

Some national retail businesses run graduate trainee management schemes for entrants with a suitable degree. These are usually a combination of skills training and work placement in one or more of a company's stores. Individuals undertaking this path normally enter a store manager position after developing experience as a department manager and deputy store manager during their training.

More information

Skillsmart Retail
Fourth Floor
93 Newman Street
London W1T 3EZ

Tel: 0800 093 5001

www.skillsmartretail.com

SALES ASSISTANT

The nature of the work

To be a good sales assistant it's important that you're able to work as part of a team, and that you're helpful, friendly and polite. You also need to reliable, honest and responsible.

The places you could work include supermarkets, fashion stores and department stores, and you could be:

- serving and advising customers
- taking payment
- helping customers to find the goods they want
- advising on stock amounts
- giving information on products and prices
- stacking shelves or displaying goods in an attractive way
- arranging window displays
- promoting special offers or store cards
- ordering goods
- handling complaints or passing them on to a manager.

Some stores, for example mobile phone shops, DIY or electrical goods stores, would usually expect you to have a lot of knowledge about their products before you apply.

What can you earn?

- Full-time salaries can be between £11,000 and £15,000 a year
- Supervisors can earn between £15,000 and £20,000 a year

Many larger retail companies also offer benefits like staff discounts, extra pay depending on how much you sell (known as commission) and bonus schemes.

Entry requirements

When applying for jobs, it will help you if you already have experience of working with the public and of handling cash. Many stores employ temporary staff at busy times such as Christmas, and this can be a good way of getting experience that can lead to a permanent job.

You may be able to start this career through an Apprenticeship scheme. You will need to check which schemes run in your local area.

For more information, visit the Apprenticeships website.

More information

Skillsmart Retail
Fourth Floor
93 Newman Street
London
W1T 3EZ
Tel: 0800 093 5001
www.skillsmartretail.com

SHOPKEEPER

The nature of the work

Unlike sales assistants or store managers (who usually work for a large retailer), shopkeepers will normally have overall responsibility for a store. Independent retailers that employ shopkeepers include; green grocers, newsagents, butchers, bakers, booksellers, florists, and antique dealers.

As a shopkeeper, you would serve customers (either at a counter or checkout) and carry out other duties such as:

- taking payments, giving change and wrapping purchases
- answering enquiries and giving advice about products to customers

- listening to customers' needs and requests, which can indicate new sales opportunities
- calculating takings and wages
- depositing cash at the bank, book-keeping and stocktaking
- ordering stock from wholesalers, manufacturers, agents and importers.

Running your own shop would also involve keeping up to date with issues such as:

- your competitors' prices and products and using this knowledge to set the rates in your own shop
- the regulations covering trading and running a business, for example VAT and national insurance payments.

What can you earn?

Earnings can range from £13,000 to £30,000 a year. Income depends on the nature and size of the business, the product or service, and the shopkeeper's ability to make the business work in its location.

Entry requirements

You will not need any specific academic qualifications to become a shopkeeper. However, you will need good maths skills, people management and business skills. Experience of shop work, sales, administration or management would be particularly useful.

You could prepare for working as a shopkeeper by taking a part-time or short course in a subject such as sales or starting a business. You would also need financial backing in order to buy the business.

The Business Link network offers a range of business support and development services, including information about finding and setting up premises, VAT and tax, and becoming an employer.

More information

Scottish Enterprise
Tel: 0845 607 8787
www.scottish-enterprise.com

Skillsmart Retail
Fourth Floor
93 Newman Street
London
W1T 3EZ
Tel: 0800 093 5001
www.skillsmartretail.com

Business Link
Tel: 0845 600 9006
www.businesslink.gov.uk

British Independent Retailers Association
225 Bristol Road
Edgbaston
Birmingham
West Midlands
B5 7UB
www.bira.co.uk

STORE DEMONSTRATOR

The nature of the work

Store demonstrators work in department stores, supermarkets and other retail businesses, introducing products (which may new to the market or on promotion) to customers to help increase sales. They may demonstrate a wide range of different products including food and drink, domestic appliances, kitchen gadgets, cleaning products, beauty products, DIY products and tools, home improvement products and toys. Some may sell these products directly, while others may pass sales leads onto other sales team members depending on the type of product, venue and size of the organisation. Your job might involve:

- Setting up a counter or other area where demonstrations take place
- Arranging stock, posters and other publicity material to attract customers
- Demonstrating how to use a product
- Explaining the benefits of a product and answering questions about it
- Handing out leaflets, brochures, coupons and free samples
- Selling products, or passing customers to other members of the sales team.
- Talking to individual passers-by, or using a microphone to catch the attention of groups of people
- Monitoring stock levels
- Keeping sales records

You could be employed full-time by a store or retail chain, or you may be freelance and find work through an agency.

What can you earn?

- Store demonstrators starting out may earn between £10,000 and £11,000
- More experienced staff may earn around £13,500
- The highest salary for a store demonstrator in a retail chain is around £18,000 to £19,000
- Some store demonstrators earn commission or productivity bonuses. There may be other benefits such as free products, discounts and petrol allowances
- Freelanceand part-time work usually pays around £6 an hour or £60 up to £240 a day for senior specialised product demonstrators

Entry requirements

It is possible to become a store demonstrator without formal qualifications, but a lot of employers look for evidence of literacy, numeracy and excellent communication skills. Mature candidates with retail or customer service experience and great people skills are warmly welcomed. Recruiters look for people with good communication skills and an enthusiastic attitude.

You will find it useful to have previous experience of dealing with the public, and previous experience of working in retail, customer service and talking to groups of people may be required by some employers.

Although you do not usually need formal qualifications to work as a store demonstrator, for demonstrating certain products you may need to have undertaken specific training such as a Level 2 Award in Food Safety for Retail/ Manufacturing to work with unwrapped food products.

More information

Skillsmart Retail
Fourth Floor
93 Newman Street
London
W1T 3EZ
Tel: 0800 093 5001
www.skillsmartretail.com

POST OFFICE CUSTOMER SERVICE ASSISTANT

The nature of the work

Customer service assistants provide a wide range of services offered at main post offices. They may sometimes be known as post office counter clerks, or counter sales assistants.

As a customer service assistant, your day-to-day duties would include:

- selling stamps and dealing with letters and parcels
- paying out pensions and benefits
- banking and savings services

- accepting bill payments
- dealing with vehicle registrations and issuing tax discs
- travel services, such as checking passport applications and selling travel insurance and foreign currency.

In a main post office (or postshop) you would be involved in selling and advising customers on a wider range of products.

What can you earn?

- Salaries can be between £13,000 and £17,500 a year
- Post Office managers may earn up to £24,000.

Pay may vary according to the location of the post office. An allowance is paid for working in London.

Entry requirements

You do not need any specific qualifications to work in a post office, however, to pass the selection tests you are likely to need a reasonable standard of secondary education. GCSEs (A-D) in maths and English would be an advantage.

The first stage of the selection process is an online questionnaire to test your accuracy and number skills, followed by a telephone interview. If you pass these tests you will then be invited to attend a face-to-face interview.

Previous customer service experience in banks, building societies or retail would be particularly helpful.

More information

Royal Mail Group PLC
100 Victoria Embankment
London
EC4Y 0HQ
www.royalmailgroup.com

Post Office Limited
Helpline: 0845 722 3344
www.postoffice.co.uk

CHECKOUT OPERATOR

The nature of the work

If you enjoy being in a busy environment and like talking to different people, this job could be just right for you. As a checkout operator you would work on a till serving customers. This could be in a supermarket, convenience store or large retail store. They help customers with items that they have chosen and take payment for goods.

As a checkout operator, your work would normally include:

- Operating a computerised till system that has a barcode scanner
- Entering prices into the till system by scanning items chosen by customers
- Weighing and pricing certain items, such as fruit and vegetables
- Using special tools to remove security tags
- Packing and wrapping purchases
- Processing store loyalty cards, coupons and vouchers
- Taking payment.

You may also spend time away from the till, filling shelves, checking stock or working on a customer service desk.

You would need to work quickly and efficiently so that other customers in the queue do not have to wait too long. You would also need to be aware of some aspects of retail law, such as the age restrictions on buying goods like alcohol and knives. Working accurately is important, as the till must balance at the end of the day.

What can you earn?

Salaries for checkout operators may start at around £10,500 a year. More experienced staff may earn between £11,500 and £12,500, and a supervisor may earn around £16,000 a year. Some checkout operators receive benefits such as staff discounts and subsidised canteen meals.

Entry requirements

You do not usually need any qualifications to become a checkout operator, however you will need to have numeracy and communication skills. Some companies may want you to have four or more GCSEs (A*-C)/Standard Grades including maths and English. Employers like to see enthusiasm and good people skills, and it would help you if you have experience of handling cash and serving customers.

Qualifications that could be useful include:

- Level 1 Award or Certificate / SVQ in Retail Skills
- Level 1 or 2 Award, Certificate or Diploma in Retail Knowledge / SCQF Level 5 Certificate in Retail Knowledge.

You may be able to do this job through an Apprenticeship scheme. You will need to check which schemes are available in your area. To find out more, see the Apprenticeships website.

More information

Skillsmart Retail
Fourth Floor
93 Newman Street
London
W1T 3EZ
Tel: 0800 093 5001
www.skillsmartretail

CUSTOMER SERVICE ASSISTANT

The nature of the work

As a customer service assistant or adviser, you would deal with customer enquiries and any complaints. You would often be a customer's first point of contact with the company you work for.

Your work may include:

- answering customer enquiries or passing them on to another department
- giving information and helping to solve problems
- selling products or taking orders
- arranging services for customers, such as booking tickets or setting up insurance policies
- handling complaints and passing them on to a manager if required
- entering customer information onto a computer database
- taking payment for goods or services
- giving refunds.

What can you earn?

Salaries are around £18,000 a year for full-time work. Bonuses or commission may also be available in some types of business, like retail, sales or banking.

Entry requirements

Many employers will be more interested in your 'people skills' than your formal qualifications, although you should have a good general standard of education. You will find it useful if you have some experience of dealing with people face-to-face or over the telephone.

Some employers, such as banks and insurance companies, may ask for some GCSEs (A-C) or higher qualifications such as A levels or BTEC National Certificates/Diplomas.

You may be able to start this work through an Apprenticeship scheme. You will need to check which schemes are available in your area. For more information, visit the Apprenticeships website.

More information

Skillsmart Retail
Fourth Floor
93 Newman Street
London
W1T 3EZ
Tel: 0800 093 5001
www.skillsmartretail.com

Institute of Customer Service (ICS)
2 Castle Court
St Peter's St
Colchester
Essex
CO1 1EW
Tel. 01206 571716
www.instituteofcustomerservice.com

CUSTOMER SERVICE MANAGER

The nature of the work

As a customer services manager, it would be your job to make sure that customers' needs and expectations are satisfied. You could be responsible for anything from managing a customer service team and dealing with enquiries in person, to developing customer service standards for a large company.

Your typical duties would include:

- Helping to develop or update customer service policies and procedures

- Managing or leading a team of customer services staff
- Handling enquiries from customers
- Handling complaints from customers
- Advising customers on the organisation's products
- Investigating and solving customer problems escalated from other customer service staff
- Liaising with customers regarding an unexpected event, such as a security issue, a recall, or a customer being taken ill
- Authorising refunds or other compensation to customers
- Ensuring accurate records are kept of communications with customers
- Analysing key metrics to determine how well customers are being served
- Meeting with management to report on customer service and discuss improvements
- Preparing or writing information for customers
- Developing or improving feedback or complaints procedures
- Helping to recruit, train and appraise new staff
- Keeping up to date with the company's products
- Keeping up to date with developments in customer service best practice e.g. by reading journals, attending meetings and courses and any changes in relevant legislation.

What can you earn?

- Entry-level customer service managers may earn £15,000 to £25,000
- An experienced customer service manager may earn £25,000 to £40,000.

Bonuses or commission may also be available in some sectors like retail, sales or banking.

Figures are intended as a guideline only.

Entry requirements

There are no formal academic requirements to work in customer services, as most employers are more interested in 'people skills' and a positive attitude.

However, employers may require some GCSEs (or Standard Grades in Scotland), in particular English and maths, to demonstrate literacy and numeracy. Previous experience of working in a customer-facing role is valuable. Most people start as customer service assistants, and becoming a manager means demonstrating that you are willing and able to take on additional responsibility.

Apprenticeship schemes may be available, and are a great way to get into retail. Some firms offer customer services management training schemes, available to candidates with more GCSEs/Standard Grades or higher qualifications.

More information

Institute of Customer Service (ICS)
2 Castle Court
St Peter's St
Colchester
Essex
CO1 1EW
Tel. 01206 571716
www.instituteofcustomerservice.com

Institute of Leadership and Management (ILM)
Stowe House
Netherstowe
Lichfield
Staffordshire
WS13 6TJ
Tel: 01543 266867
www.i-l-m.com

Chartered Management Institute (CMI)
Management House
Cottingham Road
Corby
Northants
NN17 1TT

Tel: 01536 204222
www.managers.org.uk

Skillsmart Retail
Fourth Floor
93 Newman Street
London
W1T 3EZ
Tel: 0800 093 5001
www.skillsmartretail.com

18. SOCIAL WORK

This chapter covers five main social work jobs:

- Social worker
- Assistant social worker
- Residential social worker
- Drug and alcohol worker
- Youth and Community worker

The area of social work is very wide and there are other opportunities available. For information on the numerous other roles available contact:

General Social Care Council
2 Hay's Lane
London SE1 2HB
Registration helpline: 0845 070 0630

Skills for Care (England)
Albion Court 5
Albion Place Leeds
LS1 6JL
Tel: 0113 245 1716
www.skillsforcare.org.uk

SOCIAL WORKER

The nature of the work

As a social worker, you would provide people with advice and emotional support, and arrange care services to help people.

You could support a wide range of social service users, including:

- children and parents under pressure
- older people

- people with physical or learning disabilities
- people with mental health problems
- young adults
- homeless people
- people leaving hospital who need help to live independently
- people with drug or alcohol dependency.

You would normally specialise in working with children and families, or with adult service users.

What can you earn?

Starting salaries are often around £19,500 to £25,000 a year.

With more experience and responsibility, this can rise to between £26,000 and £40,000.

Entry requirements

To become a social worker in England, you will need to take a three-year undergraduate degree or a two-year postgraduate degree in social work that is approved by the General Social Care Council (GSCC). Many university courses are full-time, although some work-based routes with part-time study may also be available. You will typically need the following qualifications in order to study for an undergraduate degree in social work:

- five GCSEs (A-C) including English and maths

- at least two A levels, or an equivalent such as a BTEC National Diploma or NVQ Level 3 in Health and Social Care.

However, you should check entry requirements as colleges and universities may accept alternatives like an Access to Higher Education qualification or substantial relevant work experience (paid or voluntary).

If you already have a degree, you could do a two-year postgraduate Masters degree in social work. All postgraduate Masters degrees in social work need to be applied for via the Universities and Colleges Admissions Service (UCAS).

For information on how to qualify as a social worker in Northern Ireland, see the Northern Ireland Social Care Council website.

Employment-based routes

Some local authorities may sponsor employees already working for them in a social care support role to take the social work degree part-time or through distance learning. Some local authorities also recruit people directly into work-based training schemes for new social workers. Check in your local area to see if schemes like these are available.

More information

General Social Care Council
2 Hay's Lane
London SE1 2HB
Registration helpline: 0845 070 0630

Skills for Care (England)
Albion Court 5
Albion Place Leeds
LS1 6JL
Tel: 0113 245 1716
www.skillsforcare.org.uk

Northern Ireland Social Care Council (NISCC)
www.niscc.info

Care Council for Wales (CCW)
www.ccwales.org.uk

Scottish Social Services Council (SSSC)
www.sssc.uk.com

NHS Business Services Authority

(NHSBSA) Social Work Bursary
Tel: 0845 610 1122
www.nhsbsa.nhs.uk/Students

SOCIAL WORK ASSISTANT

The nature of the work

As a social work assistant, you could work with a variety of people (known as clients), including:

- families under stress
- older people
- people with physical or learning disabilities
- people with mental health problems
- children at risk.

You may be known by other job titles, such as community support worker, home care officer or social services assistant.

What can you earn?

Starting salaries can be around £16,000 a year. With experience and relevant qualifications, salaries can rise to between £19,000 and £25,000.

Those taking on additional management responsibilities may earn up to £28,000 a year.

You may work for a specialist recruitment agency. Hourly rates for agency work can be between £8 and £14.

Entry requirements

You will increase your chances of finding work if you have some experience (paid or voluntary) of working with people in a caring role. You can get more information and search for volunteering opportunities on the Do-it website.

Employers will usually consider experience to be more important than your qualifications, although they may ask for a good standard of secondary education.

Before looking for work, you may find it helpful to take a full-time or part-time college course such as a BTEC National Certificate or Diploma in Health and Social Care. This is not essential, but most social care courses include work placements so this can be a good way of getting useful experience.

For any job where you would be working (paid or unpaid) with children or vulnerable adults, you will need to pass background checks by the Criminal Records Bureau (CRB). Previous convictions or cautions may not automatically prevent you from working in social care. A driving licence would be useful for jobs based in the community.

More information

Skills for Care (England)
West Gate
6 Grace Street
Leeds
LS1 2RP
Tel: 0113 245 1716
www.skillsforcare.org.uk

General Social Care Council
2 Hay's Lane
London SE1 2HB
Tel: 020 7397 5800
Registration helpline: 0845 070 0630
www.gscc.org.uk

Northern Ireland Social Care Council (NISCC)
www.niscc.info

Care Council for Wales (CCW)
www.ccwales.org.uk

Scottish Social Services Council (SSSC)
www.sssc.uk.com

Department for Education - Children and Young People
Castle View House
East Lane
Runcorn
Cheshire

RESIDENTIAL SUPPORT WORKER

The nature of the work

As a residential support worker, your clients could include children in care or adults with physical or learning disabilities, mental health problems, addiction issues or other emotional or social needs.

With experience, you could have extra responsibilities including supervising and leading a team, and managing a budget.

What can you earn?

Full-time salaries can be around £13,000 to £18,000 a year. Senior support workers can earn between £19,000 and £24,000 a year. Hourly rates for part-time and contract work can be between £7 and £14.

Salaries may be lower in the private sector.

Entry requirements

To work in residential support, you will need paid or voluntary experience in the social work and care sector. You could get relevant experience in a number of ways, such as:

- working or volunteering at a youth club
- personal experience of caring for a family member
- working as a social work assistant
- paid or voluntary work in a care home, nursery or relevant charity.

You can get more information and search for volunteering opportunities on the Do-it website.

Most social care employers will be more interested in your work and life experience than formal qualifications. However, before you look for paid work, you may find it helpful to take a college course in health and social care, youth work or childcare. This could be, for example, a BTEC National Certificate or Diploma in Health and Social Care or the 14-19 Diploma in Society, Health and Development.

Taking a social care qualification is not essential for finding work, but most courses include work placements so this could be a good way of getting experience.

Relevant qualifications are widely available at local colleges. You could do these full-time or part-time.

For any job where you would be working (paid or unpaid) with children or vulnerable adults, you will need to pass background checks by the Criminal Records Bureau (CRB). Previous convictions or cautions may not automatically prevent you from working in social care. See the CRB website for details.

More information

General Social Care Council
2 Hay's Lane
London
SE1 2HB
Tel: 020 7397 5800
Registration helpline: 0845 070 0630
www.gscc.org.uk

Skills for Care (England)

West Gate
6 Grace Street
Leeds
LS1 2RP

Tel: 0113 245 1716

www.skillsforcare.org.uk

Northern Ireland Social Care Council (NISCC)

www.niscc.info

Care Council for Wales (CCW)

www.ccwales.org.uk

Scottish Social Services Council (SSSC)

www.sssc.uk.com

Department for Education - Children and Young People

Castle View House

East Lane

Runcorn

Cheshire

WA7 2GJ

Tel: 0370 000 2288

www.education.gov.uk/childrenandyoungpeople

DRUG AND ALCOHOL WORKER

If you want to help people, and you are a calm and caring person, this job could be ideal for you. As a drug and alcohol worker, you would help people tackle their drug, alcohol or solvent misuse problems.

The nature of the work

As a drug and alcohol worker (also known as a substance misuse worker), you would help people tackle and recover from their dependence on drugs (illegal, prescription and over-the-counter), alcohol or solvents.

You would help clients to access services such as counselling, healthcare and education. Your job could also cover: out reach work – encouraging people (clients) with substance misuse problems to make contact with support services, assessing clients to understand their drug or alcohol misuse and

313

identifying suitable ways of moving them towards recovery; counselling and rehabilitation – giving support and dealing with the causes of substance misuse; arrest referral work – supporting clients arrested for drug-related offences;; education and training – helping client access services to help them with reading, writing, maths, IT and job search skills; healthcare – working as a specialist nurse in an addiction clinic, where you might prescribe medication and supervise detox programmes; advocacy – helping clients to use housing, employment and healthcare services, and speaking up for clients in the justice system

In some jobs you may cover several of these areas or you might specialise.

What can you earn?

Employment officers, and outreach and drop-in centre workers earn between £20,000 and £25,000 a year. Counsellors and specialist nursing staff can earn between £23,000 and £28,000 a year, and team leaders and local service managers can earn up to £35,000 a year.

Entry requirements

You could have a variety of backgrounds for starting in this role, such as nursing, criminal justice, social care, youth work or counselling. For example, you may have dealt with drug or alcohol-dependent patients as a nurse, or worked in the probation service dealing with offenders after their release.

If you have personal experience of addiction or dependency you could also apply for this type of work, as applications are usually welcome from people who have been through treatment successfully.

Volunteering is an excellent way to gain relevant experience, make contacts and eventually find paid work. It gives the employer a chance to see your skills and motivation, and lets you decide whether this is the career for you. Most drug and alcohol support organisations offer volunteering opportunities and training.

You can find volunteering opportunities by contacting local substance misuse organisations. You can also visit the Do-it or Talktofrank websites to search for organisations by postcode or town.

For more information about working in this field, see the Federation of Drug & Alcohol Professionals (FDAP), DrugScope and Alcohol Concern websites.

More information

Federation of Drug & Alcohol Professionals
www.fdap.org.uk

DrugScope
www.drugscope.org.uk

Alcohol Concern
www.alcoholconcern.org.uk

YOUTH AND COMMUNITY WORKER

The nature of the work

You would generally work with young people aged 13 to 19, although in some jobs they might be as young as 11, or up to age 25. Your tasks would depend on the needs of the young people, but might include:

- organising sports, arts, drama and other activities
- advising and supporting young people
- offering counselling
- working with specific groups, such as young carers or those at risk of offending
- developing and running projects that deal with issues like health, bullying, crime or drugs
- managing volunteers and part-time workers
- keeping records and controlling budgets
- trying to get grants and funding

You might also be making contact with young people in meeting places like parks, shopping centres and on the streets. This is known as detached youth work.

What can you earn?

Youth support workers (those who are not fully qualified youth workers) can earn between £15,000 and £18,000 a year for full-time work. Salaries for qualified youth workers are usually between £22,000 and £34,000 a year. Senior and management salaries can be from £35,000.

Entry requirements

To become a professional youth worker in England you will need to gain at least a BA Honours degree in youth work that is recognised by the National Youth Agency (NYA). Depending on your previous qualifications, you could take either a BA Honours degree (three years full-time, or longer part-time) or a postgraduate certificate, diploma or MA if you already have a degree in any subject (one year full-time, or longer part-time)

Degree course entry requirements can vary, so check with each university or college. You may be accepted without formal qualifications if you have relevant work experience and the potential to succeed on the course.

If you have previous youth and community work qualifications at Diploma of Higher Education (Dip HE) or Foundation Degree level, you will not need to gain a degree in order to stay qualified.

It is important for you to get experience (paid or unpaid) of working with young people. You will often need at least one year's experience in order to apply for professional youth work courses and jobs. Find out about local opportunities for voluntary or part-time youth work by contacting your local youth service or by visiting the Do-it website.

Another option is to start as a part-time or volunteer youth support worker without any qualifications. You could then take work-based qualifications in youth support work, and if you wanted to, you could complete professional youth work training later on.

More information

National Youth Agency
Eastgate House 19-23
Humberstone Road Leicester
LE5 3GJ
www.nya.org.uk

Youth Council for Northern Ireland
Forestview Purdy's Lane Belfast
BT8 7AR
Tel: 028 9064 3882
www.ycni.org/

****

19· SPORT AND LEISURE

Sport related jobs are becoming more popular with young people and provide an entry into what is a fascinating area of employment. In this section we cover:

- Fitness Instructor
- Health Trainer
- Outdoor Activities Instructor
- Personal Trainer
- Sports Physiotherapist
- Swimming Coach/Teacher

For more details of opportunities in the sport and outdoors fields go to:

SkillsActive
Castlewood House
77-91 New Oxford Street
London
WC1A 1PX
Advice line: 08000 933300
www.skillsactive.com

FITNESS INSTRUCTOR

The nature of the work

As a fitness instructor, you would lead and organise group and individual exercise programmes to help people (clients) to improve their health and fitness. Your work could involve a range of activities or you could specialise in a particular one, like:

- keep fit
- aquacise (exercise in water)
- weight training

- yoga
- Pilates

You could also work with specialist groups of people, such as older adults, children, people with disabilities or people referred by doctors.

Your job could include:

- fitness assessments, consultations and introduction sessions for new clients
- demonstrating activities for clients to follow
- showing clients how to use exercise machines and free weights properly
- supervising clients to make sure that they are exercising safely and effectively
- leading group exercise classes, such as circuit training, aerobics or spinning
- creating personal exercise programmes
- giving advice on healthy eating and lifestyle

In smaller health or fitness clubs you may also carry out routine duties, such as at reception and the swimming pool, and health and safety checks.

What can you earn?

Starting salaries can be around £13,000 a year. This can rise to between £14,000 and over £20,000 a year. Freelance instructors can earn £10 to £20 an hour.

Entry requirements

To qualify as a fitness instructor, you could:

- either complete a nationally recognised qualification before starting work
- or start as an assistant instructor and complete work-based qualifications

Nationally recognised qualification

The Level 2 Certificate in Fitness Instructing is the preferred industry standard, and is approved by the Register of Exercise Professionals (also known as the Exercise Register). There are four categories for this certificate - gym, exercise to music, aqua, and physical activity for children.

The qualification will allow you to join the Register of Exercise Professionals (REPs) at level 2, which will show employers that you are competent and qualified to do your job. See the REPs website for more information.

Before you can work as an instructor, you will also need public liability insurance and a first aid certificate, which includes a cardiopulmonary resuscitation (CPR) certificate.

If you plan to work with children or other vulnerable groups, you will need Criminal Records Bureau (CRB) clearance. See the CRB website for details.

Work-based qualifications

You may be able to start as an assistant instructor and complete qualifications whilst working under the supervision of a qualified instructor. When you have completed your qualification you can apply to join the REPs at level 2.

You may be able to start in this job through an Apprenticeship scheme. You will need to check which schemes are available in your area. For more information about Apprenticeships, visit the Apprenticeships website.

More information

Register of Exercise Professionals (REPs)
3rd Floor
8-10 Crown Hill
Croydon
Surrey
CR0 1RZ
Tel: 020 8686 6464
www.exerciseregister.org

OCR Information Bureau
Tel: 024 7685 1509
www.ocr.org.uk

SkillsActive
Castlewood House
77-91 New Oxford Street
London
WC1A 1PX
Advice line: 08000 933300
www.skillsactive.com

YMCA Fitness Industry Training
www.ymcafit.org.uk

Vocational Training Charitable Trust (VTCT) 🖻
3rd Floor
Eastleigh House
Upper Market Street
Eastleigh
Hampshire
SO50 9FD
Tel: 023 8068 4500
www.vtct.org.uk

Central YMCA Qualifications (CYQ)
www.cyq.org.uk

Active IQ
www.activeiq.co.uk

City & Guilds
1 Giltspur Street
London
EC1A 9DD
Tel: 0844 543 0000
www.cityandguilds.com

NCFE
www.ncfe.org.uk

Edexcel
www.edexcel.com

HEALTH TRAINER

The nature of the work

As a health trainer, you would advise people about healthier lifestyle choices in order to improve their general health and wellbeing.

Your work within the community could focus on issues such as:

- improving the amount of exercise people take
- the importance of practising safe sex
- helping people stop smoking
- the positive effects of lowering alcohol intake
- the benefits of breastfeeding
- improving access to healthy lifestyles in communities with the greatest needs.

You would encourage people to understand and adapt their behaviour by providing information and practical support on a one-to-one basis, as well as in groups. Your work to improve the health of the community could also include:

- connecting people to relevant local services
- helping people understand how their behaviour effects their health
- supporting and motivating individuals to change harmful habits
- explaining the benefits of healthier food and lifestyle choices
- encouraging greater community integration and sense of togetherness
- recording activity levels and results, and using these to motivate clients.

What can you earn?

- Health trainers can earn between £15,600 and £18,600 a year
- Supervisors can earn between £21,000 and £27,500.

Many health trainer jobs are offered on a part-time basis, so earnings would be a portion of full-time rates (known as 'pro rata' payment). This means that actual annual income may be less than above.

Entry requirements

To become a health trainer, you will need:

- knowledge of the health issues facing the community
- good communication skills in English (and for some jobs, a second community language)
- experience (paid or voluntary) of working with local community groups.

For advice on voluntary opportunities, you can contact the voluntary services coordinator or manager at your local NHS Trust.

Some employers will prefer you to have GCSE grade C in English, and you may also be asked for an NVQ Level 3 or equivalent qualification.

You could have an advantage when looking for work if you have qualifications or work experience in an area such as:

- personal training
- fitness instructing
- nutritional therapy or dietetics.

See the related job profiles for details about qualifications and training in these careers.

More information

Skills for Health
Goldsmiths House
Broad Plain
Bristol
BS2 0JP
Tel: 0117 922 1155
www.skillsforhealth.org.uk

NHS Careers
PO Box 2311
Bristol
BS2 2ZX
Tel: 0345 60 60 655
www.nhscareers.nhs.uk

Health Learning and Skills Advice Line
Tel: 08000 150850

OUTDOOR ACTIVITIES INSTRUCTOR

The nature of the work

As an outdoor activities instructor, you could provide:

- activities to help people enjoy their leisure time
- self-development activities
- courses for youth, social and probation services

Your work would include:

- planning and preparing activities to suit needs, and abilities
- explaining, advising on and demonstrating activities
- instructing in one or more specialist areas, such as sailing or climbing
- making sure that all equipment and facilities are safe

- explaining safety procedures
- checking weather conditions, assessing hazards and managing risks.

You may also have to deal with accidents, and support people who may be nervous about taking part in activities.

What can you earn?

Starting salaries can be around £12,000 a year.

Experienced instructors can earn around £18,000 a year, and senior instructors can earn £25,000 a year or more.

Accommodation and food may be provided.

Figures are intended as a guideline only.

Entry requirements

You should be at least 18 (21 if you need to drive a minibus) and would usually need:

- skill in at least one outdoor activity - although the more activities you can offer the better
- coaching or instructor qualifications approved by the relevant national governing body
- a first aid certificate
- a life-saving certificate if you instruct water-based activities.

If you will be working with children, young people or other vulnerable groups, you will need Criminal Records Bureau (CRB) clearance.

It would be useful if you can drive a minibus and tow a trailer, as you may need to transport equipment.

It may also help you if you have been involved in activities such as Duke of Edinburgh's awards, membership of activity clubs, or volunteering at outdoor activities centres. Some instructors have previous experience in youth work, teaching, sports coaching or training, or as physical training instructors in the armed forces.

Examples of instructor qualifications include:

- Mountain Leaders Training Board Mountain Leader Award
- British Canoe Union Level 2 Coach Award (kayak, canoe or both)
- Ski Instructor and Snowboard Instructor qualifications.

You could complete the qualifications through sports or activity clubs, or at an accredited outdoor education centre. You would usually need at least 12 months' experience in the activity before you take the award. Check with the NGB for your sport for details of courses and qualifications. NGB contact details are on the Sport England website.

You may be able to complete NGB qualifications as part of a college or university course in sport, leisure and recreation. Courses include BTEC National and Higher National Certificates and Diplomas, foundation degrees and degrees and postgraduate qualifications.

See the Outdoor Sourcebook produced by the Institute for Outdoor Learning's (IOL) for details of colleges, universities and other organisations offering training for outdoor activities. The IOL website also has careers information and a job section.

More information

sports coach UK
www.sportscoachuk.org

SkillsActive
Castlewood House
77-91 New Oxford Street
London
WC1A 1PX
Advice line: 08000 933300
www.skillsactive.com

Institute for Outdoor Learning (IOL)
Warwick Mill Business Centre
Warwick Bridge
Carlisle
Cumbria
CA4 8RR
Tel: 01228 564580
www.outdoor-learning.org

PERSONAL TRAINER

The nature of the work

To become a personal trainer you would first need to be a fitness instructor with a high level of experience and advanced qualifications.

As a personal trainer, you would first talk to clients to find out about their fitness level and health history. You would then:

- set realistic short-term and long-term goals and plan programmes
- give clients advice on health, nutrition and lifestyle changes
- help clients with their workouts
- check and record clients' progress. In some cases you might work full-time as a gym instructor and do personal training outside your normal hours of work.

What can you earn?

Personal trainers are usually paid by the hour for each session with a client. There are no set salary scales and earnings depend on location, number of clients and whether the trainer is self-employed or works for a gym. Self-employed (also known as freelance) instructors can earn between £20 and £40 an hour. Some instructors with high profile clients can earn between £50 and £100 an hour.

Personal trainers in full time employment can earn between £18,000 and £40,000 a year.

Entry requirements

To become a personal trainer you would first need to be a fitness instructor with a high level of experience and advanced qualifications (at least a level 3 certificate).

Doing a course that allows you to be a member of the Register of Exercise Professionals (REPs) will improve your chances of employment. Membership of REPs shows employers and clients that you are a competent instructor who has recognised qualifications and meets good standards of practice. REPs is also known as the Exercise Register.

You can join the REPs at different levels, depending on your qualifications. With a Level 3 Certificate in Personal Training you can join at level 3. You can complete industry-recognised awards offered by some employers and universities, and you can complete courses through a number of colleges and private training providers. See the REPs website for information about membership and for details of qualifications and approved training providers.

You can also find advice on choosing courses on the National Register of Personal Trainers website.

Another option is to do relevant BTEC HNCs or HNDs, foundation degrees, degrees and postgraduate qualifications in exercise and sports science, sports therapy or sports studies. If you have a relevant degree and at least six months' up-to-date work experience you may be given provisional REPs membership at level 3. To gain full membership, you will need to show competence by completing a work-based qualification.

To work as a personal trainer you must have public liability insurance and a first aid certificate. This must include a cardio-pulmonary resuscitation certificate (CPR).

You may be able to do this job through an Apprenticeship scheme. You will need to check which schemes are available in your area. For more information, visit the Apprenticeships website.

More information

Register of Exercise Professionals (REPs)
3rd Floor 8-10 Crown Hill
Croydon
Surrey
CR0 1RZ
Tel: 020 8686 6464
www.exerciseregister.org

OCR
Tel: 024 7685 1509
www.ocr.org.uk

SkillsActive
Castlewood House
77-91 New Oxford Street
London
WC1A 1PX
Advice line: 08000 933300
www.skillsactive.com

YMCAfit
www.ymcafit.org.uk

Vocational Training Charitable Trust (VTCT)
3rd Floor
Eastleigh House
Upper Market Street
Eastleigh
Hampshire
SO50 9FD

Tel: 023 8068 4500

www.vtct.org.uk

Central YMCA Qualifications (CYQ)

www.cyq.org.uk

Active IQ

www.activeiq.co.uk

City & Guilds

www.cityandguilds.com

NCFE

www.ncfe.org.uk

National Register of Personal Trainers

www.nrpt.co.uk

SPORTS PHYSIOTHERAPIST

The nature of the work

To become a sports physiotherapist, you will need to have an interest in health science. You will need good communication and 'people' skills. You will also have the ability to look after the health and well being of patients.

As a sports physiotherapist, you could work with top professional sports people, amateurs or people who do sports as a leisure activity.

Your work would include:

- examining and diagnosing injuries
- planning treatment programmes
- using treatments such as manipulation, massage and heat treatment
- advising how long it could take to return to sport after injury
- keeping full records of patients' treatment and progress.

If you deal with sports professionals, you would work in a team with coaches, other health care professionals and sports scientists. You could specialise in a particular sport, or in a particular aspect of physiotherapy, such as rehabilitation.

What can you earn?

Physiotherapists working in the NHS earn between £20,710 and £26,839 a year. Specialist physiotherapists earn between £24,331 and £33,436 a year. Visit the NHS Careers website for full salary scales for physiotherapists in the NHS. Salaries in the private sector can be similar but may be higher.

Entry requirements

To become a sports physiotherapist, you first need to qualify as a chartered physiotherapist by completing a physiotherapy degree approved by the Health Professions Council (HPC). When you have completed the degree, you will be eligible for state registration and membership of the Chartered Society of Physiotherapy (CSP).

See the HPC and CSP websites for details of approved degree courses. Entry requirements may vary, so check with individual colleges or universities.

Competition for places on physiotherapy degree courses is strong, so it would help you if you have relevant health care experience before applying, for example as a physiotherapy assistant. As a physiotherapy assistant, you may be able to take a part-time degree alongside your job. Ask your local NHS Trust for details.

For all courses you will need Criminal Records Bureau (CRB) clearance at the beginning of the course, and again before registering with the HPC.

The NHS would usually pay your course fees, and there is also a means-tested bursary to help with the cost of living while you train. Visit the NHS Business Services Authority website for detailed information about eligibility for the NHS bursary scheme.

If you have a first or upper second class honours degree in a relevant subject (such as a biological science, psychology or sports science) you may be eligible for an accelerated postgraduate programme. Contact the CSP for more details.

More information

NHS Careers
PO Box 2311
Bristol
BS2 2ZX
Tel: 0345 60 60 655
www.nhscareers.nhs.uk

SkillsActive
Castlewood House
77-91 New Oxford Street
London
WC1A 1PX
Advice line: 08000 933300
www.skillsactive.com

Health Learning and Skills Advice Line
Tel: 08000 150850

Association of Chartered Physiotherapists in Sports Medicine
www.acpsm.org

Chartered Society of Physiotherapy
14 Bedford Row
London
WC1R 4ED
Tel: 020 7306 6666
www.csp.org.uk

SWIMMING TEACHER OR COACH

The nature of the work

As a swimming teacher or coach you would:

- teach or coach one-to-one or in groups
- identify participants' abilities
- plan and deliver sessions appropriate to the level of swimmer
- make sure safety standards are followed in all sessions
- check that life-saving equipment is in working order
- provide explanations and demonstrate swimming techniques
- set ground rules for each session
- correct faults in swimming techniques and improve performance
- evaluate sessions and give feedback
- organise and supervise assistants and helpers.

You may also need to deal with minor injuries and accidents.

What can you earn?

Most swimming teachers and coaches work part-time and are paid an hourly rate. Rates can be between £10 and over £30 an hour.

Entry requirements

You can qualify as a swimming teacher by completing qualifications awarded by:

- the Amateur Swimming Association (ASA)
- the Swimming Teachers Association (STA).

The ASA also awards swimming coaching qualifications.

You would start with either of the following:

- ASA/UKCC Level 1 Certificate for Teaching Aquatics
- ASA/UKCC Level 1 Certificate for Coaching Swimming.

333

Completing a qualification at level 1 will qualify you to support fully-qualified teachers or coaches.

Visit the ASA website for details of qualifications and centres offering training.

Alternatively, you can qualify as a swimming teacher by doing STA teaching qualifications. See the STA website for full details.

To work with children or other vulnerable people you will need clearance from the Criminal Records Bureau (CRB).

More information

Swimming Teachers' Association (STA)
Anchor House
Birch Street
Walsall
West Midlands
WS2 8HZ
Tel: 01922 645097
www.sta.co.uk

SkillsActive
Castlewood House
77-91 New Oxford Street
London
WC1A 1PX
Advice line: 08000 933300
www.skillsactive.com

****

20. TEACHING

This chapter covers three main teaching jobs:

- Primary School Teacher
- Secondary School Teacher
- Teaching Assistant

The area of teaching is very wide and there are other opportunities available, such as college lecturing. For information on the numerous other roles available contact:

Teaching Agency - Get into Teaching
Teaching Information Line (freephone): 0800 389 2500
www.education.gov.uk/get-into-teaching

PRIMARY SCHOOL TEACHER

The nature of the work
You would work with children aged between five and eleven in state and independent schools, and be responsible for their educational, social and emotional development while in your care.

You would teach subjects covered by the primary national curriculum at Key Stage 1 (ages 5 to 7) and Key Stage 2 (7 to 11) — subjects such as English, science, music and art. In some classes, you may have a teaching assistant to help you.

Depending on your qualifications and experience, you may work as a subject specialist teacher.

As well as teaching you would:

- plan lessons and teaching materials
- mark and assess children's work
- manage class behaviour
- work with other professionals, such as education psychologists and social workers
- discuss children's progress and other relevant matters with parents and carers
- attend meetings and training
- organise outings, social activities and sports events.

As a primary teacher, you could also work with children under the age of five (Early Years Foundation Stage) in settings like a children's centre or a reception class in a school.

What can you earn?

The main salary scale is from £21,588 to £31,552 a year (£27,000 to £36,387 in inner London and £25,117 to £35,116 in outer London). Teachers who reach the top of the main salary scale may be able to move on to a higher scale, ranging from £34,181 to £36,756 (£40,288 to £43,692 in inner London). There are also separate scales for teachers who have advanced skills or progress into leadership roles, and additional payments for those who take on extra responsibilities.

Entry requirements

The most common way to become a primary school teacher is to do Initial Teacher Training (ITT) and gain Qualified Teacher Status (QTS). The following ITT routes lead to QTS:

- undergraduate degree
- postgraduate award
- work-based programme.

For all routes you will need:

- GCSEs (A-C) in English, maths and a science subject or equivalent qualifications. Check with course providers which qualifications they will accept
- passes in numeracy and literacy skills tests
- Enhanced Disclosure checks through the Criminal Records Bureau (CRB).

You will also need experience of working with young children through paid work or volunteering for example, at a local school or on a holiday play scheme. The Teaching Agency has useful advice about contacting schools for work experience.

Work-based routes

There are several options you can look at if you prefer to train and work in a school at the same time. These options are very popular and there is a lot of competition for places.

School-Centred Initial Teacher Training (SCITT)

SCITT is a classroom-based training programme that takes one year, and is aimed at those who already have a degree related to a national curriculum subject.

The programmes are run by groups of schools and colleges within a local area and you would spend time in one or more of the schools while doing your training.

School Direct

This option replaces the Graduate Teaching Programme and has two alternatives:

- School Direct Training Programme
- School Direct Training Programme (with salary – starting in September 2013).

You will need a degree for either option, and for the paid training route you will also need a minimum of three years' working experience. The aim is to attract people into teaching, who can bring in skills and knowledge from commerce and industry.

You can apply directly to schools offering the programmes and work while you are training. Both options take around 12 months to complete and lead to QTS.

Contact the Teaching Agency for a list of schools taking part in School Direct.

Teach First

Teach First is a charity that runs a two-year teacher training and leadership programme for graduates with a good degree (2:1 or higher). Training is based within schools located in areas facing social and economic challenges. See the Teach First website for more details.

Teachers who have teaching qualifications from another country should check the career pportunities pages of the Department of Education website for details about extra training that may be needed to work in schools in England and Wales.

Moving from further education into school teaching

Since April 2012, lecturers in further education who hold Qualified Teacher Learning and Skills (QTLS) status, and are members of the Institute for Learning, can be employed in primary or secondary schools as fully qualified teachers. See the Department of Education pages on QTLS recognition for more information.

Visit the Teaching Agency website for full details of all entry routes into teaching and funding for training.

Northern Ireland

For details of routes into teaching in Northern Ireland see the Department of Education Northern Ireland website.

Transferring to another age group

You do not need to do further training to transfer to teaching another age group. However, schools recommend that you get some experience of the age group you are intending to teach. This could be on a voluntary basis.

Some local education authorities and teacher training institutions may offer short conversion or refresher courses.

Returning to teaching

If you are a qualified teacher wanting to return to teaching after a career break you can find information on the Teaching Agency website. This includes details of returners' courses and other available support.

More information

Teaching Agency - Get into Teaching 🖵
Teaching Information Line (freephone): 0800 389 2500
www.education.gov.uk/get-into-teaching

Department of Education Northern Ireland (DENI) 🖵
Rathael House
Balloo Road
Bangor
BT19 7PR
Tel: 028 9127 9279
www.deni.gov.uk

Graduate Teacher Training Registry (GTTR)
Rosehill New
Barn Lane

Cheltenham
Gloucestershire
GL52 3LZ
Tel: 0871 4680 469
www.gttr.ac.uk

SECONDARY SCHOOL TEACHER

The nature of the work

Your work would be in state or independent schools, teaching children aged from 11 to 16, or up to 19 in schools with sixth forms. You would:

- specialise in teaching one or two subjects
- teach classes of different ages and abilities throughout the school
- prepare pupils for exams like GCSEs and A levels.

Some areas of England and Wales have middle schools. These take children from ages eight or nine up to ages 12 or 13. As a teacher in a middle school you would teach the primary or secondary curriculum, depending on the age of children in your class.

What can you earn?

The main salary scale is from £21,588 to £31,552 a year (£27,000 to £36,387 in inner London and £25,117 to £35,116 in outer London).

Teachers who reach the top of the main salary scale may be able to move on to a higher scale, ranging from £34,181 to £36,756 (£40,288 to £43,692 in inner London).

There are also separate scales for teachers who have advanced skills or progress into leadership roles, and additional payments for those who take on extra responsibilities.

See details of all the salary scales on the Teaching Agency website.

Entry requirements

The most common way to become a secondary school teacher is to do Initial Teacher Training (ITT) and gain Qualified Teacher Status (QTS). The following ITT routes lead to QTS:

- undergraduate degree
- postgraduate award
- work-based programme.

For all of these routes, you will need:

- GCSEs (A-C) in English and maths (and science, depending on your teaching subject) or equivalent qualifications
- passes in numeracy and literacy skills tests
- Enhanced Disclosure checks through the Criminal Records Bureau (CRB).

You will also need experience of working with young people through paid work or volunteering for example, at a local school, through youth work or on a holiday scheme. The Teaching Agency has lots of advice about contacting schools for work experience. It also offers up to 10 days' classroom experience in certain secondary subjects through the School Experience Programme.

Undergraduate degree route

You can study for a university degree and gain QTS at the same time by doing one of the following courses:

- BA (Hons) degree or BSc (Hons) degree with QTS
- Bachelor of Education (BEd) degree course.

These are usually full-time courses and take three to four years.

To get onto a degree course, you will usually need at least two A levels and at least five GCSEs (A-C). Universities may accept other qualifications such as

341

an Access to Higher Education course. Check with course providers for their exact requirements.

Postgraduate routes

If you already have a degree related to the national curriculum, you can gain QTS by doing a Postgraduate Certificate of Education (PGCE) course. Courses take one year, full-time or two years, part-time. A small number of flexible courses are available mainly aimed at those already working as unqualified teachers.

You can search for all PGCE courses and apply online on the Graduate Teacher Training Registry (GTTR) website.

Find out more about national curriculum subjects on the following website:

Work-based routes

There are several options you can look at if you prefer to train and work in a school at the same time. These options are very popular and there is a lot of competition for places.

School-Centred Initial Teacher Training (SCITT)

SCITT is a classroom-based training programme that takes one year, and is aimed at those who already have a degree related to a national curriculum subject.

The programmes are run by groups of schools and colleges within a local area and you would spend time in one or more of the schools while doing your training.

School Direct

This option replaces the Graduate Teaching Programme and has two alternatives:

- School Direct Training Programme
- School Direct Training Programme (with salary – starting in September 2013).

You will need a degree for either option, and for the paid training route you will also need a minimum of three years' working experience. The aim is to attract people into teaching, who can bring in skills and knowledge from commerce and industry.

You can apply directly to schools offering the programmes and work while you are training. Both options take around 12 months to complete and lead to QTS.

Contact the Teaching Agency for a list of schools taking part in School Direct.

Teach First

Teach First is a charity that runs a two-year teacher training and leadership programme for graduates with a good degree (2:1 or higher). Training is based within schools located in areas facing social and economic challenges. See the Teach First website for more details.

Overseas Trained Teacher Programme (OTTP)

Teachers who have teaching qualifications from another country should check the career opportunities pages of the Department of Education website for details about extra training that may be needed to work in schools in England and Wales.

Moving from further education into school teaching

Since April 2012, lecturers in further education who hold Qualified Teacher Learning and Skills (QTLS) status, and are members of the Institute for Learning, can be employed in primary or secondary schools as fully qualified teachers. See the Department of Education pages on QTLS recognition for more information.

Visit the Teaching Agency's Get into Teaching website for full details of all entry routes into teaching and funding for training.

Northern Ireland

For details of routes into teaching in Northern Ireland see the Department of Education Northern Ireland website.

More information

Teaching Agency - Get into Teaching
Teaching Information Line (freephone): 0800 389 2500
www.education.gov.uk/get-into-teaching

Department of Education Northern Ireland (DENI)
Rathael House
Balloo Road
Bangor
BT19 7PR
Tel: 028 9127 9279
www.deni.gov.uk

Graduate Teacher Training Registry (GTTR)
Rosehill
New Barn Lane
Cheltenham
Gloucestershire
GL52 3LZ
Tel: 0871 4680 469
www.gttr.ac.uk

TEACHING ASSISTANT

The nature of the work

As a teaching assistant you would support teachers and help children with their educational and social development, both in and out of the classroom. Your exact job will depend on the school and the age of the children.

Your job may include:

- getting the classroom ready for lessons
- listening to children read, reading to them or telling them stories
- helping children who need extra support to complete tasks
- helping teachers to plan learning activities and complete records
- supporting teachers in managing class behaviour
- supervising group activities
- looking after children who are upset or have had accidents
- clearing away materials and equipment after lessons
- helping with outings and sports events
- taking part in training
- carrying out administrative tasks.

You would also support children with particular needs, working with them individually or in small groups.

In some schools you could have a specialism, such as literacy, numeracy or special educational needs (SEN). If you are bilingual, you might do more work with children whose first language is not English. At secondary level, you're likely to concentrate on working with individuals and small groups and, depending on the subject, you may assist with practicals, for example in science. A teaching assistant might also be called classroom assistant or learning support assistant.

Higher Level Teaching Assistant

As a Higher Level Teaching Assistant (HLTA) you would have more responsibility. This could include:

- working along side teachers to support learning activities

- helping to plan lessons and prepare teaching materials
- acting as a specialist assistant for particular subjects
- leading classes under the direction of the teacher
- supervising other support staff.

You would also assess, record and report on the progress of children you work with.

What can you earn?

Salaries for full-time teaching assistants range from £12,000 to over £17,000 a year. Salaries for full-time HLTAs can be between £16,000 and £21,000 a year. This will vary depending on the Local Education Authority (LEA) and the responsibilities of individual jobs. There is no national pay scale and wage rates are set by each LEA. Teaching assistants who work part-time, or are paid only for term-time, earn a proportion of full-time rates. This is known as pro rata payment.

Entry requirements

LEAs and individual schools decide which qualifications and experience they want applicants to have. You can get an idea of what you are likely to need by looking at jobs advertised locally or by checking your LEA's vacancies online.

Previous qualifications in nursery nursing, childcare, play work or youth work can be useful for finding work. If you have enough experience of working with children or can show employers that you have the right personality and potential, you may be able to start work without qualifications. Volunteering to help in a local school for a few hours a week is a good way to start.

The following qualifications are also available for those not yet employed in the role and for those just new to the job, whether paid or volunteering:

- Level 2 Award in Support Work in Schools
- Level 3 Award in Supporting Teaching and Learning in Schools.

Most paid jobs will require you to have qualifications in literacy and numeracy at GCSE or equivalent.

You may be able to become a teaching assistant through an Apprenticeship scheme. The range of Apprenticeships available in your area will depend on the local jobs market and the types of skills employers need from their workers.

You can find more information on careers and qualifications for school support staff on the Department for Education and Skills4Schools websites.

More information

Department for Education - support staff
Support Staff Enquiry Line (freephone): 0800 389 5335
www.education.gov.uk/get-into-teaching

Local Government Careers Information
www.lgcareers.com

****

21. TRAVEL AND TOURISM

The areas of travel and tourism generally attract dynamic people with a sense of adventure. the field is wide, from travel agent to tourist guide. For the right people the rewards are great. In this section, we cover the following jobs:

- Travel Agent
- Tour manager
- Tourist Guide
- Resort Representative
- Air cabin crew
- Airline Customer Service Agent
- Cruise Ship Steward
- Hotel Manager
- Hotel Porter

For more details of jobs in the tourism industry go to:

International Association of Tour Managers (IATM)
397 Walworth Road
London
SE17 2AW
Tel: 020 7703 9154
www.iatm.co.uk

TRAVEL AGENT

The nature of the work
As a travel agent, you could be based at places like high street travel agents or call centres. Your work would include:

- helping customers to find a suitable package holiday or to plan independent travel

- checking the availability of the chosen holiday by telephone or computer
- making bookings using a computer system
- collecting deposits (a portion of payment) and filling in booking forms
- contacting customers when their tickets arrive, and collecting final payments
- informing customers of any changes such as cancelled flights, and arranging alternatives.

You would also advise customers about passports, travel insurance, visas, vaccinations and tours. You may also arrange refunds and handle complaints.

What can you earn?

Starting salaries can be around £13,000 a year. Experienced travel agents can earn between £15,000 and £25,000 a year, and salaries for those in senior jobs can be £30,000 a year or more. Travel agents often get commission based on meeting performance targets. They may also get discounts on holidays.

Entry requirements

You would not usually need any particular qualifications, although it may be useful if you have GCSEs. Employers will want to see that you are enthusiastic, and have the right personal qualities and skills for the job.
It could help you if you have experience in customer services or sales, and if you are able to speak other languages.

The most common way to start as a travel agent is to find work with a travel agency and train on the job. However, you could take a full-time college course before you look for work. This is not essential, but it may help you get a job. Relevant courses include:

- Level 2 Diploma in Travel and Tourism
- Level 3 Diploma in Travel and Tourism
- Level 2 Certificate in Travel Services.

You may be able to start this job through an Apprenticeship scheme, such as the Level 2 Apprenticeship in Travel Services. For more information, see the Apprenticeships and UKSP websites.

More information
People first
2nd Floor
Armstrong House
38 Market Square
Uxbridge
Middlesex
UB8 1LH
Tel: 01895 817 000
www.people1st.co.uk

UKSP
www.uksp.co.uk (careers information)

Springboard UK
http://springboarduk.net

City & Guilds
1 Giltspur Street
London
EC1A 9DD
Tel: 0844 543 0000
www.cityandguilds.com

TOUR MANAGER

The nature of the work

As a tour manager, you would be responsible for making sure that travel arrangements for groups of holiday-makers run as smoothly and enjoyably as possible. You would accompany passengers throughout their tour, keeping them informed about details like arrival and departure times and places of interest.

You would usually work on coach tours that can last from between two or three days to over a month, but could also work on tours by rail or cruise ship.

Your job would involve:

- joining the group at the start of their journey, welcoming them, and announcing details of travel arrangements and stopover points
- making sure all travel arrangements run according to plan, and that the accommodation, meals and service are satisfactory
- helping with passport and immigration issues
- helping with check-in to accommodation
- giving a spoken commentary on places travelled through or visited (although local guides may also be used)
- promoting and selling excursions to tour members
- advising about facilities such as sights, restaurants and shops at each destination
- organising entry to attractions and additional transport, such as car hire
- keeping records.

You would need to be available at almost any time to give advice, solve problems and deal with emergencies like loss of passports or money, illness or difficulties with accommodation.

In some companies you may be known as tour director rather than tour manager.

What can you earn?

Tour managers salaries can start at around £15,000 a year, rising to around £20,000 with experience.

Income varies considerably from company to company, and also depends on the areas and types of tour the manager covers. Earnings are often based on a daily allowance, plus free board and lodgings for the duration of the tour and other relevant expenses.

Entry requirements

You would not usually need any particular qualifications to become a tour manager, but you would need a good standard of general education.

You would also usually need:

- experience of working with people
- an interest in geography, history and history of art, and the ability to research these for the region covered by the tour
- a good working knowledge of foreign languages if working overseas
- experience of working abroad (if the job you are applying for is based overseas).

Qualifications related to leisure, travel and tourism are available at all levels, including GCSEs, A levels, NVQs, BTECs, degrees and postgraduate qualifications. You could find it useful to complete one of these, but this is not essential.

You may be able to get into this job through an Apprenticeship scheme. The range of Apprenticeships available in your area will depend on the local jobs market and the types of skills employers need from their workers. To find out more about Apprenticeships, visit the Apprenticeships website.

More information

International Association of Tour Managers (IATM)
397 Walworth Road
London
SE17 2AW
Tel: 020 7703 9154
www.iatm.co.uk

People 1st
2nd Floor
Armstrong House
38 Market Square
Uxbridge

Middlesex
UB8 1LH
Tel: 01895 817 000
www.uksp.co.uk/ (careers information)
www.people1st.co.uk

Institute of Travel and Tourism
PO Box 217
Ware
Hertfordshire
SG12 8WY
Tel: 0844 4995 653
www.itt.co.uk

TOURIST GUIDE

The nature of the work

Tourist guides show visitors around places of interest, such as towns and cities, historic buildings, gardens, religious sites or museums and art galleries.

As a tourist guide you could:

- work in one place such as a castle or historic house, or
- accompany groups on day tours to interesting places or sites.
- You would escort groups around the site or area, and give information about history, purpose, architecture or other points of interest.
- Guided tours could be:
- sightseeing tours
- tours for special interest groups
- themed walks.

You could also work as a 'driver guide', taking small groups of tourists on guided tours around places of interest in a car or minibus.

What can you earn?

Rates of pay vary depending on the employer and the location. Most tourist guides are self-employed and charge fees. See the Association of Professional Tourist Guides website for details of recommended fees for qualified guides.

Entry requirements

You would not need any set qualifications to start training as a tourist guide, but you would need a good standard of general education.

It would be an advantage if you have experience in jobs that involve dealing with the public and giving presentations. It could be useful if you speak a foreign language fluently, but this is not usually essential.

You can do courses and take exams which are accredited by the Institute of Tourist Guiding. Depending on the type of guiding you want to do, you could work towards qualifications such as:

- Level 2: Fixed Route Commentary, Interpretation and Presentation – for paid or voluntary work, guiding visitors round attractions such as galleries, cathedrals or stately homes, or on fixed route tours such as river trips and open top bus trips
- Level 3 Flexible Route Commentary, Heritage Interpretation and Presentation – for work as a guide in areas such as city and town centres, or in visitor attractions, historic buildings or heritage sites
- Level 4: Blue Badge in Tourist Guiding – for all aspects of guiding.

In some places, such as Westminster Abbey and York Minster, Blue Badge guides are the only guides allowed (apart from in-house staff).

Courses are run by local and regional tourist bodies, colleges and other institutions. Visit the Institute of Tourist Guiding website for details of accredited courses. See the Guild of Registered Tourist Guides website for details of regional tourist boards.

Most courses are around 20 weeks long, although some can take up to two years. They are part-time, with evening lectures and practical training at weekends. Blue Badge courses in London run once a year, but in other areas they only run when there is a demand for guides.

If you work on a site where in-house guides are employed, you may receive training from the owner of the site.

More information

Institute of Tourist Guiding
Coppergate House
16 Brune St
London
E1 7NJ
Tel: 020 7953 8397
www.itg.org.uk

People 1st
2nd Floor
Armstrong House
38 Market Square
Uxbridge
Middlesex
UB8 1LH
Tel: 01895 817 000
www.uksp.co.uk/ (careers information)
www.people1st.co.uk

Association of Professional Tourist Guides
33-37 Moreland Street
London
EC1V 8HA

RESORT REPRESENTATIVE

The nature of the work

As a resort representative, you would look after holiday-makers at their holiday destination (usually abroad).

Your work would include:

- meeting groups of holiday-makers when they arrive at the airport
- accompanying holiday-makers by coach to their accommodation
- holding a welcome meeting to give information about resort facilities and local attractions
- meeting holiday-makers at pre-arranged times to make announcements and deal with enquiries and problems
- keeping an information board and a folder of useful information up-to-date at each hotel
- arranging, and sometimes accompanying, excursions and sightseeing trips
- arranging car or ski hire if necessary
- being on-call to give advice and deal with emergencies like lost passports or money, illness or difficulties with accommodation.

You would also keep records, and write reports of complaints and incidents such as illness.

What can you earn?

- Resort representatives can start at around £12,000 a year
- Experienced representatives can earn £16,000 or more.

Resort representatives are also provided with free accommodation and insurance, and sometimes earn commission, for example by selling tours and arranging car hire.

Entry requirements

You would not need any set qualifications to become a resort representative, although employers may expect you to have GCSEs (A-C) or similar qualifications, particularly in English and maths. You would usually need a good working knowledge of one or more foreign languages.

For most jobs you should be at least 20 years of age. To work as a children's representative you may be accepted from the age of 18 or 19, and would usually be expected to have a qualification in childcare.

You could have an advantage if you have relevant experience, such as in another area of travel and tourism, or in customer service or administration. You may need specialist knowledge or skills for some holidays – for example, as a winter sports representative you may need to be able to ski at an advanced level.

Colleges offer a range of courses related to travel and tourism, including BTEC certificates and diplomas, BTEC HNCs/HNDs, foundation degrees and degrees. Although you may find these useful when looking for work, they are not essential.

More information

People 1st
2nd Floor
Armstrong House
38 Market Square
Uxbridge
Middlesex
UB8 1LH
Tel: 01895 817 000
www.people1st.co.uk
www.uksp.co.uk/ (careers information)

Springboard UK
http://springboarduk.net

Association of Independent Tour Operators
www.aito.co.uk

Federation of Tour Operators
www.fto.co.uk

Guild of Registered Tourist Guides
The Guild House
52d Borough High Street
London
SE1 1XN

Tel: 020 7403 1115
www.britainsbestguides.org

AIR CABIN CREW

The nature of the work

As an air cabin crew member you would help make sure that airline passengers have a comfortable, safe and pleasant flight. Before a flight you would:

- go a meeting about the flight and schedule
- check that there are enough supplies on the plane and that emergency equipment is working properly
- greet passengers and direct them to their seats
- demonstrate emergency equipment and procedures to passengers.
- During a flight you would:
- make sure that passengers are comfortable and deal with any requests
- serve food and drinks, and sell duty-free items
- make announcements on behalf of the pilot
- reassure passengers in the event of an emergency, and make sure that they follow safety procedures.

At the end of a flight you would:

- make sure that passengers leave the plane safely and with all their hand luggage
- write a flight report, including about any unusual incidents
- add up and record food and drink orders, and duty-free sales.

Between flights, you may have some spare time to relax and explore the destination you have flown to.

What can you earn?

Starting salaries can be between £12,000 and £14,000 a year. With experience, this rises to between £15,000 and £21,000 a year. Senior crew can earn up to £25,000 a year. Overtime and flight allowances can increase salaries.

Entry requirements

Entry requirements can vary between airlines so you should check with them directly. You will usually need to have a good standard of basic maths and English. Some airlines may ask for GCSEs (grades A-C) in maths and English, or equivalent qualifications.

You will also need:

- a good level of fitness, normal colour vision and good eyesight
- the ability to swim at least 25 metres
- a smart appearance
- a valid passport that allows you to travel anywhere in the world.

You should not have any visible tattoos or body piercings.

You must be over 18 to work as an air cabin crew member, and some airlines set the minimum entry age at 21. Height and weight requirements also vary between airlines, so you should check with them.

Some airlines look for air cabin crew who can speak a second language. Previous experience in customer service is also helpful, and nursing, or hotel and catering experience may be particularly useful.

Although not essential, there are several college courses that could help you gain useful skills for this career. These include:

- BTEC Level 2 Certificate in Preparation for Air Cabin Crew Service
- City & Guilds Level 2 Certificate/Diploma in Air Cabin Crew (New Entrants)
- NCFE Level 2 Certificate for Airline Cabin Crew.

Check with local colleges for more information.

More information

People first
2nd Floor

Armstrong House
38 Market Square
Uxbridge
Middlesex
UB8 1LH
Tel: 01895 817 000
www.people1st.co.uk

NCFE
www.ncfe.org.uk

Royal Aeronautical Society
4 Hamilton Place

AIRLINE CUSTOMER SERVICE AGENT

The nature of the work

As an airline customer service agent, you would usually work for an airline, or for a ground services agent on behalf of an airline. Your job would include:

- dealing with passenger enquiries about flight departures and arrivals
- checking passengers in
- giving seat numbers
- providing boarding passes and luggage labels
- telling passengers about luggage restrictions
- weighing baggage and collecting any excess weight charges
- taking care of people with special needs, and unaccompanied children
- calming and reassuring nervous passengers.

You may sometimes help passengers through immigration and customs, or escort passengers who have night flight connections. You could also specialise in different areas of airport work, such as computer control.

What can you earn?

Airline customer services agents can earn between £12,000-£18,000

Entry requirements

There are no fixed entry requirements for becoming an airline customer service agent. However, employers may ask for GCSEs (A-C) in subjects like English and maths, or equivalent qualifications. Some may ask you to take a medical test.

Employers may want you to have previous experience of working in a customer service role and the ability to speak a foreign language. They may also look for applicants who live near the airport or have their own transport. This can often be important as shifts may be outside normal public transport hours.

You may be able to get into this job through an Aviation Operations Apprenticeship. You will need to check if this is available in your area. For more information, visit the Apprenticeships website.

For more details about airline careers, see the GoSkills website.

More information
People 1st
2nd Floor
Armstrong House
38 Market Square
Uxbridge
Middlesex
UB8 1LH
Tel: 01895 817 000
www.people1st.co.uk

CRUISE SHIP STEWARDS

The nature of the work

Cruise ship stewards work either in cabin service or in the bar area of cruise liners.

As a cabin steward your work would include:

- keeping guests' cabins clean and tidy
- making beds
- supplying fresh linen
- vacuuming floors
- replacing stocks of supplies such as shampoo and soap.

Working in the bar area, you would:

- serve passengers with drinks
- clear and wash glasses
- help keep the bar well stocked and tidy
- deal with payments and operate the till.

You would work as part of a team, under the supervision of a head housekeeper or bar manager.

With some cruise companies the job title 'steward' refers to customer service or reception staff. In these roles, your duties could include informing passengers about the services offered on board, arranging excursions and dealing with guests' queries and complaints.

What can you earn?

Rates of pay vary between shipping companies, and according to duties. Bar staff may earn around £800 a month, plus free accommodation and meals. Cabin stewards may earn between £600 and £1,100 a month, depending on experience.

Earnings may be supplemented by tips.

Entry requirements

You will not need any particular qualifications to become a passenger liner steward. However, there is a lot of competition for jobs, so it would be useful to have previous relevant experience, for example in catering, hotel or bar work.

Some employers might prefer you to have qualifications, such as:

- Level 2 Certificate in General Food and Beverage Service Skills
- Level 1 NVQ Certificate in Accommodation Services.

Your ability to work towards certain qualifications may be considered, such as:

- Level 2 NVQ Diploma in Food and Beverage Service Skills
- Level 2 NVQ Diploma in Housekeeping.

You can apply to companies directly, or through agencies that recruit for cruise liners.

More information

Springboard UK
http://springboarduk.net

People 1st
2nd Floor
Armstrong House
38 Market Square
Uxbridge
Middlesex
UB8 1LH
Tel: 01895 817 000
www.people1st.co.uk

HOTEL MANAGER

The nature of the work
Hotel managers oversee all aspects of running a hotel, from housekeeping and general maintenance to budget management and marketing.

Large hotels may have a manager for each department, reporting to the general manager. In smaller hotels, the manager is more involved in the day-to-day running of the hotel, often dealing directly with guests.

As a hotel manager, your tasks would typically include:

- setting annual budgets
- analysing financial information and statistics
- setting business targets and marketing strategies
- managing staff
- organising building maintenance
- making sure security is effective
- dealing with customer complaints and comments
- making sure the hotel follows regulations such as licensing laws
- securing corporate bookings for entertainment and conference facilities.

In larger hotels you will spend a lot of time in meetings with the heads of departments.

What can you earn?

Trainee and assistant hotel managers can earn around £19,000 a year. Managers of small hotels or deputy managers of larger ones can earn from £20,000 to around £35,000. Senior or general managers can earn £60,000 or more.

Entry requirements

You could become a hotel manager in either of the following ways:
- working your way up to management level from a more junior position
- entering management after completing a HNC/HND, degree or postgraduate qualification.
- Relevant degree and HNC/HND subjects include:
- Hospitality Management
- International Hospitality Management

- Hotel and Hospitality Management
- Hospitality and Licensed Retail Management.

You can also complete foundation degrees in subjects such as Hospitality Business Management. These are vocational courses that are usually studied over two years. You can study part-time whilst in relevant employment or full-time with work placements. To search for foundation degrees, HNDs and degrees see the UCAS website.

An Apprenticeship might help you build the skills you need towards this role. You may be able to get into this job through an Apprenticeship scheme such as the Level 3 Apprenticeship in Hospitality & Catering (Supervision & Leadership). The range of Apprenticeships available in your area will depend on the local jobs market and the types of skills employers need from their workers.

More information

Springboard UK
http://springboarduk.net

People 1st
2nd Floor
Armstrong House
38 Market Square
Uxbridge
Middlesex
UB8 1LH
Tel: 01895 817 000
www.people1st.co.uk

Institute of Hospitality
www.instituteofhospitality.org

HOTEL PORTER

The nature of the work

As a hotel porter, based in reception or at the porters' desk, you will often be the first person to greet guests at a hotel.

Your work will include:

- helping guests by carrying luggage
- advising on hotel facilities
- arranging taxis
- running errands, such as taking and picking up dry cleaning
- taking messages
- giving directions
- answering queries and making reservations.

If the hotel has a conference suite, you may be responsible for moving and setting up equipment. In a large hotel, your duties may be more specialised.

What can you earn?

- Starting salaries can be around £12,000 a year.
- With experience, this can rise to around £16,000.
- Head porters at large hotels can earn around £22,000.

Shift allowance, overtime and tips can increase earnings.

Entry requirements

You do not need qualifications to be a hotel porter, although employers will usually expect you to have a good general education and the following may be an advantage:

- Level 2 Award in Introduction to Employment in the Hospitality Industry
- Level 2 Award in the Principles of Customer Service in Hospitality, Leisure, Travel and Tourism

You may have an advantage when looking for work if you have experience of working with the public and a knowledge of the local area will be useful so that you can answer guests' questions and give them directions.

- You may be able to get into this job through an Apprenticeship scheme such as a Level 2 Apprenticeship in Hospitality & Catering (Front of House Reception). The range of Apprenticeships available in your area will depend on the local jobs market and the types of skills employers need from their workers.

More information

Springboard UK
http://springboarduk.net

People 1st
2nd Floor
Armstrong House
38 Market Square
Uxbridge
Middlesex
UB8 1LH
Tel: 01895 817 000
www.uksp.co.uk/ (careers information)
www.people1st.co.uk

****

22. VETINARY

To work in this area, a main prerequisite is a love of animals. The rewards are great for the right person. In this section we cover the following jobs:

- Vetinary Nurse
- Vetinary Surgeon
- Vetinary Physiotherapist

For more details about careers in the vetinary profession go to:

British Veterinary Nursing Association (BVNA)
82 Greenway Business Centre
Harlow Business Park
Harlow
Essex
CM19 5QE
Tel: 01279 408644
www.bvna.org.uk

VETINARY NURSE

The nature of the work
Veterinary nurses help veterinary surgeons (vets) by providing nursing care for sick, injured and hospitalised animals. They also play an important role in educating owners on good standards of animal care and welfare. If you love animals and want to look after their health, this could be ideal for you.

As a veterinary nurse, your duties would include:

- preparing and carrying out nursing care plans
- holding animals and keeping them calm during treatment
- giving injections and drugs (as instructed by the vet)

- getting blood, urine and other samples from animals, and carrying out laboratory work at the practice
- sterilising instruments
- taking x-rays
- preparing animals for operations
- helping vets during operations
- carrying out minor procedures such as removing stitches.
- talking to clients about the care and progress of their animals

You would often have other responsibilities, including:

- taking care of animals staying in house (feeding, cleaning their accommodation, grooming and exercising)
- holding clinics for suture removal, post operation checks and weight management
- giving owners advice about caring for their animals

You could also have administration and reception duties.

What can you earn?

Veterinary nurses can earn between £14,000 and £22,000 a year, depending on experience. Senior veterinary nurses can earn around £25,000 a year. Accommodation may be provided.

Entry requirements

You can qualify as a veterinary nurse either through work-based training or through higher education. Both of these lead to Royal College of Veterinary Surgeons (RCVS) registration as a veterinary nurse.

Work-based training
You could work towards the RCVS Level 3 Diploma in Veterinary Nursing whilst you are working. This is an apprentice style option, and you will need to find employment at a training practice first. To find training practices in your area, contact RCVS Awards or check their website.

To undertake the diploma, you would need to have five GCSEs at grade C or above, including English, maths and two science subjects, or equivalent qualifications, which include:

- ABC Level 2 Certificate for Animal Nursing Assistants
- City & Guilds Level 2 Diploma For Veterinary Care Assistants.

When you are looking for work as a trainee or assistant, it could help you if you have relevant experience. This could be as a volunteer with a local vet, or in other kinds of work with animals, such as at local kennels or RSPCA centres.

Higher education

Instead of work-based training, you can complete an RCVS-approved veterinary nursing degree or foundation degree, which includes work experience placements. This combines RCVS-approved training with the academic qualification. It will take you longer to qualify than through work-based training, but it could give you more career opportunities, such as research or teaching. To do a higher education course you would usually need:

- at least two A levels or equivalent qualifications, preferably in chemistry and biology
- and five GCSEs (A-C) including English language, maths and two sciences

Check the exact requirements with individual colleges and universities.
See the RCVS website for a list of approved courses. You can search for course providers on the UCAS website.

More information

Lantra
Lantra House
Stoneleigh Park
Nr Coventry
Warwickshire

CV8 2LG
Tel: 0845 707 8007
www.lantra.co.uk

Royal College of Veterinary Surgeons (RCVS)
Belgravia House
62-64 Horseferry Road
London
SW1P 2AF
Tel: 020 7222 2001
www.rcvs.org.uk

British Veterinary Nursing Association (BVNA)
82 Greenway Business Centre
Harlow Business Park
Harlow
Essex
CM19 5QE
Tel: 01279 408644
www.bvna.org.uk

British Equine Veterinary Association (BEVA)
Mulberry House
31 Market St
Fordham
Ely
Cambridgeshire
CB7 5LQ
Tel: 01638 723555
www.beva.org.uk

VETINARY SURGEON

The nature of the work
If you would love working with animals and want a challenging medical job, this could be perfect for you. Veterinary surgeons, also known as vets, look

after the health and welfare of animals. Most work in general practice, with domestic pets, farm and zoo animals.

As a vet in general practice you would:

- diagnose and treat sick and injured animals
- operate on ill or injured animals
- carry out a range of tests such as X-rays and scans
- provide care for in-patients
- carry out regular health checks, give vaccinations and give owners advice on care and diet for their animals
- check farm animals and advise how to stop diseases spreading
- neuter animals to stop them breeding
- carry out euthanasia (painless killing) for terminally ill and severely injured animals
- supervise veterinary nurses and support staff
- keep records of the treatments that you carry out.

You could also be involved in inspecting hygiene and care standards in zoos, kennels, catteries, riding stables, pet shops and cattle markets.

Some vets work full-time for the Department for Environment, Food and Rural Affairs (DEFRA), helping to control animal diseases and protect public health interests. In this role they would work in either the Veterinary Field Service (VFS) or at Veterinary Investigation Centres (VICs).

Vets who work in public health aim to prevent and control animal and human diseases. Their work could involve investigating animal and human disease outbreaks, such as foot and mouth disease, or assessing the safety of food processing plants and abattoirs.

Vets in industry develop, test and supervise production of drugs, chemicals and biological products.

What Can you earn?
Newly qualified vets can earn around £30,000 a year. Experienced vets can earn around £48,000 a year. Earnings for senior partners in a practice can be

over £50,000 a year, depending on the size of their practice. Employers may provide accommodation and transport.

Entry requirements

To work as a vet you must be registered with the Royal College of Veterinary Surgeons (RCVS).
To register, you must have a degree from a veterinary school at one of the UK universities approved by RCVS, or an equivalent overseas qualification that the RCVS recognises. See the RCVS website for details of approved degree courses.

Your degree would take five years to complete (six years at Cambridge), and include both clinical and practical training.

To do a degree course you would usually need:

- five GCSEs (A-C) including English, maths, chemistry, biology and physics (or a combined science, double award)
- and at least three A levels (AAB), including chemistry and one or two in biology, physics or maths.

Some universities will consider other relevant qualifications, such as a BTEC Diploma in Animal Science/Animal Management with distinction grades. You will need to check exact entry requirements with universities.

If you do not have the required grades or subjects, some universities offer a six-year course. The first year will prepare you for the five-year degree.

If you have a first or upper second-class honours degree in a science-related subject, you may be exempt from part of the veterinary degree course.

You would also need to gain a considerable amount of work experience in different veterinary practices, and in handling healthy animals on livestock farms or other animal establishments.

More information
Royal College of Veterinary Surgeons (RCVS)
Belgravia House
62-64 Horseferry Road
London
SW1P 2AF
Tel: 020 7222 2001
www.rcvs.org.uk

British Equine Veterinary Association (BEVA)
Mulberry House
31 Market St
Fordham
Ely
Cambridgeshire
CB7 5LQ
Tel: 01638 723555
www.beva.org.uk

British Veterinary Nursing Association (BVNA)
82 Greenway Business Centre
Harlow Business Park
Harlow
Essex
CM19 5QE
Tel: 01279 408644
www.bvna.org.uk

Society of Practicing Veterinary Surgeons
The Governor's House,
Cape Road,
Warwick,
Warwickshire,
CV34 5DJ
Tel: 01926 410454
Email: office@spvs.org.uk
www.spvs.org.uk

VETINARY PHYSIOTHERAPIST

The nature of the work

As an veterinary physiotherapist (also known as an animal physiotherapist), you would assess and treat animals with injuries or movement problems.

As a veterinary physiotherapist, you would mainly treat horses and dogs, including both pets and 'working animals', such as race horses and greyhounds. However, you could also work with other animals such as cats and farm or zoo animals.

Your tasks would typically include:

- planning exercise programmes
- using manual and electro-therapy methods to reduce pain, increase flexibility and restore normal movement
- giving advice on changes to animals' environments to help them perform tasks more easily.

You would only be legally allowed to carry out treatment for diagnosed conditions or injuries if animals are referred by (or with the permission of) a veterinary surgeon.

What can you earn?

Salaries vary enormously for this type of work, and for self-employed private practitioners they will depend on workload. As an example, a survey of ACPAT (Association of Chartered Physiotherapists in Animal Therapy) members showed a wide range of charges for physiotherapy sessions:
initial consultations (from 30 minutes to 2 hours) from £20 to £70.50
follow-up consultations (from 30 minutes to 1.5 hours) from £20 to £60.

Entry requirements

There are two ways to become a veterinary physiotherapist:

- Chartered physiotherapist working with animals

You must first qualify and gain experience as a chartered physiotherapist in human physiotherapy. See the physiotherapist profile, and the Chartered Society of Physiotherapy website, for details.

You would then need to learn to apply your professional and practical therapy skills as a chartered physiotherapist to working with animals, by completing postgraduate training in veterinary physiotherapy.

- Postgraduate Diploma and MSc courses in Veterinary Physiotherapy are offered by the Royal Veterinary College (RVC) and the University of the West of England (run at Hartpury College, Gloucestershire). Check with the universities for their entry requirements.

To complete the course you must:

- attend one weekend a month over 18 months at the Royal Veterinary College in Hatfield, Hertfordshire
- complete 25 hours' private study, including completion of assessed coursework
- pass an exam.

As a MSc student you would also complete a thesis or dissertation.

Successful completion of either the Diploma or MSc would entitle you to become a Category A member of the ACPAT and to use the title veterinary physiotherapist.

Alternatively, you may be able to train with a fully qualified (Category A) member of the Association of Chartered Physiotherapists in Animal Therapy (ACPAT) and complete the ACPAT education course over a period of two years. To do this, you must have trainee (Category B) membership of the ACPAT.

When you have completed the training, you would be able to apply to upgrade to Category A membership of the ACPAT, and become an independent practitioner.

Training without a qualification in human physiotherapy

If you have a good working knowledge of animal care and handling, and a higher or further education qualification, you could complete the Canine and Equine Physiotherapy Training (CEPT) Advanced Certificate in Veterinary Physiotherapy. Check the CEPT website for details.

More information

Royal Veterinary College
Hawkshead Lane
North Mymms
Hatfield
Herts
AL9 7TA
Tel: 01707 666333
www.rvc.ac.uk

Chartered Society of Physiotherapy
14 Bedford Row
London
WC1R 4ED
Tel: 020 7306 6666
www.csp.org.uk

Association of Chartered Physiotherapists in Animal Therapy (ACPAT)
www.acpat.org

****

Index

"I'm not dead, and my name's not Katie. You must be confusing me with someone else."

"I know you blame me for what happened, but if it hadn't been for Nash . . ." His shell-shocked expression vanished, replaced by suspicion. "He's behind this, isn't he?" No mistaking the menace in his voice.

Okay. Not just a scary tattooed biker. A scary tattooed *psycho* biker. Regan's heart threatened to jackhammer its way past her rib cage, but she kept her voice calm and steady. "I have no idea what you're talking about."

"I don't know how he managed it, but he brought you back, didn't he? What's the plan? What's he up to?"

"I really don't have any answers." Regan spoke evenly, willing him to believe her. "I'm—"

"The hair threw me at first, but hair color's easy enough to change. Only . . ." He scowled. "Your eyes are wrong."

"My—"

"*You* aren't Katie."

"I never said I was. You're the one—"

He narrowed his eyes to black slits. "What the hell is going on?"

Good question. "Look, I don't know what your problem is, but I don't have time for—"

He clamped one big hand around her upper arm and pulled her close. "You're playing dumb, but I heard you ask for directions to Juniper Basin." He spoke just above a whisper. "Tell me, if you're not in

cahoots with Nash, then why the hell are you headed
out to his dig site?"

"I don't see how that's any of your concern."

"Don't you now?" His mouth smiled, but his eyes
didn't as he leaned closer, trailing his fingertips down
her cheek, brushing a thumb across her lower lip.

Her panic bubbled over, escaping as a scream.

He laughed. "Yell all you want, blondie. Jukebox is
amped up so loud they can't hear you inside, and my
boys are the only ones out here. Sad to say, they're not
much for rescuing damsels in distress."

"Harper!" one of the other bikers called. "You
need help?"

"I'm good," he said.

"So *you* claim." The gang's raucous laughter ebbed
away as they moved from the entrance.

Somewhere beyond Regan's line of sight, the Harleys rumbled to life, reminding her of the obligatory
chick-dismemberment scene from every cheesy biker
film she'd ever seen. *Please, God, don't let me die a
Hollywood cliché.*

Harper grinned, as if he knew exactly what she
was thinking, as if her fear fueled his pleasure.

Desperate now, she used the hand still buried in
the depths of her bag to search unobtrusively for a
weapon. Lip gloss? No. Hairbrush? Maybe. Keys?
Another maybe. Or . . . She jammed the handle of the
brush against the soft leather of her purse. "Take your
hand off me," she warned.

The biker laughed. "Or what?"

"Or I'll blow a hole through your chest." She pointed her fake gun at his breastbone.

Maybe it was just the light reflecting off the neon palm trees or maybe the biker really did turn a little green around the gills. Regan wasn't positive. All she knew for sure was that he released her arm.

"Now back off."

He studied her, his face expressionless.

"What?" she said.

"I had this figured all wrong. Nash doesn't know you're coming, does he? If he did, you wouldn't have had to ask for directions to the dig."

She didn't say anything.

"So what's your angle, blondie?"

"I don't have an angle."

"Bullshit. Everyone's got an angle."

"I don't know what you're talking about."

"You don't know Nash, either. If you did, you wouldn't try to scam him. You have no idea who you're dealing with, what he's capable of. He's not who you think he is."

"Thanks for the warning, but Mr. Nash isn't my problem at the moment. You are. So move."

He raised his eyebrows. "Or you'll shoot me? Go ahead. Have at it."

He was calling her bluff, and she had nothing. Worse, he knew it. A feral glint sparked in his dark eyes. "Bzzz. Sorry. You lose."

This wasn't a game, damn it. Anger triggered a spurt of adrenaline. She dropped her purse and, wielding the six-pack with both hands, swung at his face.

But he was too fast for her. Capturing her wrists, he twisted them up over her head. She lost her grip on the bottled water. It bounced off the hood, then hit the pavement with a crack. She jerked and kicked, desperate to free herself, but he slammed her hard against the car, immobilizing her with his hips.

"Let me go!" Her breath sawed in and out.

"I don't think so." He grinned again. Then slowly, deliberately, he ran one finger down her throat, lingering on her racing pulse.

Oh, God. She shuddered.

He ducked his head, licking along the path his fingertip had taken. "Spicy," he murmured, making it sound obscene.

A door banged open to her left. Two of the kitchen staff, one male, one female, emerged from a service entrance. Their voices rose and fell in a good-natured squabble over whose turn it was to clean the effing grease trap.

"Hel—"

The biker clapped a hand across her mouth, smothering her cry. A major miscalculation on his part.

She bit down hard enough to draw blood and elicit a yelp of pain.

"Shit!" He snatched his hand away and stumbled back a step, just far enough for her to deliver a knee to the groin. He doubled up with a moan.

"Is there a problem?" the woman called.

"Get an ambulance," Regan said. "This poor man's bleeding."

"You're making a mistake," the biker warned.

"Won't be the first time."

Doubled over, hands braced on his thighs, Harper raised his head to watch the blonde's taillights disappear. She thought she'd escaped. She hadn't. He'd let her go. There was a difference.

"Are you all right, mister?" the female restaurant worker called a little hesitantly. Probably confused about what had just gone down, not sure whether he was the villain or the victim.

"You need us to call 911?" Her male counterpart took a cautious step forward.

"No, thanks," Harper said. "I'm fine. Little difference of opinion's all it was."

"She said you were bleeding," the man said.

"Just my hand. Nothing serious." Shoving himself upright, Harper sucked at the cut, then turned his back on the pair by the door and headed around the building. His boys were all lined up, ready to go, at the far end of the parking lot.

Sarge, his second in command, shot Harper a challenging look. "So what the hell is going on? You tell us, 'Wait here. I'll handle it,' then you let her get away?"

"Didn't exactly let her do anything. Bitch bit my hand, then kneed me in the balls."

"Want one of the boys to follow her?" Sarge asked.

"No need."

"No need?" Sarge scowled. "First decent prey we've spotted in days, and you let her go."

Harper nodded languid agreement. "Yeah."

Sarge, a former Army Ranger, glared at him. "The hell you say!"

"Chill, amigo." Chupi, the shortest of the gang members and the only illegal in the group, often understood Harper's motivations better than the others even though he spoke only limited English. "Boss got plan, sí?" He grinned eagerly, revealing a mouthful of teeth he'd filed to sharp points.

"Oh, yeah," Harper agreed.

The Branson twins, Billy and Bobby, straddled their bikes. Their shiny ebony heads gleamed under the security light. Identical wolfish grins lit their faces.

Butcher—nobody knew his real name, not even Harper—spat out a wad of Copenhagen, cleared his throat, and spat again. "This plan of yours involve any slicing and dicing?"

"Hell, yeah," Harper promised. "You can make mincemeat of the bitch if you want once the rest of us have had our fun."

"Don't mind going last." Butcher scowled suddenly. "Just don't knock her out. Won't be no fun if she don't scream."

Harper nodded his understanding of Butcher's problem. The poor bastard couldn't get his rocks off unless foreplay included a certain amount of creative carving, a quirk that had gotten him blacklisted at every whorehouse west of the Rockies and earned him a stint in San Quentin.

"Son of a bitch!" Sarge revved his bike. "Just tell us

the fucking plan. While we stand here shooting the breeze, she's getting away."

"No," Harper said, "she's not. I poked a hole in her gas tank. She won't get far. In fact, she might be stranded already, waiting for a posse of kind gentlemen like us to come to her rescue."

A broad smile split Sarge's ugly face. "Hoo-ah!" he shouted.

Harper's gang took up the cry, yipping and howling like a pack of coyotes.

Favoring his still-tender equipment, Harper mounted his bike and started her up. He stared into the darkness. *I owe you one, blondie.*

And he always, always paid his debts.

Regan wondered how many miles equaled "to hell and gone" and if she'd recognize her turnoff when she came to it. At least, thank God, the heat had begun to diminish the moment the sun had set. In the last half hour, the temperature had dropped a good fifteen degrees.

She tried to ignore the myriad eyes gleaming in the glare of her headlights. On an intellectual level she knew they belonged to nocturnal feeders—deer and coyotes, skunks and kangaroo rats. But the less rational part of her brain wasn't convinced. It whispered of monsters lurking in the dark. . . .

The real monsters first appeared in her rearview mirror as six bobbing points of light. Six motorcycle headlights, she soon realized. Whooping and hollering, the bikers she'd last seen at the truck stop in

Chisel Rock circled her car, cutting in front of her, passing so close that she instinctively stepped on the brake and jerked the steering wheel to the right. As she hit the loose rock at the edge of the road, dust billowed up, obscuring her view out the windshield, choking her. She twisted the wheel back to the left and tromped on the gas pedal, hoping to outrun them.

A vain hope. Something thumped heavily on the roof of the car. A tire iron? A rock? She couldn't tell. Something else slammed into the windshield. She couldn't identify it either. Something heavy enough to ding the glass, though. A spiderweb of cracks appeared around the point of impact.

The side windows, she thought, scrabbling for the buttons that controlled them.

One of the bikers swooped up next to her, keeping pace with the Corolla. He leaned toward her, grinning maniacally. One tattooed arm suddenly snaked in the driver's-side window. The biker made a grab for the steering wheel. She swerved sharply to the right while searching feverishly with her left hand for the button that controlled the automatic windows. After what seemed like endless minutes but couldn't have been more than a second or two, she located the right button.

The biker made another grab for the wheel. In agonizing slow motion, the driver's-side window slid shut, pinning his forearm between the top edge of the glass and the window frame. He shrieked as, held fast, he was pulled from his bike. The riderless Harley struck the Corolla a glancing blow—struck the biker as well, judging by his shrill curses—and bounced away.

Regan steered with her right hand and punched buttons blindly with her left, finally locating the window control again. She released the pressure on the biker's arm, and he fell away with an eldritch scream, followed closely by an ominous thump-thump as the rear wheels bumped over his body. She punched the button again, succeeding this time in closing the window all the way.

She drew a shaky breath. Windows closed. Doors locked. As long as she didn't stop . . .

Another unseen projectile hit the car, this one starring the rear window.

She jammed the gas pedal all the way to the floor. The car shot forward, then without warning gave a hiccupping cough and died. The little Toyota decelerated and rolled to a stop.

Howling in triumph, the five remaining bikers circled the car. They thumped on the roof, leered in the windows, and shouted obscenities.

Panicked, she ground the starter. *Please, God, let it start.* Had they somehow damaged the engine? Had she? Again and again she turned the key. The starter ground, but the engine refused to catch.

The thumping and caterwauling ratcheted up a notch as the biker called Harper produced a yard-long length of pipe and began a determined assault on the Corolla's windshield. Two blows, three, and the glass shattered. Large chunks fell away.

Regan ducked beneath the dashboard, protecting her face from the falling glass with one hand while punching in Nash's number on her cell phone with the other. She doubted she'd get through. She'd tried—unsuccessfully—to make a call to her dad earlier, and chances were she wouldn't find service halfway to hell and gone, either. But damn it, she wasn't going down without a fight.

TWO

Charles Cunningham Nash hiked the narrow path between the river and the cliff, his flashlight illuminating the ancient petroglyphs that had lured him to this site in the first place. Crickets sang in the grass along the water's edge, and somewhere out in the middle of the stream, a fish surfaced with a plop. Peace enveloped him, soothing his frayed nerves.

He looked forward to this nightly ritual, this hour of solitude. Not that he didn't enjoy the enthusiasm of his crew of archaeology students, but their incessant chatter could get irritating at times.

Irritating. Like that persistent Cluny female.

Though as annoying as he found the woman's frequent calls, he had to admit he rather liked her voice, soft and low and musical. As long as he didn't actually listen to what she had to say . . .

A pebble rattled down the escarpment to land at his feet, and Nash went perfectly still, all his senses alert. He strained, listening for something—anything—out of place, but no discordant note disturbed the night.

Tilting the flashlight's beam upward, he scanned the sheer rock face. No movement. Nothing.

He sniffed at the air. Again nothing, at least not at first. Then the breeze swirled and eddied. A faint but distinctive scent teased his nostrils. Body heat. Adrenaline. Excitement. Someone—or some*thing*— was tracking him, pacing a parallel course just out of sight along the top of the cliff.

Nash clenched his jaw and narrowed his eyes. Forewarned was forearmed. And he was better armed than most.

He wedged his flashlight into the rocks so that its beam fanned out across the water, figuring that, with any luck, his stalker would assume he'd decided to linger a while.

Instead, he slipped noiselessly back down the path. Once safely out of earshot, he scaled the cliff and doubled back.

The prey had become the predator.

A young mountain lion crouched at the lip of the cliff, shoulder and leg muscles tensed, head down, ears tilted forward. A beautiful beast—elegant, powerful, dangerous.

The cat must have sensed him. Its head came up, but too late. Nash had already launched his attack, leaping onto the animal's back, grabbing its head.

The mountain lion screamed and thrashed, trying to free itself, but Nash hung on. Still screaming, frantic now, the big cat rolled, crushing Nash into the rocks.

The sudden unexpected pain triggered rage.

Teeth clenched, muscles straining, Nash gave the cat's head a vicious twist. Ligaments and tendons snapped, vertebrae cracked, and the animal went limp.

Breathing hard, Nash shifted the mountain lion's bulk, rolling the body onto its back. Then, with a guttural growl, he buried his teeth in the big cat's throat. He ripped and tore, feeding in a mad frenzy, guzzling blood, savoring its warmth, its sweetness.

For months now he'd been existing on frozen plasma thawed to room temperature or heated in the microwave. He'd almost forgotten how intoxicating the taste of fresh blood could be, rich, delicious. Shuddering in near ecstasy, he drank his fill.

Finally, hunger sated, he sat back on his haunches, gazing down at his victim. The cat stared up at him, its face frozen in a rictus of terror, its throat ripped open, its body sprawled in an ungainly tangle across the rocks. Ugly in death.

His fault.

A sick wave of self-loathing engulfed him. His stomach churned. Oh, God, what had he done? He was a man, damn it, not an animal.

"I had no choice."

But saying it aloud didn't make it true. He hadn't needed to kill. He'd wanted to kill.

Yes, the cat had stalked him, but Nash knew he could have escaped, just melted away into the shadows. After all, hadn't he had decades of experience eluding Harper, a predator a thousand times more dangerous than a mere mountain lion?

Instead, he'd allowed himself to follow his most primitive instincts. He'd hunted the animal, killed it, feasted on it. And now he had to live with what he'd done, acknowledge what he was. A ravening beast.

He shuddered again.

He should have stayed in Romania, where his kind were tolerated, even admired, and where lynx and bears and wolves ran free. Fair game.

But Native American legends about a spring with healing powers had drawn Nash from the safety of his luxurious Carpathian hideaway to this desolate section of northern California. If the spring existed and if it could perform even half the miracles legend suggested, he might one day be able to live a normal life free of these fierce, unnatural cravings. If . . .

Following clues from old manuscripts and even older petroglyphs, he'd narrowed his search to this site. Of course, he'd been aware of the danger inherent in returning to the United States, of once more entering Harper's sphere of influence, but he'd deemed the possible benefits worth the risk. For months, he'd managed to keep a low profile. But then that damned tabloid reporter had gotten creative with the facts, and the day after the absurd alien-city nonsense hit the front page of the *Inquisitor*, the networks had picked up the scent. Nash had soon found himself sharing the media spotlight with anorexic supermodels, steroid-popping ballplayers, and celebrity parents who named their offspring after vegetables.

And though by that time it was already too late,

he'd refused all subsequent interviews. Regan Cluny had tried her best to change his mind. She'd claimed she wanted to lay the alien rumors to rest, to salvage his reputation as an expert on Paleolithic spirituality, and he believed her. She'd built a successful career finding the grain of truth at the heart of sensationalized stories. Her articles had appeared everywhere from *The New Yorker* to *National Geographic.* But his reputation as a scholar was the least of his worries.

Harper was nobody's fool. After such major media exposure, he'd have no trouble tracking Nash. Time was running out. If Nash didn't locate the spring soon . . .

With one last regretful glance, he left the cat's carcass for the vultures, then scrambled down the cliff to retrieve his flashlight.

Archaeologist Thomas Davis opened an email from Brett Salinger, one of his University of Reno colleagues.

"Hey, Tommy," Brett wrote. "Wish you were here." Here being the island of Kauai, where Brett was in charge of a state-sponsored dig. "We're up to our asses in bureaucratic bullshit. Could use some of your expertise in cutting through the crap. The deal is, we want to tunnel below an abandoned temple to look for bones, but the local kahuna is raising a stink. The usual *kapu* schtick—"

The door to the single-wide trailer they were using as their Juniper Basin headquarters swung open and Nash strode in. One glance at his friend and the hair along the back of Tom's neck stood straight up. "Problem?"

Nash slammed the door. "No, why?"

"There's blood on your shirt."

Nash glanced down. "Blood?"

"On your collar."

Frowning, Nash headed for the bathroom.

Tom followed.

Standing in front of the mirror, Nash stared at the bloodstains.

"You ever wonder where that nonsense about vampires not casting reflections got started?" Tom said, a lame attempt to lighten the atmosphere.

Nash didn't respond.

"Probably Hollywood, huh?" Tom forced a smile. "Land of myth and silicone."

Still Nash said nothing.

"Okay, man, you're scaring me. What's wrong? Are you hurt?"

In the mirror, Nash's tortured gaze met his. "The blood's not mine. A mountain lion was stalking me. I . . ."

Oh, God. No wonder he was acting so strangely. He must have . . . "Turned the tables on the cat. Hey, it's all right. These things happen." To vampires. "Don't beat yourself up."

Nash shook his head, then, brushing past Tom, headed back to the office. "Is everything okay here in camp?"

The worried note in Nash's voice kicked Tom's anxiety up a level. "Far as I know." He sat down behind the computer and closed out of Outlook Express. "Why?"

"I don't know. Just a feeling." Nash pulled a folding chair closer to the desk and sat down. "It's probably nothing . . ."

Tom mentally reviewed the last hour. "Same old, same old. Big water-balloon fight was raging over by the showers a while ago until Laura took one in the face and threw a minor hissy fit. Then Winston started spinning tales around the campfire, and I came in here to check my email. Oh." He paused. "Now that I think about it, one call did come in before I got here. There's a message on the machine."

A chill ran down Tom's spine at the expression on Nash's face. "A call from whom?"

"Nobody important," Tom said. "Just that writer who's been bugging you on and off for the past couple of weeks."

"What did she want?"

"The usual," Tom said. "You."

Nash leaned across the desk to punch the message button on the answering machine.

"You have one message," the machine said. "One message."

There was a pause, then, "Mr. Nash? This is Regan Cluny."

"Not much of a message," Tom said. "Six words."

"No." Nash was frowning again. "Six words, a gasp, some raucous background noise, and then silence."

Tom shrugged. "So she got cut off."

"Yeah." A muscle twitched in Nash's cheek. He crossed to the kitchenette, separated from the main office by a waist-high counter, pulled a bottle of bourbon from a cupboard, grabbed a glass from the shelf by the sink, and poured himself a drink.

He raised his glass in a mocking salute but stopped before taking a swallow, the drink suspended halfway to his mouth. "Do you smell that?"

"Smell what?"

Nash took a deep breath. "Smoke?"

Tom relaxed. "Well, that's hardly a surprise. There's a campfire right outside."

Nash set his glass on the counter, walked across to the door, threw it open, and sniffed at the breeze. "Not wood smoke. Gasoline, plastic, fabric. Somewhere upwind."

Tom shook his head. "I don't smell anything."

Ignoring him, Nash headed outside.

Nash dug his keys from his pocket as he hustled toward his Jeep Wrangler, parked next to the tool trailer on the far edge of the compound. Halfway there, he caught another faint whiff of smoke. Definitely not his imagination.

Driven by a sense of urgency, he climbed behind the wheel and set off at a good clip, heading toward the secondary road that led to Chisel Rock.

By the time he hit the cattle guard at the top of the incline, the acrid odor was unmistakable. And once he rounded Calliope Rock, the fire came into full view. The closer he drew to the flaming wreckage, the greater his feeling of dread. He'd find no survivors here. The vehicle was a complete loss, totally engulfed in flames.

He stopped the Jeep ten yards away, grabbed a shovel from the back end, and headed toward the burning car.

A sudden gust picked up sparks and scattered them across the dusty track, toward the dry grass that flanked the road. Nash swore under his breath. A range fire was bad news. A range fire that swept across the plateau to consume the dig would be catastrophic, destroying months of careful work. Still swearing, he shoveled dirt at a steady pace until he'd smothered the last of the flames.

It wasn't until he finally stopped to rest, leaning wearily on the shovel, his arms and shoulders trembling with fatigue, that he noticed the car's missing windshield.

Ramming into livestock could wreck a car—even knock out a windshield—but in such a case, the cow seldom came out ahead of the vehicle. Yet there was no cow in sight—dead or alive. No large wildlife species, either. No injured mountain lion or mule deer. But if the car's driver hadn't run into an animal, what had knocked out the windshield?

Unless the driver hadn't been wearing a seat belt . . . When propelled with sufficient force a human head could shatter glass.

He peered into the charred wreckage, front seat and back. No body—with or without a severely contused head. Just a blackened lump that might once have been a backpack or small carry-on bag and the toasted remains of a laptop.

Nash stared at the evidence . . . or lack of evidence. "What the hell happened here?"

The breeze whispered through the sagebrush, a faint sibilance that set his nerves on edge.

"Hello?" he said, feeling a fool. "Is anyone there?"

No answer, but then he really hadn't expected one. It's just the wind, he told himself. Just the wind.

But though the breeze might account for the whispering sounds, it didn't explain what had happened to the driver. *This,* he thought, *is how stories of alien abductions get started.* The truth was probably a good deal simpler. Either the driver had walked away from the crash and was by now halfway back to Chisel Rock or the driver had been ejected through the shattered windshield.

Only here was an odd thing. The broken glass was inside the car, not outside, which pretty much eliminated his second theory.

The rear door on the driver's side hung open. Perhaps the driver had been ejected that way. If so, it behooved Nash to do at least a cursory search of the area before he went back to the dig to call the authorities on the landline.

He tossed the shovel in the back of the Wrangler, grabbed a flashlight from the glove compartment, and began searching the area in ever-widening circles.

He found the body on his third circuit. Half naked, bruised, and bloody, the dead woman lay curled up, like a pill bug, at the base of a stunted mahogany. Both wrists and ankles bore ligature marks, her throat, ghastly puncture wounds. Shallower cuts crisscrossed her body. But it was the tic-tac-toe game on her back, the *X*'s carved with a knife, the *O*'s burned into her flesh with the tip of a cigarette, that turned his stomach.

"What sort of monster. . . ?" he started. Then the truth knocked the air out of him. *Oh, God. Monster indeed. Harper.*

As he played the flashlight's beam over the body, he suddenly remembered the aborted message on his answering machine. Was this Regan Cluny? No, surely not.

The light washed across the woman's cheek, and she flinched.

"Damn!" He dropped the flashlight. It bounced once and went out.

She was alive. Somehow, some way, she was alive.

THREE

She was alive. Regan knew this for a fact because no way could she be dead and hurt this much.

She opened her eyes, vaguely uneasy to find herself in a hospital room with a snaking jungle of tubes and wires attached to various parts of her body. She'd thought she was done with doctors for a while. So how had she ended up here?

Disjointed memories flashed through her brain. The truck stop in Chisel Rock. Her unnerving encounter with the biker named Harper. The bobbing lights in her rearview mirror. The roaring Harleys, the shattered windshield, and then . . .

She frowned, trying to remember what had happened next. At first her brain produced nothing but a terrifying void. But even more terrifying was what came next, a tsunami of horrific memories.

Rough hands dragged her from the driver's seat and threw her to the ground. When she fought back, punching, kicking, screaming, and swearing, the bikers ganged up on her, nearly jerking her arms and legs from their sockets as they spread-eagled her in the dirt. A hideous silence descended then, heavy breathing the only sound as she stared up at a ring of leering faces. Their eyes had stared back, hot, fierce, and bestial, red in the backwash of the Corolla's taillights.

"Ms. Cluny?" Someone touched her wrist. "Ms. Cluny? Are you awake?"

Good question. Regan blinked, then angled her head toward the voice. A male nurse swam into view, tall and slim, the thick dark hair on his forearms in sharp contrast to the streaky blond hair on his head.

"How did I get here?" she asked. Wherever here was.

"A Good Samaritan brought you in. Apparently he spotted your car on fire and found you lying unconscious nearby. I think he's talking to someone from the sheriff's department right now. As soon as you feel up to it, I'm sure the authorities will want to take a statement from you as well. How much do you remember of what happened?"

How much? Not everything. Not even close, but, "Too much," she said.

By the time Nash finished telling Deputy Palmer all he knew of the circumstances surrounding Regan Cluny's attack—or at least all he dared to reveal—it was nearly four in the morning. He stopped by the emergency room to check on her, but they'd already moved her upstairs for what was left of the night. The receptionist offered to call up to the third floor to ask the nurse in charge if Ms. Cluny was still awake, but Nash declined. She needed her sleep, and he needed to get back to the dig.

He arrived at camp half an hour before dawn, just as the crew was trickling into the dining tent for breakfast. Tom, his dark hair still damp from the shower, came hustling up to Nash. "What took you so long?"

"Hey, I made it back before sunrise."

Tom fell into step beside him. "Don't joke. I was worried. How's the Cluny woman?"

Nash had called from the ER in Cascade to let Tom know what had happened. "She needed a transfusion, of course. Lost a lot of blood in that 'wild animal attack.'"

"That what they're calling it?"

Nash nodded. "The cops figure a cougar must have chewed on her neck sometime between the bikers' departure and my arrival on the scene, and Regan Cluny hasn't told them any different. I'm not sure why."

"Maybe she knows your secret. Maybe she's known all along."

"She says she doesn't remember the attack. I couldn't tell if she was being truthful or not." He shrugged. "The rest of her injuries are relatively superficial. The doctor says she'll be as good as new in a few days." He paused. "She was lucky. Harper's victims don't usually escape alive."

"Harper," Tom said, his voice bleak, his expression even bleaker.

"We knew it was inevitable." Nash kicked a rock.

It rattled across the path to lodge in a clump of rabbitbrush. "From the second my face showed up on network television, it was only a matter of time."

"But we're so close," Tom said. "I can feel it."

Nash could feel it, too.

"We can't quit now," Tom insisted. "If we take the proper precautions, tighten security . . ."

"That might buy us a little time, but—"

"All we need is a little time."

"He's a madman, Tom. If we cut it too close, there will be consequences. Horrible consequences. It's not just Regan Cluny's life that's in danger."

Tom frowned. "You know, that's the thing I don't understand. Why *is* Regan Cluny's life in danger? Why would Harper waste his time on her? I thought he only targeted people you cared about. Damn it, you'd never even met the Cluny woman until last night. How does hurting her advance his agenda?"

"Harper has no way of knowing I'd had no previous contact with Ms. Cluny, and after meeting her, he's convinced she's important to me."

"But why? Don't tell me she inadvertently put her life in danger by feeding him some cockamamie story."

"No."

"Then. . . ?"

Nash took a deep breath and released it slowly. "She could pass for Katie's twin."

"Well, hell," Tom said.

"And damnation," Nash added.

• • •

Tom should have been out supervising the survey crew. Instead, he sat in the nearly deserted dining tent, staring at the stone-cold sludge at the bottom of his coffee mug as if it might miraculously supply answers to the questions plaguing him, number one being, how much did Regan Cluny really know about Nash? Did she suspect he was a vampire? Was that why she'd been so determined to get an interview? Why she'd kept her mouth shut about how she'd received those puncture wounds in her throat?

He tilted the mug one way and then the other. No miracles manifested themselves. So . . . unlikely, he decided. Rational people—and from what he'd been able to learn, Ms. Cluny qualified—simply didn't think that way. God knew *he'd* had a hell of a time coming to terms with the truth.

Four years ago, shortly after the publication of his first book, *Big Myth Understanding: The Correlation Between Native American Legends and the Actual Events That Inspired Them as Evidenced by Archaeological and Geological Clues,* Tom, then an assistant professor of anthropology at the University of Reno, had received an email from Nash, who claimed to have copies of old manuscripts containing legends not mentioned in Tom's book, legends that pertained to the same areas of northern California and southern Oregon that had been the focus of Tom's research.

After corresponding for several months, Nash had offered to fly Tom to Romania, so he could examine the manuscripts himself.

Tom, of course, had jumped at the chance.

The manuscripts spoke of a hidden spring with healing properties, and Nash wanted to know if there was any concrete basis for the myth. Tom had had his doubts, but he'd promised to dig deeper once he returned to the United States.

Then, the night before he was scheduled to fly home, he and Nash had been accosted in a restaurant parking lot by a knife-wielding teenager high on something. The kid ordered them to hand over their valuables. When Tom, worried about losing his passport, hesitated, the would-be robber slashed at him. Nash threw himself between Tom and the kid, taking the knife square in the chest. Terrified, the kid took off before Nash hit the pavement. Tom remembered kneeling next to Nash, staring at the knife buried to the hilt in Nash's chest and thinking, shouldn't there be more blood?

But minimal blood or not, he never would have believed what happened next if he hadn't seen it with his own eyes. Nash had pulled the knife from his chest and tossed it across the lot, then shoved himself to his feet as if being stabbed through the heart were nothing more than a minor annoyance.

Nash tried to pretend Tom hadn't seen what he thought he'd seen, but Tom knew better. He'd ripped Nash's shirt open, only to find that the wound had already scabbed over.

They'd argued most of the night, Tom demanding explanations, Nash sidestepping the issue. It was only when Tom had threatened not to help search for the mythical spring that Nash had finally confessed his dark secret. Even then, it had taken months of research to finally convince Tom that the Charles Cunningham Nash who'd fought in the Union army during the American Civil War was the same Charles Cunningham Nash alive today. Some things were hard for a rational man to wrap his mind around, and the existence of vampires was definitely right up there at the top of the list. . . .

"Excuse me? Dr. Davis?"

Danielle Lefévre, hands down the most attractive female in Juniper Basin, stood in the doorway. Though friendly enough with the men on the crew, she never crossed the invisible line between friendship and romantic relationship. And with him, she was particularly standoffish. Even Nash, she called by his given name, but Tom was always "Dr. Davis."

"Tom," he said, as he always did, then added, "Dr. Davis is my mother."

Which surprised a smile out of her.

"What? You didn't think I had a mother?" he teased.

"I didn't realize you had a mother who was a doctor."

"Orthodontist," he said.

"I guess that explains your perfect teeth."

The better to eat you with, my dear. Okay, where the hell had *that* come from? was his first thought, followed immediately by, thank God I didn't say it out loud. Only then he started thinking maybe he *had* said it out loud, because Danielle was looking at him as if . . . whoa! She was looking at him as if she saw him as a man, not just some stuffy thirtysomething guy with a doctorate. He shoved his coffee mug out of range so he wouldn't absentmindedly take a swallow of toxic sludge, then cleared his throat. "What do you need?" he asked, not realizing how abrupt he sounded until he saw Danielle's expression morph from friendly to embarrassed.

"I just thought . . . you seemed . . . I don't know . . ." She shifted her gaze, but not before he noticed that her big brown eyes looked suspiciously glassy. "Sorry I bothered you." She turned to leave.

Not thinking, just reacting, Tom jumped up and put a hand out to stop her. "Don't go," he started to say, but the words died in his throat. The instant he put his hand on her arm, his brain short-circuited. A steady stream of sexual energy radiated from her flesh to his. And she felt it, too. He could tell by the dumbfounded look on her face.

Then her gaze met his, strengthening the connection. Her lower lip trembled. "I . . . ," she said.

"Me, too," he said.

Her arm was trembling now.

He thought maybe his hand was shaking as well.

"Weird," she said, her voice a whisper.

"Yeah, but good weird."

"Uh-huh," she agreed. "Very good weird."

And suddenly her mouth looked so soft and pink and kissable that he couldn't resist. He leaned a little closer.

"For crying out loud, are you people going to mess

around in here all day? I'd like to get the tent cleaned up before it's time to start fixing lunch."

Abruptly, Tom released his grip on Danielle's arm and turned to face Winston Hirsch, the crotchety old Paiute Nash had hired as camp cook. "We were just going," Tom told him.

He turned back to say something to Danielle—he wasn't sure what—but she'd already disappeared.

Regan lay curled up on the king-size bed in her second-floor motel room. Even with the windows closed and the air-conditioning set on high, she could hear kids squealing as they splashed around in the pool down in the courtyard. Peaceful, it wasn't. But as small-town motels went, the Manzanita Inn in Cascade wasn't too bad, especially compared to St. Ignatius Hospital. Clean sheets, room service, and a good solid lock on the door. What more could she ask?

Except maybe a massive dose of painkillers. She hurt all over, though the puncture wounds on her neck were the worst. They'd given her some heavy-duty brain-fuzzing stuff at the hospital. The problem was, if she took enough of the meds to dull the pain, she'd dull her brain at the same time, and she needed her wits about her if she were to figure out what had really happened. And why.

The bikers had tortured her. They'd tried to kill her. But they hadn't raped or robbed her.

Why? She had no idea. It didn't make sense.

She sifted through her confusing memories of the

previous night. After the initial attack, all she remembered clearly was a set of twins with shaved heads and bulging muscles. One twin had immobilized her hands while the other straddled her. She'd felt the bulge of his arousal grinding against her crotch, smelled the stale beer on his breath, the rancid odor of his sweat. And that was where her memories grew a little hazy and a lot unreliable.

She frowned, trying to focus. Teeth. She remembered teeth, ugly yellowed incisors and long pointed canines. Like fangs.

And pain. She remembered the pain, a searing agony that had tipped her into sensory overload.

She must have blacked out for a time because the next thing she could recall was the biker rolling around in the dirt and clutching his stomach. He'd vomited, and some of the foul mess had splattered her arm.

Then, just when she thought she'd met her horror quota for the night, the man had screamed, a horrible, high-pitched shrieking that stopped abruptly when he burst into flames. One second her would-be rapist was howling his head off, the next he was ashes. Front-page tabloid fodder. Spontaneous human combustion.

Not that she'd shared that particular memory with anyone. Not with the doctor in the ER. And definitely not with the Mammoth County deputy who'd taken her statement. For obvious reasons, an all-expenses-paid trip to the funny farm being number one on the list.

It had been a nightmare scenario. Or maybe just a nightmare. And damned if she knew—

Someone knocked on the door. Not the tentative tapping typical of the housekeeping staff but a much more aggressive thumping.

Regan's heart fluttered in panic. The bikers, she thought, come to finish what they'd started. She staggered to her feet, her gaze darting around the room as she searched desperately for somewhere to hide.

"Ms. Cluny? Are you in there?" Okay, reality check. The bikers wouldn't knock. They'd just barge right in. And they definitely wouldn't call her "Ms. Cluny." Therefore . . .

More thumping. "Ms. Cluny, it's Nash. We need to talk."

Nash? As in Charles Cunningham Nash?

She limped to the peephole to verify his identity. It was Nash, all right, looking every bit as tall, dark, and dangerous as he had on TDN's *Inside Scoop*.

"Ms. Cluny? I know you're in . . ."

She opened the door.

". . . there," he said, one fist raised to pound again on the door.

Regan stood dumbstruck. On television, he'd looked tall, dark, and dangerous. Through the peephole, he'd looked tall, dark, and dangerous. But up close and personal, tall, dark, and dangerous didn't begin to describe the man.

Tall and broad shouldered, muscular but lean, Charles Cunningham Nash looked more like a pro athlete or a film star than her conception of a reclusive multimillionaire obsessed with Paleo-Indian mythology. And as if that incredible body, long and lithe and powerful, didn't provide enough temptation, the man was blessed with an equally arresting face, all harsh, intriguing angles—prominent cheekbones, stubborn chin, heavy arched eyebrows, stern mouth. He didn't overwork those smile muscles, she was guessing. Though the grim mouth wasn't half as disturbing as his eyes—an icy Nordic blue that contrasted sharply with his dark complexion and even darker hair, just starting to gray at the temples.

"We need to talk," he said, more demand than request, and she realized she'd been staring.

"I'm not dressed for company." She wasn't dressed at all aside from her bandages and the terry-cloth robe that had come with the room.

"It's important," he said.

So she moved aside to let him in, suspecting that if she didn't, he'd run right over her. As she closed the door to the hall, she tried to figure out why she felt so nervous all of a sudden. Wasn't this what she'd wanted, a one-on-one interview? Though the bare feet and borrowed bathrobe hadn't been part of her plan. "Have a seat."

No need for him to ask where. The room boasted only one chair.

Regan perched on the edge of the bed. "Before you get started, I'd just like to say thank you for showing up when you did last night. The doctor assures me my injuries aren't life threatening, but if I'd lain out there all night . . ." She shuddered. If she'd lain there all night, the bikers might have come back to check on her, and if they'd found her before Nash had, she wouldn't be sitting here now.

"I'm no hero, Ms. Cluny." From anyone else, this would have come across as modesty, but Nash's tone made it sound more like a warning.

"Thank you anyway," she said. "And not just for transporting me to the emergency room. The deputy I spoke with earlier told me you were the one who found my handbag abandoned in the weeds. I really would have been lost without my credit cards and insurance information. Not to mention the flash drive with all my notes." And the tiny silver cross that was the only tangible remembrance she had of her mother.

"As I said, I don't deserve any special thanks." He leaned forward, fixing her with that strange pale gaze.

Her skin prickled. Her heart rate accelerated. Conflicting emotions bubbled to the surface: fear, curiosity . . . desire.

"What can you tell me about the men who attacked you?"

Okay, focus, Regan. This is not personal, despite the crazy seductive message you thought you read in his eyes. She took a deep breath. "They knew you. At least their leader did. Harper."

Nash's expression didn't change by so much as the flicker of an eyelash, and she wasn't sure what to make of that.

"He warned me that there was more to you than meets the eye."

"That's true of most people."

"Yes, but . . ." She frowned, trying to remember Harper's exact words. "He said I didn't know who you were, what you were capable of." She paused. "Any idea what he meant by that?"

"Do you?"

"He spoke as if he knew you, but you're a wealthy scholar. He's a psycho biker. I don't see the connection."

"Harper wasn't always a . . . psycho biker."

"Then what happened? What changed him?"

"That's irrelevant."

"Nothing's irrelevant if it'll help the cops nail him. Have you told them what you know of his past?"

"Again, irrelevant. It doesn't matter how much the authorities know about Harper Wakefield. They won't catch him unless it suits his purposes."

"You talk about the man as if he were some sort of supervillain."

Nash said nothing.

"I told the deputy who took my statement that Harper mentioned you by name."

"I know. He questioned me about it at some length." He raised an eyebrow. "In fact, I gather I'm now what's termed 'a person of interest.'"

A sharp twinge of remorse pricked her. "I didn't mean to—"

"All you did was tell the truth. Not a problem," he said. "The authorities don't worry me. Harper's the one who poses a threat. I'm sorry you got hurt."

"So am I," she said. She wanted to ask him about

Katie, the woman Harper had claimed she resembled, but since Nash hadn't remarked on the resemblance, she wasn't sure of the best way to introduce the topic. "Do I remind you of anyone?" she asked finally, deciding to take the straightforward approach.

His sudden stillness told her she'd surprised him.

"Because when Harper first accosted me outside the Oasis, he said I looked like someone named Katie."

"There's a passing resemblance," Nash said.

"That's all? Harper seemed to think I was a dead ringer for her."

"There's a resemblance, but there are differences, too. Katie was a brunette. You're a blonde. Her eyes were brown. Yours are green. Plus you're a few inches taller."

"He said she was dead. Is that true?"

Nash nodded, tight-lipped, his eyes cold.

Regan hesitated a second, afraid if she pushed any harder, he'd shut down on her, but she had to try. Otherwise, she'd never know. "Who was she? Who was Katie?"

He didn't say anything at first. The silence went on for so long that she thought he wasn't going to answer. But then, "A woman," he said. "A very special woman. We were both in love with her, Harper and I. She chose me, and he never forgave me for that."

There was more to the story; she was sure of it, but he'd said all he intended to on the subject. She was equally sure of that.

"You think Harper attacked me because I resemble

her, don't you? You feel responsible. But it wasn't your fault."

"I wish I were convinced of that." Concern drove a deep crease between his eyebrows.

"I was on his radar even before he mistook me for Katie."

Nash narrowed his eyes. "Are you saying he actually thought you *were* Katie?"

"For a few seconds, yes. He made all these wild accusations, crazy stuff."

"Do you remember what he said? His exact words?"

Regan tried, but so much had happened since. "No. Sorry. I think I can give you the gist of it, though. At first he thought you'd brought Katie back from the grave to torture him. Once he realized how impossible that was, he accused me of being in cahoots with you. Then finally he remembered that he'd heard me ask for directions out to the dig. That's when he accused me of having my own agenda. An angle, he called it."

"And do you have an angle, Ms. Cluny?"

"I want that interview. I want my story."

He studied her face for a moment, then nodded once. "I believe you. Unfortunately, Harper never will. He's seen you. There's no way he'd accept the fact that we aren't involved."

"Involved?"

"Romantically. Sexually."

Was this some sort of come-on? Because she was so not . . . Regan stared into those blue, blue eyes and found herself thinking, yeah, okay, the idea wasn't *that* distasteful. In fact . . . She tore her gaze away from his. She had to think this through logically, and she couldn't do that with her hormones amped up into the red zone. "Why would Harper make such an assumption unless. . . ? Oh, God." She frowned. "It wasn't your fault; it was mine. When I asked for directions to the dig, I . . . If I hadn't pretended you were expecting me, I wouldn't have been a target."

"Maybe," he said, "and maybe not. Face it, if he and his gang were looking for sport . . ."

"Baseball's a sport," she snapped. "Attacking innocent women is a crime."

An indefinable emotion shadowed his face for a moment. "How's your neck?"

She fingered the gauze bandage that hid her wounds. "Sore."

"The doctor said it looked like an animal bite. How much do you remember?"

"About the attack? Thankfully not much," she said, wishing it were true. "But we already discussed this."

His expression was impossible to read. Did he suspect she was lying?

"The sheriff's deputies found two Harleys at the crime scene, one a few yards from your car and a second one in less than pristine condition abandoned a couple hundred yards up the road."

She told him about the biker who'd tried to grab her steering wheel.

"No body turned up."

"Maybe he was only hurt, not killed." Or maybe,

like the bastard who'd tried to rip her throat out, he'd gone up in smoke—unless, of course, she'd hallucinated that whole ashes-to-ashes, dust-to-dust part.

"But it doesn't make sense. Why didn't they kill you?"

She glanced up sharply.

He looked as taken aback as she was, as if maybe he hadn't intended to put that particular question into words.

"They tried," she said. "Harper tossed me into the backseat of my rental car, then doused it with gasoline and set it on fire. He thought I was unconscious, but I was faking it. As soon as he and his gang rode off, I escaped." Though thanks to shock and blood loss, she hadn't gotten far. She frowned. "What puzzles me is why they didn't steal my purse. I had two major credit cards with me. Not to mention a wad of cash."

"Maybe they weren't after money," he said.

"They didn't rape me, either."

"No?"

She'd surprised him. She could tell by his sudden stillness. "They planned to, I think, but changed their minds for some reason."

He frowned. "What were you wearing?"

"You saw me."

"I mean . . . before."

Before they'd ripped off half her clothes, he meant. "Raw silk trousers and a cami. It was hot, so I'd taken off my jacket. But I don't see what—"

"Jewelry?"

"Earrings," she said.

"Nothing else?"

"What are you getting at?"

He ignored her question.

"Mr. Nash?"

"Just Nash," he said. "You need to get dressed."

She stared at him in confusion. "What?"

"You can't fly to New York in your bathrobe."

"It's not my bathrobe. It came with the room. Not that it matters, since I have no intention of flying back to New York, with or without a bathrobe, not until I get my story."

"We've been through this half a dozen—"

"Yes, and as I recall, the last time you told me to go to hell."

"I didn't mean—"

"So . . ." She paused, afraid if she didn't take a few seconds to regroup, she was going to break down, damn it, and if she started crying, she wasn't going to be able to stop any time soon. So . . . deep breaths. Okay. She scowled at Nash. "Go to hell, you said. Well, what can I tell you? Been there, done that. I think I've earned a shot at a story, don't you?"

"But it's not safe—"

"Nonsense. You're old enough to know that safety's an illusion."

A wary expression, quickly suppressed, flickered across his face, there and gone so fast she thought maybe she'd imagined it. "Meaning?" he said.

"Meaning no one's ever truly safe. My plane could crash on the way back to New York. I could choke on a peanut, get run over by a truck, die of a brain tumor. Safety's an illusion."

His icy blue eyes probed her face, as if he were seeing past the surface, plumbing all her darkest secrets.

She held her breath for an endless moment.

Then, "Get dressed, Ms. Cluny," he said, his voice harsh, at odds with the weary sadness of his eyes.

"I'm not going to New York."

"You can't stay here."

"I'll damned well stay if I want to."

"I thought you wanted a story."

"I do."

"You won't find one in Cascade," he said mildly. "Come on. Get your stuff together. It's a long drive to Juniper Basin."

"Juniper. . . ? I thought—"

"Security at this place is a joke. You're probably not safe at the dig, either, but at least there I can keep an eye on you."

She glanced at the unbolted door. "You think Harper will try again?"

"I have no doubt whatsoever."

"But why? Because he thinks we're involved? That's ridiculous. Can't you just tell him we're not?"

His pale gaze burned slowly down her body, then back up to her face. "He wouldn't believe me. I'm not sure *I'd* believe me."

She studied his face for a moment. "Okay, you win. It's dangerous here. I'm convinced. Stand up and turn around."

"Excuse me?" He looked so startled that she smiled.

"There's something wrong with the hinges on the bathroom door. It won't close, and I prefer not to change in front of an audience."

He stood, then angled to face the window. "Harper's an extremely dangerous man, a remorseless killer. I'm glad for your sake that you've decided to be reasonable about this. I'm sure I can find someone to drive you to the airport."

"I'll take you up on that," she said, "as soon as I get what I came for."

"What?" Surprised, he whipped around, catching her in her panties and what was left of her cami.

"They cut the straps," she said, as if he'd asked for an explanation.

But if her near nakedness bothered Nash, he gave no indication of it. "You're not going back to New York?"

"Of course I'm going back to New York."

"Good. Then—"

"As soon as I get my story."

He crossed the room in two strides and latched onto her arms. "Are you insane?"

Good question. Because instead of thinking, whoa, I'm being manhandled by a near stranger the authorities consider a person of interest, she was thinking instead, whoa, let's hear it for sexy cheekbones and soul-searing blue eyes.

"Answer me," he said.

Her cami slid south, and he sucked in a breath. For an instant, she thought he was going to kiss her.

Or maybe devour her. She couldn't quite interpret the expression on his face.

Abruptly, he released her arms and turned away. "Get dressed," he said.

With a population just over 7,000, Cascade was the largest town between Susanville and the Oregon border. Billing itself as the gateway to the Modoc National Forest, the town sprawled across a dry lake bed at the foot of Coyote Butte, an extinct cinder cone. In the distance, the majestic pine-forested slopes of the Cascade Range created a jagged skyline. Truly awe-inspiring scenery, though Nash doubted his passenger was in any mood to appreciate the stark contrasts of her surroundings. "How are you doing?" he asked.

Regan Cluny sat strapped into the passenger seat of the Wrangler, making full use of the headrest. She opened one eye. "Are we there yet?"

Not for another hour and a half. "We're still in Cascade," he told her. "I stopped at Wal-Mart to pick up a few things. Do you want to come in?"

The other eye came open. She stared at him as if he'd just suggested she go wading in a sea of poisonous vipers. "I'll pass," she said, and closed her eyes.

Nash left the Jeep running, the air conditioner blowing full blast, the doors locked, even though he really wasn't worried about Harper at this time of day.

Midafternoon wasn't his favorite time of day, either. Thank God for sunscreen.

He dashed to the store's main entrance, his sunglasses in place, his cap pulled low. One hundred and one blistering degrees today, according to the TV weatherman. A new record high for this date.

Twenty-five minutes later, he unlocked the Jeep's driver's-side door with his duplicate key and set a large shopping bag in Regan Cluny's lap.

"What's this?" she asked, rousing herself.

"Survival gear," he said.

She pulled items from the sack as he worked his way out of the parking lot. "Very chic," she said, frowning at a triple-pack of men's white T-shirts.

"Chic's for New York. Out here you want cool."

"So why bother with sweatpants and a sweatshirt?" She held up a navy blue hoodie and matching drawstring pants.

"This is the desert. It can get cold at night."

"If you say so." She dug deeper in the bag. "Two pairs of khaki trousers. Size ten? Excuse me? I am *so* not a size ten."

"Loose pants are cooler than snug ones."

"Easier for the snakes to crawl up, too," she muttered, then dug deeper in the sack. "Crew socks and running shoes?"

"You can't walk around the dig in those," he said, referring to her ridiculous high heels. How women could balance on stilts like that . . .

"And underwear." Two stretchy white sports bras and a pack of Hanes sporty cotton briefs for women. "*Nun* underwear."

"They didn't have much of a selection," he lied.

The truth was, he'd been sorely tempted by the racks of satin and lace, the skimpy thongs. But this wasn't about what turned him on; it was about survival.

Regan Cluny stuffed her new clothes back in the bag, then set it on the floorboards between her bare feet and her discarded stilettos. Pearly pink nail polish, he noted, not the scarlet he'd have expected. Interesting, since pearly pink toenails didn't really jibe with that belly-button ring he'd glimpsed earlier in her motel room. Unpredictability. He liked that in a woman.

"I don't suppose you thought about toiletries," she said. "They gave me a toothbrush at the hospital, and I have a few things from the motel, but not enough to last more than a day or two."

"We keep a supply of basics at the dig site. You're welcome to help yourself."

"Shampoo?" she said.

"Shampoo, soap, toothpaste, the works," he said.

Apparently reassured, she subsided once more into silence. When he glanced her way a few minutes later, she was sound asleep, her head tipped back, her slender throat exposed, the puncture wounds on her neck hidden by the gauze bandage.

Once again he found himself wondering why Harper and his gang hadn't drained her when they'd had the chance. It didn't make sense. But then, a lot of what Harper Wakefield had done in the last 140-odd years didn't make sense.

Someone had tasted her. The fang marks had told him that much. Plus, he knew for a fact she'd been given a couple of units of blood in the emergency room. Frankly, she looked as if she could use another unit or two. Porcelain pale, she seemed as fragile as glass.

His fault. If it weren't for him, Regan Cluny never would have crossed paths with a monster like Harper.

FOUR

"Wake up, Ms. Cluny. We're almost there."

Not only did Charles Cunningham Nash have a great body and killer cheekbones, he also had one of the sexiest voices she'd ever heard, deep and a little gravelly.

She opened her eyes, rolled the kinks out of her shoulders, and sat up a little straighter. Then, as their surroundings impinged on her consciousness, "Oh," she said. "Wow. That must be Calliope Rock. Josh, the kid from the Oasis Truck Stop, mentioned it, but somehow I didn't expect it to be so impressive."

"Almost a hundred feet tall and half again as wide."

"Stop," she said. "I need to capture this on film." Her camera, thank God, had been in her purse, not her carry-on. "Only other place I've seen such a fantastic example of columnar basalt is the Devil's Postpile in the Sierras. And that's gray, not this spectacular rusty orange."

He glanced across at her, one eyebrow raised. "You're a geology buff?"

"Last year I did a story debunking supposed Sasquatch activity in that area. Turned out to be a couple of over-the-hill hippies growing pot on forest service property." Regan climbed out of the Jeep. She was still sore, but the nap had helped.

She took a couple of shots of the rock formation, then paused to absorb the austere beauty of the landscape. The gravel road they'd been following wound a serpentine route across an undulating plateau, rocky and sparsely vegetated with sagebrush and juniper. To the west rose the Cascades, dark and secretive in the distance. Much closer at hand, a scattering of cinder cones, some black, others rusty red, reared up from the plateau like sand castles built, then abandoned, by a race of giant children. And above it all, the sun burned a hole in a cloudless sky the exact same blue as Nash's eyes.

Nash stepped out of the Jeep, pulling his cap low. "Extraordinary, isn't it?" he said.

She met his gaze across the Jeep's hood. Time seemed to stand still. "Amazing," she agreed, not sure if she meant the scenery or his eyes.

He held her gaze for a moment longer, then climbed back in behind the wheel. "Wait until you see the petroglyphs."

Regan Cluny stood just outside Nash's tent, glaring in through the flap. "You can't seriously expect me to share your tent?"

He shrugged. "I'm the only one in camp who doesn't already have a tent mate . . . except Winston, our cook. He'd probably be willing to double up. I can ask him, if you'd like. Of course, his tent's only half the size of mine. Plus, he snores."

"But—"

"Your choice," he said.

She scowled but didn't say anything as he brushed past her to dump the Wal-Mart sack on the cot across from his.

"Dinner's not for another hour. Feel free to un-pack"—she glanced at the sack, then back at him, her scowl deepening—"or get some rest. After we eat, I'll give you a tour of the dig. If you're feeling up to it, that is." Superficial injuries, the ER doctor had said, but that didn't take into account the probable psychological scarring.

"I'm fine," she told him with more stubbornness than conviction.

"Get some rest."

"How can I sleep? It's stiflingly hot in here."

"Stiflingly hot out there, too," he said. "That's why they call it the desert."

Regan had just stowed the last of her new underwear in the top drawer of a little chest along one wall when someone said in a raspy contralto, "Knock-knock. May I come in?"

She glanced up to see a curvy little brunette with big brown eyes and a sprinkle of freckles across the bridge of her nose. She looked about fifteen, an illusion not supported by that phone-sex voice.

"Hi," Regan said.

"Hi yourself. I'm Danielle, by the way. Danielle Le-févre, grad student at UC Berkeley. Perpetual student, according to my grandmother." She grinned. "The woman's got a point. I'll be twenty-six in October."

"And I'm Regan Cluny—"

"The writer who's been trying to get Nash to agree to an interview."

And hadn't that worked out just great so far? "Have a seat." Regan indicated a camp chair that stood near a card table at the far end of the tent.

Danielle sat, tucking one leg up under her. "I'm the self-appointed welcome wagon, by the way, come to meet, greet, and discover your darkest secrets."

Regan managed a smile. "Sorry to disappoint you, but I'm secret-free."

Danielle gave a throaty chuckle. "Everyone has secrets. Take me, for instance. This innocent facade of mine masks a serious addiction." She leaned forward, lowering her voice to a whisper. "Chocolate, more specifically, M&Ms." She pulled a crumpled bag from the pocket of her shorts. "Want some?"

"No, thanks."

Shrugging, Danielle popped a couple of candies into her mouth. "Okay, secret number two. Only it probably doesn't really count as a secret since Tom's the only one in camp who's in the dark."

"Tom?"

"Tom Davis. Dr. Davis, the archaeologist in charge

of the dig. He doesn't know it yet, but he's mine. So hands off."

"No problem," Regan said. "I'm here for a story. That's all."

"You say that now, but you haven't seen Tom. He's really hot . . . as we say in the 'hood."

Regan laughed. "What 'hood would that be? Beverly Hills?"

"Malibu," Danielle confessed. "And there you have it. Born to wealth and privilege. The last of my dirty secrets. So turnabout's fair play. What're your secrets?"

I'm dying. How's that for a shocker? But what scares me even more, I think the tumor embedded in my brain may be warping my perceptions. That or the drugs I take to slow the cancer's growth. Last night—and this is where the story gets truly weird—I could have sworn a vampire sank his fangs in my throat.

Danielle looked at her so strangely that for a second Regan wondered if she'd spoken out loud. "You okay?" Danielle said.

Regan touched the bandage on her neck. No, she wasn't okay. She wasn't even within hailing distance of okay, because, damn it, either she was losing her mind or monsters were real, and neither conclusion was exactly reassuring. "A little tired," she said. And a whole lot scared. Nash was right. If she had any brains, she'd forget the stupid story and hightail it back to New York.

• • •

Regan woke with a start just as a giant snake coiled itself around her body and started to squeeze.

A dream, she realized. Just a dream.

She sat up, forcing herself to take slow, even breaths. How long had she been sleeping, anyway? The tent's interior lay deep in shadow and the temperature had dropped from stifling to bearable. Must be nearly sunset.

She probably ought to go collect some toiletries and find something to eat. Only problem with that plan was, she was way too comfortable to move. Potent stuff, those pain meds. Potent and effective. She didn't hurt at all, just felt a little drowsy, a little disconnected. She hugged her pillow and let herself drift once again toward sleep.

A stealthy rustling disturbed the silence, jerking her back to full consciousness.

Snake?

Impossible. She'd zipped the tent up tight after Danielle left.

Hadn't she?

Regan peered toward the door flap and saw it move. Again she heard a faint susurrus . . . like slick, polished scales brushing across rough canvas.

Oh, shit.

A weapon. She needed a weapon.

"Regan?" someone whispered. "Are you awake?" Nash poked his head in through the opening, then pulled the zipper down the rest of the way.

Regan released her breath in a whoosh of relief.

"Completely," she said. A zipper, not a snake. Feeling like an idiot, she relaxed her tensed muscles.

"Are you hungry? I brought dinner."

"You didn't have to do that. I could have grabbed something later."

He handed her a paper plate covered with aluminum foil. "Later's not really an option. The dining tent's closed for the night."

"In that case, thanks." Regan shot him a quick smile. "I'm starved."

"That's a good sign. Hope you like enchiladas."

Regan peeled back a corner of the foil.

"Oh, wait. I almost forgot." Nash dug in the pocket of his shirt. "Here." He handed her a plastic knife and fork wrapped in a wad of paper napkins.

"Thanks," she said. "Smells good." She tried to remember the last time she'd eaten. If you didn't count the revolting lukewarm cream of wheat they'd served her for breakfast this morning at the hospital—and she didn't—she hadn't had anything of substance since the prepackaged chef's salad she'd picked at during her extended layover in Denver yesterday.

"I'm going to go catch up on some paperwork," Nash said, "but I'll be back in a little while to take you on that tour I promised."

"Can't wait," she said around a mouthful of enchilada. But he was already gone.

Two perfunctory knocks and the trailer door opened, breaking Nash's concentration. He glanced up, half expecting Regan Cluny. Instead, Tom stood in the doorway, his expression equal parts worry and irritation.

"Come in," Nash said. "And shut the door. You're letting all the cold air out." The office was the only air-conditioned space on the site. People could survive without air-conditioning; computers couldn't.

Tom, his heavy black eyebrows knit in a frown, shut the door with more force than necessary, then stood there, looking tense and angry, his back pressed up against the wall.

"What's wrong?" Nash asked. "Has Winston gone on another bender?"

"This has nothing to do with Winston," Tom snapped, which seemed totally out of character. Easygoing Tom Davis wasn't really the snappish type.

"Okay." Nash shoved his paperwork aside and sat up a little straighter. "But something's bothering you. Why don't you tell me about it?"

Scowling, Tom threw himself down on the folding chair across from Nash's desk. "Not it. Her. Regan Cluny. That *writer*." He made it sound like a dirty word.

Nash heaved a weary sigh. "What's she done?" She'd looked so sleepy when he'd delivered her dinner. Frankly, he hadn't expected trouble from her quite this soon. Yet here she was, already ruffling feathers.

"Why the hell did you bring her to Juniper Basin? I thought the plan was to get rid of her. Do you really want to be outed? Hell, she already knows too much."

"She knows nothing," Nash said. "She passed out. She doesn't remember what happened to her last night."

Tom shot him an incredulous look. "Or so she says. Damn it, Nash, she's a trained journalist. Poking her nose into things that are none of her business is pretty much her job description."

Nash sighed. "Look, she refused point-blank to return to New York, and I knew if she stayed in Cascade, Harper and his boys would finish what they started. Under the circumstances, bringing her here, placing her under my protection, seemed the best solution."

"Best solution? Are you insane?" Tom slammed his fist against the wall so hard the whole side of the trailer shook. "This woman may look like Katie, but she's not your lost love miraculously reincarnated. Think about it rationally. You don't even know for certain that she isn't working with Harper. Maybe he hired her precisely because she resembles Katie. Maybe she's part of a plot to destroy you."

"Before you get too enamored of your conspiracy theory, consider this: Harper and his gang of bloodsucking thugs attacked Regan Cluny last night."

Tom uttered a grunt of disgust. "But they didn't kill her, did they?"

Once Regan had eaten, she put on the jogging shoes Nash had bought her. Unlike the T-shirts and khakis, they fit surprisingly well . . . as did her new underwear. So either the man was a really good guesser or he had more experience in buying women's clothing than she'd realized.

Like maybe he was married.

No way! was her immediate gut-level response, a response backed up by her research, sketchy as that was. She'd done an online search, of course, and found no mention of a marriage, past, present, or future. No mention of any long-term romantic relationships. No mention of any short-term romantic relationships, for that matter.

But all that really proved was that when you were lucky enough to have had a great-grandfather who'd struck it rich in the Klondike, you could afford to pay off the paparazzi and keep your private life private.

"Are you ready for that tour?"

She glanced up guiltily at the sound of Nash's deep baritone. "Sure. I was just about to . . ."

Nash stepped through the tent flap, and Regan immediately noticed an oxygen shortage. Why did he have to be so damned gorgeous?

He studied her face, his expression inscrutable. "You seem . . . nervous. Is something wrong?"

Dear God, the man wasn't a mind reader, was he? "Wrong? No, I feel much better since I ate. Compliments to the chef."

"I'll be sure to pass that along," he said.

She stood up. "So. Which way do we go?"

"What would you like to see first? The aliens' underground control center? The flying-saucer launch pad?"

She stared at him. "You're joking, right?"

"Right." A sardonic smile twisted his mouth. "Follow me." As shadows gathered, he led her toward the edge of the camp proper, then along a well-worn dirt path.

"Where are we going?" she asked as the path veered away from the lights of the camp.

"To look at some rocks."

No shortage of those. They lined the path and littered the camp, fanning out here and there in piles of loose scree at the base of the ridges that bordered the basin on three sides.

Regan followed Nash across a rope bridge unsteady enough to make her thankful for her running shoes, then along a narrow path sandwiched in between the river's edge and the cliff wall. As they trudged along, the last of the light faded. Nash switched on a flashlight and handed it to her.

"Don't you need it?"

"I brought two," he said.

One by one the stars came out, until the sky was full of twinkling lights. Hundreds of stars. Thousands. Maybe even millions. More than Regan could count. Certainly more than she'd ever noticed before.

The ledge widened to accommodate a thicket of willows that overhung the river. Crickets chirped. Frogs croaked. A hungry mosquito nailed her on the arm.

"Damn bloodsucker," she muttered under her breath.

Nash stopped so abruptly that she bumped into him. He turned to stare at her and the glare of his flashlight caught her full in the face. "What did you say?"

"Move the light, would you? You're blinding me." A second mosquito dive-bombed her head, and she swatted at it. "You don't have any insect repellent, do you? The mosquitoes are eating me alive."

"Mosquitoes," he repeated, as if he were unfamiliar with the species.

"Yes, damn it." A third mosquito whined past her ear, and she smacked at it.

"They aren't bothering me. Are you wearing perfume?"

"No." Where would she get perfume?

"Must be your shampoo that's attracting them then."

"You don't use shampoo?"

"Only the unscented kind."

He slipped off the long-sleeved denim shirt he wore over his white T-shirt and handed it to her. "Here," he said. "Put this on. It's not insect repellent, but . . ."

At five feet four, Regan had never considered herself a small woman, but Nash's shirttail hung to her knees. The sleeves extended well beyond her fingertips. Wearing his shirt made her feel small and vulnerable. Worse, the fabric smelled like him, a warm, seductive masculine scent that enveloped her in a sensual cloud. She shivered, even though she was anything but cold.

"Ready?" he said.

She nodded.

They plodded on in silence. Normally a hike like this wouldn't have taxed her stamina, but her poor bruised body was a long way from normal. And to make matters worse, her pain meds were wearing off. The wounds on her neck throbbed, and her muscles protested with every step she took. "How much farther?" she asked, trying hard not to pant like a dog.

"Not much." Nash didn't even glance around.

"How far is 'not much'?" she persisted.

"You said you wanted a story, but if you're not up to the research, just say so, Ms. Cluny, and we can turn around. I'd be more than happy to have someone drive you to the airport. If you leave now, you could probably catch an early morning flight out to New York."

"You're not getting rid of me that easily."

He grunted an unintelligible response.

"What was that?"

"Never mind," he said.

She grinned to herself. The more she could get under his skin, the less likely he was to guard his tongue and the more likely she was to get her story.

"How much farther? Are we close?"

"Save your breath, Ms. Cluny. We'll get there when we get there."

"Are you saying I ask too many questions?"

"I'm saying you ask the same questions. Over and over. As in endlessly repetitious."

"Part of my journalist's training," she said. "If you ask the same question often enough, eventually you discover the truth."

Nash halted in his tracks. Slowly he turned to face her.

In the brief instant before his flashlight's beam effectively blinded her, she could have sworn his eyes glowed red in the dark. Gooseflesh rose along her arms.

"Weird," she said.

"What's weird?" He moved the light out of her eyes.

"Nothing. I thought . . . It must have been an optical illusion." She frowned. "How much farther?"

He heaved an exaggerated sigh. "Just around the bend."

Around the bend. Which was another way to say delusional. *That's me,* she thought. *Delusional.* What other explanation could there be for all the bizarre things she'd "seen" lately? Men with inch-long canines, spontaneous human combustion, glowing red eyes.

Some of her distress must have shown on her face because Nash frowned. "I didn't think . . . are you up to this?" He sounded genuinely concerned this time, not so much like a man who was looking for a reason to ship her back East.

"I'm fine," she said. *Physically.* "Or almost. A few days' rest and I'll be good as new." Or as good as she got.

"You're having trouble breathing," he said. Then, "Damn. The altitude. I forgot. We're nearly a mile high here. It can take a while for people to adjust. Maybe we should do this another time."

"We've come this far," she said. "I'm tired, yes, but it seems foolish to turn back when we're so close."

He studied her face by the light of the flashlight. "If you're sure . . ."

"I am, but . . ."

He raised his eyebrows in a silent question.

"Could we take it a little slower? Please?"

A shadow of what might have been compunction passed across his face. "No problem," he said.

They followed the riverbank for another hundred yards. Here the river narrowed. So did the path. The sheer rock cliff angled in toward the river, encroaching on their headroom while the path itself became little more than a rocky eight-inch ledge.

"End of the line?" she said.

"Almost." Nash shone the light on a crack in the cliff. Some hardy shrub she didn't recognize clung, limpetlike, to the rock above. Its roots dangled from the crevice like a witch's snarled locks. "Get a good solid grip on the roots," Nash said, "and use them to support part of your weight as you inch around the overhang."

She stared at him. "Did I mention I flunked out of Tarzan school?"

"You'll do fine," he said. "Piece of cake."

Regan eyed the formidable cliff and the equally formidable river, fast-moving here and full of rocks. She was a strong swimmer, but . . .

"Chocolate?" she said.

"What?"

"That piece of cake," she explained. "I need a strong incentive. Is it chocolate?"

"You ask too many questions, Ms. Cluny."

"And you provide too few answers, Mr. Nash."

"The petroglyphs are on the other side of the bulge."

"Petroglyphs?"

"Rock picture writing."

"The same petroglyphs that were shown in the *Inquisitor*?"

He nodded. "Though they don't look much like the published images. All those pictures were digitally enhanced to support the reporter's fabrications."

"Okay," she said. "Incentive enough. For honest-to-God petroglyphs, I'll give it a shot. And hey, what's the worst that could happen? I lose my grip, conk my head on a rock or two, and get pulled unconscious from the water a couple of miles downstream by some helpful passerby."

"There is no 'couple of miles downstream,'" Nash said. "The river empties into a sinkhole and goes underground about two hundred yards ahead."

"Well, damn," she said.

"Just use the roots for balance. It's perfectly safe. I promise. Watch what I do, and replicate my actions as closely as you can."

He grabbed a handful of roots, then, feeling his way one step at a time while leaning backward at a forty-five-degree angle, he worked his way around the bulge. "See?" he called. "No big deal. Your turn."

"My turn," she muttered. She shut off her flashlight and stuffed it in the pocket of her khakis. Even without the flashlight's beam, visibility was fair. A gibbous moon hung suspended in the eastern sky, reflecting silvery light across the rugged landscape. Regan reached into the crevice and grabbed a handful of roots. Dry and knobbly, they provided a good, secure grip. She tugged sharply, and they held.

Clinging to the roots, she inched her way toward Nash. She would have made it, too, if her foot hadn't slipped. For a brief, terrifying moment, she swung out from the cliff and hung suspended between the glittering stars above and the glittering water below.

Then Nash grabbed her firmly around the middle. "Let go," he said. "I have you."

Regan released her death grip on the dangling roots and wrapped her arms around Nash instead, hugging him tightly.

"Are you all right?" he asked.

"Fine. I thrive on near-death experiences."

"Do you?" he said in a raspy voice.

Her laughter evaporated under the intensity of his gaze. Little jolts of awareness tingled along her nerve endings.

Nash tilted his head forward, and she thought for one mad second that he was going to kiss her. Kiss her and keep on kissing her, rip off her clothes and take her right there on the riverbank. Instead, he closed his eyes, hiding the wild yearning she'd glimpsed there, a wild yearning echoed in the rapid pulsing of her heart. He loosened his grip on her waist, gently removed her arms from his neck, and took a step backward.

"Nash?"

He glanced up, one eyebrow raised in inquiry, his expression composed, his gaze impersonal. "Yes?"

Had she imagined all that wicked promise, all that scalding-hot sexual tension? "I . . ."

"Yes?" he said again. Not cold, not even unfriendly, just . . . reserved, professional, and very, very off-limits.

Regan was thankful for the dim light, which camouflaged her embarrassment. What was wrong with her?

"Check it out," Nash said.

She stood there for a second, frozen in place, not sure what he was talking about. Then he pulled the flashlight from his pocket, switched it on, and fanned its light across the rocks beside them.

At first she saw nothing but light and shadows. But gradually she realized the light and shadows formed patterns, pictures and symbols carved into the surface of the rock itself.

"I thought they'd be paintings. In the *Inquisitor*—"

"The details didn't show up well in the photos, so the photographer added some digital enhancements."

"Like the flying saucers," she said. "No, wait." She peered at a pattern of five ovals.

"The shapes are there," he said, "but I doubt they're supposed to represent flying saucers."

"They *look* like flying saucers. What else—"

"Flying boulders," Nash suggested. "What geologists call volcanic bombs. See those triangular shapes on the right?"

"The ones that look like mountains?"

"Right. Like the cinder cones that surround us. Like the Cascade Range to the north and west. Like the Medicine Lake volcano to the south. The mountains in this part of California are volcanic in origin. Isn't it more likely that the petroglyphs tell of a violent eruption, one that filled the air with molten rocks, rather than an alien invasion? Look around you. Do you see any evidence of alien culture? No. And yet there's ample evidence of volcanic activity." He pointed at the cliff. "Layers of basalt and ash-flow tuff." He picked up a yellowish rock, examined it for a second, then tossed it onto the ground. "Pumice." He shone his flashlight on the opposite ridge. "More basalt."

Regan peered closely at the carved symbols. "But they're all the same size and shape," she argued. "Wouldn't your volcanic bombs vary?"

"Not necessarily," he said. "They tend to be egg shaped."

"Eggs tend to be egg shaped, too," she said. "Maybe—"

A mosquito whined past Regan's ear. A second attacked her forehead, stinging painfully as a sonic boom echoed in the distance. Instinctively she put a hand to her head and felt something wet and warm.

"Blood." Nash stiffened. His nostrils flared. "I smell blood."

"Mine," Regan said. "Something bit me. A mosquito, I think."

"That was no mosquito. Get down!" he said, dragging her to the ground and shielding her body with his. "Someone's shooting at us."

"But—"

"Lie still," he said. "I'm going to see if I can pinpoint his position."

"Don't get your head shot off!"

"I'll be careful."

"Careful, hell! He's got a gun. So what if you do pinpoint his position? How's that going to help? What do you plan to do then? Toss your flashlight at him?"

"No," he said evenly. "But if I know where he is, I can figure out which way to move to get out of range."

She grabbed his arm as he started to raise his head. "Are you crazy?" she demanded in a whisper.

FIVE

"I know what I'm doing," Nash said.

Regan's eyes looked huge and vulnerable. "You'd better," she said, releasing her grip on his arm, "because if you get your head shot off, there's no freaking way I can get back around that bulge on my own. Seriously," she said. "Be careful."

"Always am."

He raised his head slowly, all his senses alert.

Nothing happened. No shots broke the hush. No sound and no movement.

Nash scanned the river in both directions, then checked the ridge on the opposite side of the basin. He spotted the shooter almost immediately. About halfway up the hill, Harper Wakefield stood silhouetted against the pale backdrop of sagebrush and dry grass, making no effort to blend into his surroundings.

Harper must've spotted Nash about the same time

Nash spotted him, because he brandished his rifle, waving a silent acknowledgment.

Cocky bastard.

He didn't shoot, though. Katie's protection spell prevented his hurting Nash just as it prevented Nash from hurting Harper. Physically, at least.

Unfortunately, over the years Harper had discovered other ways to inflict pain, the most effective of which was systematically destroying those Nash cared for most—his family, his friends. Nash knew most people considered him cold and aloof. Thanks to Harper's vendetta, intimacy was a luxury Nash couldn't afford.

He swore softly under his breath, cursing both Harper and the idiot tabloid reporter who'd set him on Nash's trail. Because now his entire crew was at risk, not just Regan Cluny, whom Harper mistakenly believed to be his lover.

"What's happening?" Regan started to get up.

"Stay down!" he warned. Harper was an excellent shot, and Regan was a prime target. He'd missed once; he wasn't likely to miss a second time.

Nash shifted his attention to Regan for only a split second, but when he glanced back across the basin, Harper had already disappeared. The deserted hillside seemed to mock him.

Regan sat on top of Nash's battered desk while he doctored her forehead.

"You need to visit the ER. I'll get one of the crew to drive you into Cascade."

"I don't need a doctor," she said. "It's a scratch. You said so yourself, a scratch from a flying rock fragment, not a bullet."

"Yes, but—"

"The bleeding stopped half an hour ago. It doesn't even hurt." Much.

He dabbed at her wound with a cotton ball soaked in hydrogen peroxide. "You need to leave, Ms. Cluny. It's too dangerous for you here."

"I'm not the one who's cursed," she said.

He froze. "What do you mean?" He spoke lightly, evenly, but his eyes were wary.

"I'm a journalist, Mr. Nash. I did my homework. I researched you. And your family."

"I have no family, Ms. Cluny."

"That's what I meant by cursed. Historically speaking, members of the Nash family don't live long."

"Bad luck," he said.

"Dying of pneumonia's bad luck," she said. "Dying by violence is a curse."

Harper reached the seemingly abandoned farmhouse just before dawn. His gang was still out hunting, but he knew Elizabeth would be waiting for him, anxious to know what he'd learned. He parked his bike out of sight in the barn, then hurried down the stairs into the bowels of the house where she waited.

The new master suite, formerly a cellar, was perfect for their purposes, being both large and windowless. Elizabeth had furnished it with antiques, including a few family pieces, most notably the nineteenth-century mahogany four-poster upon which they'd bled her parents dry in the first of countless murderous duets. Though the bed was rather ornate for his taste, he liked what she'd done with it—the satin and lace duvet, the diaphanous silk draperies, all the same celestial blue as her eyes.

A Tiffany floor lamp glowed in one corner next to a cream satin–striped armchair, a dog-eared copy of Stephen King's *Salem's Lot* abandoned on the floor beside it, but Elizabeth lay on the big bed, her eyes closed, her long hair loose on the pillows. At first he thought she was asleep, but then her eyelashes fluttered open and she smiled. "Harper," she said. "I thought you'd never come."

"My evening was more eventful than I expected."

"You'll have to tell me about it," Elizabeth said. "Later." Shoving back the covers, she sat up, patting the spot next to her.

He needed no further invitation. She was naked, temptation personified, all voluptuous curves, seductive eyes, and red lips. Her luscious breasts played hide-and-seek behind the heavy dark hair that hung past her shoulders in artful disarray.

Harper stripped, then joined her on the bed.

She sighed with pleasure as he gathered her close, but when he brushed his fingertips across her skin, skin so soft, so pale, so translucent that he could see the faint tracery of blue veins at her throat and wrists, she uttered a cry of frustration.

"Too slow." She pushed her lower lip out in a pout, then deliberately scraped her teeth across the tender fullness. A drop of blood welled up, just a single drop, but the scent of it filled the room. "I'm in the mood for fireworks, Harper. I want Chinese New Year and the Fourth of July all rolled into one. I want blood. I want pain. I want satisfaction."

His heart pounded, his groin tightened, and he lost what little restraint he had left. Growling deep in his throat, he grabbed for her, but she slid out of his grasp, laughing, taunting him.

"So greedy," she scolded.

"But you said . . ." Baring his teeth, he reached for her again, and again she eluded him.

"Say please," she said.

Please? *Please?* The scent of her blood was driving him insane. His heartbeat roared in his ears.

Smiling, she licked her lip, shivering ecstatically at the taste of her own blood. "See what you're missing?"

"You're killing me," he said.

"I don't know about that. You look pretty lively. At least parts of you do." She nudged his erection with the tip of one finger.

He made another grab for her, but once again, she eluded him. "Say it," she demanded.

"It," he said.

Her eyes narrowed, flashing blue fire.

"Brat," he said.

"Insults won't get you what you want," she warned.

But Harper wasn't worried. This little game of hers cut both ways. She was as aroused as he was. Maybe more so. All he had to do was bide his time and . . .

Elizabeth crawled closer, then, smiling sweetly, slashed at his chest with her nails. Blood welled up along the cuts.

Elizabeth moaned. Then leaning closer, she slid her tongue across his wounds, licking and sucking.

"More," he said when she stopped.

A smile tilted her full lips. She crawled on top of him, trapping his erection between her thighs, thrusting her breasts forward. "Say please," she said softly. He could smell the blood on her breath, almost taste it in her throaty whisper.

"Please," he said, a guttural rasp.

"Yes." Eternally young, eternally beautiful, eternally ravenous, Elizabeth fell upon him hungrily. He met her ferocity with his own. Pain and pleasure, pleasure and pain. Exquisite torture combined with an incomparable ecstasy.

Harper lost himself in a crimson haze, a world where all that mattered, all that existed was blood. Blood and sex. Minutes, hours, days. Time had no meaning.

From his chair behind the desk, Nash studied Regan Cluny's face, pale and drawn in the unflattering glare of the fluorescent lights of the office. She looked more than a little the worse for wear with bandages on her forehead and throat, but her eyes, those strange sage green eyes of hers, still burned with a lively curiosity.

How much did she know? How much had she guessed? More than once she'd made a provocative remark. Coincidence? Maybe. Or then again, she could be baiting him, trying to trip him up.

"Would you like something to drink?" he asked. "I could reheat some coffee in the microwave."

"Tempting," she said, heavy on the irony, "but I'll pass." She met his gaze head-on. "Why are you trying to change the subject?"

"Was I?" He gave her what the grad students called his freeze-ray death glare, but it didn't faze Regan Cluny.

"You were. What are you trying to hide, Mr. Nash?"

"Nash," he said, wondering where she was going with this but careful not to betray any curiosity. "No mister."

"Not Charles?"

"Just Nash."

"I assume Charles is a family name."

He nodded.

"Thought so," she said, "because when I Googled 'Charles Cunningham Nash,' I got lots of hits, including records that date back to the Civil War."

She knows something. Or at least suspects something. He raised an eyebrow. "Surely I don't look that old."

"Of course not." She did an exasperated eye roll. "I'm talking possible ancestors. Through the decades, there have been any number of Charles Nashes, and most of them have been dogged by misfortune."

"Cursed," he said, his voice edged with skepticism.

"In a manner of speaking. One of the Charles

Nashes was a Union army officer. After the war, he returned to his family home near Latrobe, in Westmoreland County, Pennsylvania, to find that his parents, the family servants, and his mother's pet spaniel had all been murdered."

"So the poor bastard shared my name. Doesn't make him my ancestor. Nash is a common name, and Pennsylvania's a long way from California."

"There were old tintypes on the website. Allowing for differences in haircuts, clothing, and age, that 1865 Charles Nash could be your twin."

"The resemblance was that strong?"

"Twin or, more likely, your great-great-great-grandfather," she said.

He rubbed his jaw as if he were considering the possibility. "It's possible, I suppose. Charles *is* a family name."

"And that's not all," she said. "In the early part of the twentieth century, another Charles Nash made headlines in San Francisco when he was accused of murdering his fiancée of two months, a young woman from a wealthy Nob Hill family."

"I know the story," he admitted. "That Charles Nash *was* a relative. However, he was never brought to trial. The police released him."

"He had an alibi," Regan said.

"Yes. Ironclad. Unfortunately the police never caught the real killer. As a result, many people, including the girl's family, continued to believe him responsible for her murder. The situation grew so unpleasant that he was finally forced to leave the city."

Nash paused, took a deep breath, then met her gaze. "He didn't do it," he said earnestly. "He didn't kill her."

She blinked in surprise. "I never suggested he did."

"Then. . . ?"

"I was only half joking when I called it a curse," she said. "Maybe not so much a family curse as a curse on the name Charles Nash. Generation after generation, men named Charles Nash have lost those closest to them—family, friends."

He stared at her, not saying anything. What could he say that wouldn't increase her suspicions? Desperate for a distraction, he shoved himself to his feet. "Hungry?" he asked. "I'm not much of a cook, but I could zap some microwave popcorn."

"I'm not hungry," she said, "but feel free to fix some for yourself."

Nash wasn't hungry, either, but fixing it gave him an excuse to move away from her and into the kitchenette.

Regan angled her chair around so she could see him. "Thirty-odd years ago, a Charles Nash was living in an apartment on Park Avenue," she said. "Someone broke in one night and killed his housekeeper."

How could he forget? Musicals really weren't his thing, but some friends had conned him into going to see *The Wiz*. He'd come home late, to find the apartment door hanging open, the smell of death everywhere. Harper hadn't just killed fifty-two-year-old Molly Rafferty; he'd butchered her. "You *have* done your homework, haven't you?"

"I assume that Charles Nash was your father."

"He moved to Europe within the month."

She studied him closely. "That's why you're so aloof. You think if anyone gets close to you, that automatically makes them fate's bitch. You really believe you're cursed, don't you?"

"With that imagination, you should be writing fiction."

"The shooter tonight was real enough. I don't believe in curses, but"—she frowned—"I think you just might be a dangerous person to get close to."

"In that case, you'd be wise to keep your distance."

She stared up at him. "Hard to do when we're sharing a tent."

Gradually, the bloodlust faded and sanity returned. Elizabeth lay sprawled facedown on the rumpled sheets. Harper lay on top of her, his teeth still sunk in her creamy shoulder. He relaxed his jaw, relinquishing his grip on her tender flesh. Rolling onto his side next to her, he licked at the bite wounds to hasten their healing.

She all but purred her satisfaction. "Now then," she said, "tell me. Did you see Charley? Did you talk to him? Did you tell him how much his beloved Betsy misses him?"

Jealousy burned in Harper's chest even though he knew it was illogical to envy Nash. He and Elizabeth had never had the sort of relationship Harper and Elizabeth shared. Nash had never felt the erotic torture of her teeth lightly razoring him, then licking away the pain, licking and tasting and sucking until he lost himself in a red-hot haze of bloodlust. Nash had never helped her seduce and murder, never watched the shuddering ecstasy that gripped her as she bathed in the blood of innocents.

"I'm not interested in anything Nash has to say," Harper told her. "I want him dead, and I think I may have finally figured out how to get it done."

Elizabeth laughed. "You've been trying to kill him for a hundred and forty-two years and have failed miserably. What makes you think this time's any different?"

"My earlier attempts failed because of Katie's protection spell," he said patiently. "I can't kill him, and he can't kill me."

Elizabeth sat up with a sinuous grace. "So you settled for second best—killing those he cares about. And of course, with his overgrown sense of responsibility, he blames himself for their deaths. He's in agony, and you're on top of the world for about ten seconds until you remember that he's still alive. So again I say, what's different this time?"

"There's a woman involved."

"An attractive woman?"

"Not just attractive. She's the spitting image of Katie."

Elizabeth narrowed her eyes.

"Now, don't go all green-eyed monster on me," he said. "Katie and I are ancient history."

Elizabeth shrugged in feigned disinterest. "So kill the Katie look-alike."

"It's more complicated than that," he said. "Besides, I already tried to kill her, and it didn't work."

"Good God, you're not talking about the blonde who toasted Bobby Branson, are you? I thought you said you'd eliminated her already."

"I set her car on fire with her inside, but apparently she escaped."

"Too bad." She shrugged again. "The best-laid plans . . ."

"No." He sat up. "It's not bad. Don't you see? If I'd succeeded in killing her, I'd have lost my best chance of killing him."

"I don't get it."

"I can't kill Nash, but *she* can."

Elizabeth stared at him blankly. "How?"

"Same way she killed Bobby." He raised his eyebrows, giving her a smug look.

"Oh," Elizabeth said, and then again, "Oh!" Understanding lit up her face. "How deliciously Machiavellian!"

Juniper Basin boasted two luxuries not found on most archaeological dig sites—flush toilets and hot showers. While availing herself of the latter, Regan managed to soak the newly applied bandage on her forehead. Fortunately, she still had a good supply of antiseptic cream and bandages. Once she got back to her tent—correction, Nash's tent—she could replace the soggy bandage on her forehead and the one she'd removed from her neck, too. Only . . . how was she going to reach the injuries on her back?

Damn it.

She needed help. Nash's help. But just imagining the way his big hands would feel spreading ointment on her bare skin was enough to give her goose bumps, despite the warm water cascading down her body.

Okay, this was doable. She'd take a double dose of pain meds so that by the time she asked Nash to help with the bandages, she'd be too zoned out to notice the way it felt when he touched her.

Because jumping the man she wanted to interview was definitely not the way to go.

Good plan, she told herself as she turned off the shower, gently toweled herself dry, and dressed in her baggy new sweat suit.

Excellent plan, she told herself as she dug out her first-aid supplies, rebandaged her forehead and throat, dry-swallowed two pills, then plopped down on one end of her cot to wait for Nash to return from wherever he was.

She was yawning an average of ten times a minute, plus her hair was almost dry—and, she noted, growing out nicely—when Nash finally returned, fresh from the shower, dressed only in a pair of faded denim jeans, his bare chest damp. Not to mention muscled. And sexy as sin.

So much for her plan.

His gaze met hers. She could have sworn his eyes darkened from ice blue to a deep azure, but it was probably only a trick of the light—in this case a single Coleman lantern.

"It's late. I thought you'd be asleep by now," he said.

"I waited up on purpose. I need help replacing the bandages on my back . . . if you don't mind?"

His jaw tightened for a second. "No problem."

Then why was his body language at odds with his words?

"I have all the stuff right here."

He crossed the tent. "Slip your jacket off and turn around."

Or vice versa. She wasn't wearing anything under her hoodie.

Regan wriggled around until she had her back to Nash. Then she unzipped the jacket and slipped out of it, hugging the soft fabric to her breasts.

He drew in his breath with a hiss.

"What's wrong?" She glanced back over her shoulder. "Am I bleeding again?"

"No." He sounded as if he were strangling.

"Are you sure? Your voice—"

"It's not as severe as I originally thought."

"Yes, the ER doctor said—"

"The cuts are shallow, hardly more than scratches. I doubt they'll leave scars, and all but one of the burns is scabbed over."

"The one in the center of my back is still raw," she guessed. "It hurts more . . . than . . . the—" She faltered to a stop, unable to maintain her train of thought with his hands on her skin. Who'd have guessed such big hands could be so gentle?

"Did I hurt you?" he asked.

"No, I . . ." Warm and gentle.

"You stopped in midsentence."

"I forgot . . . what I was going . . . to say." Warm and gentle, but not soothing. More like arousing. Her breathing quickened. Tiny shudders of anticipation rippled through her. Her nipples tingled though he hadn't even come close to touching them. What would happen, she wondered, if he sat down behind her? How would she react if he reached around, tugged the hoodie from her hands, and cupped her naked breasts? Would she burst into flames?

"There," he said, smoothing the last bandage in place. "You can get dressed now."

Or not.

What would he do if she dropped her sweatshirt and turned around?

Only one way to find out.

I can't believe I'm doing this. The sweatshirt fell away from her suddenly nerveless fingers. She turned.

Disappointment struck with an almost physical impact. She was alone in the tent.

"Mary Katherine?"

Katie O'Malley glanced up from her embroidery, a linen pillowcase meant for her dowry chest, to see her father standing in the doorway of the sitting room. The expression on his face frightened her almost as much as his unaccustomed use of her given name. "What is it, Papa? What's the matter?"

"You must terminate your engagement immediately."

"Papa?" Surely she'd not heard him correctly.

"Lieutenant Charles Nash is no longer welcome here."

"Papa! How can you say such a terrible thing? Charles not welcome? You've always held him in the highest regard. I once overheard you telling Mama you loved him like the son you never had."

"That was months ago. The situation has changed. Since Georgia seceded from the Union—"

"Politics," she said with a dismissive flip of her hand. "What have politics to do with Charles or me? States' rights? Slavery? You can't tell me my betrothed is suddenly unwelcome because he opposes slavery, not when you yourself have been an outspoken opponent of the practice for as long as I can remember. How many times have I heard you denouncing it from the pulpit?"

"Matters are more serious than you realize, my dear. Rumor has it Confederate forces have forced the surrender of Fort Sumter. Lincoln will never countenance such a slap in the face. War is now inevitable."

War? With Charles, a recent graduate of West Point, stuck irrevocably on the opposite side of the conflict? No! Katie's heart lurched. She pressed both fists to her breast.

"You're bleeding," her father said.

What did he expect? Her heart was breaking.

But the blood wasn't pouring from her chest. In her distress, she'd accidentally jabbed the embroidery needle through her finger. Blood welled from the wound, staining the fine linen pillowcase meant to grace her marriage bed. Ruined now. Ruined.

SIX

"Wake up," someone said.

On some level, Regan knew that gruff voice was trying to rouse her, but the pain meds, combined with bone-deep exhaustion, muffled its urgency. She hovered in the twilight zone between sleeping and waking, one part of her brain battling toward consciousness while another part fought equally hard to recapture her dream.

Only bits and pieces remained. Images. Emotions. She'd pricked her finger on a needle, the remembered pain almost unbearable, disproportionate to the injury. Then her blood, huge drops of it, had fallen like crimson rain onto white linen, blossoming into splotchy flowers. Funeral flowers. And grief had sunk its talons in her heart.

"Wake up," someone said again, more insistently this time. "Deputy Faraday wants to talk with you."

Regan didn't know any Deputy Faraday. Didn't know the voice in her ear, either.

With an effort, she turned over and raised her heavy lids, squinting until a face swam into focus. It—and presumably the voice—belonged to a short, squat Native American man who fell somewhere between senior citizen and old as dirt.

"You're awake."

"You think? I'm not so sure."

A reluctant smile rearranged the lines on his face.

"You must be Winston." Not a tough deduction since he was wearing an apron and smelled of bacon.

He nodded a greeting. "Winston Hirsch."

"Regan Cluny. Did the deputy say what he wanted?"

"He's here to investigate the shooting last night."

Better late than never. "Okay. Tell Deputy Faraday I'll be there ASAP."

"He's waiting in the office," Winston said. "You know where that is?"

She nodded, and the old man let himself out of the tent.

Nash leaned back in his chair, watching Deputy Faraday from between narrowed lids. Part of that was because he'd had fewer than five hours of sleep in the last two days and could barely keep his eyes open, and part of it was because he didn't much care for the way Faraday's gaze kept straying from Regan's face to her chest.

Why couldn't the dispatcher have sent the same innocuous middle-aged deputy who'd asked questions the night of the biker gang's attack? But no, instead they'd ended up with an oversexed cowboy who looked way too much like Matthew McConaughey to suit Nash. Didn't the Mammoth County Sheriff's Department have rules against deputies sporting beard stubble on duty?

How long was it going to take this bozo to get Regan's statement down, anyway? Didn't the deputy have anything better to do than stare at . . . oh, my God! No wonder the guy was all überfocused and laser-eyed. Regan Cluny wasn't wearing a bra. He could see her nipples clearly outlined against the thin white cotton of her T-shirt. Twin peaks—round and soft and full and . . . Hell, at this rate they were never going to get rid of the damned lawman.

He shoved himself to his feet. "Would you like something to drink, Deputy?"

"No, thanks."

Instead of returning to his seat behind the desk, Nash grabbed a folding chair and planted himself between Regan and the deputy. Regan shot him a puzzled look that he pretended not to see as he angled his body in such a way as to obstruct the lawman's view of Regan's breasts. Luckily, the change in position in no way interfered with his own view.

"Any idea why someone might have taken a shot at you, Ms. Cluny?" Faraday asked.

"No," Regan said. "But then I have no idea why that gang of bikers tried to kill me, either. I assumed this attack had been arranged by the same lowlife who set my rental car ablaze."

Faraday's gaze sharpened. "You saw him?"

"Well, of course I saw him. It's all in my earlier statement. He first approached me in the parking lot at the Oasis Truck Stop in Chisel Rock."

"No," Faraday said. "I meant the shooter last night. Did you see him? Could you pick him out of a lineup?"

"No, I didn't see anyone, but . . ."

"But what, Ms. Cluny?"

"Who else could it have been? I don't have enemies here. I haven't been around long enough."

"Maybe the shooter wasn't aiming at you," Faraday suggested. "Maybe Mr. Nash was the target."

"Maybe," she said.

"Wealthy men make more enemies than beautiful young women," the deputy said.

Nash glared at him. Not that there was anything wrong with Faraday's conclusion. Rich men did make enemies, and regardless of the actual target, last night's incident had been meant to hurt Nash. It was the "beautiful young women" part of the deputy's speech that irritated him. Where did Faraday get off, flirting at taxpayers' expense?

"Or," the deputy said, "maybe the shots weren't meant to hurt you, just to warn you off."

"Warn us off what?" Regan asked.

"I'm not sure," the deputy said, "but we've had a number of strange calls lately, most of them centered at this end of the county."

"Strange in what way?" Nash said.

Faraday shrugged. "It's been all over the paper."

"So enlighten me," Nash said. "I haven't seen a newspaper in weeks."

"Strange lights in strange places," Faraday said. "Rumors of chupacabra activity. At least three separate cases of exsanguinated livestock."

"Exsanguinated . . . ?" Regan said. "As in someone bled them dry?"

"That's where the chupacabra rumors got started," Faraday explained.

"What's a chupacabra?" Nash asked.

"A goat sucker," Regan said.

"Goat sucker?" he said, thinking he must have misheard her.

"A blood-drinking monster," Faraday said. "Nightmarish creatures that supposedly migrated up here from Central America. Real fairy-tale monster stuff, glowing red eyes and teeth like razors. If you polled the county's Hispanic population, I'm guessing better than half of them would swear chupacabras exist. In fact, I could probably find at least one person who claimed to have seen one."

"Surely *you* don't believe in monsters, Deputy," Nash said.

Faraday pursed his mouth and lifted one shoulder in a halfhearted shrug. "No, but something—or someone—drained three cows and a calf not ten miles from here."

Regan lingered in the office after the deputy left to check out the scene of the crime. She didn't believe in chupacabras any more than she believed in vampires, werewolves, or Bigfoot colonies, but something peculiar was going on in this secluded corner of northern California. "What's your theory, Nash? What do you think killed those cattle?"

"A mountain lion or maybe a pack of feral dogs," he said promptly.

"And did a mountain lion or pack of feral dogs attack me, too?"

"The bite marks on your neck suggest some sort of wild-animal attack," he said slowly, "but it was a very different sort of animal who played tic-tac-toe on your back." He frowned. "You're sure you don't remember what happened?"

"Only bits and pieces. Nothing that makes sense. Frankly, I'm not positive how much of what I 'remember' is real and how much is the product of hysteria." Or drug-induced hallucinations. Her oncologist had warned her of possible side effects.

"Did the bikers have any dogs with them?"

"Not that I saw." She touched the bandage on her neck. "You don't seriously think Harper sicced his pet pit bull on me, do you?"

"I wouldn't put it past him."

He was a good liar. She'd give him that. But his eyes betrayed him. He couldn't hold her gaze. "Why don't you level with me?"

"I can only speculate about what happened. I didn't witness the attack," he said, "only its aftermath."

"I'm not just talking about what the bikers did to me, though I suspect you know more than you're telling about that, too. I mean, what the hell are you doing here in the middle of nowhere?"

He did meet her gaze then. "Haven't you read the tabloids lately? I'm searching for proof that aliens colonized earth thousands of years ago."

She gave an exasperated sigh. "I don't believe that any more than you do, but I don't think you've invested all this time and money just to dig up a small, unimportant Paleolithic site. You're looking for more than spearheads and grinding stones."

He raised an eyebrow. "And you base this theory of yours on. . . ?"

"According to my research, your main field of interest is mythology."

"True."

"And Dr. Thomas Davis, the man you put in charge of the excavation, is well known for finding correlations between ancient legends and archaeological evidence."

"True again."

"So what are you really searching for?"

He studied her face for a moment, then nodded, as if he'd made up his mind. He rummaged in the top drawer of his desk. "Here. Read this." He shoved a sheaf of dog-eared pages into her hands.

"What is it?" she asked. The copies, presumably scans of the original document, were of poor quality, almost impossible to read even if the words hadn't been penned in a looping, old-fashioned script, faded with age and . . . "Written in Latin?" No wonder Nash had been so willing to share. Who, outside the

Vatican, read Latin? Two years of Latin in school and about all she remembered was *veni, vidi, vici.* I came, I saw, I conquered.

"The original manuscript was written by Father Rodrigo Padilla, a Franciscan missionary who worked at the San Carlos mission near Monterey back in the 1700s," Nash explained. "Fascinated with Native American mythology, he documented hundreds of stories, including Modoc legends about a prehistoric race called the Old Ones. It was those legends that sparked my interest in Juniper Basin."

Regan studied the pages in her hand. The word *draco* appeared several times. "*Draco*?" she said. "As in dragon?"

"Or large snake. You read Latin?" Nash said, sounding surprised.

"No. I can tell *tempus fugit* from *e pluribus unum,* but that's about the extent of my knowledge." She frowned. "Tell me you're not searching for a pit of vipers."

Amusement sparked in his eyes. "We're not searching for a pit of vipers. We're searching for a spring, what Father Padilla's manuscript refers to as the 'Font of Miracles.'"

"Miracles?" Surely that didn't mean . . . "Oh, my God! You're looking for the fountain of youth," she accused. No wonder he hadn't set the record straight during his interview on the *Inside Scoop.* Talk about a pathetic, self-deceptive goal. What did he think? That if he found the spring, he could live forever?

"That's one interpretation of the phrase, but not, I think, what the priest meant by it."

"No?" She eyed him with undisguised skepticism. "Then what?"

"According to the legends Father Padilla collected, the spring had therapeutic power. Warriors injured in battle regained their strength more quickly after bathing in its waters. The sick and infirm also benefited from treatment. Think about the implications."

She was.

"If there's even a grain of truth to the story—"

A big if. Monumental. "There's a reason these stories are classified as myths," she said.

"No argument there."

Regan studied his face. He hadn't tried very hard to convince her, had he? Which suggested that maybe he didn't want her to buy into the myth. Maybe he wanted her to write him off as a flake, so she'd forget the story. Maybe this was just a devious attempt to get rid of her.

"Nice try," she said.

"What?" His blue eyes mirrored nothing but confusion.

Damn, the man was good.

Nash wasn't sure what had prompted him to show Regan the Father Padilla manuscript, but her response had been interesting. Instant rejection. The woman didn't believe in miracles. Which suggested that she didn't believe in monsters, either. He'd suspected all along that she remembered more about the bikers' attack than she was willing to admit, but he'd misjudged the reason for her silence. He'd assumed she didn't trust him. But trust wasn't the issue at all. Apparently, the logical side of her brain wouldn't allow her to admit the existence of the supernatural.

And that should have been reassuring, since it meant she wasn't there to expose him as a blood-sucking fiend.

But it also left her vulnerable. She might not be-lieve in monsters, but monsters definitely believed in her. Twice now Harper had come after her. Chances were, she wouldn't escape a third try.

But she was safe enough for the time being. Nash squinted through the blinds at the sunshine flooding the compound. Harper would be in bed now, sleeping off the excesses of the night.

And Elizabeth?

No, he refused to think about Elizabeth. The saucy thirteen-year-old he remembered bore no re-semblance to the bloodthirsty temptress who shared Harper's bed.

Yet even knowing that Harper and his gang posed no threat, Nash had hated sending Regan off to tour the site with Danielle. He'd wanted to keep her in sight. But sunblock offered only short-term protection. By the end of an hour's hike, his perspiration would have diluted its efficiency. In which case, Regan would undoubtedly have noticed when the tip of his nose burst into flames. Might even raise enough suspicions for her to put two and two together despite her deter-mined rationality.

He stared unseeingly at his computer screen.

What was it about Regan Cluny, anyway? Three times now he'd come within a hairbreadth of kissing her, once in her motel room, once out by the petroglyphs, and then once again in his tent when she'd slipped out of her sweatshirt and he'd realized she wasn't wearing anything underneath. Face it, the woman was a walking temptation.

And yes, she looked like Katie, but . . .

No buts. She looked like Katie, she smelled like Katie, she felt like Katie, and he was willing to bet she tasted like Katie, too. Not that he was going to find out. That was one boundary he couldn't afford to cross, because, damn it, she wasn't Katie. Bottom line, he didn't want Regan. Not really. He wanted his Katie.

And Regan didn't want him, either. Not really. She wanted her story.

So, fine. They were on the same page.

And it wasn't because he was attracted to Regan that he'd Googled her. No, he was just trying to figure out why she was pursuing this story so relentlessly when most people would have said to hell with it by now.

He concentrated on the computer screen in front of him.

Now, that was interesting. He hadn't known her father was a well-known Hollywood director. For some reason he'd assumed she'd lived in New York all her life, but no. Regan Cluny, daughter of Desmond Cluny and screenwriter Karin Hanson, had been born in Southern California, though apparently after her mother died of cancer, Regan had been sent back east to boarding school.

No siblings, and oddly enough, considering that her father was a Hollywood legend, no stepmothers.

No mention of any marriages for Regan, either, though he did find one photograph online of her hobnobbing with the rich and famous at a charity event two years ago. In an evening gown with her hair falling halfway down her back, the resemblance to Katie was even more striking.

He wondered why she'd cut her hair.

"So the purpose of all this"—Regan spread her arms to encompass the grid of stakes and string curving around the edge of the basin, the grad students busy with shovels and buckets, screens and brushes—"is to locate the fabled Font of Miracles."

Danielle gave a throaty chuckle. "I think you've seen too many Indiana Jones movies."

"But Nash said—"

"Nash isn't an archaeologist, and he definitely isn't an archaeology student."

"Meaning?"

"He's bankrolling the dig because he's got some burr up his butt about an old legend, but we're involved because practical, on-site experience is as essential to education in our discipline as lectures and research. We've made some pretty amazing discoveries, too—over two hundred spear points, arrowheads, and stone tools, twenty-nine house pits, and a wall of abstract petroglyphs buried under a layer of ash, indicating that they predate the catastrophic seven thousand BP eruption of Mount Mazama."

Regan scribbled furiously in her notebook. "BP?"

"Before the present. In archaeology, it's a time line based on carbon dating; 7000 BP means seven thousand years prior to 1950, when humans began screwing up the atmosphere with nuclear testing."

"You mentioned the eruption of Mount Mazama. That was the volcano that blew its top, forming Crater Lake, right?"

"Actually," Danielle said, "snowmelt collected over time in the sunken caldera to create what we know today as Crater Lake, but yes, essentially, you're right."

"So you're not looking for the magic spring?"

Danielle shrugged. "Not so much not looking as not finding. This area is a spring-a-palooza, but so far none of the springs we've explored has met Nash's criteria."

"So you *are* looking for the springs?" Regan persisted.

Danielle grinned. "Of course we are. With all that money on the line, we'd be foolish not to."

"Money?" Regan scribbled a dollar sign on her notebook, followed by a question mark.

"At the beginning of the summer, Nash promised thousand-dollar bonuses all around if we found the legendary spring. Then a couple of weeks ago, he upped the ante to five thousand apiece."

A couple of weeks ago. About the time his face hit TV screens across the country.

Nash was avoiding her. After finishing the tour with Danielle, she'd gone looking for him, determined to ask about his sudden decision to up the bonuses for finding the spring. But Nash was nowhere to be found. Not in the office, not in his tent, not in the makeshift lab presided over by Dr. Laura Spangler, an anthropology professor from Berkeley.

So instead she'd wandered around the site, asking questions, scribbling notes, and taking photographs. The crew was, without exception, friendly and eager to answer her questions, in sharp contrast to Dr. Davis, whose responses ranged from wary to antagonistic.

"Have I offended you in some way?" she'd finally asked.

He'd blinked in surprise, then said, "You don't belong here. And every minute you stay increases the danger."

"Danger?"

"Harper has you in his crosshairs."

"Who *is* Harper?" she'd demanded. "And what's his connection to Nash?"

Davis had scowled at her, a scowl so fierce that a lesser woman would have turned tail, but Regan was accustomed to dealing with truculent interviewees. "Who's Harper?" she'd repeated.

"Go home, Ms. Cluny," Davis had said. "You'll live longer."

Want to bet? The words had teetered for a second on the tip of her tongue, but she'd managed to keep them from tumbling out.

By noon, her energy reserves were seriously depleted. Food helped, but what she really needed was a nap. So after lunch, she returned to the tent she was sharing with Nash and lay down to rest. When she woke some eight hours later, the sun was balanced like a big red ball atop the mountains to the west, dinner was long over, and Nash was still playing hide-and-seek.

Winston, who wasn't as crotchety as he liked to pretend, offered to make her a roast beef sandwich, but she settled instead for bottled water, an orange, and a bag of trail mix.

Makeshift dinner in hand, she headed for the river, where she settled on a flat rock in the shade under the rope bridge. Carefully she picked all the raisins out of her trail mix and shared them with a couple of inquisitive magpies.

At a guess, the temperature still hovered somewhere in the eighties, but it seemed much cooler in the shade with a whisper of a breeze coming off the water. Something plopped out in the middle of the river. She glanced up, startled, then realized it was only a fish snatching a quick snack from the cloud of gnats hovering just above the water's surface.

Despite the beauty of her surroundings, dissatisfaction settled around her like a dark cloud. She'd slept away half the day, damn it. Not to mention that the man she most needed to question was avoiding her. At this rate, she'd never get her story.

She finished her meal quickly, then leaned over the edge of the rock and plunged her hands into the water, scrubbing vigorously, then shaking off the excess water before drying her hands on her khakis. The river's surface smoothed out. Her reflection swam into focus. Beyond it, a disembodied second face seemed to float just beneath the water.

She screamed and jumped to her feet, her fight-or-flight instinct kicking in. Then in the space between one heartbeat and the next she realized what she'd really seen. A second reflection. She spun around, peering up at the bridge.

Nash hung over the side, regarding her with a bemused expression. "You okay down there?"

"Aside from nearly having a heart attack, yeah, I'm great."

"Sorry if I startled you." He didn't look sorry. In fact, he looked pretty damned pleased with himself. Regan wondered how pleased he'd be if she nailed him between the eyes with one of the rocks edging the riverbank.

"Where have you been all day?" she demanded.

"By all day, do you mean this morning when I drove into Cascade for supplies? Or this afternoon while you were sleeping?"

"You saw me sleeping?"

"Actually, Danielle saw you sleeping. When you didn't show up at dinner, I sent her to look for you."

So he hadn't been avoiding her. "I'm coming up,"

she said. "Trying to talk to you like this is giving me a stiff neck."

"Watch out for snakes," he said. "They like the rocks."

She picked her way carefully up the bank. "No snakes," she announced as she stepped onto the bridge.

Nash stood near the center, leaning against the rope railing and staring down at the river. He didn't respond for a second or two, just peered down at the glassy green water. "Here it is nearly dusk," he said finally, "and there's not another soul in sight."

"Wrong. You're here."

"You didn't know that when you left camp."

"Well, no, but—"

"There've been two attempts on your life just in the past few days. Did it even occur to you that wandering around by yourself might be dangerous?"

"I-I—" She stammered to a stop. "It's only a few hundred feet. I didn't think—"

"You should have, damn it." He met her gaze, no trace of amusement in his expression now. "The truth is, there's no guarantee you're safe with me."

"But you're—"

He met her gaze, and for a second his eyes gleamed red, reflecting the dying sun. "You don't know me, Regan. You don't know me at all."

SEVEN

Nash decided to make an early night of it in hopes that he'd be asleep before Regan came to bed. He'd just settled into a very satisfactory dream involving Regan and the hot tub at his Big Sur estate when Tom barged into the tent and all but dragged him off his cot.

"What?" Nash said. "What's going on? Is everyone all right?" He sniffed at the air. No blood. Just the usual scents of dust, sagebrush, and juniper, with a faint overlay of wood smoke from the evening camp-fire. He glanced over at Regan's cot. Empty. "Have you seen Regan?" Some protector he was.

"She's in the dining tent interviewing Winston, I think," Tom said, shrugging off Nash's concern. "Listen, forget her for a minute. A couple of the kids found a cave." Tom's voice quivered with excitement.

Nash sat up and started pulling on clothes. "How big?"

"Not very. Little more than a pocket, really. Tyler Ciccone's the one who made the discovery. He and

Jenny Weston went off on their own to do a little star-gazing, the kind that necessitates a condom or two. Anyway, at some point Tyler excused himself to go take a leak. He squeezed out of sight behind a scraggly juniper along the cliff, and there it was."

"Is there any indication the early inhabitants used the cave?"

"Definitely," Tom said. "Despite the fact that the entrance would have been underwater back when the lake was full. There's a steep twenty-foot climb to the cave proper, but the good news is, the interior is covered in pictographs, most of them in mint condition, protected as they've been from the elements."

"Did you recognize any of the symbols?"

"Petroglyphs and pictographs fall more into Laura Spangler's area of expertise, but I'm pretty sure I saw both the stylized serpent symbol and the graph for water."

"Any chance it's a map to the sacred spring's location?"

"I don't think so," Tom said, and Nash's hopes took a dive.

"Damn," he said.

"It's not a map, directing us to the sacred spring," Tom said. "It is the sacred spring itself."

Regan stood under the shower, letting the water wash over her and trying not to think, not to worry. "You don't know me, Regan. You don't know me at all," Nash had said. And clear as day she'd heard the words "Yes, I do, Charles."

What was it called when you heard things that weren't there? Auditory hallucinations? Insanity?

Could be her pain meds causing it. Could be the blood loss. Could be a lot of things, some worse than others.

Worry's a waste of energy. That's what her dad always said. And as annoying as the man could sometimes be, he was right about that one. Worry couldn't change a thing. She might as well spend her time and energy on something more productive.

So cheer the hell up, Regan. She forced a smile, grinning hard enough to make her cheek muscles ache. She felt so ridiculous, standing there with the water splashing against her teeth that she laughed for real. Funny thing was, it did make her feel better.

She emerged from the shower to find the camp in an uproar. The grad students seemed to be scurrying in ten directions at once, like a colony of ants whose hill has been disturbed.

"What's going on?" she asked a tall, thin Japanese boy with thick rimless glasses and an incongruous soul patch.

"We're rich," he said, grinning maniacally.

"You won the lottery? What? I don't get it," she said, but he was already too far away to hear.

Halfway back to Nash's tent, she ran into Danielle Lefévre. "What's up?" Regan asked.

Danielle flashed a grin. "They found the spring. Can you believe it?"

"The legendary spring? But earlier you said—"

"Apparently Nash was right and I was wrong."

She grinned again. "It's in a cave, just as the legend predicted. And apparently there are pictographs, too. Dr. Spangler's out there now doing a preliminary examination."

"Out where?"

"Just beyond the grid near section N six. I'm headed that way. You can come along if you want."

"I want," Regan said. "Can you wait? I'll be right back."

Danielle agreed, so Regan took off at a lope, toweling her hair dry as she ran. Nash was gone, she noticed the minute she pushed through the tent flap, his sleeping bag rumpled, as if he'd left in a hurry. She hung her towel over the back of a chair, quickly doctored the wound on her throat, grabbed the digital camera from her purse, and rushed back to Danielle. "Ready whenever you are."

Danielle, used to the altitude and the rocky terrain, set a brisk pace that had Regan breathing hard by the time they reached section N6, where a crowd had gathered at the base of the cliff. Regan bent over, bracing her hands on her aching thighs as she fought to catch her breath.

"You okay?" Danielle asked.

Regan flashed a smile in between huffs. "Just winded. Not accustomed to the altitude yet."

The crowd milled around, laughing and talking excitedly, creating a partylike atmosphere.

Danielle disappeared into the throng, reappearing almost immediately. "This way." She grabbed Regan's arm and dragged her through the sea of bodies toward a scrubby, lopsided juniper that grew close to the rocky cliff. Crushed branches gave off a sharp, medicinal scent. "Make way, folks." Danielle towed Regan through a tight cluster of people and into the space between the tree and the cliff. Here, someone had rigged a spotlight that illuminated a narrow opening in the rock. "Careful," Danielle said. "Watch your step. The surface is pretty rough."

Regan stared at the crack in the cliff. Her heart rate accelerated, not with excitement but with a totally irrational fear. She shuddered.

"Come on," Danielle said, pulling at her arm.

"No," Regan said. "Really, I—"

"Don't be silly. After hiking all this way? You know you want to see the spring as much as I do."

"You go on. I'll catch up with you later."

"But—"

"I'm claustrophobic," Regan admitted. "If I try to squeeze myself through that fissure, I'll have a panic attack. But"—she handed Danielle her camera—"if you'd snap a few pictures, I'd be forever in your debt."

"Deal," Danielle said, and wriggled sideways through the crevice.

Just watching her gave Regan a shuddery butterflies-in-the-stomach feeling. She turned away, intending to find a nice flat rock to perch on while she waited, but she bumped into another of the grad students, this one a burly blond who nearly flattened her. He grabbed her arm to steady her, then grinned and shoved an opened can of Coors into her hand. "Doesn't this totally rock? Come join the party."

Less a party than a chaotic mob scene in Regan's opinion. "Thanks, but no thanks," she said, returning the beer to him, then working her way toward the edge of the crowd. "Have you seen Nash?" she asked the kid she'd spoken to earlier, the one with the soul patch.

"Not for a while." The kid shrugged. "Last I knew he was up at the cave. Funny thing is, he didn't look as happy as you'd expect, what with the big discovery and all. Maybe he's not looking forward to paying out all those five-thousand-dollar bonuses." He raised his beer in a farewell salute, then went off to join his fellow revelers.

Regan chewed thoughtfully at her lower lip. Something didn't add up. They'd found the spring they'd been searching for. They'd proved the legends true. And yet, Nash wasn't happy. She didn't for a second believe it was the thought of paying bonuses that was bothering him. Therefore, it must be something else.

But what?

She spotted Nash then on the far side of the crowd. Soul Patch was right. Nash didn't look happy. As she watched, he detached himself from the group and headed toward the river.

She longed to follow, but wandering off into the darkness by herself was not an option. On the other hand, since she didn't have the nerves to squeeze into that cave, there wasn't much point in hanging around here, either. So the smartest thing to do would be to return to camp and get some sleep.

Figuring there was safety in numbers, she joined a group headed back to camp to replenish their beer supply. Though there were only three of them, they made more than enough noise to scare off any wild animals, and that included Harper.

But when she was halfway back to camp, she spotted Nash again. Head down, hands stuffed in the back pockets of his jeans, he stepped off the far side of the rope bridge and headed down the path along the river, the one that led to the petroglyphs.

Maybe he was going off on his own to reflect on the ramifications of the big find. Or maybe not. He wasn't exactly displaying the body language of a man whose dream had come true.

A sharp twinge of concern brought her to a faltering halt.

One of the kids glanced back over his shoulder. "Something wrong?"

"I'll catch up with you guys, okay?"

"Whatever."

Regan headed on an angle for the bridge, but by the time she'd reached it, Nash was already out of sight.

Nash leaned against a big boulder that edged the path. Though the sun had been down for hours, the rock still radiated warmth. Unfortunately, that warmth did nothing to alleviate the chill of his disappointment.

So close. He'd come so close. This time he'd really thought he had a chance. But maybe he was only fooling himself. Maybe he'd never had a chance at all.

Maybe it was time to face facts, time to come to terms with his situation.

A rustling on the hillside above him put all his senses on high alert. Harper, he thought. But it was only a doe bringing her fawn down to the water to drink. The deer passed within five feet of him, almost close enough to touch. Beautiful creatures, the pair of them, graceful, elegant, and every bit as skittish as he was.

As he watched, the doe froze. She stared in his direction, her ears cocked forward, her muscles tensed, ready to run. Had he inadvertently made some noise?

She stayed that way a second or two while the fawn drank and nibbled at the tender green grass on the riverbank. Then the doe gave a little twitch of her ears and lowered her head to drink.

The night was peaceful but far from silent. Crickets sang in the grass along the water's edge, and the cool night breeze made a steady drone as it wove its way through the branches of the pines, junipers, and mahoganies that clung to the hillside. A frog croaked a greeting and was answered by a second. A fish flopped and rolled somewhere downstream.

Then a shower of loose rocks rattled down the bank ten yards or so from where Nash stood. The miniavalanche bumped and clattered down the slope, landing in the river with a series of small plinks.

The doe panicked, herding her fawn back up the hill. In an instant, they were gone.

Harper, Nash thought. Who else would be sneaking around out here at this time of night?

He ducked behind the boulder, ready to pounce. Nash might not be able to eliminate Harper, but maybe he could pound a little sense into the beast, if nothing else, convince him that Regan Cluny was only a bit player in their little drama.

Liar, his conscience taunted him. Bit players didn't keep the lead up all night, tossing and turning in frustration. The truth was, Regan had a much larger role to play. He just wasn't sure at this point what that role was going to be.

The footsteps approached Nash's hiding place. The arrogant bastard wasn't even trying to be stealthy. Or maybe he didn't realize Nash was so close. One more step and he'd be within range. . . .

Nash launched himself in a flying tackle that sent both of them sliding down the bank to the grassy strip that edged the water.

He landed on top, his legs tangled with Harper's but his hands free. He fumbled for the other man's wrists, determined to immobilize him.

"Stop it!" A sharp gasp. Not Harper's voice. Not Harper's wrists, either. And definitely not Harper's body pinned beneath him. Much too soft and curvy.

"Regan?" He lifted his torso off hers and saw that her T-shirt had ridden up in the struggle, baring one perfect breast.

He shut his eyes for a few seconds, but the image lingered, tantalizing and seductive. Desire flared. He knew how she'd taste—hot and sweet. He knew, too, how she'd feel, straining against him, her nipples tightening under his tongue even as the slender column of her throat beckoned. He wanted. He needed. He hungered. He ached.

He stared at her, and she stared back, surprise, fear, and fascination written across her face.

"Nash?" she whispered.

"Hmm?"

"Your eyes," she said. "They're glowing red."

"An optical illusion." He leaned closer, close enough to nibble at her full lower lip.

"But—"

He outlined her mouth with the tip of his tongue, then sucked at her lip, savoring the sweetness tinged with a hint of fear.

"No," she said, but her denial lacked conviction, accompanied as it was by a moan of pleasure.

"Yes." Nash transferred both her wrists to his left hand, freeing his right so he could touch her, feel the texture of her skin, the throb of her racing heart.

He cupped her breast, and she stiffened in surprise. "Kiss me back," he murmured against her mouth, and felt her shudder. "Kiss me," he said again, his words demanding, his voice husky with need.

Her lips moved against his, tentatively at first, but then as his fingers teased her nipple, as his hips rubbed against hers, the friction unbearably arousing, she deepened the kiss.

Oh, yes. He drank her in, and she tasted just as he'd known she would. Deliciously contradictory. Sweet and seductive.

He played with her nipple and felt it swell to full arousal. "You want me."

"Yes," she said, her voice a ragged whisper.

"Almost as much as I want you." He released her wrists just long enough to strip off her T-shirt, giving him better access to all that soft, smooth skin. "I'm going to make you moan," he promised, then smiled at her startled expression. "I'm going to make you beg." The pulse in her throat fluttered in anticipation as he lowered his mouth to her left breast.

Regan uttered a sobbing sigh when he sucked the nipple into his mouth, and when he increased the torment by teasing her right breast between his thumb and fingers, she moaned and writhed and arched her back.

Her skin was hot and silky smooth. She smelled so good, the rich, spicy scent of female arousal. He licked and kissed his way up her chest, lingering at the hollow of her throat, sucking, tasting, feeling the thrum of her heartbeat under his tongue. Gently, he peeled away the bandage on her neck, revealing her wounds.

"No!" Regan protested.

"It's all right," he said. "I'm not going to hurt you." But he wasn't sure if she believed him. She quivered beneath him, her breathing fast and shallow.

The bite had begun to heal, though the punctures were still red and slightly swollen. Seeing again the marks Harper's henchman had left on her flesh reignited Nash's fury, but he held himself in check, carefully pressing gentle kisses all around the damaged tissue, then delicately licking the wounds themselves, knowing his saliva would hasten their healing.

Regan realized what he was doing and tried to pull away. "No," she said.

"Relax," he whispered. "Enjoy." Then he soothed her with his touch, kissing and stroking her.

"Enjoy?" she repeated breathlessly and then again on a sigh. "Enjoy."

Nash shifted his position so he could focus once more on her mouth. At first he merely brushed his lips across hers in feather-soft kisses, but gradually he increased the intensity and duration of his assault, plundering her sweetness, demanding a response she seemed more than willing to surrender.

At the same time, he used his free hand to play with her nipples, teasing them unmercifully. She moved beneath him, moaning softly and thrusting her body hard against his. She was losing control, rising to a climax. He could hear it in the quickened cadence of her breathing, feel it in the furious flutter of her heartbeat.

Then she stiffened, stifling a scream as the waves of pleasure hit. Her breath sobbed in and out as she squirmed beneath him, rocking hard against his erection. "Please," she begged, her voice ragged. "I want you inside me."

"Not yet."

He unzipped her slacks, then slid his hand inside her panties. Once more Regan's shudders increased in intensity. Again she stifled a scream, this time biting down hard on her lip.

Blood. The scent filled his head, feeding his darkest desires. With a choked growl, he shifted position and lunged for her throat.

Then, just as he was about to claim her in a blood bond, "Charles," she whispered.

Shock waves reverberated through his body. *Charles?* He released her wrists and jerked himself away from her.

Her eyes were shut, her mouth curved in a smile he knew well, mischievous, innocently sexy. Then her eyelashes fluttered. She opened her eyes. Dark eyes. Much darker than Regan's.

Katie? But how?

She blinked again, and his reality shifted. Regan was back.

An illusion. That was all it had been. But it had saved her . . . and him. He shuddered to think how close he'd come to . . . "I'm sorry," he muttered.

"For what?" Regan stared up at him, eyes wide, her swollen lips curved in a puzzled half smile.

"I can't do this. *We* can't do this."

EIGHT

"Have sex, you mean?" Regan said. "Isn't it a little late to change your mind?"

Nash rolled off of her, tossing her discarded clothing at her. He wasn't making eye contact, and that worried her. Had she said or done something to turn him off? She'd tried to hold on, tried hard, but it had been so long and she'd wanted him so badly. . . .

"Nash?" she said again.

"This was a mistake," he said.

She stared at him, but he still wouldn't look at her. She was a mistake. That's what he really meant.

"Get dressed."

Stiffly, she turned away from him. Her hands were all thumbs, clumsy and inept. "I . . . ," she started, then found herself unable to finish. Tears welled up, blurring her vision, clogging her throat.

Nash put a hand on her arm. "Regan—"

"No." She pulled away. She didn't want his pity, damn it.

Humiliated, embarrassed, angry, hurt, she clambered at full speed up the steep bank. A mistake at this altitude. By the time she reached the path, she was panting as hard as if she'd just done an hour on the treadmill.

"Regan, stop," Nash called.

I don't think so, she thought, though she had no choice but to slow her pace.

Behind her, Nash scrambled up the bank, catching her within seconds. She offered no resistance when he grabbed her shoulder and spun her around. "Are you all right?" he asked in what might have been genuine concern. "Sounds like you're having trouble breathing."

"I'm fine, just not used to the elevation." Or rejection.

"You took off so fast. I thought . . ."

"What?"

The moonlight fell full on his face, revealing a surprising mix of emotions—confusion, concern, and . . . was that guilt?

"What?" she said again.

"I thought maybe I'd hurt you."

He thought *maybe*? "News flash, Nash. Rejection hurts. You don't get a woman all hot and bothered, then suddenly go, 'Oh, wait. I think this is a mistake.' Like what kind of mistake? Did you suddenly decide I wasn't good enough for you? What's the problem? Is my hair too short? My breasts too small? Or maybe I'm just a lousy kisser."

"None of the above," he said. "It's not you; it's me. I was wrong to start something I couldn't finish."

"Couldn't finish? Why?"

"For one thing, I don't have any protection with me."

So he hadn't really been rejecting her. He'd been protecting her. She gave a shaky laugh. "Even so, there's more than one way to—"

"Not with me," he said. "There's no way. No safe way. Getting involved with me would be a fatal mistake."

A fatal mistake? What was that supposed to mean? "So it's not just a condom problem," she said slowly.

"No, Harper—"

"Harper? He's tried to kill me twice already. Our having sex isn't going to increase the threat."

"You don't understand."

"You're right. I don't."

He shook his head. "I can't explain."

"Can't or won't?"

"Can't." The stone-face expression was back, a clear signal that he considered the discussion over.

Well, tough. "I've done enough research to be fairly certain you're not involved with anyone else."

"No, I—"

"Female or male." Okay, yes, she *was* trying to get under his skin.

Apparently, she succeeded, too, because his eyebrows rose nearly to his hairline. "I'm not gay."

"Isn't that what I said?" She shrugged. "But if you're not involved with someone else, what's left?" A depressing possibility sucker punched her. "Oh, my God. Disease. That's the problem. You're afraid . . ."

"Something like that," he said. "We can't be intimate. It wouldn't be safe."

He knew. Oh, God. Somehow—from the ER doctor? Deputy Faraday?—he knew. But she wasn't a leper, damn it. Her cancer wasn't contagious.

Just terminal.

Regan turned on her heel and started walking back toward camp. Nash kept pace with her, his flashlight's beam illuminating the path. Neither of them said anything for a long time. Finally Nash broke the silence.

"What were you doing wandering around out here by yourself? You know it's not safe."

"Maybe safety's not my first priority."

"Lucky for you, it *is* mine." He uttered an exasperated sound. "Answer my question. Why were you out here?"

"I was looking for you."

"For me? Why?" He sounded more confused than confrontational. They had reached the rope bridge and could no longer walk two abreast. Nash took the lead, Regan following close behind.

"Because I was worried about you. Everyone else was celebrating the discovery of the spring, but you looked . . . I don't know . . . shattered. Broken. When I saw you heading up the river path by yourself, looking all grim and mysterious, I followed."

"Not so much grim and mysterious as disappointed and angry," he said.

"Disappointed?" she echoed. "Angry? But why? I thought this was your dream come true. You look for the spring. You find the spring. You celebrate." She paused. "So what am I missing?"

"There is no spring," he said.

She stared at the back of his head. No spring? "But—"

"Sometime over the last few thousand years, it dried up. There are mineral stains on the cave wall, evidence that water once seeped from cracks in the rock, but the water's all gone. Maybe it's seasonal. Maybe come spring . . ." He shrugged. "Or maybe seismic activity diverted the flow permanently. All I can tell you is, there's no water dripping down the wall of that cave."

"So? You've still got the pictographs, right? You've still got your proof."

"Proof that the spring existed? Yes. Proof that the legends are true? No."

Nash stepped off the end of the bridge, then turned to help her negotiate that tricky final step. She took his hand, grateful for the assistance as she stepped from the swaying planks to solid ground.

She wasn't prepared for the zap of sexual electricity. One casual touch. Instant zing.

He'd felt it, too. That was why he'd dropped her hand so quickly.

She glanced sideways at him. "What would constitute proof? What exactly do those legends of yours promise?"

"Long story," he said.

She shrugged. "We've got all night." And apparently they weren't doing anything else. "Mind if we rest for a while?" She lowered herself to the ground without waiting for a response.

Nash sat just far enough away to avoid any inadvertent physical contact. More proof that she affected him as powerfully as he affected her.

"According to Father Padilla, the Old Ones, those who were here before the Europeans, even before the present-day tribes, lived on the banks of a silver lake. Life was good. No war. No hunger. No illness."

"Where does the spring come in?"

"Apparently it, along with the lake, was the source of their prosperity. The Old Ones revered the hidden spring as a sacred site. Mothers immersed their newborns in its waters to ensure a long and healthy life. Warriors bathed their wounds in it to speed the healing process."

"So at least in the Father Padilla version, the spring was more a health spa than a fountain of youth."

He nodded.

"And the snake?"

"He was the spoiler, the one who ruined the Old Ones' idyllic existence."

"So it's a Garden of Eden story?"

"There are some similarities," he said, "but more differences. As legend has it, one day a giant serpent came slithering into the village of the Old Ones, demanding to speak to the chief. The serpent claimed that a hunting party had skewered three of his brethren for sport, then left the snakes to die a lingering death, writhing in agony beneath the hot sun."

"And?" she prompted when he fell silent.

Nash stared down at the river. "The serpent demanded justice, saying the chief must forfeit the hunters' lives."

"But the chief refused," she guessed.

"The leader of the hunting party was the chief's only son. He couldn't sentence his own flesh and blood to death."

"So what did he do?"

"He seized his war club and crushed the snake's head. But the serpent's vengeful spirit lived on, calling upon Mountain to avenge his death and the deaths of his brethren.

"So Mountain shook and rattled, tossing out great burning stones that killed many and set the village on fire. The land heaved and cracked. A great hole opened, swallowing the river that fed the silver lake. Eventually, the lake, too, disappeared and with it, the Old Ones. The serpent's revenge was complete."

"What about the spring?" she said.

He shrugged. "Its secrets vanished with the Old Ones."

"Okay." She chewed thoughtfully at her lower lip. "So now that you've found the spring, you have proof that the legends are at least partly true. There really were people living here during the late Pleistocene. Shouldn't you be happy about that?"

"We already knew there was a village. The artifacts and bone fragments we've found prove it. But the spring . . ." His voice trailed off.

And then it all clicked. "Oh, my God," she said. Font of Miracles. Healing power. Disease. Not *her* disease. *His.* "What is it?" she said. "What's wrong with you? Why are you searching so desperately for a miracle?"

"Doesn't matter," he said. "I didn't find it."

She recognized despair when she saw it; her heart ached for him. "I'm sorry."

Nash glanced up at her softly spoken words. The expression in his eyes made her want to cry.

She leaned forward and touched his hand, a gesture meant only to comfort, but he jerked as if she'd Tasered him.

And suddenly he looked so fierce, so wild, so out of control that her stomach did an elevator drop, a twenty-story free fall. His pale eyes seemed to burn into hers, so intense she couldn't look away, so passionate she didn't want to.

"Nash?"

Groaning softly, he reached for her, crushing her lips to his.

Once again, desire licked a fiery path along her nerves.

"Nash!" a strident voice shouted. Tom Davis, damn his soul.

Nash started, like a man jolted out of a dream. Then, swearing viciously under his breath, he scrambled to his feet. "What do you need?"

How about what I *need?* Regan folded her arms and hung on tight, afraid if she didn't she might fly into a thousand pieces. If there'd been a boulder handy, she'd have bashed her head against it in sheer frustration. Damn and damn and damn again.

Tom's flashlight bobbed along ahead of him as he advanced toward them. "It's not what I need. It's what I found." His voice vibrated with excitement.

"What?" Nash said.

"Bones," Tom told him. "The skeleton of a big snake."

Harper, who'd been watching the little drama below the bridge from his vantage point on top of the rim-rocks, wondered what would have happened if Nash's archaeologist buddy hadn't shown up when he had. Nash was attracted to the girl. No doubt about that. But was he attracted enough to lose control? To succumb to his baser impulses?

All he had to do was taste her. One good taste and he was a dead man.

Not that the girl had any clue how lethal she was. Judging by the way she'd reacted to the interruption, Harper was fairly certain she didn't want Nash dead. So what was she after?

Was she purposely using her resemblance to Katie to . . . to . . . to what? That's where he got stuck every time. What did Regan Cluny want from Nash? Money seemed the most likely answer, but somehow it didn't feel right. Still, what else could be driving her? Unless . . .

Could she somehow have learned Nash's secret?

When Tom, Nash, and Regan arrived back at the cliff near section N6, the festivities were still in full swing. Regan suspected the discovery of the bones had given the merrymakers a second wind. Still, who would have guessed archaeology students were such party animals?

Everyone seemed to be talking at once, their voices loud, their mood giddy, no doubt thanks in part to all the empty beer cans and wine bottles littering the area.

Nash leaned down, speaking directly into Regan's ear in order to be heard above the din. "I want to take a look at the bones in situ. You're welcome to tag along."

"No, thanks," she said quickly. Small, enclosed spaces were bad enough. Small, enclosed spaces that harbored snakes—even long-dead snakes—were even worse. "I'll wait out here."

Nash studied her face. "Don't wander off by yourself."

"No," she said. "I'm sure it's much safer here with all the drunken grad students."

He laughed, and Regan's heart stopped beating for a full five count. She'd never seen him laugh before. The man was good-looking even when he scowled, but laughing, he was breath-stoppingly gorgeous, Rhett Butler, Zorro, and Prince Charming all rolled into one. "You've got a point," he admitted, "but wait for me anyway, okay?"

Who could refuse that smile? "Okay," she said.

Nash and Tom squeezed through the crack, and Regan looked around for a familiar face. She didn't have to look far.

"There you are!" Danielle handed Regan her camera. "I thought maybe you'd left. Follow me. This way." She towed Regan off to the fringe of the crowd, where they could carry on a conversation without screaming at the top of their lungs, and plopped down on a fallen juniper. "Got some great shots, including one of the skeleton."

"Thanks." Regan checked the log for wildlife before taking a seat next to Danielle.

A frown suddenly appeared on Danielle's face. "This story of yours. You're not planning to sell it to some sleazy rag, are you?"

"Not unless you consider *National Geographic* a sleazy rag," Regan said. "Why?"

"I'd hate to see you make a fool of Nash, which, considering that we've officially entered woo-woo territory, wouldn't be that hard."

"How does a snake skeleton vault us into woo-woo territory?" Regan asked.

"Not just a snake skeleton. A humongous snake skeleton," Danielle corrected her. "I mean, the thing's got to be thirty feet long. Maybe even longer."

"Like the giant snake in Father Padilla's legend."

Danielle nodded. "And even though the discovery supports the legend, the serpent angle's just odd enough to attract attention from the tabloids. Tom's asked the crew to keep a lid on it, but details are bound to leak out, and when they do, I guarantee the admittedly strange facts will morph into something truly bizarre . . . like talking snakes or laser-eyed snakes or maybe even snakes from outer space."

She snorted again. "Yeah, an alien-reptile invasion."

"Don't scoff," Regan said. "When I was preparing for my interview with Nash, I stumbled across a website devoted to the theory that a race of saurians once inhabited caves beneath the Panamint Mountains near Death Valley."

"Saurians?" Danielle said.

"Intelligent beings, possibly descendants of the dinosaurs that once roamed the earth, or maybe even the remnants of an alien civilization."

"Real *X-Files* stuff." Danielle grinned.

"Oddly enough, the website popped up when I was researching Native American legends."

"I'll have to ask Tom about it. Native American legends are his specialty. He's part Modoc, you know." Danielle sighed. "And a hundred percent sexy."

Dr. Davis? Sexy? The man was attractive enough, but when measured against the Nash yardstick, he came up sadly short.

Danielle shot her a knowing look. "You can't see it, can you? Tall, dark, and grim is what gets you hot and bothered." She stopped. Her teasing smile faded. "Don't get me wrong, Regan. I like Nash, but if I were you, I'd think twice about getting involved with him."

"Why?"

"I don't know. It's just . . ." She frowned. "He's always so damned serious. Don't you think that's strange? I mean, if I were a multimillionaire, you couldn't scrape the smile off my face."

"Maybe Nash has reason to be serious."

"Like what?"

Like being plagued by a mysterious illness? Like being stalked by a psychotic biker?

Someone had set a lantern on a ledge. Its light illuminated the white and ochre pictographs that covered the gray stone walls and the mineral stains that showed where water had once leaked out through the cracks in the rock. "Where's the snake?" Nash asked.

"This way." Tom squeezed through a narrow opening at the back of the cave.

Nash followed.

A larger cavern opened off the first. Nash shone his flashlight over the walls. More pictographs here, and butted up against one wall, the remains of an enormous reptile. In life, it would have been larger than any species currently found in North America, larger than any snake Nash had ever seen outside a zoo. He knelt next to the bones. "Remarkably well preserved," he said.

Tom nodded. "Except for the skull."

"Looks like someone took a sledgehammer to it," Nash said. Splintered bone fragments fanned out in a ragged semicircle.

"War club, according to legend."

"Right." Nash shoved himself to his feet and walked across to examine the nearest pictographs.

"Damn," Tom said. "You're scowling again. What's your problem? We just made the discovery of a lifetime."

Nash turned his frown on Tom. "The spring's dried up."

"Now," Tom said, "at the end of the summer. That doesn't mean it won't be running like a miniature waterfall come spring."

"And if it's not?"

"Then you'll find another way. Chances are, the water had no special properties anyway," Tom said quietly. "Legends shouldn't be taken literally."

"No," Nash agreed. He fell silent for a moment. "I assume we're sending in samples for analysis."

"Of course," Tom said. "Laura collected scrapings already."

Nash studied the snake skeleton. Stumbling across the cave had seemed like an act of providence. But the discovery of a giant snake skeleton . . . that was edging into too-good-to-be-true territory. "Why are the bones here?"

Tom shrugged. "Presumably because this was a sacred spot."

"But think about it. Unless the snake was actually killed here, why would they have gone to all the trouble of moving the corpse?" Nash demanded. "It's hard enough to crawl up to the main cavern now. In those days the entrance would have been underwater, making the journey twice as difficult, especially for someone dragging a dead snake the size of this one."

Tom shone his lantern around the cave, pausing to illuminate the rubble filling the far end. "That may be the answer to your seeming conundrum. Perhaps the lake entrance wasn't the entrance the Old Ones used. Their entrance, the original entrance, probably lies somewhere beyond that caved-in section. At some point the earth shifted enough to collapse the tunnel."

"Maybe," Nash said, but something didn't feel right.

NINE

Still half asleep, Tom stumbled into the office at a quarter past five, only to find Nash already hard at work. Tom grunted a greeting, then shuffled into the kitchenette, beckoned by the aroma of freshly brewed coffee. He poured some into a Styrofoam cup and downed half of it before speaking again. "You're up early."

"Haven't been to bed," Nash said.

"Something wrong?" Tom pulled a chair up to the desk where Nash was working.

"I'm not sure." Nash scowled at the map spread out across the desk. "At first finding the cave and then the bones seemed providential, but the more I thought about it . . . I don't like coincidences. I don't trust them."

Tom spread his hands palms up. "Where's the coincidence? We've spent months searching for the spring."

"But until we drew media attention—"

He studied Nash's troubled expression. "This isn't about the spring, is it? Or at least not entirely. Regan Cluny," Tom said. "That's who has you all worked up." He took another long swallow of his coffee. "Don't think I didn't notice the almost palpable tension between the two of you last night at the bridge. Dead giveaway." He grinned. "That and the grass in her hair."

Nash met his teasing gaze with a scowl. "It's no laughing matter. I came within a hairbreadth of biting her."

Tom shrugged. "So tell Ms. Cluny to pack up and leave. As many people as she's interviewed, as many questions as she's asked, she already has enough information for three or four articles."

"I suppose you're right."

"Hell, yes, I'm right." Tom finished the last of his coffee, then tossed the empty cup at the target taped to the wall. It hit two inches below the bull's-eye and a hair to the left before dropping neatly into the wastebasket. "And Davis sinks the two-pointer to win the game."

"Lucky shot," Nash said.

"Luck, my ass." Tom pinned him with a penetrating look. "What has you confused is this random resemblance between Regan Cluny and your Katie. But it's sheer coincidence. It doesn't mean—"

"It's not just—"

"I know she's gotten to you with that fragile blonde act and those big blue eyes, but—"

"Green eyes," Nash said. "Dusty sage green."

"Damn, if that doesn't prove my point, nothing does. Try thinking with your brain, man. She's a distraction, and with Harper hot on your trail, you don't need a distraction. Tell her to leave. I know you're worried about her safety, but Harper's not going to follow her all the way back to New York."

"No," Nash admitted, though he didn't look convinced.

"Better for her, better for you." Better for the dig. Tom trusted Nash. He did. Under normal circumstances. But a vampire suffering from testosterone overload was a disaster waiting to happen. "We're agreed, then? You'll talk to her?"

"I'll talk to her," Nash said.

Angry and resentful, Katie O'Malley felt like a naughty child forced to do penance as she sat at the big desk in Papa's study. Outside, the sun shone. Bees hummed among the magnolias just now starting to blossom, and birds—wrens, sparrows, robins, and jays—flitted back and forth. Inside, the blank sheet of parchment Papa had laid out seemed to mock her, as did his well-worn King James Bible, casually opened to Ephesians 6:1: "Children, obey your parents in the Lord: for this is right."

Right? What was right in what she was being forced to do?

Charles Nash was a good man, and she loved him with all her heart. The color of his uniform couldn't change that. Nor could her father's tirades, her mother's tearful pleading.

But she would acquiesce to their demands, at least until she'd squirreled away enough money for the journey north. If only there were some way to apprise Charles of her plan . . .

She stared at the paper, realizing the futility of that desire almost as soon as it sprang to mind. Papa would surely read this letter and any other she might try to send. He and Mama had been watching her like hawks ever since he'd demanded that she sever her ties to Charles.

It wasn't fair. It wasn't right. But she had no choice, none at all. She picked up the pen, dipped it in the inkwell, then wrote, "Darling Charles, my heart is breaking as I pen these words. Papa says I must end our engagement." One fat tear rolled down her cheek and splashed on the word "engagement," blurring it beyond recognition.

Regan woke with tears on her cheeks. She couldn't remember the details of her dream, but its emotional components—resentment and an almost unbearable sadness—lingered even after she'd dressed and made up her cot.

Nash's rumpled bedding looked just as it had last night when she'd stopped by to grab her camera. Apparently, he hadn't returned to bed. After walking her back to camp last night, he must have returned almost immediately to the cave.

He hadn't said much on the walk to the compound, but after what had happened between them on the petroglyph path, she'd expected some acknowledgment, a quick embrace, a fleeting kiss, before he headed off again into the darkness. Instead, he'd muttered a gruff "Don't wander off," as if she were a disobedient child. An irritating and disobedient child.

Idiot, she thought, not sure if she meant Nash or herself.

Normally the dining tent was bursting at the seams by a quarter to six in the morning. Today it was virtually deserted. Off to one side, her friend Soul Patch raised a finger in greeting, then continued spooning cereal into his mouth with a martyred determination.

Regan had little appetite for breakfast herself, but she ate anyway. She still had a handful of pills to take, and they wouldn't settle well on an empty stomach.

"You look a little green around the gills this morning." Danielle plonked down a tray loaded with French toast, eggs over easy, and smoked link sausages.

Regan, who was having enough trouble downing cornflakes, nearly gagged at the smell.

"What's wrong? All the partying get to you?" Danielle grabbed a pitcher from the center of the table and drowned her French toast in maple syrup.

Regan uttered a noncommittal response. She hadn't done any partying, not in the sense Danielle meant. She'd never been much of a drinker, but nowadays she avoided alcohol entirely. Doctor's orders.

"Fun while it lasted," Danielle said, "but it's back to the old grind today." She stabbed a sausage. "For you, too, I guess. How's your story coming?"

"Slowly," Regan said. The truth was, she had more

than enough material to flesh out an article on the dig, especially after the big discoveries yesterday. What she was still searching for was a human-interest angle. And Nash just might provide it. Handsome as sin, rich as Croesus, and apparently afflicted with an ailment no doctor could cure, he had funded this excavation in his quest for a miracle. Or so she'd gathered from what he'd said last night.

Only he didn't look sick. And he didn't act sick, either. In fact, he'd seemed pretty lively there for a while.

So the question was, what was Nash's deep, dark secret, and what impact did that secret have on his decision to fund the dig?

Plus, she wouldn't mind knowing exactly why Harper was so hell-bent on Nash's destruction. Because of Katie, Nash had said, the woman from their past, the woman she apparently resembled. Only there had to be more to the story than jealousy and unrequited love.

Didn't there?

Okay, then. First order of the day: a serious cards-on-the-table talk with Nash.

"I almost slept in this morning," Danielle said. "Glad now I didn't." She nodded toward the entrance where Dr. Tom Davis stood blinking as his eyes adjusted from the early morning light outside to the relative darkness inside the tent. She smiled at him. And he smiled back, then headed their way.

As Tom approached, Regan applied herself to her cornflakes and did her best impression of invisible.

With any luck, she wouldn't even have to make eye contact.

"Morning," Danielle said. "What's on the docket for today? Are we working the cave?"

"Some of us are," he said, "though you're assigned to section B sixteen."

"Unfair! You get to examine petroglyphs and bones while I'm stuck sifting through bushels of earth for a few obsidian flakes?"

"It's a dirty job, but somebody's got to do it."

"Ha-ha." Danielle made a disgusted face, and Tom Davis laughed, making Regan think maybe he wasn't so bad after all. At least he had a sense of humor.

"Ms. Cluny?"

Regan glanced up. So much for invisibility. "Yes?"

Davis was still smiling, but all the warmth and charm were gone. He'd edged into smirk territory, as if he knew something she didn't know, and whatever the big secret was, she wasn't going to like it. "When you're done here, Nash would like to see you in the office."

Nash had spent the long hours of the night creating a transparent overlay for his topographical map of the area. The overlay, based on information from the county assessor's office, labeled the land according to ownership. The property encompassing the dig site was marked "Summers Land Development," SLD being a subsidiary of C. C. Nash, Incorporated. A large section to the north and east was public land under the control of the Bureau of Land Management.

The rest of the surrounding properties were farms and ranches ranging from twenty to three hundred and sixty acres.

The properties he was most interested in were those within hiking distance of the dig, particularly those to the southwest since that's where the so-called chupacabra activity had been reported. Nash was no expert on goat suckers, but he did know vampires. If Harper and his gang were hiding out nearby, they'd be feeding nearby as well.

He marked the three most likely possibilities, properties deeded to Kevin Ransom, Everett and Marigold Casper, and T. E. Spinelli. Then he checked the local phone directory for corresponding telephone numbers. Ransom and Casper he found, but there was no listing for Spinelli, which was a little suspicious. Who didn't have a phone in this day and age? Of course, maybe it was a new listing or an unlisted number. Or maybe Spinelli relied on cell service.

Or . . . maybe Spinelli was a front for Harper.

Nash put in a call to the sheriff's department, hoping Deputy Faraday might know something about the three landowners, Spinelli in particular, but he hit a dead end. Faraday was out on a call. The woman who answered the phone said she'd leave him a message to contact Nash as soon as possible.

Nash was just hanging up when a brief knock on the door heralded Regan's appearance.

"Dr. Davis said you wanted to see me."

Damn. He'd told Tom that he'd speak to Regan

about leaving, a task that he now suspected was going to be easier said than done. "Ah, yes," he said. "Have a seat."

She dumped a bundle of stakes and a roll of twine off a folding chair and onto the floor, then, positioning the chair across the desk from him, sat down. She tapped his makeshift two-layer map. "Does that show details of the dig site?"

"The dig and the surrounding area," he said. "I'm playing detective, trying to figure out where Harper might be headquartered."

"When you do, let me know."

He cocked an eyebrow in an unspoken question.

"I'll sic the cops on him."

"It's a deal," he said, even though he knew the Mammoth County Sheriff's Department stood no chance against Harper.

A smile lit Regan's face. Even so, she looked exhausted.

"Did you get any sleep at all last night?"

"I look that bad, huh?"

"You couldn't look bad if you tried," he said, meaning it, though judging by her expression, she didn't believe him.

"So," she said. "Why the summons? Am I in trouble? Did I break some unwritten archaeological-dig-site law?"

"You're not in trouble yet, but if you hang around here much longer, you will be." He frowned at the thought of all the ways Harper could hurt her.

"You want me to leave."

"I do. You have plenty of material for your story. It's time to move on."

"What about us? What about what happened last night?" She was playing it tough, but it didn't take a genius to see the hurt that lay just beneath the surface.

"Nothing happened," he said slowly. Though he still wasn't sure how he'd been able to stop when he had. "Nothing happened," he repeated, "and nothing's going to happen."

He could feel the pain reflected in her eyes as if it were his own. He thought for a second that she was going to cry. Then her eyes iced over and her jaw set in a stubborn line. "All right. That's clear enough," she said. "Here's the deal, then. Answer my questions and I'll leave without an argument."

Apparently reading his lack of response as agreement, she pulled out a notebook and pen. "What's your big secret, Nash? What are you searching for? What do you want? Tell me, and maybe I can help you find it."

I want you, he thought. *I want you in ways you can't begin to imagine, thank God, because if you did, you'd run screaming in the opposite direction.*

Only . . . wasn't that the plan? To get her to run far, far away, where neither he nor Harper could hurt her? Hell, maybe he *should* tell her the truth.

Right, and what happens if her writerly curiosity overpowers her fear?

"Nash? Did you hear what I said?"

"I heard." He frowned. "I'm going to be blunt here,

and I apologize in advance if I hurt your feelings. The thing is, I don't need your help. I don't want your help. Yes, I'm attracted to you, but for reasons I won't go into, we have no future. Under other circumstances . . ." He shrugged. "But right here, right now, you are a liability. The sooner you go back to New York, the better." There, he'd said it. And she wasn't crying and she wasn't screaming and she wasn't storming out. He stared at her uneasily. "Regan?"

"Ms. Cluny," she snapped in the tone of voice normally reserved for the choicer epithets, a hearty "Fuck you," for example.

"I can have Danielle drive you down to Reno."

"I'll take you up on that," she said, "as soon as I have the answer to my question. But until then . . ."

"Be reasonable."

"Reasonable Regan. That's me. Answer my question and I'm gone." She paused. "No response? Well, I can't say I'm surprised." She stood. "Once I get my notes organized, I'll start working on my article. You won't mind if I use your computer, will you, since my laptop burned up along with my rental car?"

"Regan, I don't think—"

She headed for the door. "That's settled, then." She flashed a phony smile in his direction, then slammed the door so hard the whole trailer rattled.

Adrenaline saw Regan through a morning of walking the dig and asking questions. The facts were fascinating, more interesting by far than the science fiction nonsense in the tabloid story. Besides the snake skeleton, the site had yielded a number of random bones, many of them from large, now-extinct mammals, presumably a food source for the "Old Ones."

"But you say you've found only one human skeleton?" she asked her old friend Soul Patch, whose real name turned out to be Preston Nakahara. He was carefully cataloging the latest finds, working in the meager shade of a canvas awning. "Doesn't that seem odd to you? I mean, this appears to have been a good-size settlement. Wouldn't you have expected to have discovered more human remains?"

"We think they cremated their dead, possibly by sending their flaming funeral pyres floating off across the lake à la King Arthur," he said. "Hand me that magnifier there on the crate, would you?"

Regan passed him the magnifier, and he carefully examined what looked like an ordinary chunk of obsidian.

"Tool marks," he said. "Interesting."

"If they routinely cremated their dead, though," she said, "how'd your human skeleton slip through the cracks?"

"That's it." He shot her a big, goofy grin. "He slipped through the cracks. Literally."

"I don't follow."

"We found him in a lava tube. We theorize that he ventured inside looking for something, stumbled into a hole, and broke his neck."

"But if this happened as long ago as you say—"

"Ten thousand years, give or take," he said.

"If they're that old, wouldn't the bones have turned to dust?"

"The cave preserved them," he explained. "It was sort of like keeping the remains in a refrigerator for ten millennia."

"Poor man," she said. "How tragic to die that way, separated forever from your loved ones. Have you gotten any flak from the local tribes? Anybody demanding his body be released for proper burial?"

"No, though it's happened elsewhere. We've been lucky so far . . . if you don't count all Nash's unwelcome media attention, that is." He passed her the rock and the magnifying glass. "Here. Check it out."

Even magnified, the rock just looked like an ordinary chunk of obsidian.

"Cool, huh?"

"Umm," she said, handing it back.

"Funny thing about that skeleton." Preston set the obsidian carefully back in its nest of shredded paper. "The man was fairly big—we estimate eight or nine inches above five feet and heavy boned, with good teeth."

"What's so strange about that?"

"Nothing. Why?" Preston stared at her blankly.

"You said—and I quote—'Funny thing about that skeleton.'"

"Oh." He nodded. "Right. I meant because of his skull."

"Why? Was he a Neanderthal or something?"

"No, he was definitely *Homo sapiens*. But instead of the broad cheekbones typical of present-day Native

Americans, he had a long, narrow Caucasoid skull."

Regan stared at Preston. "So you're saying the Old Ones were Caucasians?"

"Now you sound like the guy from the *Inquisitor*, leaping to unwarranted conclusions. No, that's not what I'm saying. You can't make sweeping conclusions based on a single skull, but if this skull is representative, it would mean that the Modocs were likely not direct descendants of the Old Ones. That isn't to suggest that the Old Ones were some clan of lost Vikings. They could just as easily have immigrated to North America from Southeast Asia or the South Pacific, for that matter. The jury's still out."

By noon, Regan's energy was running low. Feeling weak and shaky, she swallowed a handful of pills, then proceeded to the dining tent, where she forced herself to eat homemade vegetable soup and a grilled cheese sandwich.

After lunch, she went back to the office. There she commandeered the computer, easy enough to do since no one else was around. Before starting her article, she did a quick Google search on early Americans and learned that Preston was right about the jury being out. Nobody disputed the old theory about people crossing a land bridge over the Bering Strait during the Ice Age, but since the discoveries of several Pleistocene and early Holocene skulls at various sites throughout the West, skulls that didn't display the characteristic short, wide facial structure of northern Asia, scientists had come up with a plethora of theories to explain the discrepancies and used the wonders of modern forensic anthropology as evidence, all of which merely served to convince Regan that archaeology was an inexact science.

Just as she was finishing up her preliminary outline, Tom Davis came through the door. He saw her, did a classic double take, then demanded, "What are you doing in here?"

"I have permission from Nash." Which she did. Sort of.

"I thought you were leaving."

"Change of plan."

"Meaning?"

"I'm *not* leaving. Not yet. Not until Nash tells me his big secret." She felt like adding that grinding his teeth was hard on his enamel but managed to restrain herself. Instead, she saved her document, closed out of Word, and stood. "If you'll excuse me, I think I have just enough time for a nap before dinner."

He watched in silence as she made her way to the door. Hopefully, her baggy pants disguised the shaky weakness of her legs.

"Be careful, Ms. Cluny," he said just as she put her hand on the doorknob. "Some secrets should stay hidden."

She glanced at him over her shoulder, planning to deliver a smart-alecky comeback, but changed her mind when she saw the expression on his face. Gone was the antagonism. He looked genuinely concerned.

"Things aren't always what they appear," he said.

TEN

Regan's nap hadn't done much to raise her energy level. She'd hoped dinner would help, but so far, she was still hovering about halfway between exhausted and comatose.

"This grilled trout is fantastic," Danielle said. "You should try it, Regan."

Regan picked an almond sliver out of her salad. "I'll get there." Eventually. She'd never cared much for fish. "I'm still a little groggy after my nap."

"I can't sleep during the day." The comment came from one of the female grad students, a stocky strawberry blonde with freckles and a sunburned nose.

"Not a problem for me," Tyler Ciccone said. "Sleep all day, play all night. That's my lifestyle of choice."

Regan tried a bite of the trout. It was better than she'd expected, though it still tasted like fish.

"Man, are you in the wrong line of work or what?" her buddy Preston said to Tyler. "Archaeologists and dedicated hedonists fall on way opposite ends of the spectrum."

"No sh . . . kidding," Tyler said. "This summer's been a huge eye-opener. I'm changing programs come fall. Archaeology's totally not what I expected. Too much sweating. Not enough adventure."

Preston nodded. "Indiana Jones syndrome, a common affliction. You were secretly hoping to be chased by Nazis across two continents."

"Was not," Tyler said.

"Were too," Preston insisted.

"Knock it off," Tom ordered from the other end of the table, where he'd been eating in a distracted daze while working a sudoku puzzle. "I can't concentrate."

Regan forced herself to take another bite of fish.

"What are you guys going to do with your five grand?" Tyler asked.

"Pay off some school loans," Danielle said promptly.

"Ditto," Preston said.

"Double ditto." The strawberry blonde was starting on dessert.

"Boring," Tyler said. "Me, I'm going to spend about a month in Thailand, scuba diving by day and partying by night."

"I thought you were a sleep-by-day guy," Preston said.

"Got it covered," Tyler said. "I'll sleep on the dive boat on the way to and from the reef."

The banter between the two boys continued, but

Regan lost track. Nash had just entered the dining tent.

He stopped at Tom's end of the table. Regan tried to catch his eye, but she might as well have been part of the scenery for all the attention he paid her.

"Tom," he said, "could you stop by the office when you've finished eating? Just got Laura's preliminary report on the snake skeleton, and I'd like to go over her findings with you."

"If I met face-to-face with a snake that size in real life," Danielle said, "I'd have a heart attack."

"Pretty freaky," Preston agreed.

"Sure," Tom told Nash. "I'll finish up here and be right over."

Something was up. Nash looked and sounded the same as he always did, but Regan's nose was twitching up a storm. Something—besides her half-eaten dinner—was fishy.

Nash was already seated behind the desk, pouring himself a bourbon by the time Tom showed up at the office. "You want a drink?" Nash offered.

"Sure, not the hard stuff, though." Tom helped himself to a cup of coffee, then pulled a chair up to the desk and sat down. "What's up?"

"I had a hunch somebody was jerking us around. That's why I asked Laura not to let any grass grow under her feet." Nash handed Tom a copy of her preliminary report.

"What the hell?" Tom shot Nash an incredulous look. "According to this, the snake is a reticulated python. What's a native of humid Southeast Asia doing in the high desert of California?"

"Good question. But the real kicker comes a couple of paragraphs down. Seems those 'ancient' bones we found aren't ancient at all. Like I said, somebody's jerking us around."

"But the pictographs . . . ," Tom said.

"Laura's ninety percent convinced that they're fakes, too, though whoever drew them knew what he was doing." He paused. "Who's been off site recently?"

"You think one of the crew set this up?"

"Who else could have?" Nash said.

Tom paused with his coffee cup halfway to his mouth. "How about Regan Cluny?"

"She lacks the specialized knowledge necessary to create the illusion. And besides, she hasn't left camp."

"She could have paid someone else to set it up." Tom took a swallow of his coffee.

"Why would she?"

"To spice up her story, of course."

Nash shook his head. "She's an award-winning writer. She doesn't need to resort to gimmicks." But he could tell Tom wasn't convinced. "You didn't answer my question. Who's left camp in the last two weeks?"

Tom shrugged. "Everybody. Half the crew went to the rodeo in Cascade the Saturday before last. Even Winston. His grandson's a bull rider."

"And the other half?"

"Were off this past weekend. Some of the girls

took the Explorer to Redding. Danielle organized a big shopping trip."

Nash frowned. "So the bottom line is, everyone had opportunity."

"Opportunity for what?" Tom took another sip.

"To pick up the reticulated python skeleton."

"Where, though? That's not exactly something you could find at the local supermarket." Tom finished his coffee in one long gulp, then set the cup down on the desk.

"I suspect that whoever staged this probably already had the snake skeleton," Nash said. "When they heard the legend of the serpent and the Old Ones, they decided to cash in."

"Cash in?"

"On those five-thousand-dollar bonuses."

Tom rolled the empty Styrofoam cup between his hands. "Damn it, I think you're right. It wasn't Regan Cluny. It was one of the grad students. How stupid do you have to be to compromise a dig and destroy your academic career for a lousy five K?"

"I shouldn't have offered the bonuses."

"Don't blame yourself. Money can't corrupt an honest person." He left, so upset he didn't stop to lob his empty cup at the target on the wall as he usually did.

Nash reached across the desk, grabbed the cup, swiveled around in his chair and aimed for the bull's-eye. The cup hit dead center, then dropped into the wastebasket. "Nash sinks a three-pointer. And the crowd goes wild."

"Woo-hoo," someone said behind him.

He spun around to see Regan standing in the doorway.

"Sorry. That's as close as I get to going wild," she said. "Am I interrupting something important, or can anyone play?"

He tucked Laura's report into a folder and set it aside. "What do you need?"

"Some straight answers. First, you show up at dinner and do the mysterious 'Meet me in the office, Dr. Davis' thing. Then Tom clumps out of here so depressed he doesn't even have the energy to shoot a dirty look in my direction." Her gaze met his. "Something's going on, and I want to know what. Did one of the local tribes file a lawsuit to try to gain possession of your Paleo-Indian remains? Did Deputy Faraday get a line on the bikers' whereabouts? Did Harper issue some scary ultimatum?"

"None of the above," he said.

"Like you'd tell me even if I guessed right," she said.

"How would you like to spend a long weekend at Big Sur?"

She studied his face for a moment. The room was so silent he could hear the hum of the refrigerator in the kitchenette, the ticking of the clock on the wall by the door.

"No response?" he said.

"I'm confused," she said. "This morning you were doing your level best to get rid of me, and now you're issuing invitations. Was that a 'Let's go away for a weekend of crazy sex' invitation? Or more of a diversion, a sort of 'Let's get the nosy writer out of camp before she figures out what's going on' invitation?"

"Neither," he said, which wasn't precisely the truth, but . . . "I have a vault full of research material at my place in Big Sur. Old books and manuscripts, interviews, oral histories on tape. I have copies of some of the information here, but something's come up, a glitch of sorts, and I feel the need to delve more deeply into my research."

"You mean in case you missed something the first hundred times," she said.

He raised his eyebrows. "Something like that. And I don't want to leave you here alone."

"In case Harper decides to take out the security guards and half the crew to get to me."

"I was more worried about your wandering off."

"Hey, I am *not* one of those too-stupid-to-live heroines from a slasher flick."

"And yet twice you've wandered away from camp by yourself." He shrugged. "If you don't want to go to Big Sur, say so and I'll make other arrangements."

"What sort of other arrangements? Accuse me of some bogus crime and have the sheriff lock me up for the weekend?"

"No, I was thinking more along the lines of dropping you off at a hotel in San Francisco."

"My story's not in San Francisco," she said slowly, but her expression was so guarded, he couldn't tell what was going on inside her head.

"So that's a yes?"

"When do we leave?"

"In about thirty minutes," he said.

She blinked in surprise. Then a smile tilted the corners of her mouth. "Wow. Way to sweep a girl off her feet." She headed for the door. "Guess I'd better go pack my . . . Wal-Mart sack."

She disappeared, and Nash started wondering if he'd lost his mind. Yes, Regan might be in danger from Harper if he left her behind, but taking her with him. . . ? That might prove an even more dangerous alternative.

Harper hated driving the van. The damn thing steered like a bowlegged elephant. But Elizabeth refused to ride on the back of his Harley. Wearing a helmet mashed her hair.

"You promised me a treat," she said. "I'm sick to death of pig blood. I don't see why we can't have cow blood once in a while."

"Because we can't risk any more reports of chupacabra activity. Someone in the sheriff's department might put two and two together."

"Chupacabras." Elizabeth rolled her eyes. "People are such fools."

"But delicious fools," he reminded her.

She flared her nostrils. "Or so you promised."

"Petulance doesn't become you, sweetheart. It's not my fault none of the potential donors at the Oasis was to your taste."

"Flabby old men, wrinkly old women, and acne-faced teenagers," Elizabeth complained. "Is it any wonder I lost my appetite?"

"Which is why we're headed for Cascade. A larger population equals more potential donors." He might have elaborated on that, but they'd reached a twisty stretch of road with a rocky cliff on one side and a steep drop-off on the other. Unfortunately, the van's steering wheel seemed to have a mind of its own, and that mind was dead set on checking out the slope on the wrong side of the guardrail.

Elizabeth leaned closer, rasping her fingernails lightly across his denim-covered thigh. "Harper," she whispered in his ear, "why don't we just keep driving until we hit L.A.? Lots of tasty little morsels down there. No need for a girl to go hungry."

Each pass of her nails sparked a little shock wave of pleasure. "Keep your hands to yourself, sweetheart. I'm trying to drive," he protested as they kissed the guardrail.

"Spoilsport." She kept up the rasping with one hand while burrowing into his pocket with the other.

He went rock hard in two seconds flat.

With the ease of long practice, Elizabeth loosened his belt, popped the snap on his jeans, and tugged down his zipper.

"No," he said, a halfhearted protest because hell, he knew what was coming and damned if he really wanted to stop her.

"Yes," she said. Then she put her face in his lap and buried her teeth in his swollen flesh.

Pain blinded him for a second, but only a second. Then her mouth and lips closed around him. The alternating agony and ecstasy seemed to last forever. Harper drove on autopilot.

He climaxed in a final explosion of pain and pleasure and heard Elizabeth's crooning sigh of satisfaction.

Moving languidly but with exquisite grace, she sat up, then zipped him back into his jeans. He watched in fascination from the corners of his eyes as she used the tip of her tongue to delicately lick the last of his blood from her lips.

Then her eyes widened and her lips formed an *O*. "Watch out!" she said, seconds before they ran over something with an ominous ba-dum, ba-dum. Like railroad tracks only not as solid.

"Damn, I think we hit a deer." He slowed, easing the van to the side of the road.

"Not unless deer stick their thumbs out," Elizabeth said.

"What?"

"It was a hitchhiker. I saw him right before you ran him down. Young guy. Big, blond, athletic-looking."

Harper backed slowly, thankful for the late hour and the consequent dearth of traffic. He watched the crumpled form grow closer in the rearview mirror. Not so much athletic-looking as dead-looking. The young man's head had taken a direct hit.

He stopped the van and Elizabeth piled out. "Road kill," she said, a lilt in her voice.

• • •

Katie, who'd spent her morning paying a duty call on Widow Rankin, one of her father's housebound parishioners, got caught in a rainstorm on her walk home and arrived back at the parsonage with her bonnet soaked, the hem of her gown splattered with mud. Someone had left a strange horse and buggy tied up outside.

Her breath caught on a sharp inhalation. She pressed both hands to her breast. *Charles,* she thought. *Charles has come for me.*

Unlikely, her common sense warned.

But possible, her heart argued. Charles loved her, and there was nothing Mama and Papa could do to change that or the fact that she loved him back.

Charles.

Heedless of her muddy shoes and wet clothing, Katie marched through the empty parlor, heading straight back to the kitchen, where Delia was rolling out pastry at the big table in the center of the room. "Have you seen Mama?"

"Lordy, child. What happened to you? You look like a drowned rat."

Katie stripped off her bonnet and tossed it onto one of the ladder-backed kitchen chairs. "It's raining. Again." They hadn't seen the sun in a week.

"I told you to take your papa's big black umbrella, didn't I now? But you never listen to a word I say. Nobody listens. Might as well be talking to myself." Delia thumped her rolling pin down on a lump of dough.

"I'm sorry, Delia. I surely should have heeded your

advice," Katie said. "By the way, Widow Rankin was mightily pleased with your huckleberry preserves."

"'Course she was," Delia said. "Probably the first she's seen since Polly died. That new girl of hers don't do nothing she don't have to." Delia dug a rag from one of the capacious pockets of her apron and handed it to Katie. "Wipe your shoes, child. You're making a mess of my kitchen."

Katie sat on the bench next to the back door and dutifully cleaned the mud from her slippers, trying not to think about the conniption fit Delia would throw when she saw the mess in the parlor. "Where's Mama?" she asked.

"Miss Amy come down with the headache a while back. I fixed her some willow bark tea and told her to get some rest, but that girl's just like you. She never listens to a word I say." Delia, a free woman now, though born into slavery, had taken care of Mama since she was a child. "I expect Miss Amy's up in her sitting room working at her 'broidery. I tell her that close work's going to ruin her eyes, but she don't pay me no more mind than she does them magpies chattering away in the berry patch."

Delia's last few words chased Katie up the back stairs, which she took two at a time, despite her tight corset and voluminous petticoats. She raced down the upstairs hall with Mama's oft-repeated words echoing in her ears—*Gentlemen have no respect for a hoyden, Mary Katherine*—and burst into Mama's sitting room. "Whose horse and buggy is that out front?"

Her mother glanced up sharply from her needlework, a frown furrowing her brow. "It's not ladylike to run, Mary Katherine. Gentlemen have—"

"—no respect for a hoyden. Yes, I know, Mama. Who's here?" Katie fully expected to be dressed down for her saucy tongue. Instead, an odd expression rippled across her mother's face, neither trepidation nor sorrow but with elements of both. "Mama?" Despite the muggy August heat, a tiny frisson of alarm shivered down Katie's spine. "Is something amiss?"

"Your cousin Harper's come to call," Mama said. Harper Wakefield wasn't really Katie's cousin, not by blood. His mother had married Mama's brother, Spencer Mayhew, after her first husband, Harper's father, had died of the cholera two years before Katie was born. Which made them kissing cousins, according to Harper, a claim Katie had never disputed. Of all her relatives, he was the only one who made her laugh, the only one who didn't bore her to tears with endless lectures on propriety. She doubted Harper, a born charmer and a shameless flirt, even knew what propriety was. "He brings news of Charles," Mama said.

Katie's heart lurched. Charles. Somehow she'd known this had something to do with Charles. But mercy, wasn't it more than passing strange to hear his name again on Mama's lips? For months now, he'd been "your former fiancé," "that friend of Harper's," or, more often than not, "that Yankee."

"Where is Cousin Harper?" Katie asked. "In Papa's study?"

"Yes, but—"

Katie left before her mother could finish the sentence, unwilling to hear the "You mustn't disturb them" part. She clattered down the front stairs to Papa's office. The door was shut, which was customary when Papa was working on a sermon but unusual when he was entertaining a guest. She tapped once, then let herself in without waiting for an invitation. Cousin Harper, after all, wasn't a real guest. He was family. And more important, he brought news of Charles.

Papa glanced up, a frown on his brow. He and Harper had been sitting in wing chairs facing each other across a mahogany piecrust table, but as soon as she entered, both men stood. According to the grandfather clock against the wall behind Papa, it was scarcely a quarter to eleven, and yet Papa had poured out two glasses of Mama's elderberry wine. Cousin Harper's was half empty. "You're interrupting," Papa said.

"I'm sorry. I couldn't wait. Mama told me Cousin Harper brought word of . . ." Her voice trailed off to silence. One look at Cousin Harper's shadowed eyes and she knew. Her heart seized up. "The news is bad, isn't it?" She glanced from one familiar face to the other, searching for some glimmer of hope. "Charles? He was captured, wasn't he?"

Her father plucked at his waistcoat, avoiding her eyes. "We'll discuss this later."

"Now," she said, a little shocked at her own boldness. "We'll discuss it now. He was captured, wasn't he?" she repeated.

"No," Cousin Harper said, his expression indecipherable.

"Injured?"

Cousin Harper inclined his head. "At Manassas."

Injured, she thought. Charles injured. She stared at the window behind Papa's desk. Raindrops coursed down the glass, distorting the view of the garden.

Papa forbade any talk of war in the parsonage, but she'd heard whispers around town. Though accounted a major victory for the Confederacy, both sides had suffered considerable losses in the battle at Manassas. Considerable losses and horrific injuries. Bodies mangled. Limbs severed.

But she didn't care how severe Charles's injuries might be. She'd love him no matter what. Charles with a mangled arm or a missing leg was still her Charles. "How bad is it?"

Katie glanced up in time to catch a glimpse of the grim look that passed between her father and Cousin Harper.

"How bad?" she whispered, her voice nearly inaudible over the thunder of her racing heartbeat.

"He died of his wounds." Even Cousin Harper's voice, rich and smooth as molasses, couldn't soften the blow.

Katie gasped for air. She couldn't breathe, couldn't think. Charles dead? How could this be? Surely there must be some mistake. How could he have died without her knowing it? Pain, shock, and confusion roiled around in her head. "I don't believe you."

Her father closed his eyes for a second and gave his

head a weary shake. "Mary Katherine—" he started, but Cousin Harper cut him off.

"Allow me, sir. Charles was my friend. I loved him, too."

"Very well," Papa said, and left the room, closing the door behind him.

"I don't believe you," Katie repeated stubbornly. "Charles isn't dead. He can't be. We're going to be married. Mama and Papa forced me to break our engagement, but once this horrible war is over, we're going to be married, Charles and I, no matter what anyone says."

Cousin Harper stepped closer to brush a curl back off her cheek. "It hurts me to see you this way," he said, his kindness convincing her of the truth as no words could have done. "Don't cry, Katie."

"I'm not," she lied even as tears slid down her cheeks.

He gathered her close, pressing her face against his linen shirtfront. He smelled of starch and hair oil and elderberry wine, a strangely comforting combination.

"Tell me," she said when the worst of it was past. "I want to know."

He held her away from him, his hands clenched on her shoulders. A muscle twitched at the corner of his mouth. His eyes reflected some private torment. "You don't."

"Please?" she said.

Cousin Harper closed his eyes for a moment. When he opened them again, he seemed to have himself well in hand. "Charles's injuries were severe, his death a mercy." He hesitated. When he spoke again, his voice was rough with suppressed emotion. "Half his skull was blown away. Even if he'd lived"—he shuddered—"he wouldn't have been normal."

Cousin Harper had been right the first time. She really didn't want to know.

"Half his skull was blown away."

Regan woke with a start to find herself strapped into the passenger's seat of Nash's small private plane. "Did you say something?" she asked.

But Nash had on headphones and didn't hear her question, which meant the voice she'd heard had been inside her head. "Half his skull was blown away."

She knew that voice, that soft Southern drawl. Her cousin. Her kissing cousin.

Only trouble with that was, Regan didn't have any cousins, kissing or otherwise. Both her parents had been only children, and she'd continued the tradition. No siblings. No cousins. No Southerners, for that matter. Her mother had been a native Californian, and her dad was the product of a Belfast orphanage.

She leaned back against the headrest, trying to retrieve the rest of the dream, but it was gone. Only dregs of negative emotion remained—horror, regret, and an almost unbearable sadness.

She touched Nash's arm to get his attention.

"What?" He lifted his headphones away from his ear.

She decided "I think I'm going crazy" probably fell

into the too-much-information category. "How much farther?" she asked instead.

"See the lights down there?" he said. "That's the Bay Area. Another few minutes and we'll touch down in Monterey. Malcolm's meeting us with the car."

"Malcolm?"

"Caretaker, driver, and general factotum."

"English?" she said.

His mouth twitched in one of his almost-smiles. "Very."

The noise woke Katie, a pattering sound. She slipped out of bed to investigate. At first she thought maybe it was raining, but when she pulled open the shutters to peer outside, no clouds obscured the moon. Like a ripe peach, it hung suspended above the rooftops of the sleeping town.

The pattering came again. Pebbles. They bounced off the glass and rattled down the shingled roof of the veranda.

Katie opened the window and leaned out.

Cousin Harper stood grinning up at her. He doffed his hat and bowed low.

"Go away," she said, "before you wake Papa."

"Your parents' room is on the other side of the house."

"You're remarkably well informed, sir."

"And you, my dear, are simply remarkable."

Surprised by his audacity, Katie stared. Was Cousin Harper flirting with her? "Have you been drinking?"

His laughter floated like dandelion fluff on the

soft September breeze. One year and one month since she'd seen him last. One year and one month since she'd learned of Charles's death. "Come down and play, Katie," he said. "It'll be like old times."

Times from her childhood, he meant. Times when she'd stayed at Harmony Hill, the Mayhew family plantation on the banks of the Savannah River. Times when she and Harper, unbeknownst to the adults, had sneaked out at night to indulge in forbidden adventures—catching lightning bugs down by the river, playing hide-and-seek in the rose garden, and once, climbing all the way to the top of Pearly Ridge to make wishes on shooting stars.

Why not? she thought. Lord knew she could use a little adventure in her life.

"Wake up, Regan."

Why not? she thought. Lord knew she could use a little adventure in her life.

No, wait. That was her dream. Pebbles rattling against her bedroom window, a fat yellow moon, and . . . No, she'd lost the rest.

"Regan? We're here."

She opened her eyes to see Nash's face just inches from hers. She smiled sleepily, thinking that if she had the energy, she'd pull him a little closer, close enough to bring his mouth within kissing range.

Judging by the sparkle in his eyes, Nash's thoughts were running along similar lines.

"Would you and the young lady care for something to eat, sir?" Nigel Malcolm, Nash's very British caretaker, spoiled the moment. Possibly on purpose.

Nash unfastened her seat belt, then helped her out of the Land Rover. "Hungry, Regan?"

"A little maybe." It was after eleven, and she hadn't eaten much dinner.

"Something light, then, Malcolm," Nash instructed. "Soup perhaps?"

"Very good, sir." Malcolm gathered up their luggage, Nash's carry-on and Regan's sack. She could have sworn the caretaker's nose twitched in distaste when he noticed the Wal-Mart logo.

"Ms. Cluny and I will have our supper in the library," Nash said.

"Yes, sir. Very good, sir." Malcolm disappeared around the back of the house, but Nash led her up onto the deck that stretched across the front of the big two-story glass-and-wood structure. Nestled in a grove of redwoods, it was perched high on a mountainside, the ocean below. Even by starlight, the view was spectacular.

Regan leaned on the deck railing, breathing deeply of the pine-scented air. "This is an incredibly lovely spot," she said, turning to Nash. "If this property belonged to me, I'd never want to leave."

"I had the house built just this year, though I've owned the land for some time." He gazed down at the ocean, his expression pensive.

"I'm surprised you'd bother. You don't spend much time in the U.S."

"I have houses in every corner of the world," he said. "I don't like staying in hotels."

She laughed. "Can't say I'm a big fan of hotels, either, though there are some perks I enjoy, room service, for example. And not having to make my bed."

"That's why I pay Malcolm the big bucks."

She laughed again. "Somehow I suspect there's more to that relationship than money. He seems very protective of you. Tom Davis, too. Apparently, you inspire loyalty."

"Tom and Malcolm are both good men. Too good maybe. Too loyal. I worry about them."

"Why on earth? Their loyalty is safe with you. You'd never betray them."

"Of course not, but . . ." He paused. "Every time I let myself get attached to someone . . . Maybe you weren't so far off the mark when you said I was a dangerous man to get close to." He gripped the railing with both hands.

She placed her small hand over his big one. "I'm pretty close right now, and the only danger I foresee is you shutting me out before I get any closer. I'd really, *really* like to get to know you better."

Nash turned his hand over and gave hers a squeeze. "I'd like that, too," he admitted, "but there are problems."

"Harper, you mean?"

"He's one problem certainly."

"What's his deal anyway?" she asked. "You both fell for the same woman. She chose you, as what sane woman wouldn't, and then she died. But none of that really explains why he's so determined to make your life a living hell."

"Is there a question in there?"

"Yes. Motivation. What is Harper's?"

"Off the record?"

She stiffened. "Absolutely. I'm not working now."

"You're just curious," he said.

She pulled her hand out of his and turned to face him. His eyes seemed to glow red for a second. "I want to know everything about you because I like you . . . most of the time."

His lips twitched. "This particular moment being an exception to the rule?"

"Yes," she said bluntly.

"You can't blame me for not wanting to see my darkest secrets revealed in a magazine article."

"No, but I can be pissed as hell that you'd think I would betray your trust that way. You should know better." She turned away to stare at the ocean through a glaze of tears.

"Why should I know better, Regan? I don't really know you at all. You dig and you dig, determined to unearth my deepest, darkest secrets. You act as if it's your right. But you reveal little or nothing of yourself."

He had a point, damn it. "Okay," she said tightly. "What do you want to know? I'm a native Californian. My mother's dead—she was a writer, too, screenplays, though, not magazine articles—and my dad's a semi-bigwig in Hollywood, not Steven Spielberg big but big enough to have received five Oscar nominations. No wins. Yet." She shrugged. "He lives in L.A., and I live in New York, which probably tells you all you need to know about our relationship. I love strawberries, snorkeling, reading, silver-and-turquoise jewelry, Paris, and old Cary Grant movies. I have a passion for all things moose, am an inveterate list maker, and loathe reality shows with a purple—"

"Regan?" He put one hand on her shoulder, then gently turned her to face him. "I'm sorry if you thought I was questioning your integrity."

She blinked repeatedly. *I will not cry. I will not cry.*

"I guess what I really want is for us to get to know each other better. I'd like us to be friends."

Friends? Who was he kidding? Since when did friends ignite a firestorm of passion every time they kissed? Every time they touched? Friends? Had he lost his freaking mind? "Friend this," she said, reaching for him.

The kiss, begun as a lesson in semantics, soon took on a life of its own, evolving into something both sweet and dangerous. A fierce need consumed her. In that moment, she wanted Nash more than she'd ever wanted anything in her life, more than a Pulitzer or a six-figure income, more than her father's approval, even more than a normal life span.

The raging desire wasn't all one-sided, either. She could tell that much from the way he kissed her back. One perfect night. That's all she asked. One perfect night with this oh-so-perfect man and she could die happy.

Nash lifted her onto the railing. Then, nudging her thighs apart, he moved between her legs.

Regan draped her arms around his neck, running

her fingers through his silky hair. One stray lock fell across his brow. She brushed it back, mesmerized by the fierce promise in his eyes.

I want you, she thought.

She burned with anticipation, ached with desire. "Touch me," she whispered, then gasped in delight when he shoved up her shirt and bra and applied himself to her breasts. He used his mouth and tongue to tease one, his thumb to torment the other. Pleasure shuddered through her, rich and dark.

He sucked harder.

A moan escaped her lips, surprising her as much as the pleasure that had provoked it. Her eyes flew open, and she found herself face-to-face with Malcolm.

The French doors stood open behind him. Light spilled out onto the deck. "Your food is ready, sir." Not by so much as a twitch of his lip did he betray a hint of discomposure at finding them in such a compromising position.

Nash straightened, pulling her clothes back into place with a couple of discreet tugs. Only then did he turn to face the caretaker. "Thank you, Malcolm. We'll be in shortly."

"Will you have any further need of my services this evening, sir?"

"No, you've done quite enough for one night." Nash's tone was silky smooth, but Regan didn't think she was imagining the barb lurking beneath the surface of his words.

Malcolm must have heard it, too. He immediately

lowered his gaze and mumbled something about seeing them in the morning.

"Well," Regan said as soon as the double doors closed behind the caretaker. "That was embarrassing."

"But fun," Nash said.

"Yes, you have a very interesting take on friendship."

His expression grew thoughtful. "I guess I was wrong about that. Friendship is too tepid a word to describe our relationship."

"You think?" Together they generated enough heat to affect global warming.

But as she studied his angular face, her heart sank. No lingering warmth lit his eyes. No hint of it softened his stern mouth. Nash had shut himself off again.

"How would you describe our relationship, then?" She regretted asking almost as soon as the words left her mouth.

He frowned. "Risky, teetering on the verge of disastrous."

"I like risky," she said.

"How about disastrous?"

"I'm willing to chance it."

"I'm not joking." He spoke almost harshly.

"Neither am I," she said.

His gaze held hers for a moment longer, then he swore softly under his breath. "Let's eat."

ELEVEN

In the 142 years since Nash had become a vampire, he'd never wanted to possess a woman as much as he wanted to possess Regan Cluny. And therein lay the rub.

Had his emotions not been aroused, they could have had sex six times a day every day from now until the end of time without his posing the slightest danger to her. But a man—a vampire—who wanted a woman the way he wanted Regan couldn't be trusted not to initiate a blood bond. Hell, he'd already come within an ace of biting her once. A second time she might not escape unscathed.

He watched her now as she picked at her supper, consommé and finger sandwiches. Finger sandwiches. Malcolm's sick sense of humor at work. It was a wonder the man hadn't served them blood pudding.

"What?" Regan said. "Do I have crumbs on my lip?"

"No, why?"

"You're staring."

"If it bothers you, I'll stop."

"It doesn't bother me, exactly. I mean, it does bother me but not in the pissed-off sense of the word. More the hot-and-bothered sense, if you get my drift."

Her desire made her vulnerable, more vulnerable than she realized. It would be so easy to lose himself in the depths of those sage green eyes, to sink his teeth into that delicate throat and feast on her.

Some hint of his thoughts must have shown in his face because Regan's eyes widened. "Nash?"

Damn it. Damn *him*. He stood. "If you've finished eating, I can give you a quick tour of the house, but then I really need to get to work."

"Your research. Of course. That's why you came here in the first place." She averted her gaze, but not before he saw the wounded expression in her eyes.

Nash hardened his heart. Hurt feelings were nothing compared to the damage he might cause if he lost control.

Regan got up and wandered over to the nearest bookcase, pulled a book down, and began leafing through it. "Quite a collection you have here." She returned the book to the shelf, then trailed a finger across the spines of several volumes. "*Guide to Demonology; The Lilith Legend; Vlad, the Impaler; Vampyre.*" She glanced up. "I sense a theme."

"You like Cary Grant movies," he said. "I like myths and legends."

"Fair enough." She shot him a smile, then continued her exploration.

Nash froze, hardly daring to breathe, when she paused to study the portrait of Katie that hung above the fireplace. He'd meant to ask Malcolm to move it into storage, damn it.

"Who's this?" she asked. "An ancestor of yours?"

"Mary Katherine O'Malley was her name."

Regan frowned. "That name rings a distant bell, but I'm not making the connection. Was she famous? Someone I would have learned about in history class if only I hadn't spent all my time doodling in the margins of my notebook? A spy for the Confederacy, perhaps? Or John Wilkes Booth's leading lady?"

"You don't see the resemblance?" How could she not?

"Resemblance to whom?" She stared at the portrait, furrowing her brow, tilting her head one way and then the other. "I guess she reminds me a little of Catherine Zeta-Jones in the first *Zorro* movie. Or maybe Vivien Leigh in *Gone with the Wind*."

Okay, now she was teasing him, though damned if he could figure out why. "She looks like you, Regan."

"Like me?" She turned to him, her expression incredulous. "No she doesn't. We're complete opposites. She's a brunette with a heart-shaped face, soft features, and rounded cheeks. I'm a blonde with an angular face, sharp features, and a squared-off chin. We look nothing alike. Absolutely nothing." She frowned. "But that name. I swear I've heard that name before."

"You're not afraid, are you?" Cousin Harper asked as they strolled hand in hand under the honeysuckle archway that separated the parsonage lawn from the adjoining cemetery.

"Should I be?" Smiling, Katie flicked a flirtatious glance up at him.

"Not of ghosts." The moonlight reflected off his eyes. For a second, they seemed to glow red.

She gave an involuntary shiver.

"What's wrong?" He drew her to a stop at the base of an ancient oak, big and broad, older than the cemetery, older than the town.

"Nothing," she said, afraid to meet his gaze, afraid of what she might see there.

He backed her against the tree, his big warm hands rubbing lightly up and down her arms. "You're safe with me, Katie. We're kissing cousins, remember?" He brushed his lips across her cheek.

"I remember." But she didn't feel safe. She felt dangerously out of control.

He kissed her again, this time on her eyelids, the tip of her nose, her earlobes, her throat.

Her heart fluttered in her breast like a bird in a trap. And she wanted something, something more, and though she couldn't name it, she ached with the wanting.

Then his lips brushed her mouth, not really a kiss, just a fleeting touch. She thought she would die if he didn't kiss her. She knew she would die if he did.

"Charles," she said, as much of a reminder to herself as to Cousin Harper.

"He's dead, Katie," Cousin Harper whispered. "But you're alive, and so am I. Shall I prove it to you?"

"No," she said, but he kissed her anyway, stealing her will, stealing her soul. His hands were everywhere, touching her in ways she'd never been touched, sparking sensations she'd never imagined.

She teetered on a precipice. Her breath sobbed in and out. A terrified yearning consumed her. She wanted. She needed. "Please," she said.

Cousin Harper, who'd been licking a hot path along her collarbone, raised his head and smiled at her. "Whatever happens," he said, "remember that I love you."

"Love me?" Was that what this yearning was? Love?

Then he sank his teeth in her neck, and Katie screamed.

Pain and pleasure. Agony and ecstasy.

Regan woke with a start, one hand pressed to her throat. She'd been dreaming again, though as usual, the details escaped her. The residual emotions were very different this time, though. Contradictory. She frowned into the darkness, trying to get a grip on them. Pleasure, she thought, and fear, too. Pain and excitement.

She sat up, disoriented for a moment. She wasn't sure where "here" was, but it definitely wasn't the tent she'd been sharing with Nash.

For a second, panic gripped her. Then she remembered. This enormous shadowed room was part of the guest suite in Nash's house at Big Sur, and that soft soughing sound was the wind trailing through the redwoods on the mountainside below her open windows.

Nash had shown her around the house, then left her alone in this luxurious suite.

She slid out of bed, shivering in the thin slip of a nightgown she'd found waiting for her on the bed. Nash had called ahead to arrange a surprise. Apparently, Malcolm had gone shopping. In addition to the nightgown and matching robe, he'd bought her some decadent underwear, a pair of trendy jeans—*not* size 10—a simple rose silk cami, and a short, flirty little dress the same color as her eyes, with shoes to match.

Gorgeous clothes, gorgeous room, gorgeous view. What was missing from this picture? A gorgeous man, maybe?

Regan wrapped herself in the silky aqua robe, then wandered restlessly around the shadowed room. Nash wanted her as much as she wanted him. She was sure of it. When he'd suggested this trip, she'd had such high hopes.

Then he'd played the friendship card. What was up with that?

She groaned in frustration. Obviously not what counted.

He wanted her. She knew he wanted her, but for some reason he held back.

Why, though? That was the question.

Some misplaced sense of nobility? Maybe he saw her as a long-term-relationship girl, not just an easy lay.

Which under normal circumstances would have

been flattering. And true. Only her circumstances were anything but normal. The sad truth was, for her, any relationship was going to be strictly short-term. Best-case scenario, six to eight months, according to the specialist. So damn it, what was he worried about?

Regan paused. Nash was concerned because he didn't know she was living on borrowed time. Maybe if she told him the truth . . .

Only if she did come clean, she'd never know for sure that he hadn't been motivated solely by pity, would she?

Was that really what she was looking for?

Regan examined that scenario from every perspective. Did she really care why he slept with her? Okay, yes. Some small part of her did care. But the greater part of her, that aching, wanting, desperate part of her, didn't give a rip. So by majority rule, she'd take Charles Cunningham Nash any way she could get him.

She resumed her pacing, back and forth, back and forth, finally pausing for a moment by the window to breathe deeply of the cool air, rich with the scents of pine resin, damp earth, and roses.

Her suite was located on the second floor, directly above the broad front deck. But it wasn't the stunning view of the moonlit ocean that drew her attention. It was Nash. He sat slumped on the top step, despair in every line of his body.

Her chest tightened in sympathy.

Before she could talk herself out of it, she was dressed and heading downstairs.

• • •

Nash smelled Regan—her distinctive scent, feminine and seductive—even before he heard her light step behind him. He turned to greet her, but the words died in his throat, choked by a wave of desire. Even in baggy khakis and a man's T-shirt, Regan had made his pulse race. In tight low-cut jeans and a barely there cami that revealed her belly-button ring, she was temptation personified.

"Can't you sleep, either?" she asked, perching on the step next to him.

"Haven't been to bed yet," he said.

"Research not going as planned?"

"I've looked through every relevant book in the library, every piece of primary source material in the vault."

"And nothing helped," she guessed.

"Finally came out here to clear my head."

"But that isn't helping, either."

"No," he agreed. And neither was she.

"You could bounce ideas off me. Sometimes it helps me clarify things if I talk them out." She hugged herself, rubbing her hands up and down her upper arms.

"Cold?"

"A little. I didn't think I'd need my hoodie. Left it in Juniper Basin."

Where I, apparently, abandoned all my common sense. He knew he was playing with fire, but he slipped his right arm around her anyway.

She relaxed against him with a sigh, snuggling

close. Her thigh nudged his with disturbing familiarity. Her breast pressed against his side, accentuating the half-moon of fine pale skin that rose with such tantalizing promise above the low neckline of her camisole. Her hair, soft and fragrant, brushed his chin. He closed his eyes, overwhelmed by the sight of her, the feel of her, the smell of her.

Bad move, he thought, pulling her close like this. Hard to think with all his blood heading south.

"So tell me all about it," she said, and for a split second, he thought she was asking about his arousal. "Did you find any more references to the spring?"

"The spring," he repeated.

She tilted her head to give him a questioning look. "Isn't that what we were talking about?"

"Yes. Of course." He reached past the haze of sexual awareness and gathered his scattered thoughts. "The Old Ones had no written language. Neither did the tribes who moved into the area after them, so all the stories were handed down by word of mouth. Inevitably, they changed over time."

She nodded, sending another drift of sweet, seductive Regan scent in his direction. "Like that children's game gossip."

"Exactly. Details were added, others omitted. It's impossible to know for certain what's fact and what's some raconteur's imaginative embellishment."

"You know the spring is real because you found it. And the snake, too. Danielle said the skeleton's huge."

"Huge, yes," Nash told her. "But not ten thousand

years old. Someone—most likely one of the grad students—planted a python skeleton."

It didn't take her long to work it out. "For the bonus money."

"I think so, yes."

"How about the pictographs?"

"Also faked, we think."

She paused to digest that information. "But in a way, that's good news. If the spring you found isn't the real spring . . . I mean, maybe the real spring isn't dried up."

"And maybe there is no real spring."

"Maybe," she agreed. "Or maybe you overlooked something. Could be it's one of the other springs you've already explored."

"No," he said. "All the stories refer to a cloistered spring. That was one of the details I came here to check."

"Cloistered?"

"Hidden. Covered. Secret." He shrugged. "Thus eliminating all the known springs in the Juniper Basin area except the dried-up one inside the cleft in the rock."

"Are you thinking maybe it's the real spring after all?"

"I'm afraid so."

"Why afraid?"

"First of all, because convincing anyone that it's the legendary spring now that the site's integrity has been compromised will be almost impossible. Second, because the spring is dried up. Useless." He fell silent.

"Nash?" Regan's soft voice broke into his absorption. "I know it's a disappointment, but it's not the end of the world."

No, just the end of his hopes for a normal life, a life where he could make love to a woman, this woman, without worrying about hurting her.

Regan tucked her right hand in his left, a simple, trusting gesture.

But he didn't deserve her trust.

Nash stood abruptly, pulling Regan to her feet. "Let's walk," he said. "Maybe a little exercise will spark a brainstorm." And as long as they were moving, he might be able to keep his hands to himself.

"Okay," she said, looking a little confused and a lot adorable.

"Wait here a minute. I'll be right back."

When he reemerged from the house, he found Regan leaning against the deck railing, staring down at the ocean. She turned at his approach. "This place is so beautiful," she said.

You're so beautiful, he thought. But what he said was, "Here," and handed her a sweatshirt, one of his.

Regan smiled, and his heart skipped two beats in a row. "Thanks," she said. "My goose bumps have goose bumps." He helped her pull the sweatshirt over her head. It was huge on her, hanging halfway to her knees. But unfortunately, it did nothing to dim her allure. She still looked sexy as hell.

"Shall we?" he said.

"Where are we going?"

"It's a surprise." He led her around the house and up the hill.

"Good." She smiled. "I like surprises."

They climbed steadily for several minutes, his flashlight's beam bouncing ahead of them to light the way as they worked their way through the trees. Ferns grew heavily underfoot. The rich scents of pine and damp earth filled the air.

"What were you hoping to find?" Regan asked suddenly. "In your primary sources, I mean."

He shook his head. "A hint, a clarification, something to tell me I'm on the right track."

"But you didn't."

He helped her over a fallen log.

"Just the same vague references to the spring's location and, in the Father Padilla manuscript, repetition of the words *secrete* and *occultus*."

"Meaning hidden?" she said slowly.

"Yes, why?"

"Because it occurs to me that maybe Father Padilla was being purposely obscure. Maybe there's another level of meaning in his manuscript, and the repetitions of *secrete* and *occultus* are like a code or something." She gave a self-deprecating laugh. "Or then again, maybe I've read *The Da Vinci Code* one too many times." She stopped suddenly and grabbed his arm. "What's that noise?"

My heart overreacting to your touch? "What noise?" he asked, his voice only a little huskier-sounding than normal.

"That low rumbling. Can't you hear it?"

"Ah, that would be the surprise," he said. "Come on. Follow me. We're almost there."

He led her up a slight incline, then along a rocky ledge. The noise grew steadily louder. "All right, close your eyes now. Don't open them until I tell you to." He guided her up the last steep section, one arm around her waist. To prevent her falling, he told himself, not because the feel of her body, even through the bulky sweatshirt, was a major turn-on.

"Are we there yet? Can I peek?"

"Not yet." He laid the flashlight down behind him. Now that they were clear of the trees, the moon provided more than enough illumination. Nash positioned her directly in front of him, where she would have the best vantage point. Unfortunately, her position also placed her backside snugly against his front, awakening inappropriate thoughts and even more inappropriate physical responses. "All right," he said, trying to ignore his arousal and to deny the sudden bloodlust triggered by the sight of her long, slender throat. "Open your eyes."

She gasped in surprise and pleasure. "Oh, my God! It's spectacular. Judging by the sound, I expected a river, maybe a canyon and some whitewater, but not a waterfall. Especially not a waterfall that looks, at least from this angle, like a stairway straight to heaven."

"The early inhabitants would have agreed with you. They called it the Spirit Ladder. Legend has it, this is where the Great Spirit first descended to earth."

She turned in his arms, her smile incandescent. "Thank you, Nash. Thank you for bringing me here."

The night breeze was cool, the mist off the falls even cooler, but his body was on fire.

Regan didn't know she was flirting with destruction, smiling up at him like that. He, on the other hand, was fully aware of the potential for disaster, but need trumped conscience, and he kissed her anyway, consequences be damned.

Each taste, each touch fed the fire inside him. It blazed up hot, then hotter still, a raging inferno. He burned for her.

"Nash," she whispered the instant he relinquished her mouth. "Don't stop."

"Wasn't planning to." He lifted her high in his arms and carried her to the center of the glade. He'd thought—in at least one dark corner of his brain he'd thought—that he'd make love to her this weekend, but he'd never dreamed it would be here in this high meadow with a full moon overhead and the drama of the falls as a backdrop.

He laid her gently on the grass, then stretched out beside her, supporting himself on one elbow so he could study her face, watch the emotions that played across it—excitement, anticipation, desire.

He brushed a tendril of hair back off her face, then traced the elegant angle of her cheekbone, the delicate line of her jaw. "You're beautiful," he said.

Her eyes softened. Her lips curved.

Slowly he drew the pad of his thumb across her lower lip and felt her tremble. What emotion, he wondered, had sparked that response? Fear? Desire? Or some hybrid of the two?

Once again he brushed his thumb across the velvety fullness of her lip.

But this time Regan surprised him by catching his thumb between her teeth and sucking gently.

The sensation sent a sharp pang of desire spiking through him. Some of that naked need must have been reflected in his expression because Regan's eyes widened.

He leaned closer. Their mouths met with no hesitation, as if they'd been made for each other, as if they were two halves of the same whole.

Nash's heartbeat thundered in his ears, drowning out any remnant of caution. He needed her, damn it. Needed to see her, feel her, which he couldn't do with all the damned clothes in the way.

He jerked both sweatshirt and cami up in one impatient tug, then drew a sharp breath. Oh, God, she was exquisite, perfect in every way, from those angled hip bones and that taut stomach to the tempting indentation of her navel and those beautiful, beautiful breasts.

Luscious. Tantalizing.

He touched first, learning her curves, her hollows, her sensitive spots, her textures. Then he tasted, learning the flavor of her skin, the spicy sweetness of her excitement.

The longer he explored her body, the more ragged her breathing grew.

"Please," she begged.

"Please what?" he asked, his voice muffled as he nuzzled her softness.

"I need . . . ," she sobbed. "I want . . ."

Suddenly Regan moved frantically beneath him.

"What's wrong?" he asked, belatedly realizing what she was doing when she pushed her jeans down her legs.

He unzipped his own jeans, freeing his erection, then he eased himself into her warmth a little at a time, afraid to go too fast, afraid he'd lose control.

Regan moaned. "Please," she said again. Then she arched up to meet him, taking him even deeper.

Blood pounded in his head. Need overwhelmed him. Hard and fast he moved. Too fast, too fast, but he couldn't hold back. Didn't want to hold back.

"Yes!" Regan clenched herself around him, coming in a series of convulsive shudders, her cries muffled against his neck.

One last thrust and Nash climaxed in a rush so powerful it was nearly pain.

Instinctively, he reared back to sink his fangs in her throat, a low growl escaping him.

Then his gaze fell upon the scars on her neck.

Guilt and shame struck a powerful blow. Damn him to hell. He'd almost . . . he'd almost . . .

Regan smiled up at him. She looked sated and drowsy, her eyes shut. She drew a long, shaky breath, then whispered something about dying happy.

"You're not going to die," he said fiercely.

She opened her eyes and studied his face solemnly. "Everyone dies," she said.

• • •

Nash walked Regan up to her room, left her with a kiss and an admonishment to get some rest, then headed back down to the library to tackle his research again.

Malcolm was waiting for him, his demeanor that of a disapproving parent.

"Save your breath," Nash said.

"I beg your pardon?" Malcolm raised his eyebrows a full half inch, looking snooty as hell even in faded pajamas and an ancient flannel robe.

"You should be in bed."

"And so I was until the telephone started ringing off the hook."

Nash's heart lurched. "Trouble at the dig?"

"Wrong number." Malcolm set his teacup down with an irritated clatter. "The point is, had there been a problem at the dig, you wouldn't have been here to learn of it."

"I had my cell phone with me."

"No." Malcolm's gaze flicked toward the cell phone nearly buried in the clutter on the desk. "You didn't." He fixed Nash with a sharp look. "Does she know?"

"Regan?"

"Yes, Regan, unless, that is, you have some other poor unsuspecting female hidden somewhere about the premises. What's got into you, sir, bringing a woman into your home? You've never done that before. Does she know what you are?"

"No," he said.

"Are you going to tell her?"

"No!"

"Then what in hell are you playing at?"

"I'm not playing. I'm—"

"Oh, my God." Malcolm's eyebrows rose once more, even higher this time. "Don't tell me you've convinced yourself you're in love."

"I don't know," Nash said, trying to be honest. "I have feelings for her certainly, very powerful feelings. At first, I assumed it was because she looks so much like Katie, but—"

"Like Katie?" Malcolm interrupted. "*Your* Katie? Are you quite mad? The two women look nothing alike."

"Regan couldn't see the resemblance, either, though Harper spotted it right away."

Malcolm frowned. "Harper sees a resemblance, too, you say?"

Nash nodded.

"Interesting."

"In what way?"

Malcolm pursed his lips and steepled his fingers. "What do you know of reincarnation theory?"

"About as much as you know about quantum physics."

"All right, consider this. What if Regan is Katie reincarnated? That might explain why you and Harper, the two men who loved Katie O'Malley, can see her in Regan Cluny, a woman who's in no way physically similar."

"But she is similar," Nash argued. "Granted, Regan is a blonde, taller, more slender . . ." His voice trailed off. "There really isn't any resemblance, is there?"

"None," Malcolm replied unequivocally.

"Then why do I see one?"

"Because you're seeing her essence. Different person, same essence."

"So, going with your theory," Nash said, "does she 'recognize' me?"

"On some deep, subconscious level, I imagine she does," Malcolm said. "I mean, think about it. Think about how quickly your relationship has progressed."

"Meaning?"

"Don't try that innocent face on me," Malcolm said. "You came in here reeking of sex. Granted, I don't know the woman as well as you do, but my initial impression doesn't lead me to surmise that she's someone accustomed to bestowing her favors—"

"'Lead me to surmise'? 'Bestowing her favors'? Which one of us is a hundred and sixty-seven years old?"

"You know perfectly well what I mean."

Yes, Nash did know what Malcolm meant. "I didn't use a condom. I didn't even think of it."

"Is that a problem?" Malcolm shrugged. "I've always understood that a vampire can't impregnate a normal human, and your kind is immune to human diseases, so . . ." He shrugged again.

"She didn't think of it, either."

"I expect she's on birth control."

Regan *had* packed a lot of prescriptions for the weekend. "You're probably right."

"Did you bite her?" Malcolm asked.

"No!"

"But you wanted to."

Hell, yes. Not just wanted to, tried to, though he didn't tell Malcolm that. Some things were best kept hidden. Like the fact that he was a vampire. Or the location of a legendary spring? "I really need to get some research done." He glanced pointedly at the pile of papers on his desk.

"Of course, sir," Malcolm said, giving the "sir" a little more emphasis than he normally did. He gathered up his teacup and saucer and headed for the door, then paused on the threshold. "Should you start feeling peckish, there are several packets of blood in the minifridge under the bar."

"Thank you, Malcolm. That was very thoughtful."

"You should tell her," he said. "Tell her before she finds out for herself."

Nash pressed his lips together in a tight line to prevent any profanities from escaping. The worst part was, Malcolm was right, damn him to hell and back. "Good night, Malcolm," Nash said firmly.

"Better for some than others, sir," Malcolm said, prim, smug, and British to the core.

Katie opened the heavy front door of Harmony Hill to find a raggedy, scruffy-faced scarecrow of a man standing there in a tattered Union uniform. He didn't look dangerous, but looks could be deceiving, as she'd learned the hard way. "The war is over, sir. We have nothing left to surrender."

"Katie?" The man took a lurching step forward.

"Do I know you, sir?" Absurd. The only Yankee she'd ever known was Charles, and he'd been dead for . . . "Charles?" Despite the dramatic weight loss, despite the unkempt hair and beard-stubbled cheeks, she should have recognized those blue, blue eyes of his immediately. Her heart beat so hard and fast she thought surely it would batter its way past her ribs. "Oh, Charles, I thought you'd died at Manassas." Laughing and crying all at the same time, she threw her arms around him and hugged him tight. "Harper said . . ." Harper had said a lot of things, many of them untrue. Why was she surprised to discover he'd lied about this, too?

Charles held her so tightly she could barely breathe. "Ah, love, I thought I'd never find you."

"Come in, come in," she said, ushering him inside once he'd finally relinquished his hold on her.

"I didn't expect you to answer the door." His pale eyes glistened with unshed tears. He seemed even more overwhelmed than she.

"There's no one else. The servants are gone. Come. Sit down. You look tired."

"I walked all the way from Richmond. Libby Prison. That's where they put me after I was captured at Bull Run."

"Manassas," she said. "We call it Manassas."

"Took me two weeks to get to Magnolia Grove, only to find the parsonage deserted. Neighbors told me you'd gone to live with relatives here at Harmony Hill after your parents died, so I kept on walking."

"You should have gone home to Pennsylvania. Your family must be frantic."

"I'm not going anywhere without you, Katie. Swear

to God. If you want to come with me to Pennsylvania, we'll do that. But if you'd rather stay in Georgia, I'm agreeable. As long as we're together, that's all that matters."

"You rest now, Charles. You must be exhausted after coming all that way. I'll bring you something to drink, something to eat." She smiled nervously, wondering how much he knew, how much she dared tell him.

He grabbed her hands to prevent her leaving. His eyes burned into hers, their message clearer than any spoken words.

Katie's heartbeat quickened. "You're not hungry."

"Not for food," he said.

A high-pitched squealing interrupted Regan's dream. Smoke alarm.

She jumped out of bed and raced downstairs. By the time she was halfway to the bottom, she could smell not only smoke, but the nauseating odor of burnt flesh as well. She rushed down the last few steps. Living room clear. Dining room clear. No fire in the entryway. None in the hall back toward the kitchen.

Then she spotted the library door standing slightly ajar. No flames visible here, either, though smoke hovered in a haze near the ceiling.

She moved in to investigate but was brought up short by the sound of angry voices.

"The flames are out. Can't you turn that damn thing off?" Nash, his voice nearly unrecognizable.

"Presently," Malcolm replied. "In such circumstances, one must prioritize."

This exchange was followed by ripping sounds and more hissing profanity, most of it Nash's.

Regan tapped on the door. "Everything okay in there?"

The alarm cut off abruptly. "We're fine," Malcolm shouted. "Fire's out. Crisis over. Go back to bed."

"Are you sure? Nash?" She bumped the door, and it swung open on a nightmare.

Nash lay slumped on the floor, half naked, his chest and arms raw and bleeding. Malcolm hunkered next to him, a filleting knife in one bloody hand, a strip of blackened skin in the other. The room reeked of smoke, smoldering fabric, and scorched meat.

Malcolm glared at her. "Get out. He doesn't want you to see him like this."

"My God, what happened?" she demanded. "What did you do to him?"

"Accident," Nash gasped. "Did it to myself. Not as bad as it looks."

"Not as bad as it looks? He's stripping off ribbons of your skin!"

"Debriding," Malcolm said. "And if you don't leave me to it, he's going to end up with scars. I need to remove the blistered flesh before it heals all puckered and twisted."

"What he needs is a doctor, damn it. Have you called 911?" Regan grabbed the phone from the desk and began punching in numbers.

"No!" Nash started to shove himself up.

Malcolm pushed him back down; then, muttering a string of "bloody hell"'s, he reached out with his knife and cut the phone line at the wall.

"You couldn't just unplug it?" Nash said.

"Time is of the essence. Unless, that is, you really want to explain your condition to the authorities."

Regan slammed the phone onto the desk loudly enough to get both men's full attention. "Have you two lost your minds? Nash, I know you're in pain, but be reasonable. You need help. And, Malcolm, I'm going to give you the benefit of the doubt here and assume you mean well, but damn it, you're not a doctor. Those burns . . ." She shuddered.

"Will heal before morning," Malcolm assured her.

Nash shot him a warning glance.

"Heal before morning? What are you talking about? Nobody heals that fast," she said, "especially not someone with burns like Nash's."

Malcolm stripped another row of blackened blisters from Nash's chest.

Nash squeezed his eyes shut and groaned. "Damn you, Malcolm."

"Don't blame me," Malcolm said. "You should have known better than to play with fire."

"Wasn't playing," Nash said through gritted teeth as Malcolm continued the debriding process. "I was holding a candle under a manuscript page to see if I could reveal a hidden message."

"Talk about a foolish stunt," Malcolm muttered.

This was insane. She was insane. Or maybe just

hallucinating. The doctor had warned her about that possible side effect. Maybe none of this horror—Nash's scorched flesh, Malcolm's bloody filleting knife—was real. Maybe she'd conjured up the whole scene from some sick little corner of her overmedicated brain.

"There," Malcolm said. "That should do it. Good as new in a few hours." He smoothed salve over Nash's raw flesh, then helped him to his feet. "Will there be anything else, sir?"

"No, thank you, Malcolm."

The manservant gathered up his makeshift medical supplies and left, closing the door to the hall behind him.

Nash propped himself against the edge of the desk, turning his back on her.

"Are you sure you're all right?" Regan looked at the pile of charred fabric on the floor, tattered remnants that had once been Nash's shirt. "What's going on here?"

"You asked about my secret a while back."

"Yes, I—"

"I'm a vampire."

Okay, yes, she didn't care how real this seemed, she was definitely hallucinating. Or maybe dreaming. Nightmaring. Was that a word? Nightmaring? She lowered herself into one of the club chairs by the fireplace.

"Aren't you going to say anything?"

"What's the point? I'm asleep."

"But it's all—"

"Asleep," she repeated. "Dreaming."

Nash sighed heavily. "Regan, it's a lot to wrap your brain around. I get that." The muscles in his broad back tensed up. "You need proof."

"And you're going to provide that how, exactly?" she asked, laughing uneasily as her panic mounted. "By staking yourself and disappearing in a cloud of dust?"

"I'd prefer to avoid such drastic measures." He moved closer, taking up a position directly in front of her. "Look at my arms, my chest," he said. "I'm already halfway healed."

He was, too. Must have been some kind of miracle salve Malcolm had put on his wounds. That or . . . "I'm dreaming," she repeated. "Anything's possible in a dream."

He studied her face, his expression serious. "Deep down you know the truth, don't you? You've known from the beginning. When Harper and his boys attacked you—"

"Harper's a vampire, too? Is that what you're saying?"

"Harper and his whole gang."

"No."

"What happened during the attack, Regan? What memories are you suppressing?"

"None. I don't know what you're talking about." But her hands were shaking and she couldn't breathe.

"Tell me what happened."

"I don't want to talk about it."

He grabbed her hands. "Tell me, damn it."

Real. He felt real. Not some incorporeal dream Nash, but flesh and blood.

"What happened that night, Regan? What didn't you tell the deputy?"

"I don't know what you're talking about," she said. "I told him everything." But she couldn't meet his gaze.

"Tell me," he said.

"I was so terrified, in so much pain. I'm not sure what part was real and what part was my mind playing tricks on me."

"One of them bit you."

"Yes," she said. "He sank his teeth in my neck." She put a hand instinctively to her throat.

"And then what?"

"I don't know. Really, I don't know. I think I passed out. The next thing I remember—or think I remember—was him bursting into flames. And then he was gone. Ashes on the wind."

Nash frowned. "Ashes? Not dust?"

"Ashes," she said.

Still holding her hands, he pulled her to her feet. Brow furrowed in concentration, he stared into the empty fireplace behind her. "Doesn't make sense," he muttered.

"It does if I was hallucinating."

"You weren't hallucinating, Regan." He gave her hands an impatient shake. "Though damned if I can explain what you saw. When the sheriff's deputies found the abandoned bike, I figured either one of the other bikers had staked its owner or the guy had accidentally impaled himself on a sharp branch, but if that were the case, he'd have turned to dust, not gone up in smoke. Your story doesn't make sense."

"Hallucinations seldom do."

His gaze met hers, and she felt the burn all the way to her toes. "How familiar are you with traditional vampire lore?" he asked.

"This is ridiculous."

"Humor me," he said. But he looked serious. Dead serious.

Okay, sure. Why not? This was all just a bad dream anyway. "Vampires are creatures of the night. They suck blood, sleep in coffins, and change into bats. The only way to kill one is to put a wooden stake through its heart, decapitate it, or expose it to direct sunlight."

"So you're familiar with the legends."

"The *Buffy* mythology's a little different. Vampires in Sunnydale are soulless demons who inhabit human bodies. Their faces assume a monstrous visage when they're ready to bite, plus they're all experts in martial arts."

"Nonsense, of course," he said. "Vampires aren't demons. And we're not the living dead, either. We're people infected with a rare parasite that makes us crave blood. Aside from acute night vision and a keener than normal sense of smell, we have no extraordinary abilities. We aren't ninja masters, and we don't turn into bats. We do live longer than normal, aging only about a year for every ten. We're quick to heal. Exhibit A," he said, pointing to the burns that seemed to be healing before her eyes. "We're invulnerable to virtually all diseases, though a stake through the heart will kill us, as will exposure to direct sunlight."

"I've seen you outside in the daylight."

"For short periods. Wearing long sleeves and sunblock."

No, she thought. Impossible. *I'm dreaming. Please, God, I must be dreaming.*

He dropped her hand to cup her chin, forcing her to meet his gaze. "I'm a vampire, Regan. I don't like it any better than you do, but it's the truth. I thought I owed you that."

"Owed me why?"

"You know why."

"Because we had sex?"

"It was more than just sex. Most women are safe with me. From me. But you elicit all these wild, undisciplined feelings. Twice now I've nearly sunk my teeth in your throat, nearly initiated a blood bond."

"A blood bond," she repeated.

"A ritual mating that combines blood and sex, pain and pleasure."

Swept up in a maelstrom of conflicting emotions—shock, horror, and revulsion, yes, but also curiosity and a degree of erotic fascination—Regan stared at him.

His eyes. Oh, God, his eyes. That searing blue seemed to see past all her pretenses, past all the lies she told herself. Deep, deep into the depths of her soul.

Time stopped dead in its tracks. Silence stretched to the breaking point. He knew her. He knew her better than she knew herself.

Suddenly terrified, Regan jerked free and bolted for the door.

"Wait!" Nash lunged after her.

"Don't touch me!" she said.

He drew up short, looking both surprised and hurt. "Don't touch you?"

"I can't deal with this right now. I need time to think, time to process."

Bitterness hardened his expression. "That's not the problem."

"Yes, I—"

"No." His eyes burned into hers. "The problem is, you're afraid of me."

"I'm not," she said.

But she lied. And he knew it.

TWELVE

Regan woke to the cries of gulls and the diffuse pearly light of a foggy dawn. She squinted at the alarm clock on the nightstand. Not quite six. No wonder she felt so thickheaded. She hadn't gone to bed until well after midnight, and even then, she hadn't gotten much rest, thanks to her drug-induced nightmares.

One particularly vivid dream came flooding back, and she sat up abruptly, clutching at the covers. The smoke alarm, Nash's burns, Malcolm's bloody knife, Nash saying, "I'm a vampire." Each detail was indelibly etched on her memory. Not like a dream at all. More like reality.

Only vampires weren't real.

Regan's heart raced. Her breathing quickened. Her hands trembled.

Were they?

Nash wasn't sure how long he'd been sitting in the library, staring out at the ocean. He just kept remembering the way Regan had torn herself away from him, the agitation in her voice, the fear on her face. He'd done that to her.

Telling her had been a mistake.

No, thinking they might be able to build a relationship, that was the real mistake.

He knew it didn't help to brood over what couldn't be changed. Didn't help to sit there staring into the darkness, either.

But still he didn't move, not until the sky began to lighten, not until the morning mist rolled in off the water, lapping at the deck, tangling itself in the trees. Only then did he head upstairs to bed.

Alone.

The sun had started to burn through the haze by the time Regan finally worked up the courage to leave her room. She need not have worried. The first floor was deserted. No Nash. No Malcolm. And no lingering odor of smoke, either.

So had it been a dream after all?

Not sure what to think, Regan made her way to the kitchen, at the back of the house. She had a fistful of pills that needed to be taken with food.

She opened the big stainless-steel side-by-side refrigerator and stared at the contents—milk, orange juice, eggs, bacon, fruit—all perfectly good breakfast selections, but nothing tempted her appetite, not even the strawberries. Better stick to toast, she thought, that was, if she could find where Malcolm had hidden the bread.

She was poking through cupboards when the door from the garage swung open and Malcolm, arms full of grocery bags, shouldered his way into the room. "Good morning," she said. "What have you done with the bread? I checked the bread box, but it was empty."

Malcolm set his load on the granite countertop. If he noticed the little pyramid of pills piled up next to the sink, he didn't mention it. "We were out," he said, "which is why I went into town so early. Which would you prefer? Wheat, white, bagel, or English muffin?"

"English muffin, please, but you don't need to fuss. I can toast it myself."

"It's no trouble," he said stiffly, the subtext being, "I don't like people messing about in my kitchen." Moving quickly but with an economy of effort, he unloaded the bags and put everything away. "Coffee?" he asked with a glance in her direction. "Tea?"

"Hot chocolate, if it's not too much trouble."

He raised an eyebrow at that. "No trouble at all. Seeing to the needs of Mr. Nash and his guests is my job and one I pride myself on doing well. Why don't you relax? Have a seat." He nodded toward the dining room.

She ignored the hint, perching instead on one of the bar stools that lined the counter, watching as Malcolm puttered around measuring cocoa powder, sugar, and a pinch of salt. She hadn't realized anyone made hot chocolate from scratch anymore.

"I apologize for not being here when you came downstairs," Malcolm said. "After last night's disturbance, I expected you to sleep in. I thought I'd be back from the grocery store long before anyone else got up."

Her heart gave a lurch. "Last night's disturbance?"

"Mr. Nash's setting off the smoke alarm and the ensuing unpleasantness."

Oh, God. Oh, God. She squeezed the edge of the counter so hard that her fingertips turned white. "It was real, then? Not a dream?"

She must have sounded as freaked out as she felt because he shot a worried glance in her direction. "You thought you'd dreamed it?"

"No," she said. "I thought it was real. I just hoped I'd dreamed it. I mean, vampires? If vampires are real, then maybe werewolves are, too, and goblins and trolls and witches. Maybe fairy tales are fact and science is fantasy."

"Begging your pardon, miss, but you're overreacting."

"Overreacting?" She laughed, a hollow sound completely devoid of mirth. "I discover in a very gruesome way that monsters are real and you say I'm overreacting?"

"Mr. Nash is no monster."

"Just a vampire."

"He can't help that," Malcolm said, "though God knows he's tried. Do you have any idea what it's like for him? For all of them? Unable to live a normal life, forced to avoid the sun, controlled by unnatural cravings. He's a good man, a strong man. Most people in his situation—"

"Most vampires, you mean."

He frowned. "Yes. Most vampires allow the dark desires to rule them, but Mr. Nash never has, not even in the days following Katie's death." He paused. "Has he told you about Katie?"

"A little," she said, frowning. "He thinks I look like her. He and Harper—you know about Harper?"—Malcolm nodded—"both think I look like her, but I've seen the portrait in the library. That's Katie, isn't it? There's no resemblance."

"None." Malcolm stirred milk into the cocoa mixture with a metal whisk, then set the saucepan on the range top. Judging by his expression, he had more to say about her so-called resemblance to Katie, but when he spoke again, it was to continue the story he'd started. "Harper Wakefield was the one who first introduced Mr. Nash to Katie O'Malley," Malcolm explained, "and it was love at first sight. Neither Katie nor Mr. Nash realized that Harper considered Katie his property, that he'd long planned to settle down with her once he'd finished sowing his wild oats."

"So when they announced their engagement, Harper was pissed," she guessed.

"Furious," Malcolm agreed. "He headed for the fleshpots of New Orleans, where he drowned his sorrows in alcohol and sated his baser appetites with the denizens of the city's underworld. One of them, a beautiful prostitute named Lorelei, was in actuality much older—and more dangerous—than she appeared. She seduced Harper into drinking her blood, thereby turning him into a vampire."

"You have to drink a vampire's blood in order to become a vampire?"

Malcolm nodded. "Vampirism is caused by a rare blood-borne parasite, though it's not as highly contagious as, say, hepatitis B. One must ingest large quantities of blood in order to become contaminated. That's why there are so few vampires, no more than three hundred thousand or so in the entire world." Malcolm poured the cocoa into a mug and handed it to her.

"Tell me the rest of the story," she said. "What happened after Harper became a vampire?"

"War broke out, aborting Mr. Nash's wedding plans."

An image of bloodstained linen teased at Regan's memory. "Katie's parents forced her to break her engagement."

Malcolm eyed her strangely as he slotted an English muffin into the toaster and shoved the lever down. "After Mr. Nash was captured at Bull Run and sent to Libby Prison in Richmond, Harper told Katie he'd been killed. She married Harper on the rebound."

"She married Harper?" Regan echoed in surprise.

Malcolm's face hardened. "Yes, though by all accounts it was a less-than-blissful union. Again and again Harper's lust for blood and sex led him astray. Again and again Katie forgave his lies, his transgressions, but then the war ended. When Mr. Nash showed up on Katie's doorstep, she realized the enormity of Harper's betrayal." He paused. "Harper caught Mr. Nash and Katie in bed together. He tried to skewer Mr. Nash with his cane, but Katie threw herself between the two. To this day, Mr. Nash blames himself for her death."

"But—"

"Harper blames Mr. Nash, too, and would gladly have sent him to hell decades ago, but he can't, you see. Katie cast a protection spell with her dying breath, a spell that prevents either man from killing the other." The muffin popped up. Malcolm buttered it, set it on a plate, and handed it to her.

"Okay, that explains a lot, though not how Nash became a vampire."

"That's not my tale to tell," Malcolm said.

Regan took a bite of her muffin, wondering what Malcolm was hiding. Had Nash, too, been seduced by the vampire prostitute? Or had Harper somehow engineered Nash's change as part of his revenge? She frowned, trying to make sense of it all. "You're saying Harper's held a grudge against Nash all this time?"

"Almost a century and a half," Malcolm said. "The protection spell prevents him from hurting Mr. Nash physically, but over the years he's perfected other ways to inflict pain."

"By destroying those Nash loves," she said. "The other Charles Cunningham Nashes I found on-line—the Civil War officer who came home to Pennsylvania to find his family slaughtered, the man in San Francisco accused of murdering his fiancée, the New Yorker who returned from the theater to find his housekeeper dead—those men were all Nash, the murders all part of Harper's revenge."

"Yes," Malcolm agreed. "Wherever Mr. Nash went, Harper Wakefield followed, destroying those Mr. Nash cared for. That's why Mr. Nash has earned a reputation as a recluse. He's afraid to get close to anyone, afraid to build relationships, afraid of endangering those he cares for. He knows how perilous it is to stay here, for example. If it weren't for his desire to locate the spring, he—"

"Here, you say? Harper threatens him here? But not in Europe?"

"Mr. Nash left the country after the New York incident and discovered to his surprise that Harper didn't follow."

"Why not?" she asked.

Malcolm shrugged. "I don't know. I've been with Mr. Nash for thirty years now. We've lived in Denmark, Scotland, and more recently, Romania, and in all that time, he's seen nothing of Harper Wakefield. Yet a month after returning to California, Harper is breathing down his neck again."

"You've been with Nash a long time," Regan said, not quite sure how to phrase her next question. "Are you a vampire, too?" she said finally, figuring the hell with it, she might as well just ask.

Malcolm's upper lip twitched in what might have been a smile. "No," he said.

"But you know about these things?"

"Vampires have been around since the dawn of time, some good, some evil, most somewhere in between. And as long as there have been vampires, there have been caretakers, humans who perform those essential tasks vampires can't."

"Tasks like debriding?"

He nodded, a rueful smile twisting his mouth. "And shopping in broad daylight, though the newer sunblocks have helped to reduce the risk of exposure."

She finished her muffin, then began swallowing pills, one after another. "You're a caretaker."

"Like my father before me and his father before him."

"Doesn't it bother you, the fact that Nash craves blood? Don't you worry that he might turn on you?"

"Mr. Nash would never do that."

"How can you be sure?"

"A vampire doesn't have to hurt people to survive. In all the years I've served Mr. Nash, I've never known him to drink a drop of human blood. Cow blood, yes. Pig blood occasionally. Even wild game, but never human."

And yet, by Nash's own admission, he'd nearly bitten her twice.

Nash slept past noon and probably would have slept through the afternoon, too, had Malcolm not awakened him. "She's gone, sir," Malcolm said. "Ms. Cluny."

"What do you mean, gone?" Nash shoved himself to a sitting position and swung his feet off the side of the bed. "Gone where?"

"I'm not quite certain," Malcolm said. "She seemed"

—he hesitated—"upset during breakfast. I did my best to reassure her, but—"

"Why'd she take off, then?"

"Perhaps she needed some time alone," Malcolm suggested.

Nash pulled on clothes at random. "But time alone where?" He rubbed a hand across his stubbly jaw. No time to shave. He hurried down the stairs, making his way to the kitchen, Malcolm close on his heels. "Did she take a car?"

"No," Malcolm said. "The Jaguar and the Range Rover are both in the garage."

"Then she's on foot." Where, though? That was the real question. Hitchhiking to the nearest airport? Wandering the beach? Lost in the forest? Kidnapped by Harper?

"Harper. Oh, my God, Harper."

"Unlikely, sir. Without a private plane, he couldn't very well have followed you. And even if he did trace you as far as the airport in Monterey, this property is listed under my name, not yours. Dead end."

Malcolm made good sense, but . . . "I need to call Tom." Nash grabbed the phone. "Search the beach," he told Malcolm. "Take your cell. Call if you find her. You have my number, right?"

Malcolm nodded.

"I'll head up through the trees once I check in with Tom. Maybe she's lost. Or hurt." Or hiding.

Regan sat cross-legged on the grass, gazing up at the Spirit Ladder. Diaphanous sheets of water seemed to tumble straight out of the sky and down the rocky stairway, first falling in a sheer white veil, then spraying out in a lacy froth.

The midday sun fell warm on her bare shoulders. Bees buzzed. Butterflies flittered. Birds chattered. A lone ant scuttled across her hand, looking for a shortcut to the land of milk and honey.

"Nash is a vampire," she told the ant.

He ignored her.

And no wonder. "Doesn't compute for me, either," she said. "Can't seem to wrap my mind around it, though it does explain a few things—for instance, all those times his eyes seemed to glow red, the funny look he gave me when I complained about the bloodsucking mosquitoes, his penchant for long sleeves, his habit of working half the night and sleeping half the day. And that time he licked my neck wounds. Heaven help me, I thought it was sexy. A little kinky, but . . ."

"Regan!" Nash's voice, harsh with an edge of panic, echoed across the meadow.

"Speak of the devil," she whispered to the ant, then turned. He stood in the shade just inside the tree line, looking even sexier and more dangerous than usual with his dark hair rumpled and beard stubble shadowing his jaw.

"I've been searching everywhere for you. What are you doing all the way up here?" he called.

"Talking to an ant. Why?"

He frowned. "I was worried about you."

"To tell the truth, I'm a little worried about myself."

She stood. "Talking to ants is one of the warning signs of mental illness, you know. Ranks right up there behind having sex with vampires."

"Regan, don't do this."

He was concerned; she could hear it in his voice. But she hadn't figured out how she felt. If she felt. Right now she was too numb.

She crossed the meadow, avoiding the thorny canes of a wild rose, a clump of poison oak. "The situation's utterly surreal," she said. "Dalíesque. The face and the fruit bowl. Do you know that painting? We're like that, you and I, neither of us exactly what we seem." She stopped within a foot of him, the sunlight falling across her face while he lingered in the shadows.

"I shouldn't have told you," Nash said. "But once you saw the burns . . ."

She met his gaze, blazing blue, brilliant as the sky above. "How are your burns?"

Nash unbuttoned his shirt to display muscular pecs and washboard abs, all covered with perfect, unblemished skin. "Healed," he said.

"Like magic."

"Dark magic. Magic with a price." He studied her face. "You said you needed time to process, but I didn't expect you to wander off on your own. It's not safe."

"Why? Harper's no danger to me here, is he?"

"I don't think so. As far as I know, I'm the only vampire in Big Sur." Bitterness colored his words.

The only vampire. The only danger.

"Why did you come here?" he asked. "Why this place?"

He knew why. He must. Memories, bittersweet now, flashed through her mind. She ignored them, focusing instead on the muted roar of the falls. "I thought maybe I could think more clearly on the mountain, that maybe if I stared long enough at the falls, my brain would unmuddle itself."

"Did it help?"

"No." She stared at him helplessly. "I didn't intend to worry you, but I couldn't stay in the house another minute. When I saw all that blood in the library, I lost it."

"But I cleaned the floor."

"Not blood on the floor. Blood in the minifridge. Packets of it, like fruit juice."

"Oh, God." He glanced at her, his expression ineffably sad. "I'm sorry."

"So am I," she said. "Though the shock did bring one thing into focus. That's why you're so anxious to find the spring, isn't it? Because you're a vampire. You're searching for a cure."

He nodded, weary resignation in the gesture.

"And Harper's trying to stop you?"

"No," he said. "Harper's trying to destroy me."

"You should go back to Europe. Malcolm told me Harper can't follow you there."

"He could," Nash said, "but he won't, not without Elizabeth, and she refuses to leave the U.S."

"Elizabeth?"

"A vampire he's loved almost as long as he's hated me."

"So Harper has an Achilles' heel. Perhaps if you threatened this Elizabeth—"

"No!" Nash said sharply, and then in more moderate tones, "I refuse to sink to his level."

She shrugged. "Go back to Europe, then."

"I will, but not yet. We're very close to finding the spring, so close I can almost taste it."

She recognized the desperation in his voice; it was an emotion she knew only too well. Sympathy welled up unbidden, and she touched his shoulder in a gesture of comfort.

A mistake. She knew that even before she did it. One touch and she was lost. Even now, even knowing what she knew, she wanted him. He filled her thoughts, her heart, her soul.

"Regan," he said. Just that. Her name. Then he pulled her into his arms and kissed her, his mouth warm and demanding.

Her resistance melted away, and with it, her doubts. She was dying anyway. Nothing could change that. So why not spend the time she had left with the man she loved? Vampire or not, Nash was the one she wanted.

As if alerted by some sixth sense, Nash glanced up just as Regan appeared at the top of the stairs. Breathtakingly beautiful—literally—she was wearing the green dress he'd had Malcolm pick up in Monterey, a flirty scrap of silk that bared more skin than it covered. Intricate jade-and-gold earrings, one of Malcolm's more inspired purchases, dangled from her earlobes. And the rest was Regan, slender and vibrant, her hair tumbling around her face in soft curls.

She didn't notice him standing in the door to the library until she hit the bottom step. She smiled then, and his heart stopped for a three count. "You look beautiful," he said.

"I feel beautiful." She crossed the entry, her heels tap-tap-tapping accompaniment. "Here, feel." Capturing his hand, she pressed it to her abdomen. "I'm wearing the matching belly-button ring as per your request, though, frankly, what does it matter? No one can see it."

"But I'll know it's there," he said. "And you'll know I know."

"You're a devious devil, Charles Cunningham Nash." Still smiling, she stretched up on tiptoes to press a kiss to his lips. "I love that in a man."

Regan eyed the trendy crowd milling about the restaurant terrace. "When you asked if I'd like to go to a little party, I was expecting something slightly more intimate."

Nash gave her hand a squeeze. "We don't have to stay long if you don't want. But since we were here in Big Sur, it seemed rude not to put in at least a token appearance. Marcia Tischler, the organizer, is a neighbor, and it's a good cause, after all, raising money for brain tumor research."

"Brain tumor research?" Regan hoped her voice didn't betray her surprise.

"Leo Tischler, Marcia's husband, died of a brain tumor three years ago. Since then, she's been tireless in her fund-raising efforts."

"I thought you lived abroad. How is it you know this Tischler woman?"

"Through Leo. He's the one who sold me the Father Padilla manuscripts," he said. "Normally I avoid affairs like this, but I thought you might enjoy it."

"Gave me an excuse to wear my pretty new dress," she agreed. "Plus, rubbing shoulders with the rich and famous? Always fun."

"Would you like something to drink?" Nash nodded toward the bar.

"Just water," she said.

He disappeared into the throng, and Regan scanned the crowd for familiar faces. Most of the people she recognized were celebrities she knew by reputation only, though she did spot one politician who was a friend of her father's. She smiled and waved at the woman.

Behind her, someone said, "Regan Cluny? Is that you?"

A British accent she'd know anywhere. Smiling in genuine pleasure, she turned. "Hugh Sterling! What a surprise!"

"You've cut your hair," he said. "I like it. Very Charlize Theron."

"Thanks. What are you doing here?"

"Rapidly becoming tipsy." He gave her one of his

trademark lopsided smiles. "One should know better than to drink on an empty stomach, but somehow one never does."

"I saw *No Prince Charming* last month. The toothpick sword fight? Hysterical. And you were fantastic, as always."

"I was, wasn't I?" He took a sip of his champagne, his expression shifting from smug to pensive. "Though I do worry a bit about being typecast as the suave leading man. Yes, I am brilliant at clever banter and sexual innuendo, but I have the chops for meatier roles. I daresay I could do a better job with *Equus* than that Harry Potter fellow. Nudity required, of course. Luckily, my ass is truly stellar. Here. Give those glutes a good squeeze." Hugh angled his stellar ass in her direction.

She laughed. "Outrageous as ever, I see. Thanks for the offer, but I'll pass."

"She'll pass on the ass." He heaved a dramatic sigh, then paused, his handsome head tilted to one side. "Actually, that's rather poetic, isn't it? She'll pass on the ass." He smiled vaguely, then wandered off to offer his ass to some other unsuspecting female.

"More pathetic than poetic if you ask me," Nash said from behind her.

"Oh, you caught that, did you?"

Nash handed her a drink. "Annoying bastard."

"He's really quite nice," she protested.

"If you say so," Nash said.

"You're not jealous, are you?"

"Of an egocentric British twit? No way. Now, if it

had been someone like George Clooney offering his ass for the squeezing . . ."

Regan scanned the crowd. "George is here?"

"Not that I know of, but—"

"Look," she said, waving at a couple on the far side of the crowd. "There's Clint and Dina."

"Regan?"

She froze. No mistaking that voice either, a whiskey tenor with the faintest hint of an Irish accent.

"Dad," she said, turning to face him with a half-hearted smile. "What a surprise."

Her father cocked an eyebrow at Nash. "You notice I didn't merit an adjective? Not a 'pleasant' surprise or even a 'nice' surprise. Just a surprise. Period." He pressed a kiss to Regan's cheek. "Introduce me to your friend."

She turned to Nash. "You notice I didn't merit a 'please' or even a 'would you.' Just an order. Period."

"Chip off the old block," her dad said, which was truer than she cared to admit.

"Dad, this is Nash. Charles Cunningham Nash. Nash, this is my father, Desmond Cluny."

The two men shook hands, sizing each other up. "I know you," her father said. "You're the one who found the alien city buried in the desert. They featured you on the *Inside Scoop*."

"Don't believe everything you see on tabloid TV," Regan said.

"What? You mean he hasn't dug up any little green men?"

"Hard to say," Nash said. "It's virtually impossible

to determine skin pigmentation from bone fragments."

Her father stared at Nash for a second or two, then burst into laughter. "Got to appreciate a man with a sly sense of humor." He turned to Regan, studying her closely. "You're looking well, much better than the last time I saw you." Three months ago in the hospital, he meant.

Nash shot her a questioning glance that she pretended not to see.

"You're looking great, too, Dad. Have you started production yet on the big Civil War epic?" she asked in an effort to distract him. "You might consider using Nash as a consultant. He's something of an expert on that era."

Nash gave her a look that promised future reprisals.

"Really?" her father said. "That's nice."

So much for distractions. Well, if at first . . . "Have you seen Hugh Sterling? He's here somewhere."

"What would I want with that pompous twit?" her dad demanded.

Nash laughed, rather uncharitably, she thought.

"I spent last weekend at the Donahues' place in the Hamptons," her father said. "Ran into Dr. Hartmann. He asked how you were doing."

"Fine," she said, smiling so hard she was afraid her cheek muscles would start twitching.

"I told him you'd gone back to work."

"That's me. Work, work, work. Though since meeting Nash"—she slipped her hand in his—"I'm beginning to understand the benefits of play."

"Glad to hear it, kiddo." Her dad's smile nearly broke her heart. "Life's too precious to waste. You're still planning to come visit me next month, right?"

"Absolutely."

"Marcia Tischler was just telling me about this New Age practitioner in Beverly Hills, uses crystals and whatnot. Not that I'm big on that kind of crap, but I figure what the hell? Anything's worth a shot."

"Who's Dr. Hartmann?" Nash asked later on the drive down the coast to the restaurant where he'd made dinner reservations.

"A therapist," she lied.

"You have a therapist?"

"Had," she said. "Past tense. I went through a rough patch a few months ago. Found out a friend of mine was terminally ill. Shook me up a little. Forced me to reexamine my priorities."

"Such as?"

"Family. Reconnecting with my dad, for one thing."

Nash glanced sideways at her. "Reconnecting?"

"My mother died when I was twelve. Neither of us handled it well. I threw tantrums. He threw himself into his work. Things got so bad between us—my fault, most of it—that he finally sent me off to a Catholic boarding school where the nuns did their best to hammer some sense into me. At the time, I felt he'd abandoned me just when I needed him the most. Took me twenty years to get past the resentment."

"Is he ill?" Nash asked.

"Not likely. The man's healthy as a horse. Never been sick a day in his life. Why?"

"He mentioned a Beverly Hills practitioner."

"Oh, that." She forced a laugh. "Dad's got this crazy idea he needs to contact my mother."

"Your *dead* mother?"

"I told you it was a crazy idea. He already tried a couple of so-called ghost whisperers. The New Age practitioner is just the latest wannabe go-between."

"I wish him luck," Nash said. "He seems like a nice man."

Regan laughed. "I doubt most of Hollywood would agree with you. He has a reputation as a shark."

"Well deserved, I'm sure," Nash said. "When you were in the ladies' room, he threatened to eviscerate me if I broke your heart."

"That's my dad."

"I miss that," he said.

"What? Threats of evisceration?"

"No, family ties."

"You don't have family, but you have Malcolm."

"And you," he said, pulling her hand to his mouth and pressing a kiss to her palm.

Nash broke the speed limit on the way home. He wanted Regan. No, more than that, he needed Regan. Desperately. Greedily. Immediately.

The how and the why of it didn't matter anymore. Maybe she was Katie reincarnated. as Malcolm seemed to think. Or maybe she was just Regan, sweet and stubborn and sexy as sin. He didn't care why he found her so irresistible. All that mattered at the moment was that he have her, and the sooner the better.

Neither of them spoke as the miles slid past in a blur, not even when Nash turned off the highway for the seemingly endless winding drive up the hill to the house.

He paused to kiss her in the garage, then again at the foot of the stairs. "You'll sleep with me tonight," he said, and it wasn't a question.

Regan gazed up at him, a smile playing at the corners of her mouth. "I don't know how much sleep we'll get."

"Is that a promise?"

She drew an imaginary X on her chest. "Cross my heart and hope to die."

"I'll take your word for it. No dying necessary," he said.

Sadness shadowed her eyes for a second. But then she smiled, and he thought he must have imagined it. "Race you," she said, and took off up the stairs.

He caught up with her on the second step from the top, grabbed her around the waist, and tossed her over his shoulder.

"Hey," she protested. But she was laughing.

He hit the light switch with his elbow, then set her on her feet just inside his bedroom.

Regan ran for the bed, ripping back the quilt and throwing herself dramatically across the sheets. "I win!"

"You cheated," he protested.

"You cheated first. Picking me up and throwing me over your shoulder was interference."

"Fair enough," he said. "I concede. What's the prize?"

"You are," she said, beckoning him with a curl of her finger.

He crossed the room, shucking clothes as fast as he could. "I love you," he said, shocking both of them.

Various emotions chased themselves across Regan's face. "Nash, I . . ."

Don't feel the same way? Was that what she meant?

"Did I mention the one big plus to making love with a vampire?" he asked quickly, not giving her a chance to put her thoughts into words he was pretty sure he didn't want to hear. He hadn't been able to interpret all of the emotions flitting across Regan's face, but he'd damned well recognized her dismay.

"Only one?" She had the longest lashes, thick and dark.

"No condoms needed," he said. "No clothes, either."

He managed to strip off his boxers and her dress before she grabbed him. "My prize, my rules," she said, shoving him onto his back. And then she was all over him, first with her hands and then with her mouth, sucking, sucking, sucking so hard he thought he would lose his mind.

So maybe she didn't love him, but damned if she didn't want him.

Pain, sharp and unexpected, stole his breath. He

reared up on his elbows, growling a protest. "Don't damage the equipment."

"But you heal so fast." Regan shot him a wicked smile, then used the tip of her tongue to lick away the pain.

He relaxed against the sheets, all but purring in satisfaction.

But when she nipped a little harder the second time, he flipped her over, pinning her to the bed. "This is war," he said.

She smiled. "*Morituri te salutamus.* That's Latin for 'Bring it on,' right?"

"Close." He found his discarded tie on the floor next to the bed and used it to bind her wrists to the headboard.

"What are you doing?" she demanded, jerking against the restraints and doing her best to wriggle out from under him.

"Fighting dirty." He raked his gaze down her torso. Her underwear showcased rather than covered, the underwire cups of her demibra emphasizing the upward thrust of her breasts while exposing her nipples, the lacy thong doing little to hide what lay beneath. "Bringing it on."

He ravaged her lips, her breasts, the damp curls beneath the lacy thong, kissing and sucking until she was sobbing for breath, begging for release.

He bent over her, sucking one nipple and then the other before licking his way down her flat stomach to the faint indentation where her belly-button ring, a thin gold circle studded with tiny jade beads, pierced her skin. He swirled his tongue into her navel, then used the tip to flip the ring up and down, up and down.

"Oh," she moaned on a sobbing breath, and then, "Oh, God!" as he pushed the lacy crotch of her thong out of his way so he could slide two fingers inside her.

"Been waiting all night to do this," he whispered. Up and down. Up and down. In and out. In and out. "All the while we were making nice at the fund-raiser. All the while we were having dinner. All the while we were driving back. All that time I was watching you in that flirty little green dress and imagining what you looked like underneath, what you felt like, what you tasted like." Up and down. In and out.

She arched her back and thrashed from side to side. Side to side. In and out. Up and down. "Please, Nash."

"Please, Nash, what?" he prompted.

"Please don't torture me like this."

"Wrong answer," he said.

THIRTEEN

Regan came in a hot, sweet, ecstatic rush. She might have screamed. She was pretty sure she screamed, but she couldn't help it. Nash did things with that tongue of his, wicked, wicked things, things she'd never experienced before. Three times she'd come to climax, the first time while she was still in her underwear, that decadent underwear hanging now from the lampshade.

"Cliché," she said.

"What is?" he mumbled against her breast.

"Underwear on the lampshade."

Without looking up, without lifting his head, he reached out and flipped it off onto the floor. "Better?"

"Much."

Heat began to swell again in response to the ministrations of his tongue and lips. Three times she'd come to climax, each time more exquisite than the last, and yet Nash still hadn't penetrated her. He still hadn't had a single orgasm.

Why, though? Because she hadn't said she loved him, too?

She'd wanted to say the words but had known it wouldn't be fair. "I love you" implied "happily ever after," not "happily for the next few months."

Or maybe he was afraid of losing control. Of initiating that blood bond he'd told her about.

But what if he did lose it? What if he did bite her? Couldn't she bear a little pain to bring him a fraction of the pleasure he'd given her?

He wanted her. She knew that without asking. His erection, thick and hard, lay warm against her belly. But still he hadn't entered her.

"Nash?" she said.

"Hmm?" His hands kneaded her breasts as he used his tongue to do that distracting flip-flop thing on her belly-button ring.

"What's the right answer?"

He shoved himself up so he could make eye contact. "There are lots of possibilities. Lots of right answers." He ran one finger down her throat, down the valley between her breasts, down her stomach, and down even further.

She drew a ragged breath, hardly able to think, let alone speak. "I want you inside me. I need you inside me."

"That's better," he said, releasing her hands with a single jerk on the knot. "Don't ask. Demand. Don't beg. Take."

"But you're stronger than I am."

"True." He rolled over onto his back. "But then, I don't plan to put up much of a fight."

She climbed astride him, rubbing her hands lightly over his biceps, his pectorals. Desire swept over her in a dizzying rush. Never had she wanted anyone as much as she wanted Nash.

She shifted her weight up on her knees, then reached again for his erection. Warm and hard and big. Carefully she lowered herself onto him, easing down an inch at a time until he filled her with his warmth.

She did a little experimental rocking and saw him wince. "Did I hurt you?" she asked.

"No." He groaned. "Feels good. Too good."

"No such thing," she said, and rocked again, this time squeezing hard as well.

He swore softly under his breath.

She smiled. Her turn to do the torturing. She squeezed again, flexing her internal muscles.

Nash groaned, then brushed the back of his knuckles lightly across the tips of her breasts, an action that sent shock waves zinging through her body.

And the battle was on.

She rocked. He fondled.

She squeezed. He suckled.

A haze of desire obscured details. Regan lost track of who did what. All she knew was she wanted, she needed. Tension coiled in her body, tighter and tighter and tighter still. She couldn't think or breathe. All she could do was react. Heat and need devoured her, the pressure building to unbearable heights before she fell off the edge into shuddering ecstasy.

And to her great and lasting satisfaction, Nash lost control as well this time—a full five seconds before she did.

She'd thought he might sink his teeth in her neck then, but he didn't. He growled low in his throat and nipped at her but not hard enough to break the skin. "I love you," he said against her breast. Or maybe he didn't. Maybe all she heard was the frenzied throb of her own heartbeat.

Nash lay spooned around Regan as she slept. He loved the texture of her skin, her warmth, her scent. He loved the way her hair curled at the nape of her neck, the contrast between the narrowness of her waist and the curve of her hip. He loved the way she responded to his touch, the way she forced him to respond. He loved her smile and her wit and the way she said what she thought even when she knew it wasn't what you wanted to hear. He loved her. Period. End of story. And he didn't care if she loved him back.

Okay, lie. He did care, but he was willing to wait, willing to give her however much time she needed to come to the same conclusion.

And if she doesn't?

His arms tightened around her convulsively. She would. She would love him eventually. Some part of her loved him already. He was sure of it.

But what if she doesn't? Do you love her enough to let her go?

Nash's heart hammered against his breastbone. Did he love her enough?

Maybe he did. After all, he hadn't buried his teeth in her throat, had he? And this despite that incredible joining, the hands-down, all-bets-off, most amazing sex of his life.

He smoothed the tumbled curls back off her forehead. "I love you," he whispered. "I love you, Katie."

No, Regan.

Damn.

"Need some help scrubbing your back?" Katie asked, shocked by her own temerity.

Charles, chest deep in hot water, glanced up. His freshly shaved face, all sharp angles and brilliant blue eyes, registered first surprise and then pleasure. "Why, Katie, you little minx you."

"I've waited so long," she said in her own defense.

"As have I, my sweet. Pay no attention to my teasing."

"I brought you a dressing gown." She draped it over the back of the same chair that held the towels she'd set out earlier. "An old one of Harper's I found upstairs."

He gave her an odd look. "You used to call him Cousin Harper."

"I did, yes," she agreed, feeling flustered but hoping it didn't show. "Living here at Harmony Hill with Uncle Spencer and Aunt Selina, I've gotten out of the habit. Naturally Harper is what they call him."

"Naturally," he agreed. "Where are the Mayhews, by the way?"

Was he concerned that they might return to find him bathing in their kitchen with her in attendance? And wouldn't that cause a scene? she thought. Aunt Selina would likely have hysterics. Uncle Spencer might even call Nash out. "They went upriver to visit their daughter Rachel. I expect them back sometime tomorrow."

"They left you alone?" he asked in surprise.

"Not truly alone. Old Silas is here. He and two of his grandsons have been helping Uncle Spencer get things organized for next spring's planting. They're living in the former slave quarters."

"But you're the only one in the house."

"Except you," she said. And it wasn't a lie. Not really. Harper had gone upriver, too. Hunting.

"Turn around," Charles said. "I'm getting out."

She turned quickly, her cheeks on fire, though not embarrassed for the reason he thought. She hated lying to him, even lying by omission, but she couldn't tell him the truth. He'd never understand.

"I daresay you've never seen a naked man."

"No," she said, not quite a lie. Harper always came to her in the dark.

"I wouldn't want to shock your maidenly eyes." She heard the water slosh as he stepped out of the tub, the scratch of the towels, the rustle of the robe.

"I'm no longer easily shocked," she said. "These past few years have stripped away most of my girlish illusions."

"Poor Katie," he said from right behind her, so close his breath stirred the hair at her temple. Then his arms came around her, warm and strong, pulling her against him. "I wish you could have been spared the horrors of war and the untimely loss of your parents."

She turned, draping her arms around his neck. "I don't want to think about the past. Only the present. That's all that exists, all that matters. You and I in the here and now. By all rights, we should be married. By all rights, this should be our wedding night."

"And so it shall be, Katie." Smiling, he swung her up into his arms with amazing ease, strong despite his half-starved appearance. He carried her up the narrow back stairs, pausing at the top. The single oil lamp on the table near the front-stairs landing did little to dispel the shadows. "Which way?"

Which way, indeed? The house was large, but her choices were limited. Only two beds were made up. So should she direct him to her aunt and uncle's room? Or to the chamber she shared with Harper? "Last door on the left," she said finally. The room she shared with Harper. Though the chamber itself was smaller, the bed was better, furnished with a nearly new feather tick.

Once inside, Charles set her on her feet, then moved to the windows, pushing the heavy draperies aside and opening the shutters to admit the moonlight.

It had been a night like this, with a full moon shining down, bright and beguiling, when she'd fallen under Harper's spell. The moon had seemed to bathe the world in silvery magic. Harper had backed her against a tree in the cemetery and done such wicked things to her, evoked such fierce reactions. Bliss and pain irrevocably intertwined. The memory of those forbidden pleasures shamed her now.

Harper had lied. He'd lied about Charles's death, and he'd lied about his intentions.

But part of the fault was hers. She'd given herself to him too easily, with no regard for the possible consequences, not that she'd had even the faintest notion how very far-reaching those consequences would be.

Charles turned to face her. "I, Charles, take thee, Katie, to be my lawfully wedded wife."

She stepped closer, gripping his hands tightly. "And I, Katie, take thee, Charles, to be my lawfully wedded husband."

"I love you, Katie," he said.

"And I love you." She was weeping. She couldn't help it.

"Don't cry. It's all right." He pulled her against his chest, holding her close, comforting her. "We don't have to do this if you don't want. We've waited this long. We can wait a little longer, long enough to find a minister to marry us properly."

"No," she said. "You don't understand. I'm not weeping because I'm frightened. I'm weeping for joy. I love you, and I don't want to wait for a minister. I don't want to wait another second."

"Then we won't."

He undressed her by moonlight, struggling a little with her corset strings and laughing over his own clumsiness. She didn't mind the awkwardness. To her, it just proved he hadn't been with many women. She might even be his first.

Her heart beat faster at the possibility that Charles had saved himself for her. Surely that was a measure of true love.

Harper claimed he loved her. Harper claimed he'd always loved her. Yet he hadn't said a word when she'd become engaged to Charles. Instead of confessing his feelings, instead of making his case, he'd run off to sulk in the brothels of New Orleans, where he'd fallen under the spell of a bloodsucking woman named Lorelei. Harper swore he'd never loved the harlot.

But he whispered her name in his sleep.

"Katie?" Charles's voice rescued her from the mire of her thoughts, bringing her back to the sweet, sweet present. They stood naked in front of the window, face-to-face, bathed in moonlight.

He trailed a finger down her throat, then cupped one breast. "I dreamed of this. Of you. But you're more beautiful in reality than in my wildest imaginings. Your skin's like silk, and you smell of jasmine. I wonder. Will you taste of honey?"

She wrapped her arms around his neck and lifted her lips to his. "Why don't you find out?"

Regan turned in his arms, murmuring something in her sleep.

Or maybe she wasn't asleep, he thought, when she wrapped her hands around his penis, stroking, rubbing, and squeezing until he was rock hard and on the verge of losing it.

"Regan, what are you—"

"Shh," she said, then, "Touch me."

So he did, exploring all her warm, soft places.

His heart pounded. His senses swam.

"Now," she said, rolling onto her back and pulling him on top of her.

He buried himself in her warmth. Tight and slick, a sinful combination designed to drive a man to the brink. Even so, his orgasm took him by surprise, an explosion of pleasure so intense it was almost pain. Was pain, he realized suddenly.

Regan, caught up in the throes of her own extended climax, was biting his neck. The sharp tang of blood—his blood—mingled with the musky scent of sex.

"Stop it! What are you doing?" Charles jerked away from her, a hand pressed to his throat.

She squeezed her eyes shut, breathing deeply. The rich, coppery odor of fresh blood fed her darkest desires. She moaned in ecstasy, then ran her tongue across her teeth, savoring the last of the heady flavor.

Regan opened her eyes, jolted back to reality by the worried expression on Nash's face. "What?" she said. It was only when her gaze dropped lower, to the blood trickling from the wound on his neck, that she realized what she'd done . . . what Katie'd done.

"I turned you, didn't I? Back then. Back when I was Katie and you were Charles. Katie was a vampire, wasn't she?" She dug her fingers into his shoulders, hoping against hope that he'd tell her it wasn't true.

"Yes," he said, eyeing her strangely. "Only how did you know that?"

"My dreams," she said. "Ever since I met you, I've been having these dreams, and until now, I couldn't remember them. I'd wake up and they would dissolve into nothingness, leaving only a hint of residual emotion in their wake. But this time, I remember. I remember all of it—Papa forcing me to break off our engagement, learning that you'd died at Second Manassas, Harper luring me to the graveyard with the promise of adventure." She stopped, and her eyes filled with tears.

"It's okay," he said.

"No, it's not." She blinked, and her eyes overflowed. Glistening trails traversed her cheeks. "He lied, and I believed him. He stole my innocence, and I forgave him. He changed me, and I embraced him. And then you showed up. Do you remember that day?"

"Could I ever forget?"

"You were the best, dearest part of my life, Charles, and I destroyed you."

"You didn't destroy anything. I'm still here." He held her close.

But she wasn't comforted. "I forced a blood bond. I gave you no choice."

"I loved you."

"Past tense," she said.

"Exactly. You're not Katie. You're Regan. And I'm not Charles. I'm Nash." He hugged her close, then kissed away her tears.

"But—"

He pressed a finger to her lips. "Go to sleep. Get some rest. It's almost morning."

"And tomorrow is another day." She uttered a little sob of laughter that bordered on hysteria. "I'm not Scarlett O'Hara, Nash."

"No, and you're not Katie O'Malley, either."

Someone rapped sharply on the door.

Nash shot a quick, concerned glance toward Regan. She stirred but didn't wake.

"Sir?" Malcolm said.

Nash pulled on his trousers and strode to the door. Opening it a crack, he peered out. "What do you need, Malcolm?"

"Tom Davis just called. A CHP officer found a body abandoned alongside the highway thirty miles out of Cascade early Saturday morning. They've identified the victim as one of the graduate students working the dig in Juniper Basin."

"Victim, you say? Was it an accident? Or do they suspect foul play?"

"Hit-and-run," Malcolm said.

"Did Tom happen to mention which grad student it was?"

"Tyler Ciccone."

Nash frowned. The young man who'd "discovered" the hidden spring. And very possibly the one who'd faked the pictographs and buried the snake skeleton.

"Call Tom for me, would you?" Nash said. "Tell him we're flying back immediately."

"Shall I wake Ms. Cluny, then?"

Regan, wrapped in a sheet, poked her head around the door. "You already have."

Nash, rumpled, bleary-eyed, and beard stubbled, walked in the office door at ten after ten on Sunday morning. Tom had never in his life been so thankful to see anyone. He started to relinquish the chair behind the desk, but Nash shook his head, then propped himself against the wall.

"Thank God you're back," Tom said. "This place is a zoo. The phone's been ringing off the hook. Cops, reporters, you name it."

"The Ciccone boy's parents?"

"I called them as soon as I heard, but the authorities had already notified them."

Nash looked as if he hadn't had any more sleep than Tom had. So either he and Regan had had a really, really good weekend or a really, really bad weekend. Tom figured now was not the best time to ask which.

"The cops are calling it a hit-and-run, but I got the feeling there's more to the story than they're releasing." Tom drained what was probably his fifth cup of coffee in the last hour. No wonder he had the jitters.

"They think he was run down deliberately?" Nash frowned. "But why?"

Tom shrugged. "I went looking for Tyler after you

left Friday, thought I'd sound him out, but he'd already taken off. According to his roommate, Alan Levy, Tyler caught a ride into Chisel Rock with Winston after dinner and was planning to hitchhike on in to Cascade. Alan claims Tyler has a girlfriend there."

"Did Winston corroborate the Levy kid's story?"

Tom nodded. "The hitchhiking part, yes. Only, according to Winston, the kid had a stuffed-to-the-gills backpack with him. More than he'd need for a weekend."

"He was running?"

"That's my take on it. Thinking back, I realized he was one of the people at the table when you told me you'd just gotten Laura's report on the snake skeleton."

"You're suggesting he panicked and took off."

"I think so."

"I guess the real question is, who ran him down and why? Was it an accident, or not?"

"What does it matter? Dead is dead," Tom said, feeling a little sick to his stomach.

Nash's eyes burned. His head throbbed. His muscles threatened to cramp up on him every time he shifted position. He needed sleep, desperately, but someone had to stay here to field calls, and Tom was in even worse shape than he was.

He must have drowsed off in his chair, because when a sharp knock on the door roused him, it was after one in the afternoon. The last he remembered, it had been ten thirty.

"Come in." He rubbed at his eyes with the back of his hand. Felt like he had a half yard of gravel in each one.

The door swung open to reveal Deputy Faraday. "You're back," he said, sounding surprised.

"Returned as soon as I heard about the hit-and-run."

"And Dr. Davis?"

"Sleeping," Nash said. "He had a long night. Have a seat."

Faraday, whose beard had graduated from stubble to scrunge, sank down on a folding chair with a muffled groan. "Been a hell of a weekend for all of us." His tone was casual, but his eyes were sharp, his gaze moving around the office as if he were taking inventory.

Nash leaned back in his chair, trying to ignore the warning prickles on the back of his neck. "What can I do for you, Deputy?"

"Mind if I get a forensics team out to examine the vehicles in the compound?"

"No, of course not. What exactly are you looking for?"

"Evidence."

Nash frowned. "You think someone from the dig deliberately ran down Tyler Ciccone?"

"I didn't say that."

"But that's what you think."

"It's one possibility." His gaze scalded Nash. "I understand you left Friday night about the same time Ciccone did."

"I didn't run over him, if that's what you're imply-ing. Ask Ms. Cluny. She was in the Wrangler with me. Besides, we drove straight north up 139 to the airport in Klamath Falls. Tyler was killed on the highway that runs west from Chisel Rock to Cascade."

"You're remarkably well informed on the details."

"Tom filled me in."

"Did you know the Ciccone boy's body was muti-lated postmortem?"

Alarm bells went off in Nash's head. "There was nothing mentioned about mutilation on the news this morning."

"It's a detail we purposely withheld from the media."

"But you're telling me. Why?"

"Ciccone's body had multiple puncture wounds inconsistent with his accident, and the coroner's preliminary examination revealed something even stranger. Though there was little blood at the scene, Ciccone suffered significant blood loss."

Harper. Harper or some of his gang members. "That's odd," Nash said carefully, "but again, why tell me?"

"The sheriff's department has seen a number of peculiar incidents this summer—reports of exsangui-nated cattle, the brutal attack on Ms. Cluny, and now this. Your dig here in Juniper Basin seems to be right at the epicenter of all the weird occurrences."

"Are you accusing me of something?"

Faraday widened his eyes in feigned surprise. "Why, no."

Nash met the other man's mockery with a level gaze. "I'm on your side, whether you believe it or not. I promise my complete cooperation. If there's anything I can do . . ."

Faraday let it hang there for a few moments. "Actually, there is one thing."

"Of course. Name it."

"Is there a bathroom handy?"

Not quite the request he'd expected, but . . . Nash nodded toward the door at the far end of the room. "Be my guest."

Faraday disappeared into the small bathroom. Nash heard the toilet flush, the water running in the sink. Then Faraday appeared in the doorway, his hands dripping water onto the vinyl flooring. "Do you have a towel?"

"On the rack to the left of the sink," Nash said.

Faraday shook his head. "I looked."

"It was there earlier." Nash crossed to the bathroom and wedged himself in past the deputy. Faraday was right. No towel hung from the rack. Nash opened the cabinet under the sink, dug out a clean hand towel, and handed it to the deputy.

Faraday dried his hands, hung the towel on the rack, then said, "Oh, mystery solved. Here's the other towel. Somebody must have knocked it off, into the wastebasket." Smiling, he retrieved the missing towel and handed it to Nash.

Faraday was a good liar and an even better actor, but Nash wasn't fooled. The deputy had deliberately hidden the towel so he had an excuse to lure Nash into the bathroom. And it was painfully obvious why. Nash glanced into the mirror above the sink. *Yes, Deputy, I do have a reflection.*

Nash had to admit the man's open-mindedness surprised him, though. Vampires? How many pragmatic law-enforcement types would even consider such an off-the-wall possibility?

Faraday left shortly after that. On his way out, he paused, one hand on the doorknob. "Someone will show up later today to examine the vehicles."

"I'll alert the rest of the staff," Nash said.

Once again, Faraday started to leave and once again, he stopped, this time with the door hanging open. "I almost forgot. You left a message asking me to call back the other day. I got busy, and it totally slipped my mind. What was that about?"

"I was wondering about the farms and ranches that border the dig," Nash said. "Have any of them changed hands recently? What can you tell me about Kevin Ransom, Everett and Marigold Casper, and T.E. Spinelli?"

Faraday held up a thumb. "The Casper family has owned their place since the turn of the last century." His index finger joined the thumb. "Kevin Ransom bought out his dad a few years back. He's lived in the area his whole life and, coincidentally, is married to the sheriff's sister." His middle finger made three. "And T.E.—that's short for Teresa Something, by the way—is a former hippie who lives in a sixties time warp. She supports herself by selling free-range chickens, raku pottery, and custom silver jewelry."

"She's not listed in the phone book," Nash said. "I thought she might be new to the area."

"Nope. Been around since before I was born. Her phone's listed under Free Spirit Gifts," Faraday said.

All of which led to a dead end.

FOURTEEN

After Faraday left, Nash looked up the so-called chupacabra attacks in the online version of the *Cascade Courier* and marked their locations in red on his two-layer map. Red stars also marked the hit-and-run site and the spot where Regan had been attacked.

He studied the seemingly random stars, looking for a pattern. Faraday had claimed Juniper Basin was the epicenter of the attacks, but that wasn't really true. Regan had been attacked within two miles of the dig, whereas Tyler's attack had occurred halfway to Cascade, almost fifty miles north and west of Juniper Basin. As for the so-called chupacabra attacks, all three had been clustered along Obsidian Butte Road, ten miles to the south, on BLM rangeland. If there was a pattern, he couldn't see it.

Regan popped her head in the door. "Oh," she said. "You're busy."

"What do you need?"

"Never mind. I'll—"

"You've been avoiding me all day. Please tell me what's wrong."

"It's nothing to do with you. It's me. I—"

"You're having second thoughts about getting involved with a monster."

"No, it's not that." She stared at him, her expression tortured. "Or not just that. It's everything. All the weirdness. The dreams and the reincarnation thing. I need time to get it sorted out in my head." She studied the well-worn vinyl flooring in apparent fascination.

"Okay. Time. You've got it. Take all the time you need. I can even bunk with Winston for a while, give you some privacy."

"You don't have to—"

"I do," he said. "I really do. Otherwise, I'll . . ." He stopped.

She shook her head, her expression ineffably sad.

Silence, awkward and uncomfortable, filled the space between them.

"But if you didn't come in here to talk about us," Nash said finally, "then. . . ?"

She tore her gaze from the cracks and gouges in the flooring to look him in the eye. "I came to Juniper Basin looking for a story with a human-interest angle, and I found one. No," she said when he started to protest. "It has nothing to do with vampires or your feud with Harper. It's a story about the attempt to connect myth and reality and how seriously that goal was compromised by a young man's reckless decision to tamper with the truth. I want to explain what Tyler

Ciccone did, how his actions affected the work here and ultimately led to his death."

"Sounds like quite a story, but are you sure you want to go public with it? Think about his parents."

"So that's a no vote."

"I didn't say that. I just want you to consider the possible repercussions. Is this a story that needs to be told, no matter what? Even if people get hurt?"

"I don't know."

He could feel her anguish as if it were his own. "Regan—"

"I honestly hadn't thought about his parents. The thing is, though, right now I really need to work. I need to concentrate on something over which I have a measure of control. I don't want to hurt you or anyone else. I just want to write my story and—"

"And what? Leave?"

"Nash, I can't—"

"What? Can't stay? Can't commit? Can't be honest about how you feel?"

"Can't do this." Regan left without another word. No warning and no drama. She didn't cry or yell or slam the door behind her.

Nash might have felt better about their chances if she'd done at least one of the three. Or not. Damn it, he was an idiot. He'd known how emotionally fragile she was, and he'd pushed anyway. If he lost her, he had no one to blame but himself.

Despite the heat—or maybe because of it—Regan slept on and off all day. Ironically, once the sun went down, she perked up enough to hit the showers, then con Winston out of some peanut butter and crackers so she didn't have to take her pills on an empty stomach. She noticed lights on in the office. Figuring that was where Nash was, she gave the trailer a wide berth. She didn't want to talk to him, not yet.

Out in the center of the compound, the crew had gathered around the campfire. She could hear the muted buzz of their voices, though she couldn't make out the words. The sounds soothed her, though, as did the cool evening breeze flowing up the basin.

She yawned. Tired. My God, she was so tired. Her muscles relaxed, and her mind drifted like a feather on the wind, gradually settling down as she sank deeper and deeper into unconsciousness.

In her dream world, it was nighttime, too, cool and dark. She was lying on a quilt in the middle of a field, the stars spread out across the sky above her and the scent of roses filling the air. Crickets sang and somewhere nearby water burbled accompaniment.

Suddenly Nash appeared, tall and dark and dangerous, looking just like his picture in the *Inquisitor*. But then, the instant he saw her, his expression changed. Gone was the darkness, the sadness, the worry. He smiled, and the warmth of it touched her heart.

"I love you," he said, the words sweet to her ears.

Emotion clogged her throat. She didn't say anything. She couldn't. She just stretched her arms wide in welcome.

And in one of those sudden dream shifts, he was making love to her, first slowly and tenderly and then hard and fast. Reveling in the feel of his skin, silky soft in sharp contrast to the hard muscle, sinew, and bone beneath, she immersed herself in sensation. He brought her to climax over and over again until she was boneless, mindless, and utterly satisfied.

And that's when the dream morphed into nightmare.

Without warning, Nash's long, clever fingers turned into claws. And instead of pleasure, they brought torment. Everywhere he touched her—her breast, her belly, her thighs—the claws ripped her flesh. The pain was unbearable, the sense of betrayal excruciating. "Why?" she sobbed. "Why?"

His only response was soft laughter.

She fought, scratching, kicking, writhing beneath him, but her strength was no match for his. The more she fought, the more he laughed.

Her blood welled up, hot and thick and warm. He lapped at it, making nauseating sounds, guttural grunts interspersed with sucking, slurping noises.

"Please, no," she said.

"No? Too late. You can't change your mind now." Then he reared up, like a snake about to strike.

Staring at him through a haze of pain, she realized it wasn't just Nash's hands that had changed but all of him. Gone was her lover, and in his place a beast, wild and dangerous. Nash's eyes glowed red. His nostrils flared. He grinned, and the silvery moonlight gleamed off inch-long fangs. A drop of blood—her blood—

dripped onto his lip, and his tongue snaked out to lick it up. "Delicious," he said.

He opened his jaws to their fullest extent. She tried to shrink away, but there was nowhere to go. The weight of his body held her fast. And just as he was about to sink those hideous fangs in her throat, she woke up, shaking and sobbing uncontrollably.

Nash hadn't seen Regan since their uncomfortable confrontation earlier in the day. She hadn't even put in an appearance at dinner. He sat in a camp chair, sipping at a bourbon and staring into the campfire, sorely tempted to ask Danielle to check on her. But if he did that, Regan would know immediately that he'd put Danielle up to it, and no telling how she'd take that. Think he was pushing probably, reneging on his promise.

He'd said he'd give her time. So he'd give her time, damn it. But that didn't mean he had to like it. He took another swallow of his drink.

"How about a story, Winston?" Alec Yates asked.

Good idea, Nash thought. Everyone had been in a state of shock since the news of the hit-and-run. One of Winston's stories might be just the distraction they needed.

Winston shook his head. "Not tonight."

"Come on, Winston, please," Preston begged. "If you don't spin a tale, Danielle's going to make us sing camp songs."

Danielle made a face at him.

"Well, all right. If you put it that way . . ." Winston

shoved himself to his feet. "A story it is. A Modoc legend."

He waited for the applause to die down, then began. "In the long-ago days, the spirits lived in an underground world. By night they sang and danced, but by day, they turned into bones. Kumush, Old Man of the Ancients, yearned for company, so he visited their realm deep within the earth."

Across the campfire, Tom and Danielle had their heads together. An interesting development. Nash had suspected for some time that Danielle was interested in the archaeologist, but until now, workaholic Tom had seemed oblivious.

Nash caught his friend's eye and raised his glass in a silent toast.

Tom frowned.

An odd reaction, Nash thought.

"Kumush enjoyed his visit with the spirits. The singing and dancing filled his heart with joy," Winston said, "but after six days and nights, he longed for the sun. He decided to take some of his spirit friends home with him. As soon as they changed into bones, he gathered them in a basket and began the long journey up to the surface."

Danielle whispered something to Tom, but he ignored her. Still frowning, he stood, then began picking his way through the crowd, heading for Nash.

"Near the top, Kumush stumbled and dropped the basket." Winston mimed the action with such enthusiasm that he nearly fell down, grabbing Tom's arm to steady himself. "When the bones hit the ground,"

Winston said, "they turned back into spirits and ran away."

Tom released himself from Winston's grip and marched over to Nash's chair.

"Is there a problem?" Nash said.

"Yes," Tom said. "I'd like to speak with you. Privately."

"In the office?"

Tom nodded.

"Once again, Kumush returned to the underground world and gathered a basket of spirit bones," Winston's voice accompanied them across the compound.

Nash led the way inside. "Have a seat," he said.

"I'll stand, thanks."

"Suit yourself." Nash took the chair behind the desk. "Guess we'll never know how Winston's story ends."

Tom shrugged. "Third time's a charm. Kumush tosses the bones out of the tunnel into the light and the spirits become the various local tribes—the Shastas, the Klamath, the Modoc." He frowned. "But we're not here to talk mythology."

"No? What's the problem?"

"You've been feeding on her, haven't you?"

"*What* did you say?" He couldn't have heard what he thought he'd heard. Tom couldn't seriously believe . . .

"Regan. You've been taking blood from her."

"Are you insane? Of course I haven't."

Uncertainty diluted the strength of Tom's scowl. "You're attracted to her. Don't try to deny it."

"I am, yes."

"And you told me yourself how close you came to sinking your teeth in her throat the night we found the spring."

"I think you mean the night we didn't find the spring," Nash said. "And yes, I nearly lost control that night, but I've been careful since."

"You took her to Big Sur."

"I did," Nash said.

"She came back looking exhausted. Danielle tells me she slept most of the day."

"Of course, she was tired. She scarcely slept at all over the weekend. We . . ."

"You what?"

"We kept busy," Nash said.

"Doing what?"

Nash heaved a weary sigh. "Hiking up to the falls, attending a fund-raiser, going out to dinner, and oh, yes, having lots of wild sex. But nothing, repeat nothing, that involved my drinking her blood."

A worried scowl drove deep lines between the archaeologist's heavy black eyebrows. "Then why is she so pale? Every day she seems weaker, more anemic than the day before. Why is that, Nash?"

"I haven't bled her. I swear."

Tom studied his face closely. "You wouldn't lie to me, would you, about something so serious?"

"I'm not lying. In a hundred and forty-two years,

I've never bled another human being. I'm not about to start with the woman I love."

"Love?" Tom repeated. "You barely know the woman. How can you love her?"

"I don't know. It doesn't make any sense." He paused. "You really think she seems to be getting weaker? She is pale, but . . ."

"To be fair, Danielle has a completely different theory. She thinks Regan is suffering from delayed stress. God knows that after what Harper and his gang put her through, she has every right to be traumatized."

"I should have noticed," Nash said. And maybe he would have if he'd been thinking with his brain.

"So," Tom said, sounding a little hoarse and a lot uncomfortable, "am I fired?"

"For what? For trying to protect Regan?"

Every time Regan managed to drift off for a few minutes, the nightmare returned. Finally, at twenty after four, she decided to quit torturing herself and do something productive, something like work on her story.

She dressed quickly. Then, grabbing a flashlight, she slipped out of the tent and into the predawn darkness.

A preternatural silence seemed to hold the camp in thrall. No breeze. No voices. Not even the chirp of a cricket or the whine of a mosquito. Regan shivered, hugging her sweatshirt around her.

She tiptoed down the row of darkened tents, toward the office. The rickety steps creaked under her weight, but the door opened silently. The desk lamp shed a muted glow. Nash's computer hummed a welcome.

"Regan?"

Her heart slammed against her breastbone, then tried to claw its way up her throat. Nash stood in the shadows, near the kitchenette. "You startled me."

He frowned. "Likewise. What are you doing here?"

"I couldn't sleep, so I decided to work, but if you're using the computer . . ."

"I was just going to check on one of the guards."

Her heart raced. "Trouble?"

"He didn't call in when he was supposed to. Chances are he just lost track of time, but I need to make sure." Nash shrugged, then disappeared into the night without another word.

He hadn't been gone a minute when the phone rang. Figuring it was the security guard checking in late, she let the answering machine pick up. But it wasn't security; it was Deputy Faraday. When he started to leave a message, she cut in. "Regan Cluny here."

"I need to talk to Nash."

"He just left. Hang on. I'll see if I can catch him."

Regan laid the receiver down and headed out the door. Not sure which direction Nash had taken, she paused on the top step to scan the area. A flashlight bobbed along the path that curved around the top of the cliff.

He had quite a head start on her, but if she hustled, maybe she could catch him.

When she paused to catch her breath a quarter mile from camp, a furtive rustling in a massive old juniper a few feet off the trail set her heart thumping erratically. She angled her flashlight into the branches and caught a flash of movement as an owl took flight. It swooped soundlessly across the basin, a dark shadow against a sky just beginning to show the pearly gray opalescence of dawn along the eastern horizon.

Dreaming of monsters. Jumping at shadows. What was her problem?

A loose branch rattled down from the top of the juniper and she jumped. Was there a second owl? Once again she trained her flashlight's beam upward.

Nothing this time. No flash of wings. No gleaming eyes.

With an uneasy shrug, she resumed her pursuit, only to be brought up short when her flashlight illuminated the "branch" that had come bouncing down from the tree. Not a branch at all, she realized, but a pair of high-powered binoculars. Someone had been spying on her every move.

Not Nash. He was still ahead of her. And not a security guard. They didn't hide in trees.

Which left Harper. Harper or one of his henchmen.

Sheer terror sent her hurtling back the way she'd come.

Too slow. Too slow. Kicking it into high gear, she abandoned the meandering path and took off cross-country, heading in a direct line for the all-too-faraway lights of camp. Stupid, stupid, stupid to cut across the open like this. If he had his rifle . . . She should have climbed down the cliff face into the basin, out of sight, out of range. Too late now.

Don't think. Just run. Run. Run like—

She tripped and went sprawling face-first into the rocks. The fall knocked the wind out of her for an instant, but she scrambled to her feet and, ignoring her scrapes and cuts, took off again. Only a hundred yards from camp now. Ninety. Eighty.

She jumped another rock and came down hard, so hard the earth seemed to shudder.

Just your imagination, she told herself, and took off again. She didn't get far.

One second she was running, the next the ground crumbled under her and she found herself falling, like Alice down the rabbit hole. Down she dropped, fifteen feet or more before plunging feetfirst into an underground pool.

No time to panic. No time to scream. The water swallowed her in a single gulp. Shock drove the air from her lungs. Her feet slammed into the bottom with a jolt that she felt from her heels to the base of her skull. She lost her flashlight. Terrified, confused, disoriented, she opened her eyes as wide as they would go, staring blindly into the inky void, no longer sure which direction was up.

Panic closed in. She was going to die. She was going to drown as ignominiously as a worm in a puddle. Alone. And no one would ever know what had happened to her.

Then a sudden wave of anger supplanted her panic. Regan battled her way to the surface, flailing at the water and gasping for air. Chill, musty air, dank as a cellar and cold as a grave, but air nonetheless.

"Help!" she screamed, her voice echoing hollowly. Helphelphelphelp.

Then her left hand struck something solid, and she latched onto what felt like a rock ledge. She dragged herself from the water with an effort, heedless of the sharp protrusions that abraded her skin. Soaked to the bone, shudders racked her body as she lay prone, her cheek pressed to the rough surface. How could it be so cold?

Her breath sawed in and out, loud in the darkness. Too loud. Scary loud. Panic-attack loud. She needed to calm down. Freaking out wasn't going to get her out of here—wherever the hell here was.

Little by little, she regained control. Her heartbeat slowed to a normal rate. Her brain began to function more rationally.

She rolled over onto her back and lay there, shivering and staring wide-eyed into the darkness. At first she could see nothing at all, but gradually, her eyes adjusted. Pale moonlight filtered down through the ragged hole above, enough illumination for her to see that she was in a cavern of some sort, though insufficient to give her any real sense of its size or dimensions.

All she knew for sure was that she was in trouble, because unless she miraculously developed superpowers, she couldn't get out the same way she'd gotten in. What was worse, no one was going to rescue her because no one knew where she was.

She lay back on the rock ledge, trying to think, trying to plan, trying to approach the problem logically, but—

A surreptitious scuffling interrupted her thoughts. She froze, listening with every ounce of concentration she could muster. There it was again, a rustling, shuffling, scratching sound. But was it inside the cavern or outside the cavern? She couldn't tell.

And the worst part was, she wasn't sure which possibility scared her more.

FIFTEEN

Nash didn't know what had sent Regan hurtling across the open plateau, but when her flashlight's bobbing beam had suddenly disappeared, he'd realized at once what must have happened. She'd fallen through the roof of a lava tube, one of many that crisscrossed the area.

He raced to the spot where she'd disappeared, afraid of what he'd find once he got there.

"Regan?" Nash lay flat on the ground and inched forward until he could peer into the gaping hole. "Regan?" he tried again. He shone his flashlight into the darkness, but it didn't penetrate far. "Regan, answer me." *Please, God, let her be all right.*

"Nash?" Her voice sounded hollow and far away.

"Are you all right?"

"I fell," she said. "The ground gave way."

"You're inside a lava tube. The roof must have crumbled under your weight," he said. "This whole section of the plateau is honeycombed by tunnels. Are you hurt?"

"Just my pride, though I'm likely to break a molar the way my teeth are chattering. It's cold and wet down here."

"Caves are cold year-round. As for the moisture, the roof has probably been spiderwebbed with fractures for a long time. Water seeped through the cracks and collected in a low spot. Nowhere else for it to go."

"I can relate," she said. "Get me out of here."

"I will, but I need to go get a rope."

"You're leaving me?" No disguising the sudden panic in her voice.

"Not for long. I'll be right back."

"Hurry," she said.

One word, but it broke his heart the way she said it, her voice shaky, full of anxiety.

Carefully, Nash backed away from the hole, then slowly got to his feet. Just as he started to turn, he heard the faint crunch of a stealthy footstep. He whipped around, but it was already too late. Something hit him hard and he staggered backward.

Nash flailed his arms, trying to regain his balance. But a second shove sent him toppling through the hole in the tunnel's roof.

Regan's scream echoed off the cavern walls, so loud he could hear it even while he was submerged. He kicked back to the surface, shaking his head to clear the water from his ears. "Regan, it's me, Nash. Where are you?"

"Over here, but—"

"A pool?" Harper's head partially blocked the moonlight. "You lucky damn son of a bitch. I figured you'd break a leg at least."

"No such luck," Nash said.

"You did this," Regan accused shrilly. "You planned it."

"No, blondie," Harper said. "I'm just taking advantage of the situation."

"Get us out of here!" Regan demanded, her tone riding the edge of hysteria.

"Are you kidding? When I finally have Nash just where I want him?" Harper paused. "Tell me, Nash, how long since your last meal?"

"Damn you." A single long stroke brought Nash to the edge of the pool. He pulled himself out of the water and gathered Regan close. "It'll be all right," he whispered in her ear, too softly for Harper to hear.

"Hell, I'm doing you a favor." Harper made some obscene sucking noises, then laughed again before ducking out of sight. "Be right back." His voice sounded faint. He was already on the move.

"We've got to get out of here," Regan said. "Do you still have your flashlight? I dropped mine."

"Lost mine, too."

"Damn." She pulled herself free of his arms and stood up. "We're sitting ducks down here. We need to get out of range, but without a light . . ."

Nash shoved himself to his feet. "I don't think Harper plans to shoot us."

"No? Then what?"

"I suspect he'll just leave us stranded."

"But someone's bound to find us."

"Sooner or later," Nash said. His eyes had adjusted to the dim light by this time, and he could tell they were, as he'd assumed, in a lava tube. A small pool, no more than seven feet by nine feet, filled the center, but there were a series of narrow ledges on both sides of the cave, formed as the level of the molten rock flowing through the tube fell. One end of the tunnel had collapsed in a pile of rubble, but the cave extended in the other direction for as far as he could see, which admittedly wasn't far. Ten feet at best. Beyond that, all was Stygian blackness.

"Welcome to hell." Harper's voice echoed eerily down from above.

"What—," Regan started. A sheet of plywood, no doubt pilfered from the supply tent, slammed down over the hole, dislodging small clumps of dirt and rock. The debris made small plopping sounds as it landed in the water. "What's going on?" Regan squeezed Nash's arm with a frantic grip. "What's he doing?"

"Sealing us in," Nash said. "Delaying our rescue."

Shovelfuls of dirt thunked and rattled as they landed on top of the plywood.

"Delaying?" Regan's voice shook. "Or eliminating? He's burying us alive. The crew won't realize what happened. They won't know where to look."

He pulled her into his arms, doing his best to calm her. "Tom's a professional. He'll notice that the earth's been disturbed. He'll find us." But Nash spoke with more confidence than he felt. Not that he doubted Tom would find them. The question was, would he find them in time?

As Harper walked in the front door of the farmhouse he'd commandeered for his headquarters, Elizabeth tore her gaze away from the television screen.

"*Hannibal*?" he asked.

"No, *Texas Chainsaw Massacre*," she said. "What's happened? Something deliciously nasty, I assume, because you're looking very pleased with yourself."

"I did it. Nash is as good as dead."

Vicious glee lit her face. "Tell me more."

So he filled her in, but she didn't react the way he'd expected. "What's wrong? Don't tell me you still have residual feelings for him after all this time."

"No." But she was still frowning.

"Then what? There's no chance they'll be able to dig themselves out, if that's what you're worried about. This tunnel's too deep."

"But it is a tunnel, right?"

"Yes, but—"

"So what if there's another opening?"

Harper swore under his breath. Elizabeth was right. He should have thought of that himself. If Nash and the blonde tried to escape, he could drive them back underground, then set off a stick or two of dynamite to seal the exit. But it would require more than one pair of eyes to watch that section of the plateau. "I'm going to go get Butcher," he said. "You round up Sarge and Billy."

• • •

"We've got to get out of here," Nash said.

"Agreed, but . . ." Regan broke off what she'd been about to say, staring wide-eyed into the darkness. "Did you hear that?"

"Hear what?"

"A slithery sound."

"Probably just a lizard."

Or a snake? "You're right," she said. "We definitely need to get out of here, and the sooner the better. But how?"

"The roofs of lava tubes are relatively fragile," he said.

"So I noticed."

"If we start walking, we may stumble across another caved-in section, one shallow enough to climb out of."

"Or," she said, "we could step into a bottomless pit."

The peculiar acoustics of the place distorted his laughter, an eerie sound that brought back vivid memories of her nightmare. She shuddered uncontrollably. "Don't," she said. She was cold to the bone and scared out of her mind, imprisoned in the darkness with a man she wasn't sure she could trust. "What happens to a vampire who's deprived of blood, Nash? Does he get sick? Weak? What?"

"I fed before we left Big Sur. I won't be desperate for a while yet."

"That's not what I asked. What happens? Do you fall into a coma? Go into convulsions?"

"Neither." He paused. "Are you sure you want to know?"

"I wouldn't have asked otherwise."

He drew a deep breath. "They say the lust for blood is a thousand times stronger than the cravings of a drug addict. I don't know if that's true, but I do know that long-term deprivation will lead to insanity and irreversible brain damage."

She'd been wrong. She really didn't want to know this. "How long?" she asked. "How long can you hold out before you need to feed again? A day? Two?"

"About that," he said, "but when I said long-term, I meant a week or more. We aren't going to be stuck in here that long. I promise. If we can't find a way out, Tom and the crew will find a way in."

Unless Harper and his gang took Tom and the crew out of the equation.

Nash and Regan had been inching their way along the lava tube for what felt like hours but probably hadn't been more than forty minutes when the tunnel suddenly narrowed. Nash discovered this the hard way by thumping his head against solid rock. "Stop," he said.

"What's wrong?" Regan's voice seemed shakier than normal. But maybe that was just the irregularity of the cave walls distorting sound.

"Our tunnel just got smaller."

"How small?"

"We're going to have to duck our heads. We may even have to get down on our hands and knees."

"Crawl?" A definite quiver, not attributable to the acoustics.

"Is that a problem?"

"Only if you're claustrophobic."

"You're claustrophobic?"

"Extremely."

"Regan, I'm sorry." But when he pulled her into his arms to comfort her, she flinched, and God, that hurt. Like a stake through his heart. "Hey, it's okay. I'm not going to bite."

"I can't handle this," she said. "It's too much."

He released her reluctantly. "Then wait here while I scout ahead."

"No!" she said quickly, grabbing his shirt. "Pitch black and claustrophobic is better than pitch black, claustrophobic, and alone."

"Even with a vampire?"

"Even with a vampire."

Harper, dogged by a sense of urgency, strode out to the barn to collect Butcher, currently on guard duty. When he pulled open the side door, the stench nearly gagged him. "What the hell. . . ?" His anger boiled over as he surveyed the gory mess in the combination workshop-barn. Pools of blood and unidentifiable globs of human residue stretched from one end of the workshop area to the other, the blood spatter reaching as high as the hayloft in places. The place reeked of urine and feces and raw meat, overlaid by the strong odor of fresh blood.

At the far end of the room lay a snoring Butcher.

In one hand he cradled an empty Jim Beam bottle. Near the other lay a bloody chainsaw. Other blood-stained tools had been abandoned on the big work-table—filleting knives, hunting knives, two axes, a hatchet, and a machete.

"Son of a freaking bitch," Harper muttered.

"Boss?" Sarge spoke from behind him. "Elizabeth said you wanted to talk to me. Oh, geez, what's that stink?" He peered past Harper. "What the hell happened here?"

"Butcher got into the whiskey and went totally ape shit."

"I warned you when you hired him that he was a loose cannon. Guy's not right in the head."

Which was pretty amusing coming from a man who got off on branding his prey with cigarettes. Or anyway, it would have been, if the possible repercussions of Butcher's actions weren't so serious.

Sarge stepped across the threshold. "Judging by the amount of blood, I'm guessing he murdered the old coot and his wife, too. Only what did he do with the bodies? You don't suppose he's gone cannibal, do you?"

Harper nodded toward the chainsaw, the bloody knives and axes. "I figure he chopped up our hostages and fed them to the pigs."

"Well, fuck," Sarge said.

Which was pretty much Harper's reaction, too.

"Never gonna be able to clean up this mess," Sarge grumbled. "Cops come nosing around, we're in deep shit."

Butcher grunted and rolled over, burying his face in the pile of moldy hay where elderly Everett and Marigold Casper had been sleeping since Harper had evicted them from the house.

"Warned you not to assign him to guard duty," Sarge muttered.

Harper shot him a quelling glance. "I hear any more told-you-sos out of you, Sarge, and I'll dust your ass." Harper frowned. Sarge was right about one thing, though. No salvaging this disaster. "Go tell Elizabeth to pack up. We're leaving."

"I thought you wanted us to make sure your friend Nash didn't escape his tunnel prison."

"Screw that," Harper said. "We need to move. Now!"

"What about Butcher? He's in no condition to travel."

"Not a problem," Harper said. "He's not going anywhere. Got any matches on you?"

"Sure." Sarge dug a book of matches from his shirt pocket and passed it to Harper, who struck one, using it to set the whole book aflame. "What the hell!" Sarge jumped back out of range.

Harper tossed the makeshift torch onto the pile of hay inches from Butcher's shaggy head, then turned and walked away.

Sometimes you just had to cut your losses.

Regan kept hoping the tunnel would widen out. Instead it grew progressively narrower, so narrow their shoulders and elbows scraped the sides, so narrow they were reduced to crawling on their hands and knees, so narrow Regan began to worry that they'd get stuck in a bottleneck, unable to move backward or forward. Her heart pounded. Her chest tightened. Her head swam. She couldn't breathe. *I don't want to die like this,* she thought. *I don't want to die at all.*

Nash stopped so abruptly that Regan ran into him. "I see light up ahead," he said. "I think the tunnel is widening out again, too."

Overwhelmed by a surge of relief, Regan could say nothing.

Nash reached back and touched her arm. "Did you hear me?"

"Yes," she managed.

"Are you crying?"

Her heart clutched at the gentle concern in his voice. "Tears of joy," she said.

He gave her arm a final squeeze, then released it. "Let's get the hell out of here, shall we?"

Only, of course, it wasn't as easy as that. The tunnel did balloon out enough for them to stand upright and side by side. But then it ended abruptly. "Cave-in," Regan said, numb with disappointment. Only gradually did it dawn on her that she could actually see her surroundings. Daylight leaked in through a narrow crack near the top edge of the rubble pile blocking the exit.

Tom was working his way through a ham-and-cheese omelet when Danielle appeared in the doorway of the dining tent. One look at her face was enough to tell him something was wrong.

She spotted him and hustled across to his table, twice bumping into crew members without stopping to apologize or even to respond to their good mornings. Something was definitely wrong.

He shoved his breakfast aside and stood at her approach. "What is it?"

"Deputy Faraday's here. He's looking for Nash. Apparently when the deputy called the office sometime before daybreak, Regan answered."

"What would she have been doing there at that hour?" Tom wondered.

Danielle shrugged. "The thing is, she asked Faraday to hold while she went to get Nash. Only she never came back on the line, and when I checked just now, the phone was still off the hook. But what really worries me is that I can't find either Regan or Nash, and I've looked everywhere. Everywhere," she repeated.

The bottom seemed to drop out of Tom's stomach. Half a dozen possible scenarios popped into his head, none of them good. "Maybe Regan's had an accident and Nash drove her to the emergency room in Cascade."

"I don't think so. Nash's Jeep is still here. So are the rest of the vehicles."

"Damn." Tom's mind raced. "I'd better talk to Faraday."

Wherever Nash and Regan had gone, they were on foot.

And the sun was up.

● ● ●

"I can't budge this one." Regan balanced on top of a pile of debris near the end of the tunnel, both arms wrapped around a massive boulder. Nash wondered if she'd noticed the shiny black lizard crouched just inches from her right hand. Probably not. The little reptile was well camouflaged.

"Let me try," Nash offered.

Regan shot him a dubious look. "Are you sure that's wise? Up here, you'll be exposed to the light."

In the last half hour, they'd cleared a space two feet wide and about six inches high. Sunshine poured into the cave through the opening.

"Light isn't a problem," he told her. "It's only direct exposure to the sun that's hazardous to my health."

"Okay." She half climbed, half slithered down the rubble pile, missing the poor lizard by less than an inch. "Your turn, then."

Nash clambered up the rocks and tackled the stubborn boulder. He managed to rock it an inch or so, but that was it. "Need something to use as a lever."

"Sorry. We're all out of crowbars," Regan said.

He raised an eyebrow. "Sarcasm? From someone who's been crawling through tunnels and moving rocks for the last two hours?"

A mildly surprised expression settled on Regan's face. "Actually, I feel pretty good, aside from a few bumps and scrapes and the fact that I'm hungry enough to eat a raw lizard."

So maybe she *had* noticed the little black reptile. "Good, because I'm going to need some help. Climb up the other side and wedge yourself with your back to the cave wall and your feet against the boulder. I'll do the same on this side. Then, on the count of three, we push."

She scrambled up the rock pile and positioned herself as he'd instructed.

"Okay, now," Nash said. "Together on three. One . . . two . . ."

On three, they shoved. The boulder, along with an avalanche of smaller rocks, went tumbling down the debris pile on the outside of the cave-in. But their celebration was short-lived. A second avalanche of rocks suddenly cascaded down from above, filling the space they'd worked so hard to clear and sweeping both Regan and Nash from their perches.

Their downhill slide ended as abruptly as it had begun. Gradually the dust settled. The rock slide had left only a small irregular opening high up near the roof of the cave. Sunlight penetrated, but only dimly. Nash shoved himself upright and peered through the murky light. "Regan?"

"Over here."

"Are you all right?"

She staggered to her feet, coughing and wheezing.

"Is that a yes or a no?"

"Call it a solid maybe." She held up her battered hands for his inspection. "I think I broke a nail."

A joke. As if she'd notice a broken nail when her hands, like his, were already raw and bleeding, damage sustained in their attempt to dig their way through the sharp volcanic rocks.

She peered toward the meager opening at the top

of the rubble pile. "Okay, that's depressing. All that work, and here we are back at square one."

"Maybe it's a sign," he said.

"Or a warning not to get complacent." She began the laborious climb back to the top. "This time we'll be more careful."

After another half hour of digging, Regan examined their new escape portal, a narrow, five-by-fifteen-inch slot at the top of the rubble pile. "It's too small," she complained.

"It'll have to do," Nash said. "If we try to remove the rocks on either end, the roof will collapse on us like it did the last time."

"But this hole is so narrow I'm not sure I can wriggle through. And there's for sure no way you can make it." She picked her way down the slope of debris in order to continue her argument face-to-face. But one look at his set expression and she knew she'd already lost. "You aren't coming, are you?"

"I can't. The sun's up. I don't like the idea of your going off on your own, but you should be safe enough. Harper and his boys aren't any better equipped to handle direct sunlight than I am. They won't come out to play until the sun sets, and we'll both be safely back at camp long before then."

"Splitting up is not a good idea." She set her jaw stubbornly. "I don't know the area. What if I get lost?"

"All you have to do is head south. Downhill."

That didn't seem right. "But we've been going steadily downhill the whole time we've been in the lava tube," she said. "So wouldn't Juniper Basin be uphill from here?"

"Yes, but it's a treacherous walk."

"By treacherous, you mean I'd have to watch out for snakes."

"That, too, of course," he said, "but the main danger is that the whole area is undermined by lava tubes. You don't want to fall through another tunnel roof."

Definitely not. "What alternatives do I have, though? I'll die of thirst before I make it to Chisel Rock."

"Chisel Rock's not an option," he said. "It's on the opposite side of the dig. But there's a county road to the south, and it's all downhill in that direction."

"Downhill. Okay," she said. "I can do this."

He framed her face between his hands, staring down at her, his eyes fiercely blue, even more fiercely protective. Then he leaned a little closer and kissed her. "I love you, Regan."

He loved her, and she loved him, which sounded like a recipe for happiness. So why did this feel like the end of the world?

Damn it, what a fool she'd been all these months since her diagnosis. She'd thought dying was the hard part.

Wrong.

Living was the real challenge.

SIXTEEN

Fifteen minutes after leaving Nash, Regan came to a barbed-wire fence. She followed it east until she hit a cross fence that headed south, straight to the graveled county road Nash had told her about.

To the east, the road ran straight between twin barbed-wire fences until it hit the base of a solitary butte. Not a single house in sight. Not even a tree to break the monotony.

The road to the west looked more promising. She spotted two clumps of trees in the distance, one, a mile or more away, a second, much closer, a quarter of a mile distant, perhaps less.

Hiking along a road, even a rutted gravel road like this one, made her feel very exposed, even though the chances of Harper roaring up on his Harley to carry her away were slim to none. Besides, she told herself, traffic was a good thing. The sooner she flagged someone down, the sooner she could alert Tom to Nash's predicament. But in the entire ten minutes it took her to reach the nearest ranch, she met only one vehicle, a battered Chevy pickup whose owner ignored her frantic waving.

An oversize mailbox stood at the junction of the county road and a narrow lane. SPINELLI, it said on the side of the box in capital letters. Just Spinelli. No first name. Not even initials. The lane wound uphill toward a two-story white clapboard house with a porch across the front. Charming in an old-fashioned, Grant Wood sort of way.

No vehicles, no farm machinery, and aside from a flock of chickens pecking for insects in the yard, no signs of life.

She rang the doorbell anyway, and when that produced no result, she banged on the door. Only after she'd given up in frustration did she notice the hand-written sign propped in the window beside the door: "Gone to town. Be back later. T. E. Spinelli."

Not helpful.

Regan tried both the front and back doors, just in case T.E. was one of those trusting souls who left doors unlocked, but no such luck.

She did find a hose hooked up at the rear of the house, though, and drank her fill before heading back down the long gravel lane to the road.

She'd barely covered half the distance to the next ranch house when a dust cloud materialized behind her. As it drew closer, she realized what it really was, a silver van being driven twice as fast as it should have been, considering the rutted road surface. She waved frantically, half afraid the driver wouldn't stop for anyone who looked as filthy and bedraggled as she did.

But the van's driver slowed, then pulled to the side of the road, giving the billowing dust cloud a chance to catch up. It covered both the van and Regan in a layer of fine grit.

Coughing and blinking, she made her way toward the van, approaching cautiously, some part of her worried that this was all too easy, that she was about to be picked up by a serial killer or, worse yet, Harper.

Then the driver's-side window slid down, and she relaxed. The woman behind the wheel was several years younger than she was, dark haired, blue eyed, and attractive. "Need a ride?"

"Desperately, and the loan of a cell phone if you have one."

The young woman shook her head. "No cell. Left it hooked to my charger, but you're welcome to a lift. I'm headed to Chisel Rock."

"Great. Thanks." Regan climbed in on the passenger's side. She'd barely fastened her seat belt before the woman pulled back onto the road. "I'm Regan, by the way. Regan Cluny."

"Elizabeth," the driver said with a smile. "Tell me. How'd you get yourself stranded all the way out here at the back of beyond?"

"Long story," Regan said, and not one she intended to share with a stranger, not even a stranger who looked vaguely familiar. "Do I know you?" she asked.

"No, we've never met," Elizabeth said.

But the nagging sense of familiarity refused to go away. Those eyes. Something about those eyes. "How far is it to Chisel Rock?"

"Not far. Ten miles maybe."

"Do you live there?" Regan asked, thinking maybe she'd seen the woman at the Oasis.

"No, I'm just visiting. I'm from Pennsylvania originally, though I haven't been back in years. And you?"

"I'm a New Yorker these days, but a Californian by birth. Grew up in L.A."

Elizabeth's face lit up. "Oh, I love L.A. So many beautiful people."

Most of them desperately searching for the big break that would never come. Regan loved L.A., too, but spending too much time there depressed her.

They spent the rest of the trip discussing trivialities. Elizabeth did most of the talking, which suited Regan just fine. She'd half expected the other woman to push for an explanation of her less-than-pristine appearance, but Elizabeth, it turned out, was far more interested in her own appearance. She spent nearly as much time peering at her own reflection as she did peering out the windshield at the road ahead. Twice they nearly hit mailboxes and once they bumped along the ditch for a good twenty feet.

When they finally reached the Oasis, Regan's relief was so great that she was sorely tempted to get down on her knees and kiss the ground. "Just drop me off in front of the restaurant," she told Elizabeth. "I'm sure there's a pay phone inside."

"Nonsense," Elizabeth told her. "Why scrounge for quarters when you can use my cell for free?"

An especially attractive offer, Regan realized, since she didn't have a cent on her. "Thanks," she said.

Elizabeth pulled into the parking space reserved for unit seven, released her seat belt, checked her reflection one last time in the rearview mirror, then stepped out of the van. Regan followed suit, all except the checking herself out in the mirror part, which she figured would be too depressing.

"Follow me," Elizabeth said, leading the way to a salmon pink door. A lime green palm tree sporting a stenciled black seven was mounted at eye level. Like the rest of the units in the motel, this one was fifties-vintage cinder-block construction retrofitted with a noisy window-mounted air conditioner.

Elizabeth keyed open the door using a real key, not a key card. "Phone's plugged in there next to the TV."

Regan crossed the shabby green shag carpet to the television. A charger lay abandoned next to the TV stand but someone had removed the phone.

"Oops," Elizabeth said. "Don't I feel silly." She dug in her little pink shoulder bag and produced the phone. "Here I had it with me all the time."

Meaning Regan could have called for help half an hour ago if Elizabeth weren't such a ditz.

She shot Regan an apologetic smile, then shifted her gaze slightly. "Hey, honey!" she greeted the new-comer. "Look who's here."

Regan turned to see who Elizabeth was talking

to, saw Harper Wakefield standing there in a pair of camouflage-print boxers, and nearly had a heart attack.

"It's Charley's little blonde," Elizabeth said, "and she's just in time for lunch."

Preston Nakahara, who, like the rest of the crew, had been beating the brush all morning, to no avail, stopped in his tracks so suddenly that Tom nearly ran into him. "Did you hear that?" Preston asked.

"Hear what?" Tom removed his cap, swiped the sweat off his forehead with the back of one hand, then put his cap back on.

"A whistle, I think." Preston cocked his head to one side. "There it is again."

Very faintly Tom heard three short blasts. "Someone's found them!"

"Could you tell where the whistle came from?" Preston asked. "Sounded like it was almost due west of here."

"It did." Tom frowned. That part of the plateau was a rolling landscape, rocky, sparsely vegetated, and riddled with lava tubes.

Some of the crew were fascinated by the caves, exploring them in their free time, certain they would find artifacts left behind by the prehistoric residents of the region. Of course, aside from that one almost perfectly preserved skeleton, they'd found nothing. According to legend, the early inhabitants had avoided the caves, believing them the antechambers to the underworld. And Nash knew that as well as

Tom did. So the question was, what could he have been doing out there in that no-man's-land?

"Not lunch," Harper reminded Elizabeth. "She's poisoned fruit, remember? One good drink and Bobby burst into flames."

"Poor Bobby," Elizabeth murmured, then turned to him with a frown. "I thought you said Regan looked like Katie."

"She does."

"Does not."

"Okay, I admit the coloring's different, but—"

"Everything's different," Elizabeth said. "Size, shape, coloring, facial features."

Harper studied the blonde. Elizabeth was right. And yet . . .

Regan Cluny stared from Elizabeth to Harper, then back to Elizabeth, apparently horror-struck. "You're a vampire, too?"

"Did you hear that, Elizabeth? She knows our secret." He turned his attention back to the Cluny woman, who was edging toward the door. "Now, stop," he said. "You don't want to run off before we've even gotten the party started." He gave her a quizzical look. "Tell me, did you figure things out for yourself? Or did Nash betray us?"

"He told me everything," she said.

Elizabeth laughed. "I doubt that."

The blonde suddenly dashed for the door.

Harper, caught off guard, lunged after her, but she eluded him.

She jerked the door open and bolted across the threshold.

"Stop her!" Elizabeth shouted.

He brought her down with a flying tackle that slammed her face-first onto the concrete sidewalk. The air went out of her in an audible whoosh. Even after he got up, she just lay there, not moving.

Elizabeth came up behind him and peered around his shoulder. "You broke her," she said.

Regan woke up with a throbbing headache and no idea where she was or how she'd gotten there. In fact, the last thing she remembered clearly was falling down the rabbit hole. But this shabby green box was definitely no Wonderland. In fact, it appeared to be the tackiest motel room in the entire Western hemisphere, though possibly the discomfort of being bound to a green metal lawn chair by a half mile of baling twine was influencing her judgment.

Slowly confusion gave way to dread. She might not remember all the particulars, but she was pretty sure she knew who was responsible for her current predicament.

Harper.

And considering that she was still alive, if not in mint condition, he must have come up with another plan, some new way to use her to get revenge on Nash.

The bathroom door opened. Regan turned, expecting to see Harper, but it was a woman, a slim, dark-haired woman with distinctive blue eyes.

One glimpse of those eyes and all the missing pieces of Regan's memory fell into place. The long hike, the silver van, the ride to Chisel Rock, the promise of a cell phone, and then . . . Harper.

"Pity about lunch," the other woman said. "I've really got the munchies."

Regan shrugged. "So bite me."

Elizabeth gaped at her for a second or two, then laughed in apparent delight. "Gallows humor. I love it." She threw herself across the foot of the bed and propped her chin on her folded hands. "I'm bored. Amuse me."

"Who are you, Elizabeth?" Regan asked. "What's your connection to Harper?"

"I'm the love of his life, of course."

"Really? I thought Katie was the love of Harper's life."

Elizabeth dismissed Katie with a curl of her lip. "She's history."

"But that's what this whole feud between Harper and Nash is about, isn't it? Katie."

Elizabeth's nostrils flared. "I said she's history and that's that. If you're not going to amuse me, I might as well gag you."

"No," Regan said quickly. "Please don't."

"Those are my orders," Elizabeth said. "As soon as you regain consciousness, I'm supposed to gag you so you can't scream. Not that anyone would hear you anyway over that air conditioner, but Harper doesn't like to take chances."

"Only you do. You're a risk taker, aren't you?"

"True." A self-satisfied smile tilted the corners of Elizabeth's mouth. "Okay, no gag, not as long as I find you entertaining."

"But it's hard to be entertaining when you're in pain."

"That is quite the bump you have on your head," Elizabeth agreed.

"Actually, I was referring to my wrists. Do you suppose you could loosen the twine just a little?"

"I don't think Harper would like that, would you, Harper?"

"Definitely not."

Regan whipped her head around to see Harper propped against the door to the adjoining room. "What do you want from me?" she demanded.

"Nothing. You're just bait."

"Strange what some men find attractive," Elizabeth said. "But then Charley always did have bad taste."

"I don't know. He tastes pretty good to me," Regan said.

Elizabeth's eyes widened for a second. Then she laughed in what sounded like genuine amusement. "I'm beginning to understand what my brother sees in you."

Elizabeth left before Regan had recovered from her shock. Nash had a sister? A sister who was on intimate terms with his worst enemy? It boggled the mind.

"She won't help you," Harper said. "You know that, right?"

Regan didn't say anything. What was there to say?

"No one's going to help you, and no one's going to come to your rescue, either, because no one knows where you are. I can do anything I want with you, and there's no one to stop me."

"Nash—," she started.

"No, blondie. Not going to happen. Unless I'm completely misreading the situation, I'd say you managed to find another way out of the cave. Am I right?"

Again, she didn't answer.

"You made it out, but Nash is still stuck in the cave. He can't escape until the sun goes down. That's it, isn't it?"

She didn't respond, but he must have read confirmation in her eyes because he laughed softly.

"You have such a wonderfully expressive face. I thought so the first time we met, and then again later when my boys were having their fun and games. Oh"—he pressed a hand to his heart—"she glowers." His laughter fed her anger. "Don't like being reminded of that experience, do you?"

"Go fuck yourself."

"Anatomically impossible and extremely rude besides." He slapped her so hard that her ears rang. "Didn't your parents teach you any manners?"

"Bastard."

"Evidently not." He backhanded her this time. Fireworks seemed to explode inside her head.

For a few endless moments her world held only pain and sparkly lights. Then, gradually, her vision cleared and the pain subsided to a throbbing. Hatred welled up, trumping both pain and fear. This monster would learn nothing from her.

Blood trickled from a cut in her lower lip.

Harper's nostrils quivered.

Aware of his fascination, she deliberately probed the damage with the tip of her tongue.

A shudder ran through him.

"Go ahead," she said, making eye contact. "Have a taste. You know you want to." And as soon as he got close enough, she'd head-butt him, knock him off balance, maybe even knock him out.

He tore his gaze from hers, drew a long, quivering breath, then turned abruptly.

"What's wrong?" she asked.

He stood stiffly, his back to her, his shoulders rigid, his fists clenched.

"Was it something I said?"

He turned to face her, once again in control of his emotions. "Nice try, but I'm not that stupid. I know your blood is lethal. Remember? I watched Bobby Branson go up in smoke? What is it? Cancer? Is that why your blood's loaded with toxic chemicals?"

Realization hit her as solidly as Harper's backhand. Bobby Branson. That would be the biker who'd sunk his fangs in her throat, the one who'd spontaneously combusted. Dear God. *Dear God.*

"That was your plan, wasn't it?" she demanded. "You thought Nash would bite me. That's why you shut us in the cave together. You couldn't murder him yourself, so you set me up to do your dirty work for you."

Harper's smile sent chills down her spine. "Where's Nash?"

"You know where he is, trapped in the lava tube." That wasn't telling him anything he didn't already know.

"You escaped. How?" he snapped.

"Dug my way out." Again, an obvious conclusion.

"Where? Where's the exit?"

"I couldn't tell you if I wanted to. I have no sense of direction."

"Or maybe just no sense." He slapped her again.

Her head snapped back, and she bit her tongue. Her anger flared white hot. "Do that again, and I'll spit blood all over you."

"Answer my questions, and you won't get hurt. Where's the exit?"

"I told you, I don't know."

"Liar, liar, pants on fire," he chanted in a singsong voice as he dug through a flowered overnight bag. "I know Elizabeth must have matches in here somewhere. Ever the romantic, my Elizabeth. She insists on bathing by candlelight, even though she knows fire's a danger for our kind. For your kind, too." He glanced in her direction, a smile playing at the corners of his mouth. "You know what a cigarette burn feels like, don't you? Imagine how much worse the pain will be when I set your pants on fire. Imagine the flames searing your skin, blistering it, blackening it. Imagine the stink of your own burnt flesh. Imagine the unspeakable agony of being roasted alive."

"No," she said. She wouldn't help him. She wouldn't. No matter what he did to her.

"Aha! I knew she had some." He pulled a long, slender box of fireplace matches from the bag.

"No!" she said again, allowing her terror to show this time.

"Then tell me what I want to know. Where's the exit?"

"I don't know. I spent hours walking in circles."

"How many hours?" He waved an unlit match under her nose.

"Two? Four? How am I supposed to answer that? I didn't have a watch with me."

He rubbed the match head across her cheek. "How far did you walk? A mile? Three miles?"

"Farther, I think. I'm not sure. It was so hot and I was so tired and thirsty."

He lit a match with an ominous scratching sound. It flared to life, the flame blazing high for a moment before settling into a steady golden-orange glow. "Describe the terrain."

She eyed the match nervously. "I don't know. Sagebrush, rocks. Then more sagebrush and more rocks."

"Last chance, blondie." Harper knelt, gathered a handful of khaki pants leg in one fist, and held the match to it. The heavy fabric, thoroughly dry now after her long hike through the heat of the afternoon, smoldered for a second, then burst into flames.

She screamed. "No! No! Put it out!"

Harper stepped back out of range and blew out the match.

"I'll tell you." She sobbed hysterically. "Whatever you want to know. Just put it out. Put it out!"

"I knew you'd be sensible about this."

The flames licked along her shin, the pain even more excruciating than she'd imagined. She rocked madly back and forth, thinking that if only she could tip over the chair, she could roll along the carpet and smother the fire.

Harper grabbed a fistful of her hair and jerked her to a stop.

"Put it out!" she screamed. "For God's sake, put it out! You win. I'll tell you whatever you want to know."

"Good decision." He released his grip on her hair and dragged the orange chenille bedspread off the bed. He wrapped it around her, smothering the flames.

Regan was sobbing so hard she could barely breathe, half out of her mind with pain, her thoughts chaotic.

Harper grabbed her chin in one hand, forcing her to look him in the eye. Then he drew another match from the box. "Tell me what I want to know." He enunciated each word carefully, menace in his voice. But it was his eyes, fierce and dark with a determination to follow through on his implicit threat, that convinced her.

She had to tell him something, but what? Her thoughts were too scattered, her brain too fragmented to come up with a plausible lie. "I don't remember much. Honestly, I don't." She sobbed as much in frustration as in a ploy to buy herself time. *Think, Regan, think.* Then the miracle happened. A lie popped full-blown into her head, a gift from her subconscious. She'd describe the cleft in the rock where Tyler Ciccone had buried the snake skeleton. Wrong place, wrong direction. She could send Harper on a wild-goose chase. "I came out through a crack in a cliff."

"Describe the cliff," he snapped.

"It faced east, I think. Very rocky, but in columns, like tree trunks turned to stone."

"What else?"

"There was a juniper tree to my right. Old and scraggly."

"Anything else?"

She squeezed her eyes shut, as if she were scouring her memory. Then she gave a little exclamation, as if she'd suddenly remembered a telling detail. His gaze locked with hers. Was he buying her act? She couldn't tell. "Birds," she said. "Falcons, I think. They were nesting in holes in the cliff." She hesitated, frowning. "And that's all I remember. I swear." Please, please, God, let him believe her.

He studied her face for a long moment. Then he patted her shoulder. "See? That wasn't so hard, now was it?"

As Harper entered the adjoining room, Elizabeth, who was sitting at the table in the corner, raised a coffee mug in a silent toast.

"You're drinking coffee? I thought you were going to feed on the housekeeper."

Elizabeth pushed out her lower lip. "She smelled of bleach. How disgusting is that? Sarge bled her out for me. The extra's in the thermos. Care for some? She was a big woman. Plenty to go around."

"Sure," he said, filling a cup.

"Did Charley's blonde tell you anything useful?" Elizabeth asked.

Harper took a cautious sip. "I've tasted worse."

"Makes a nice change from pig blood anyway," Elizabeth said.

Harper took another sip. Definitely an improvement over pig blood.

"So?" Elizabeth prompted. "Did she talk?"

"With a little persuasion, yes, she told me everything I needed to know."

"Like where Nash is?"

He laughed softly. "No, she rattled off a pack of lies, said she'd come out of the cave through a crack in a cliff."

Elizabeth took a long swallow from her mug. "How do you know she wasn't telling you the truth?"

"The only cliff nearby is the cliff that edges the basin. If she'd come out of the cave there, she'd have followed the cliff back to the dig site. Therefore, she lied."

Elizabeth licked the blood mustache off her upper lip. "Maybe you weren't persuasive enough."

"On the contrary, I was extremely . . . persuasive. The truth is, I don't care where Nash is. What does it matter? I can't touch him. I just wanted to know how much she was willing to sacrifice for his sake. Would she fall apart when things got rough? Or would she lie to protect him with her dying breath?"

Elizabeth stared at him, round-eyed. "You killed her?"

Harper drained his cup. "Not yet."

SEVENTEEN

Something terrible had happened to Regan. Nash was sure of it. She'd been gone for hours. If she'd made it to a phone, help would have been there already. Which meant she hadn't made it to a phone.

The alternatives were many and universally grim. She could have fallen and broken a leg. She could have cracked her skull and be wandering around with a concussion. She could have crossed paths with a rattlesnake or been attacked by a mountain lion. She could have suffered a stroke or a heart attack. Hell, she could have fallen into another damn lava tube.

He never should have let her go without him. He should have tried to dig the hole a little bigger. He should have made her wait until the sun set, then gone with her. She was right. They shouldn't have split up.

Sick with worry, Nash peered out the narrow slot through which Regan had disappeared. He couldn't see much, just a small portion of a rock-strewn caved-in area, all of it bathed in harsh afternoon light.

He must have nodded off at some point because he woke with a start, not sure what had awakened him. Then he saw lights bouncing around at the far end of the tunnel. He blinked, thinking at first that his mind was playing tricks on him. But the lights didn't go away. If anything, they came a little closer.

Then he heard someone say, "I think I see daylight up ahead," and he knew he wasn't imagining that. The cavalry had arrived.

"Help," he called, his voice so hoarse he barely recognized it.

"Did you hear something?" Tom's voice. Definitely Tom's voice.

"Tom!" he yelled.

"Nash?"

"Here!"

Tom covered the last twenty yards so quickly that it was a miracle he didn't brain himself on a low-hanging rock or rip his knees to shreds on the uneven cave floor. Preston Nakahara and Alec Yates followed at a saner pace.

Tom grabbed Nash in a bear hug. "You're safe, man. You're safe."

"Thank God, Regan got through," Nash said. "She's been gone so long I was beginning to worry." Understatement of the century.

Tom looked confused.

"Regan's not with you?" Preston tugged at his soul patch.

"No, she went for help. Hours ago." Nash turned to Tom. "You haven't seen her?"

Tom frowned. "No."

Fear rose up, choking Nash. "Then where is she?" he demanded. "Where the hell is she?"

Preston and Alec both took a step back.

"Yelling's not going to help. We don't know where she is." Tom placed a hand on Nash's arm. "You need to calm down."

"No," he said. "I need to find her."

Slathered with sunblock and protected by the broad-brimmed Stetson Tom had provided, Nash made it back to the office without bursting into flames. Faraday was there waiting for him.

"Got a possible sighting on Ms. Cluny," the deputy said. "Midori Yamaguchi, an elderly widow who lives out on County Road Eighteen, was on her way to town earlier today when, according to her, some crazy druggie jumped into the road and tried to wave her down. Scared the daylights out of her, so she called it in. When I read the report, it occurred to me that the so-called crazy druggie might have been Ms. Cluny. Deputies are out searching the area now."

"We can help," Nash said.

"Got it covered," Faraday told him. "What you need to do is stick close to the phone in case she calls here."

"But—"

"Did Dr. Davis mention the fire at the Casper farm?"

Nash shook his head.

"Arson. Farmhouse and outbuildings, too. A total loss. What's worse, the owners are missing and presumed dead. And it all happened not ten miles from where Mrs. Yamaguchi spotted the 'crazy druggie.'"

"You can't suspect Regan of—"

"No," Faraday said. "I suspect Harper Wakefield and his gang. It appears they were using the Casper place as their headquarters. We found the well-toasted remains of a Harley in what was left of the barn."

Nash frowned. Why would Harper have torched his own hideout? Why abandon a bike? "It makes no sense."

"Nothing about Harper Wakefield adds up," Faraday said. "Tell me, how does a man erase himself from every known database? I've searched birth records, military records, criminal records, DMV records. The guy doesn't even have a social security number."

Faraday might look like a Hollywood heartthrob, but there was a brain behind that pretty face.

Faraday studied Nash. "If he contacts you, don't be a hero. Call me."

Elizabeth wandered over to the armchair where Harper sat methodically working his way through a stack of *National Geographic*s, the only reading material available at the Oasis aside from a Gideon Bible. "Remind me to have the bike tuned up once we're done here," he said. "Got to do my bit in the battle against global warming."

"If you ask me, glaciers are vastly overrated." Elizabeth yawned.

"Bored, sweetheart?"

"Beyond bored and rapidly approaching comatose."

"Why don't you see what's on TV?"

"Because I know what's on TV." She perched on the arm of his chair. "Nothing. Nothing you can see, anyway. The reception's horrible. I hate this place." She twined her arms around his neck and blew softly in his ear. "But I don't hate you."

"Be patient, sweetheart. It won't be long now," he promised.

She toyed with the hair at the nape of his neck. "The time would go faster if you'd let me go next door and play with Charley's little friend."

"No," he said. "The isolation heightens her fear, and the more frightened she is, the harder it'll be on Nash."

"I could cut her a little. That would heighten her fear."

"Or kill her. I need her alive, preferably alive and able to vocalize, and you, sweetheart"—he pressed a kiss to her lips—"have no real concept of moderation."

Smiling wickedly, she tossed the magazines onto the floor and climbed into his lap. "Which is why you love me so much."

After the deputy left, Nash sank down on the chair behind the desk and cradled his head in his hands.

Obsessed with worry over Regan's safety, he couldn't think logically. Couldn't think at all. He'd known what would happen if he let himself get close to her. He'd known what Harper would do, what he'd done in the past. He'd known he was putting her in danger. He'd known. His fault. All of it.

When the phone rang, dragging him back to the moment, he had no idea how long he'd been sitting there, racked with guilt, consumed by fear.

He almost let the answering machine pick up, but then he thought, what if it's Faraday with word of Regan's whereabouts?

"Nash," he said, answering on the third ring.

"Are you missing something?" Harper's idea of cute.

"Damn you."

"Got someone here who'd like to talk with you. Of course, she might sound a little mumbly. When the bitch refused to cooperate earlier, I had to smack her around. Her lower lip's swollen."

"You sadistic son of a bitch."

"You got that right." Harper laughed. "So. Do you want to talk to her or not?"

"Put her on."

"Nash?"

He'd half expected a trick, but it was Regan. She was still alive. A wave of relief washed over him, and in its wake, hope began to grow.

"Nash?" she said again.

"I'm here. How are you?"

"I've been better," she said.

"I'll take that," he heard Harper say in the background, and then Harper was back on the phone.

"What do you want, Harper?"

"Same thing I've always wanted. Your head on a platter, figuratively speaking, of course. I'm willing to trade you for Ms. Cluny."

"Do you promise not to hurt her?"

"No more than I've hurt her already," he said.

"Meaning the puffy lip?"

"The puffy lip, the goose egg she got when I tackled her, and the burn on her shin. See, she didn't want to tell me the truth, so I had to resort to trial by fire."

"You fucking psychopath."

"Me? That's nothing compared to what Elizabeth wants to do to her."

Nash was so angry his voice shook. "If Elizabeth's a monster, it's only because you made her that way."

Harper laughed. "You cling to those illusions, Nash." He paused for a second or two, and when he spoke again, his voice was tempered steel. "So are we on for the trade, or should I turn blondie over to your sister?"

"We're on," Nash said. "Just tell me where and when."

Harper laughed again. "So you can call your friendly neighborhood deputy in as backup? I don't think so. Stick close to the phone. I'll be in touch."

Nash sat staring at the phone as if it were a snake poised to strike. He barely glanced up when the trailer door opened to admit Tom and a small cloud of mosquitoes.

"What are you doing?" Tom asked in the tone of voice normally reserved for the criminally insane.

"Waiting for a call."

"From whom?" Tom asked. "Deputy Faraday?"

"No. Harper."

"What makes you think he'll contact you? You don't even know for certain that he's the one who has Regan."

"Yes," Nash said dully. "I do. He called earlier. I spoke with her."

"She's alive, then?"

"Harper says he wants to do a trade. Regan for me. He's going to call back when he's worked out all the details."

"You for Regan?" Tom said. "That doesn't make sense. What's he going to do with you? Regan he can use to hurt you, but what good are you to him? The protection spell prevents him from killing you, right?"

"Yes, but—"

"So maybe the plan is to have one of his henchmen do the actual killing."

Nash shook his head. "It doesn't work that way. If someone knowingly assists him, it's the same as if he were doing the deed himself, and the spell will prevent it."

"That's some powerful magic," Tom said. "I've never read of a spell like that in any of the vampire lore."

"Because it's not a vampire spell. It's magic Katie learned from a former slave, a woman who worked for her family."

"Voodoo," Tom said.

"I guess that's what it would be called today. To Katie it was just magic. Charms and spells. No right or wrong to it. No evil connotations."

"You know," Tom said, "staring at that phone isn't going to make it ring. It's like the watched pot that never boils." He moved closer, flattening his palms on the edge of the desk. "You missed dinner."

"Wasn't hungry," Nash said.

"You want me to stick some blood in the micro-wave for you?"

"No." The thought of warm blood made him feel slightly queasy.

"Winston's in bed. Hell, everyone's in bed by now. But I could raid the cook trailer for leftovers."

"No, thanks."

"You need to eat something."

"Okay, sure. You're right," Nash said, more as a means of getting rid of Tom than because he was truly hungry.

But just as Tom shoved himself upright, the phone rang.

Nash stared at it.

"You want me to answer?" Tom asked.

"And put another person I care about in Harper's line of fire? No. God, no."

"Then you'd better pick up before the answering machine kicks in."

"Right." But it took a major act of willpower to force his hand to move. "Nash," he said into the mouthpiece, then switched over to speakerphone so Tom could listen in.

"What took you so long?" Harper asked.

"I was asleep," Nash said.

"And I'm the king of Persia."

"It's called Iran these days, and they have presidents, not kings."

"You're missing the point."

"Which is?"

"I was calling you a liar."

"I've called you worse."

"Understatement of the year," Tom mouthed.

Nash ignored him. "What's the plan?"

"You die, and I live happily ever after."

"What about Regan?"

"She lives, too, though in her case, I can't guarantee the happily-ever-after part."

"Let me talk to her."

"Not this time," Harper said. "Listen carefully. I'm not going to repeat myself. As soon as this call is over, drive to Chisel Rock. Meet me in unit seven of the Oasis Motel for the exchange. Come alone, and don't be late. Ms. Cluny's well-being lies in your hands."

"I need to talk to her," Nash said. "How can I be certain she's all right if you won't let me talk to her?"

"I guess you can't," Harper said, and broke the connection.

Nash grabbed his car keys. "Call Faraday," he told

Tom. "Ask him to meet me at the RV park behind the Oasis. No sirens. No flashing lights."

"Let me come with you," Tom said.

"No," Nash said. "Stay here and stay alert. Harper's a devious bastard. Who knows what other fun and games he has planned?"

The four hired security guards were patrolling the perimeter of the dig, but Tom had decided to keep an eye on the tents himself. Might as well, he figured, since he was too wound up to sleep.

He didn't really expect to see anything suspicious, not with the bikers holed up in Chisel Rock, but on his third circuit, his heart damn near jumped out of his chest when he spied a shadowy figure lurking near the entrance flap of Danielle's tent. He probably should have ducked behind the nearest sagebrush and waited to see what the intruder was up to, but he wasn't thinking that clearly. His brain screamed, "Danielle's in danger!" and his body responded by going on the attack. He ran up behind the intruder, grabbing him around the middle, immobilizing his arms.

The intruder's scream sounded suspiciously like Danielle, and the intruder's body definitely felt like Danielle, soft and warm and oh, God.

He released her, and she turned on him furiously. "What on earth . . . ?"

"Sorry about that. I saw someone messing around your tent and thought . . ."

Her anger evaporated. "You thought I was in

trouble. You were trying to protect me." She took a step closer, pressing all that soft warmth of hers up against him.

"I did," he said. "I was."

"That's so sweet." Danielle smiled up at him, and he thought, what the hell, why not kiss her? But then she stiffened. "Did you hear that?"

"Hear what?" The truth was, he couldn't hear much over the thunder of his own heartbeat.

She frowned. "I'm not sure."

He glanced at the half-unzipped tent flap and thought he probably should have chosen a more private spot to make his move. "Maybe your roommate turned over in her sleep?"

"Wrong direction," Danielle whispered. "The noise came from over there." She gestured toward the river.

"Deer coming down to drink?" he suggested.

"Probably," she agreed.

"What are you doing up so late anyway? I thought you went to bed a long time ago."

"I did, but I couldn't sleep."

"Neither could I. That's why I'm pulling patrol duty."

"I thought I'd go hang out at the office. Someone ought to be there in case"—she shrugged—"someone calls. About Regan, I mean."

"Good idea," he said.

Nash avoided the highway, approaching the RV park on unpaved back streets. He pulled into the empty space next to Faraday's patrol car and shut off his engine. As he stepped out of the Jeep, Faraday seemed to materialize from the shadows beneath the trees.

"Dr. Davis's phone call dragged me out of bed with the best-looking woman in Mammoth County. If this is a wild-goose chase, Nash, your ass is grass."

Nash ignored the threat. "Did you talk to the desk clerk?"

Faraday nodded. "He confirms that a man matching Harper Wakefield's description checked into the Oasis earlier today. He rented units seven and eight. There's a connecting interior door. I also checked the parking lot. Spotted three Harleys. Shall we?" he said, nodding toward the motel.

"I'll go in first. You hang back. If Harper sees you, he'll kill her for sure." If he hadn't already.

"Sounds like a plan," Faraday said. "You armed?"

"No," Nash said. Guns were useless against vampires.

Faraday shrugged. "Just as well, I suppose. First thing he'll probably do is check you for weapons."

They cut across the empty lot separating the back of the motel from the RV park, then followed the cracked concrete sidewalk around the side of the building. Faraday waited in the shadows while Nash approached unit seven. The lights were on in both unit seven and unit eight, though the blinds prevented him from seeing what was going on inside.

He thumped the door hard enough to be heard above the air conditioner. "It's Nash. Open up."

No response.

He waited half a minute and repeated the same routine.

Again, no response.

Every muscle in his body felt as if it were spring-loaded. Damn it. What was Harper up to? He tried the door. It wasn't locked.

An invitation. But an invitation to what? Was the room rigged to explode in his face?

Cautiously, he turned the knob, then gave the door a shove. The hinges creaked, but that was it.

And then he got a whiff of blood. Large quantities of it.

He peered inside, then beckoned to Faraday.

"What's going on?" Faraday asked in a whisper.

"I don't think anyone's here." Not anyone alive, at any rate. "See for yourself." Nash stepped aside to give the deputy a better view of the room's interior. Blood stained the walls, the carpet, the bedspread. Regan's blood? he wondered.

"Holy shit." Faraday drew his weapon. "Sheriff's department!" he shouted as he crossed the threshold. He did a quick but thorough search of both rooms and bathrooms, then turned to Nash. "Come on in if you have the stomach for it. Nobody's here. And for what it's worth, I don't think this is a crime scene. The blood spatter's all wrong. Wakefield set this up for the shock value."

"It worked," Nash said.

The shrill ring of the old-fashioned rotary-dial

phone on the bedside table interrupted their conversation.

Nash crossed the bloodstained carpet in two strides and grabbed the receiver. "Nash."

"Sorry about the diversion," Harper said, "but I needed to get things organized. By the time you get back to the dig, I'll be ready to make that trade."

Nash didn't listen to any more. He threw down the phone and headed for the Jeep at a dead run.

"Talk to the desk clerk," he yelled at Faraday. "He's got to know something. Check his neck."

"His neck?" Faraday called, sounding thoroughly confused.

"For bite marks," Nash said, and left it at that. If Faraday was even half as smart as Nash suspected he was, he'd figure it out.

EIGHTEEN

The sky lightened steadily as Nash drove hell for leather toward Juniper Basin. Dust billowed up in his wake as he tore across the desert faster than the law—or common sense—allowed. Harper, damn his soul, had lured Nash to Chisel Rock for one reason, to get him away from the compound. And Nash had fallen right into the trap, credulous fool that he was.

The sun was up, a bright orange ball in the eastern sky, by the time Nash arrived at the dig. Yet despite the hour, not a soul was in sight. No steam rose from the showers. No Winston bustled back and forth between his cook trailer and the dining tent. No tiny figures scurried around out on the dig itself. Even the dining tent appeared deserted.

Dread twisted his gut into knots.

Instead of parking in his usual spot, he drove right up to the office door. Then, pulling his shirt up to protect his face, he dashed up the steps, jerked the door open, dove inside, and slammed the door behind him.

He examined his hands for blisters, but the skin looked healthy. Not even a hint of redness.

Then the smell hit him, and he wasted no more time congratulating himself on his lucky escape.

So quiet that he could hear the faint hum of the computer, the room should have been an oasis of peace with its stacks of books and boxes of carefully cataloged artifacts, with the early morning sunlight leaking through the slats of the blinds and the familiar scent of coffee heralding a new day.

But the room reeked of death, the comforting scent of coffee overpowered by the more pungent odors of fear and blood.

He took a cautious step toward his desk. It looked normal, the computer on one side, the phone on the other, sticky notes, pens, and stacks of reference books and periodicals littering every free inch of its battered surface. He saw no obvious disturbance on this side of the long, narrow room. No scattered papers or overturned chairs. The boxes of artifacts hadn't been moved, and none of the file-cabinet drawers hung open.

Nothing to explain that smell.

He sniffed again, then, following his nose, moved toward the kitchenette. The closer he drew, the stronger the stench. His stomach gave a warning heave, and he forced back a wave of nausea.

And then he saw her, just an out-flung hand and wrist at first and part of an arm encased in the sleeve of a navy blue sweatshirt, the same sweatshirt he'd bought two weeks ago at the Cascade Wal-Mart. Twenty-two ninety-five on sale.

Regan.

His gorge rose again, and he tasted the bitterness of bile.

Regan.

Regan dead.

That she was gone, he never doubted for an instant. Not only was that hand not moving, but already the skin had assumed a pale, mottled appearance. And then there was the stink of blood and terror, of death and decay.

Regan dead. Just like his parents and Katie and everyone else he'd ever loved.

The dark side of his nature, the part he'd reined in for over a century, consumed him. In that moment, he hated as purely as he'd ever loved. He didn't just want to kill Harper Wakefield; he wanted to destroy him, bit by bit, in the most painful way possible. But first he needed to hold Regan one last time.

Nash approached her body slowly, noticing details he'd missed at first glance—fragments of glass from the broken coffee carafe, dried brown spatters on the beige vinyl flooring.

Then he rounded the four-foot-high partition.

The dead girl wasn't Regan. It was Danielle who sprawled across the floor of the kitchenette, staring up at him, her brown eyes wide but already clouding over. Harper, the sadistic bastard, had slit her throat so deeply that her head was nearly severed from her body. A sticky crimson lake had formed beneath her, soaking into her clothes and turning her ponytail into a sodden mass.

Tears stung his eyes. She'd been so young, so full of life.

And now, she wasn't.

Regan came to with a start, gasping and blinking furiously.

"Thought the old water-in-the-face trick might do it." Harper Wakefield stood over her, grinning smugly, an empty bucket in his hands.

"Go to hell," she said.

"I'd come back with 'ladies first,' but that's so cliched."

He hadn't used baling twine this time. Instead he'd taken rope from the supply trailer. And she wasn't tied to a chair, either. This time he'd spread-eagled her beneath the awning in front of Nash's tent and tied her wrists and ankles to wooden stakes he'd driven into the hard-packed earth. The sledgehammer he'd used lay abandoned nearby. Regan strained against the ropes binding her wrists. If she could just get her hands on that sledgehammer, he'd never know what hit him.

"Don't wear yourself out," Harper advised. "You'll need your energy for the fun-and-games part later."

"That's the part where I rip your heart out and use it for a hacky sack, right?"

He stared down at her, his eyes as hard as obsidian. "I think I liked you better unconscious." He raised his foot in an unspoken threat.

Her head throbbed already, but she'd be damned if she was going to beg this bastard for mercy. Instead, she held his gaze and said nothing.

"That's better," he said. "Blood's a bitch to clean off these boots."

Which sounded as if he'd had a lot of practice.

"Your hero just arrived." He glanced toward the office.

Regan twisted her head to follow his gaze. The rear bumper of Nash's Jeep Wrangler extended a foot beyond the end of the trailer.

"I wonder what's taking so long," he said, scratching thoughtfully at his beard stubble with the hilt of his knife. "He should have found the girl by now."

Girl?

"Little bitch threw a pot of coffee at me."

Regan noticed the red patches on the left side of his face and down his neck. Burns, second degree at a guess, but already starting to heal.

Harper focused on the office door, a speculative expression on his face. "Somebody's going to have a hell of a job cleaning up the mess. Damned shame to waste all that blood"—he licked his lips—"but I was in a hurry."

The "girl's" blood, he was talking about. Meaning he'd killed one of the grad students. Tears sprang to Regan's eyes, but she blinked them away. Or tried to. Warm moisture leaked down her cheeks.

Harper knelt beside her. "Does that make you sad?" He cupped her cheek in one hand and leaned close.

She jerked her head free.

Anger flashed in those obsidian eyes. He captured her jaw in a punishing grip. "You look so much like her, like Katie." He leaned closer yet, his soulless eyes terrifying at such close quarters. "She cried, too, when I told her Nash had been killed at Manassas. But I comforted her. Shall I comfort you, blondie?" He licked at her tears, his tongue as sandpaper rough as a cat's.

She jerked frantically at her bonds.

"What? You don't like that?" He stood up, raking her body with a dispassionate gaze.

Her struggle grew more desperate.

Harper planted a boot in the center of her chest, increasing the pressure in small increments until she quit fighting. "I told you to save your strength," he said, his gently chiding tone at odds with the viciousness of his actions. "Are you going to relax? Or are we going to have to step this up to another level?"

Regan didn't even want to think about what might constitute another level. She shook her head, the pressure making it difficult, if not impossible, to talk.

"Well, okay then." He lifted his boot, and she gulped air into her lungs. "You're a slow learner, but that's all right." He outlined her breasts with the toe of his boot. "I'm a very patient teacher."

She cringed away from him, a visceral reaction she couldn't control.

He laughed. "Just like Katie."

"How about Elizabeth?" she said. "She might not like it if you get too carried away with your instruction."

"Elizabeth's not here."

"Why not? Where is she?"

"Somewhere safe," he said. "Unlike Nash, I take good care of the women I love."

The sudden ringing of the phone shattered the silence and brought Nash out of his stupor. How long had he been standing there, staring at little Danielle's lifeless body?

The phone rang again.

Still feeling dazed and disconnected, he picked up. "Yes?"

"About time you got back," Harper said.

"Why?" Nash demanded. "Why did you kill the girl? She was nothing to me and no threat to you."

"Wrong on both counts. She *was* something to you. They all are. You're like that, Nash—assuming responsibility, doling out affection. It's like a disease. You can't help yourself." He laughed. "But I didn't kill her just to hurt you. The little bitch tossed hot coffee at me. Burned the hell out of my neck. For that alone, she deserved what she got."

"She didn't deserve to have her throat slit. How long did it take her to die?"

"Not long enough. It was fun while it lasted, though. She made some really interesting gurgling noises."

"You sick son of a bitch!"

Harper laughed in what sounded like genuine amusement.

"Where's the rest of my crew?" Nash demanded.

"Safe," Harper said. "For now. Of course, once the sun gets a little higher and a little hotter . . ."

"Where are they, Harper?"

"Packed like sardines into that ugly metal tool trailer of yours and locked in to keep them from interfering with my plans."

So many in so small a space? Once the day started heating up, without water or adequate ventilation, they'd all die. "You can't keep them locked up in there, not with the sun beating down. They'll fry."

"Not if you cooperate," Harper said.

"You won't get away with this. Deputy Faraday knows what's going on."

"It doesn't matter who knows what. By the time anyone gets here, you'll be history. Here's the deal. I'll release your crew of tame archaeologists and even tamer archaeologists-in-training. I'll even release Ms. Cluny, but only if you cooperate."

"If you touch one hair on her head—"

"Whoops. Too late. Already touched way more than a hair."

A Gorgon's knot of rage, terror, and guilt writhed in Nash's gut, his internal turmoil too intense to allow for speech.

"You still there, Nash?" Harper paused. "Guess so. I can hear you breathing. Careful you don't hyperventilate. You don't want to pass out just when we're getting to the good part." Harper paused again. "Nothing to say, hmm? Well, that's okay with me. I find your yammering a bore. Look out the office window."

Nash crossed to the big front window and parted the blinds, careful to stay out of the direct sunlight.

"What do you see?"

"An empty camp."

"Wrong direction, Einstein. Look out the back toward the tents."

Nash hurried to the small window behind his desk. No need to worry about the sunlight here. This window faced west. He pulled up the blinds, then released his breath in a groan. "Oh, my God."

Harper stood in the shade of the awning outside Nash's tent, a cell phone in one hand and a filleting knife in the other. At his feet, Regan lay supine in the dirt, her wrists and ankles bound to stakes.

"Let her go. She's no part of this."

"Then why do you care whether or not I release her?" Harper asked. "Because you love her, that's why. You want to know why I'm convinced of that?"

"Why?" Nash asked.

"Because you didn't bite her. There you were, the two of you, all alone in the cave together for hours. You could have fed on her. I expected you to feed on her, but you didn't. And I know you wanted to. The bloodlust probably drove you half insane, and yet, you resisted. Why would any man—any vampire—deny himself such pleasure?"

"It's your story. You tell me," Nash said.

"Because he—or in this case, you—values her safety above his desires. You love her, Nash. Admit it."

"I love her," he said. Why bother to deny it?

"She loves you, too," Harper said.

"Confided in you, did she? I don't think so."

"She didn't have to put it in words," Harper said. "Her actions spoke for her. She lied to protect you. Even under torture, she lied."

"Reminding me of all the times you've put her through hell is hardly the way to secure my cooperation." Nash was shaking so hard with repressed anger that he nearly dropped the phone.

"Funny thing about blondie here," Harper continued, as if Nash hadn't spoken. "I had her figured all wrong in the beginning. That first night, one of my boys tasted her. Seconds later, he was ashes. Some of those anticancer drugs will burn our kind from the inside out, you know. Like swallowing liquid fire. I suspected right then she was dying, figured that was why she'd come looking for you, that she'd somehow discovered you were a vampire and was planning to get herself immortalized, so to speak."

"That's ridiculous," Nash said. Regan would never plan anything so calculated and cold-blooded.

"Yeah," Harper agreed. "Wouldn't have worked, either, since she's a walking toxin from all the drugs the doctors have been feeding her. Still pisses me off that you didn't bite her after I went to all the trouble of sealing you in together." Harper grunted. "I hate it when a plan goes south, but I learn from my mistakes. This time, I've got myself a foolproof scheme."

"Really?"

"Absolutely," Harper said. "I can't kill you. Katie's spell doesn't allow it. But you *can* kill yourself."

"Why would I do that?"

"Because if you don't, I'm going to slit blondie's throat the same way I slit the throat of the little bitch in the office."

"No!"

"Yes, and when I'm done with her, one by one, I'll eliminate the rest of your crew. I won't stop until they're all maggot food."

Nash's brain raced in circles. A weapon. If he had a weapon, he could even the odds. A rifle would be best, because he could use it from a distance. A bullet wouldn't kill Harper, of course, but it would slow him down. The problem was, Nash didn't have a rifle. He didn't have a weapon of any sort.

No, that was wrong. There were weapons on-site—the wooden stakes they used to mark the corners of the grids and the matches Winston used to light the campfire. Unfortunately, even if Nash could get to one or the other, he could use neither. Lethal weapons were of no use to him.

So think nonlethal weapons. There were plenty of tools on the site, picks and shovels, hammers and mallets. Unfortunately, the tools were locked in the tool trailer along with his crew. And even if Harper had unloaded the trailer before locking up Tom and the others, the tools were still on the opposite side of camp, and with the sun up and his sunblock still in his tent, he wasn't exactly mobile.

Of course, the Jeep was parked right outside the door. He could drive across the compound.

No, he couldn't. The minute he started the engine, Harper would slit Regan's throat.

He started a frenzied search of the office. There must be something he could use against Harper.

"You're awfully quiet, Nash. I hope you're not getting any cute ideas. One wrong move and blondie's history."

"Don't hurt her," Nash said.

"Oops. Too late."

Nash heard a scream. He peered out the window. Blood flowed down Regan's neck in a steady trickle. Harper stooped to pick up something from the ground. He held it aloft in the same hand that brandished the bloody knife. "Skinned an eighth of an inch off her earlobe," he said. "Better pay attention, Nash. Not a whole lot of body parts the little lady can afford to lose."

"What do you want me to do?"

"Kill yourself."

"How?" Maybe if he pulled on a pair of work gloves and wrapped something around his head, he could survive the dash across the compound. If he was fast enough, he might catch Harper off guard. With any luck, he could free Regan before Harper recovered his wits. It was a long shot, but—

"I can hear the wheels turning from here. You're

planning something," Harper said. "I'd advise you not to do anything rash. I can kill her with one stroke of the knife. Is that what you want?"

"No," Nash said.

"Then pay attention. All you have to do to free her and the others is to sacrifice yourself. That's not so bad, is it? You always did like to play the hero."

"Go on."

"I want you to walk across the compound, from the office to your tent."

Okay, he could do this. He had some cotton work gloves in his bottom drawer. They'd protect his hands. And he could use one of the jackets hanging from the coat rack by the door to cover his head. Then once he was close enough, he'd have at least a chance of freeing Regan.

"All right. I can do that."

"Naked," Harper added. "No clothing. No sunscreen."

Which meant he'd be ashes before he got three steps.

"That's the deal. Take it or leave it," Harper said. "Of course, if you leave it, then your crew will stay locked up in that tool trailer until they rot. As for blondie, I was going to off her immediately, but on second thought, maybe I'll keep her . . . for a while anyway. My boys love a good game of tic-tac-toe."

Regan was so angry that she'd moved beyond fear, beyond pain. She hated Harper Wakefield with every molecule of her being.

He'd taunted Nash with threats of death for the crew and degradation for her if Nash didn't agree to his demands. But surely Nash knew better than to accede. There was no trade-off here, no deal to be struck. Harper had no honor. He wasn't going to let any of them go, no matter what promises he made now. Once Nash was dead, the crew would be, too. And her days would be numbered as well. Numbered in blood.

So while Harper focused his attention on Nash, she surreptitiously jerked against her bonds. Both wrists were bleeding now, but her anger was so fierce that it blocked the pain.

Again and again, she pulled at the stakes. Did the right one give a little?

She jerked once more and definitely felt some movement.

She was dying. Yes, she'd accepted that fact, but she'd be damned if she was going to go this way, a puppet in Harper's hands.

NINETEEN

Nash listened in silence as Harper finished giving his orders, then broke the connection. Fumble fingered in his haste, it took Nash two tries to dial 911. "This is Charles Nash," he told the dispatcher. "I'm calling to report a murder at the dig site in Juniper Basin. Deputy Faraday's been out here. He knows the way."

"I'll need some more information, sir. Could you—"

"Sorry. No time." He disconnected, then dug the gloves out of his drawer and pulled them on. Three jackets and a long-sleeved shirt hung from the coat rack. He chose a jacket at random, and wrapped it around his head. No point going up in flames without an audience. Harper wouldn't believe what he didn't see.

Nash ran around the north end of the office to the shaded west side, a mere twenty yards from Harper.

A grin split Harper's face when he spotted Nash. "Well, look who's here."

"Go back!" Regan yelled. "Don't trust him."

"Has he hurt you?" Nash dropped the shirt he'd used to swathe his head, then stripped off the gloves.

"Not as much as I'd like to hurt him," Regan said.

Harper laughed. "She's a feisty one. Bet she's dynamite in bed, too, not that you'll ever find out."

"Wrong," Regan said. "Been there, done that."

Harper booted her in the ribs.

Regan sucked in a hissing breath.

Instinctively, Nash lunged forward.

"No!" she screamed. "I'm okay. Stay back."

He stopped himself just inches from the edge of the shade. "You did that on purpose, Harper. You were trying to provoke me."

"No, I just don't like being lied to. You two haven't slept together. If you'd done the deed, you'd be ashes by now, and none of this"—he waved his arm in a sweeping gesture that took in Regan, the office, and the tool trailer on the far side of the compound— "would have been necessary. People like us can't get off without tasting. It's the nature of the beast."

Unless, Nash thought, the . . . man . . . in question truly loved his partner.

"But enough chitchat. Strip," Harper ordered.

"Not until I have your word that if I do as you say, you'll let Regan and the others go free."

Harper smirked. "Nobility must be such a burden."

"Promise," Nash insisted.

"Okay. I promise."

Nash didn't believe him. Harper had no honor, but Nash had no other options. If he did as Harper demanded, Harper might spare Regan and the others. But if Nash refused, they were dead for certain.

"Don't do it," Regan said.

"I have to. It's the only way."

"You can't trust him." Regan sounded increasingly desperate.

He kicked off his boots, then stripped off his shirt, his jeans, and his socks.

"Boxers, huh?" Harper said. "Wait till I tell your sister."

"I have no sister," Nash said. "You destroyed Elizabeth along with everyone else I ever loved."

"I didn't destroy her. I saved her. I blessed her with eternal life."

"Eternal damnation, you mean."

Harper heaved an exaggerated sigh. "She'll be so sad to hear that her Charley was judgmental to the end."

"Judgmental? You seduced her when she was a child of thirteen. You corrupted her. You forced her to help murder her own parents."

"Forced her, hell. She relished the job. That's what I've always loved best about Elizabeth. She seems so sweet and delicate, but she has the heart of a tigress."

No, Elizabeth had no heart at all.

Harper's grin faded. "You're trying to stall, aren't

you? You think help's on the way, but it's not. No one's going to save you now." He shot Nash a menacing look. "Strip off the shorts."

Nash pulled down his boxers and tossed them on the pile of discarded clothing.

"Now then. Time to prove what a hero you are. Time to sacrifice yourself so others can live."

"Don't," Regan said. "Please don't. There must be another way."

"Do it," Harper said. "No more stalling."

Nash knew he didn't have a chance. There was no way he could make it twenty yards in direct sunlight. The exposure would blister his skin before he'd gone two feet. He'd burst into flames by the time he reached the halfway mark. It was hopeless, and he knew it, but he mentally calculated the most direct route anyway.

Every time Harper focused on Nash, Regan jerked on the ropes that tied her wrists to the stakes. Harper had knotted the ropes well. They weren't the slightest bit loose, but the stake attached to her right wrist was definitely wobbly. Two or three more good, hard jerks and she'd be able to pull it out of the ground.

"Damn," Harper swore softly. "He's going to do it. I didn't think he had the balls."

Nash, he meant. She craned her neck to see past Harper.

Nash still stood in the shade on the back side of

the office. Poised to run, he looked as lean and muscled as the athletes immortalized in Greek statues.

"No," she whispered in horror as he suddenly shot
forward into the sunlight. "Go back!" she screamed.

"Burn, baby, burn!" Harper yelled.

Regan was fairly certain Nash didn't hear either
one of them. Calm and determined, his expression
never flickered. He seemed intent on covering the
maximum amount of ground in the minimum amount
of time.

"Burn, damn it, burn!" Harper screamed, an edge
of hysteria in his voice now.

But Nash just kept coming. His skin glistened with
a light sheen of perspiration, but no blisters appeared,
no smoke, no flames. An incredulous smile lit his face
as he pounded barefoot across the compound. Twenty
feet away. Fifteen. Ten.

"Stop!" Harper shouted.

Nash pulled up just inches from the shade beneath the canopy. "I did as you asked. Now release my
people."

"Fuck you," Harper said. "You cheated."

"I didn't cheat. Open your eyes, man. I'm standing
naked in direct sunlight. How is that cheating?"

"I don't know. You must have slathered on some
sort of supersunscreen or something."

"I'm not wearing sunscreen. Hell, I'm not wearing
anything." Nash took a step toward the shade.

"Don't move," Harper snapped. "Stay right where
you are." He glanced over his shoulder at Regan, a

brief glance, but enough to scare the hell out of her. Scary psycho biker had returned.

Nash froze.

Harper backed up a few steps, edging around Regan.

"Let her go, Harper." Nash spoke quietly, but Regan could tell from the expression in his eyes that he was as wary of Harper's sudden mood swing as she was. "I'm the one you have the problem with."

Harper grabbed a handful of her hair and jerked her head back. "I'm going to slit her throat right in front of you," he said, slowly drawing his knife blade toward her exposed throat, "and there's nothing you can do—"

Nash didn't wait for Harper to finish his threat. He lunged, kicking the knife from Harper's hand and knocking him off balance. He fell backward, and Nash landed on top of him. The two men rolled over and over in the dirt, Nash doing his best to rip Harper's head off.

Regan, who'd been tugging frantically at her bonds, heard a loud crack. The stake attached to her right wrist split off at ground level, giving her just enough range of motion to get her hands on Harper's knife. Quickly, she sawed through the rope holding her left hand, but before she could release her feet, Harper and Nash, still locked together, kicking and punching at each other, slammed into her. Pain exploded as Harper's booted foot landed squarely on her chest. The air went out of her in a whoosh and she lost her grip on the knife. It flew end over end through the air, landing out of reach and out of sight somewhere inside the tent.

The men rolled off her, and she shoved up on her elbows, gasping for air. She had one goal: to get loose. Desperately, she worked at the knots on the ropes binding her ankles. She broke two nails without making any progress. The ropes were tied too tightly; she wasn't strong enough to work them loose.

Nash gasped, then swore viciously. She turned to see what was happening.

Harper had managed to get his left hand on the sledgehammer and was using it to pummel Nash's back—awkwardly and inefficiently, but with enough force to get Nash's attention.

She jerked repeatedly with her feet, hoping to loosen the stakes, if not the ropes, but without result. She'd hoped one or both would break off the way the one that had held her right wrist had, but neither budged.

Okay, think, Regan. There must be a way.

She needed something sharp, something to cut through the ropes or pick away at the knots. But she had squat. No knife, no fingernail file, no hair clip. Nothing. Nothing except for her own two hands.

She stared hopelessly at her bloody wrists and broken nails. At least she'd managed to cut the rope off her left hand. Her right still had its rope bracelet intact, complete with the jagged remains of the stake she'd been tied to.

Jagged. As in sharp. Not sharp enough to cut

through the rope but maybe sharp enough to pick at those stubborn knots.

She used her left hand to twist the rope on her right around until the broken stake was on the inside of her wrist, where she could get a grip on it with her right hand. Then she scooted forward on her rear, leaning over her knee to work at the rope binding her left ankle. Her heartbeat roared in her ears. "Hurry, hurry, hurry," it seemed to say.

Nash was losing the fight. With each blow of the sledgehammer, Harper came closer to victory. Nash grabbed for the handle, trying to wrest the tool from Harper's grip.

Hurry, hurry, hurry.

Faster than she would have believed possible, the knot seemed to unravel itself and her left leg was free. One down, one to go. Regan hunched over the knot, picking frenziedly at the rope.

Hurry, hurry, hurry.

Back and forth went the sledgehammer, hitting first Nash, then Harper, as the two men grappled for control. The thunks and grunts, the raspy breathing and muttered curses played in the background as Regan struggled with the knot.

And then it was over. Harper ripped the tool free of Nash's grip and took a wild swing that caught Nash in the back of his head. He collapsed with a thud, landing face-first in the dust.

Hurry, hurry, hurry.

Harper uttered a sound that was 50 percent sob,

50 percent giggle, and 100 percent crazy. "I win," he whispered. He wriggled out from under Nash's limp body. "I win," he said again, his voice stronger and more authoritative this time.

A mere four feet away, she worked feverishly to free herself.

She must have made some noise because Harper glanced at her then, his eyes glittering from beneath half-lowered lids. Black as night. Black as the heart of evil. He looked every inch a monster, covered in blood and sweat and streaks of grime, but it was the feral expression on his face, the way he raised his upper lip to show off his canines, that sent icicles skittering down her spine.

Hurry, hurry, hurry. She hunched over her task, working with renewed energy.

Harper rose to his feet. "I win," he said, his voice cold, his face dark with menace. "And winner takes all."

He grabbed the sledgehammer in both hands, swung it back over his shoulder, and charged.

Regan wasn't scared. She didn't have time to register emotion. She didn't think. She just reacted, surging to her feet on a rush of adrenaline.

She surprised Harper, who hadn't anticipated her move. With no time to alter course, no time to pull up, the momentum of his charge carried him forward with such force that he impaled himself on the broken stake Regan still clutched in her hands.

A shocked expression contorted his face for an

instant. In the next, he was gone, his body shattering into a million fragments of dust. The sledgehammer fell to the ground with a muffled thump.

"You lose," Regan said, and slowly crumpled to her knees.

Nash had had headaches in the past that made him feel as if his head were exploding, but this current headache was worse. Exponentially worse. His head didn't feel as if it were in the process of exploding. No, this was definitely the explosion's aftermath, and maybe, if he lay very still, all the scattered bits of his brain would coalesce again on their own.

What had happened? How had he ended up in this state? Had he been run down by a logging truck?

Or . . . One of those scattered brain fragments slotted itself back into place. Harper. Sledgehammer. And oh, my God . . . "Regan." He meant to shout, but it came out more like a croak, and a lame croak at that. Second-rate bullfrog.

"Nash?"

"You speak bullfrog," he said.

"You're not making sense," she said. "I think you must have a concussion. Hang on. I'll be there as soon as I get this damned knot untied."

"Harper?"

"Gone," she said, and he wasn't sure, but he thought she sounded as if she were crying. Only why would she be crying about Harper leaving?

He tried opening his eyes. Huge mistake. He shut them again almost immediately but not soon enough. His stomach gave a warning lurch. "No heaving," he ordered.

"Heaving?" Regan sounded a little hysterical. "Oh, Nash. Don't try to talk. Just lie still."

"If I lie any stiller, I'll be dead."

"And no death jokes, please. Not after what we've been through."

"That's just it," he said. "I don't remember what we've been through." Only that wasn't strictly true. Bits and pieces were coming back to him as his brain reassembled itself. "Harper hit me with the sledgehammer, didn't he? That's what's wrong with my head."

"Yes. Just hang on. This stupid rope. Oh, there, I got it." Seconds later she sat down beside him and took one of his hands in hers. She was definitely crying. Warm tears fell like rain on his bare chest. Another chunk of his memory fell into place and with it, panic.

"Tom," he said. "The crew. They're locked in the tool trailer. You've got to go release them. Now."

"I think they've released themselves," she said. "Can't you hear all the commotion in the distance?"

He gave her hand a warning squeeze. "If we can hear it, so can Harper."

"No," she told him, her voice a little steadier. "He can't. Like I told you, he's gone, and he's not coming back."

He thought that over with his fragmented brain. Surely she didn't mean. . . ? "You dusted him?"

"It was an accident."

"But you dusted him?"

"Actually, he sort of dusted himself."

Despite the pain in his head, he smiled. "How totally Buffy."

TWENTY

Regan stepped onto the elevator on the parking level of St. Ignatius Hospital, where she'd come to visit Nash, to break the news that she was leaving. She punched the button for the third floor and the doors slid shut.

God, she hated hospitals. Everything about them grated on her nerves, from the faint, pervasive smell of antiseptic to the determined cheerfulness of the staff. They said stupid things like "You're looking chipper this morning," when the truth was, you looked like you'd just walked out of a concentration camp. They said "Try this Jell-O; it should slip right down," when they knew as well as you did that shortly after it hit bottom, it would be making a return trip. Regan had puked up a lot of Jell-O in the past year and a half.

Nash's room, 372, was located right across from the nurses' station. The better to coddle you, my dear, Regan thought as she walked into his room to find no less than four hospital personnel in attendance.

Nash glanced up, saw Regan in the doorway, and smiled.

Her heart fluttered around like a befuddled moth searching for a place to light. Dour, unsmiling Nash had rocked her world. This new, improved version threatened her entire universe.

"Hi," he said. "Dr. Frasier here"—he indicated a redhead in a teal linen suit and Manolo Blahniks—"says I can be released tomorrow if all my vitals stay within the normal range today." He was no longer hooked up to half a dozen machines, she noticed. A good sign.

She mumbled something noncommittal. She'd come here to tell Nash she was flying back to New York, a hard enough task had they been alone, impossible with all these others in the room.

But eventually the doctor left, followed closely by the floor nurse, the candy striper, and the lab tech.

"So," Nash said, "did Tom bring you in?"

"Yes. He finally got in touch with Danielle's family. They're having her body flown down to L.A. for burial, but Tom's going ahead with the arrangements for a memorial service up here, too."

"That's a good idea. It'll give the crew some closure, a chance to say good-bye." A troubled expression crossed Nash's face. "But it must be killing Tom. He and Danielle . . . He shouldn't have to deal with all the arrangements by himself."

"He wants to, I think. It keeps him busy. Don't fret." She touched his hand in what was meant to be a comforting gesture, but instead turned into a jolt of pure sexual energy. She jerked away, but not soon enough. He'd felt it, too. She could see the residual heat smoldering in his eyes.

"So what's the plan for the rest of the day? If you have some time to spare, why don't you shut the door and come on over here." He patted the edge of the bed.

"With that crowd of Nash groupies out there just looking for a reason to barge in? I don't think so."

"You could wedge a chair under the door handle." A provocative smile tilted the corners of his mouth.

The suggestion was tempting and the raised eyebrows damn near irresistible, but . . . "I still have to shop for something to wear to the memorial service. No time for hospital high jinks."

"Maybe that's just as well. With all the pain meds they've pumped into me, I'm not sure I'm up to the task."

"Have you talked to the authorities yet? The sheriff's department has had search teams combing the dig for evidence, but so far all they've found is a stolen pickup abandoned near Calliope Rock."

"Deputy Faraday came by yesterday," Nash said. "He filled me in on what happened at the Oasis after I left. Harper had splattered blood around unit seven. For shock value, I assumed. Turns out he'd murdered the middle-aged couple who own the Oasis. It was their blood he used. Faraday found the bodies stuffed in a closet in one of the empty units."

"Those poor people," Regan said.

"Their son, the teenager who was manning the motel office that night, was coerced into helping."

"Coerced?"

"He had bite marks on his neck."

Regan put a hand to her own throat.

"During the initial interview in the motel office, the kid kept glancing over his shoulder toward the family's living quarters. Faraday figured maybe there was something back there the kid didn't want him to see. So he asked if it would be okay to search the place. When the kid refused to give permission, Faraday knew something was up. He called a judge and sat right there until another deputy showed up with a search warrant."

"What was the big secret? What did they find?"

"Not what. Who. Elizabeth."

"Your sister?"

"She hasn't been my sister for a long, long time," Nash said in a harsh voice. "Harper saw to that. He destroyed her as surely as if he'd killed her."

"I know you said vampires aren't demons the way they are in the Buffyverse, but Elizabeth and Harper both seemed more demon than human to me."

"It's the curse of an extended life span," he said. "When a person knows he's going to live ten times as long as normal, he starts thinking he's superior to ordinary people, that he doesn't have to follow the rules anymore." He paused. "And the truth is, my parents indulged Elizabeth from the day she was born. She was always spoiled, but Harper corrupted her. Ruined her just to hurt me."

"And it worked," she said.

He heaved a weary sigh. "Yes, it worked, though I think his plan backfired to some extent. In the end, he loved her as much as he hated me. Loved her, indulged her. Maybe it's just as well that things turned out as they did."

"Meaning?"

"When Faraday discovered Elizabeth's hiding place, she went berserk, spouted threats, and tried to stab the kid. It took both deputies to subdue her. They finally got her in cuffs, but when they started to take her out to the patrol car, she came unglued again."

"The sun must have been up by that time," Regan guessed.

Nash nodded. "According to Faraday, they dragged her, kicking and screaming, out the door, and then, whoosh, she went up in flames. Faraday had a grip on her shoulder. Burned the hell out of his hand."

"Oh, my God. So what does the deputy think happened? If he's burned, he can't dismiss it as a hallucination the way I did."

"The second deputy swears she must have been zapped by a stray bolt of lightning, but I think Faraday has figured it out."

"Do you think he knows about you?" Regan asked.

"He's no fool."

No, but she was. What had made her think she could do this?

Nash reached out and took her hand in his. "Looks like they're going to release me in time for Danielle's memorial service tomorrow. If you wouldn't mind driving the Wrangler in, we could go home together."

Home. Regan shut her eyes for a second. Damn. "Actually"—she cleared her throat—"I won't be going back to the dig. Preston volunteered to drive me down to Reno after the services."

Nash looked confused. "Why Reno? Do you have a secret gambling addiction I don't know about?"

"I booked a flight back to New York."

"Without telling me?"

Regan gave him a big fake smile. "This is me telling you."

He didn't smile back. "I love you. Doesn't that mean anything?"

"I love you, too, but I'm dying. Harper wasn't wrong about that."

"You can't be," he said. "There must be some mistake."

"No mistake." She shook her head sadly. "I have an inoperable brain tumor. Cancerous. Just like my mother's."

She watched his face as he put two and two together. "That's why your father showed up at Marcia Tischler's fund-raiser?"

She nodded. "In the last eighteen months, I've been to every top-notch cancer specialist in the country. I've undergone rigorous treatment, including chemo and radiation."

"But what about experimental drugs—," he started.

"They've used me as a guinea pig for all of them.

The doctors agree there's nothing more that can be done."

"Then we'll go see different doctors. European doctors. They're doing some incredible things with stem-cell research in Germany."

"Stem-cell research isn't going to help. I'm terminal, Nash."

"I don't believe it," he said stubbornly, almost shouting now. "I refuse to believe it. You're so beautiful—vital and strong. How can you be dying?"

The anguish in his voice ripped holes in her heart. She'd guessed he'd take it badly, but not this badly. "We're all dying, Nash, some of us sooner than others, that's all."

"No." He frowned. "No way. When you first arrived in Juniper Basin, yes, I'll admit you seemed pale and tired, but I assumed that was a result of the injuries suffered in the bikers' attack."

"The attack didn't help."

"But now," he said, "aside from a few bumps and bruises, you seem healthy enough."

"'Seem' being the operative word," she said. "I know I should have told you sooner."

"Damned right you should have," he said. "I was honest with you about my vampirism."

"Only because I caught Malcolm stripping the blistered skin from your chest."

"I didn't have to tell the truth. I could easily have convinced you that you'd dreamed the whole thing. It's what you wanted to believe."

"Because I'm not as brave as you are, not as honest. I was going to tell you. I thought about it, but"—she shrugged—"I didn't. My mistake. I apologize. It was selfish of me. I see that now. The thing is, I thought if I could just have you for a little while, it would be enough. You'd be left with some nice memories, and I could die happy."

He made some inarticulate sound she couldn't interpret.

"But it doesn't really work that way, you know? I thought dying alone and unloved defined hell, but it doesn't. Hell is finding heaven and knowing you can't stay."

He didn't say anything for the longest time. All he did was stare out the window as if he were memorizing the view. Finally he shifted his gaze back to hers, renewed determination in his face. "But you *can* stay," he insisted. "Please. I want you for as long as I can have you, a year, a month, a day. I don't care."

"You don't get it, Nash."

"No, I really don't. I don't understand how you can leave me."

She shook her head sadly. "Because I don't want you to watch me wither away. I'd rather have you remember me as I am now."

He didn't say anything, didn't even look at her, and somehow that hurt worse than pleading or arguments.

She snagged a tissue from the box on his tray table and dabbed surreptitiously at her eyes. Damn it, hadn't she already cried her quota for the year?

Then she stiffened her spine and hardened her heart. Her dad had lost the love of his life, and he'd survived. Nash would, too.

"I don't want to leave," she said honestly. "But staying would only prolong the pain. A clean break is best."

"Really? Why don't you ask Tom about that?" Nash said. "Ask Tom if it was better to lose Danielle the way he did, or if he would have preferred more time to say a proper good-bye."

"That's not fair." She was mortified to hear her voice crack.

But Nash didn't seem to notice. He'd retreated into his memories—bad ones, judging by the haunted expression on his face. "She was wearing a sweatshirt just like yours," he said, "the one I bought you at Wal-Mart. When I first spotted her, all I could see was a wrist, a hand, and part of the sleeve. I thought it was you lying there dead. And God help me, when I realized it was Danielle instead, a part of me was relieved." He turned to her, the torment in his eyes almost more than she could bear. "So tell me, Regan, what kind of monster does that make me?"

"You're not a monster," she said quickly.

"I'm not a man, either."

"Yes, you are. You're the finest man I've ever met—strong, intelligent, brave, noble. You're a hero, Charles Cunningham Nash. Only a hero would have been willing to sacrifice himself to save others."

He frowned. "Willing but not able. I should have died. Why didn't I die?"

She forced a smile. "Because heroes never do. It's the law."

"In fairy tales maybe, but in real life, vampire plus sunlight equals ashes."

"You know, that sounded pretty whacked, using the phrase 'real life' in the same sentence with 'vampire.'"

"I suppose it did." Suddenly, he looked exhausted. "I shouldn't be alive. It doesn't make sense."

Tom thought Danielle would have approved of her memorial service. He'd bought out every florist in town. A jungle of flowers filled the funeral chapel with their colors and scents. Bright and cheery. Just like Danielle.

He'd originally planned to have one of the local ministers say a few words, but Regan had talked him out of that. What could some anonymous minister say about Danielle, she'd demanded, that her friends couldn't say better? So in lieu of a minister, one by one each member of the crew had shared his or her favorite memory.

Winston spoke of solving the mystery of the missing chocolate chip cookies by literally catching Danielle with her hand in the cookie jar at two in the morning. Jada Chavez told about the time she and Danielle had sneaked off in the middle of the day to go skinny-dipping and had ended up with sunburns in places where the sun wasn't supposed to shine. Tom didn't share, but he had a favorite memory all right, the first time Danielle had called him

Tom instead of Dr. Davis, the first time he'd realized she saw him as a man, not just a stuffy academic.

The best part of all, though, had come at the end. Preston had surprised them with a slide show of candid shots taken over the course of the summer. There was one of Danielle mugging for the camera with a Clovis point in one hand and a trowel in the other, another of Danielle starting a squirt-gun fight, a third of a spellbound Danielle sitting next to him at the campfire while Winston spun one of his tales. But Tom's favorite of all was a shot of Danielle rescuing a baby hawk that had fallen from its nest high up on the petroglyph cliff.

He might even have managed to make it through the whole presentation dry-eyed if Preston hadn't accompanied the slides with the Rod Stewart version of "Forever Young."

Regan and Nash stood talking in the shade in front of the restaurant where the crew had gathered after Danielle's memorial service. They'd already said their good-byes, but still she lingered, unable to tear herself away.

Preston, parked across the street, tapped his horn, an impatient reminder that if they didn't leave soon, they wouldn't make it to Reno in time for her flight.

"I should go," she said, forcing a smile, pretending that her heart wasn't breaking.

Nash wasn't fooled. She could tell that from the tender expression on his face and the gentleness with which he brushed the tears from her cheek. "Not yet. You can't leave yet. I have something to show you."

And right there on the sidewalk he unknotted his tie and stripped off his shirt, turning to show her the bruises. They extended the full width of his shoulders and down his back, where they disappeared beneath his trousers. She'd never seen uglier or more extensive bruising, huge mottled black-and-purple smudges.

Fresh tears sprang to her eyes. "Harper did this?" Tenderly, she brushed her fingertips across the discolored skin.

"With the sledgehammer."

"I should have staked him twice," she said fiercely.

"You're missing the point. It's been three days since the fight. I should have healed in a fraction of that time."

She frowned, not sure what he was getting at.

"Remember when I burned myself at Big Sur?"

She shuddered. "I'll never get that image out of my mind—Malcolm peeling burnt skin from your chest in strips." She shuddered again.

"Third-degree burns. And yet by the next morning, I was completely healed. So why is my body repairing itself so slowly this time?"

"I—"

"And while we're at it, why didn't I burn to a cinder when I ran across the compound?"

"I assumed it had something to do with Katie's protection spell."

"Or maybe it's because I'm no longer a vampire."

"What?" She stared at him, her mind a blank. "How is that possible?"

"I came here looking for a healing spring. I think I found it."

"Well, yes, but it's dried up, so—"

"How do you feel?" he asked, his gaze taking in every detail of her appearance.

"The bump on my head is still a little tender, but my lip's better and my abrasions are healing nicely."

Preston beeped his horn again.

Regan glanced toward his car, holding up a finger in a "just a minute" gesture.

"No," Nash said, completely focused on her. "I mean how do you feel? Are you tired? Do you have an appetite? Have you been having headaches? Problems sleeping? Nightmares?"

"What are you getting at?"

"How do you feel?" he asked again. "Because you look great. Your color's good. No black circles. No shakiness."

Regan had been too busy the last few days, too concerned about Nash, to think about herself. But now that she did . . . She frowned. Aside from a few minor bumps and bruises, she felt pretty good—excellent, in fact. She hadn't had a headache in days. And the exhaustion that had plagued her all summer? Gone.

"And why? Because your tumor's gone," Nash said.

Absurd. And yet, she couldn't deny that she felt

perfectly healthy, perfectly normal, and had ever since . . . "The pool of runoff water in the lava tube," she said slowly. "Maybe it wasn't runoff water."

"I suspect seismic activity diverted the spring," Nash said. "I think that pool was Father Padilla's Font of Miracles." He paused. "Of course, you'll need to have tests done to confirm that your cancer is gone."

"Yes." But suddenly she was confident of the results. She'd never felt better in her life. "But if I am truly as healthy as I feel," she said, considering the broader implications, "then that means—"

"We're going to get our happy ending after all," he finished, then pulled her close and kissed her like a man with no plans to let her go anytime soon.

Regan lost herself in sensation, the warmth of his touch, the sweet promise of his kisses. *I want you. I need you. I love you. I can't live without you.*

"Ahem!" Someone tapped her on the shoulder.

"Go away," Nash said.

But she eased herself free of his embrace to turn far enough to ID the shoulder tapper. "Preston," she said. "I'm sorry. I forgot all about you."

"Yeah," he said. "I got that." He checked his watch. "So are we going to Reno or not?"

"Not," Nash said, pulling her closer.

"Not," she murmured against his lips.

"Okay, then," Preston said. "I'm out of here."

A minute or so passed—hard to track time when you were in the bliss zone—and then Preston's car pulled away, accompanied by some raucous horn beeping. Regan wasn't sure, but she thought it might have been the first few bars of the wedding march. That or the Bon Jovi version of "You Give Love a Bad Name."

Later, much later, as they were driving back to Juniper Basin, Nash glanced across at her, eyebrows raised, eyes sparkling. "And you know what the most deliciously ironic part is?"

"What's that?" she asked, not sure what he was talking about but willing to play along.

"Our happy ending is all thanks to Harper."

She stared blankly at him for a moment, but then she got it. "He's the one I was running from when I took off across the plateau and fell through the roof of the lava tube."

"Yes, and he's the one who shoved me in after you."

"Curing you. Curing both of us," Regan said.

Nash's mouth curved in a wicked grin. "Imagine how pissed he'd be if he knew."

EPILOGUE

The sun fell warm on Nash's shoulders. July 25. His birthday. His 168th birthday.

He'd offered to take Regan somewhere special for the weekend, but she'd insisted nowhere was more special than the house at Big Sur. So here they were, just finishing a late brunch on the deck, while far below, three sea otters played in the waves. Closer at hand, a pair of robins plundered Regan's strawberry patch, ignoring the striped chipmunk scolding from the branch of a nearby tree. Bees hummed among the flowers in the planter, and a soft breeze, hardly more than a ripple of air, teased a loose tendril of Regan's hair.

Almost a year he'd been cured now, but every day revealed a new miracle.

"What are you staring at?" Regan asked.

"You," he said.

"Why? Do I have jam on my nose or something?"

"Or something," he said, then leaned across the table to whisper in her ear.

"Play nice," she said.

"But naughty's so much more fun."

Her cheeks turned faintly pink, probably because his "naughty" remark had reminded her why they'd been so late for brunch.

Malcolm cleared his throat. "Will there be anything else, sir?"

"We're fine, thanks."

"Very well, then." Malcolm turned on his heel and marched off toward the kitchen.

Regan's gaze followed him out of sight. Then she turned to Nash with a mischievous grin. "I thought he'd never leave."

Which sounded promising.

"I have a surprise for you."

Which sounded even more promising.

"Close your eyes. Don't open them until I tell you to."

Ah, yes. Better and better.

He closed his eyes and Regan placed something in his hands.

"Okay," she said. "You can look now."

He wasn't sure what he'd expected—a can of whipped cream maybe or some glow-in-the-dark condoms—but certainly not a book.

"*Something Wicked*," he read, then shot her a questioning look. "That's your name there just below the title. You wrote a novel?"

"The editor thinks so, but it's really a true account

of what happened to us last summer in Juniper Basin. I changed the names, of course, and the locations, but it's all there, the whole story—Harper, the vampire bikers, Tyler and the snake, all of it. I felt this overwhelming compulsion to tell the story, you see, but if I'd written it as an article, I'd have had to leave out all the good stuff. This was a sort of compromise. So? What do you think?"

Nash opened to the first page and read aloud. "'The late-afternoon sun beat down like a curse. A hundred and two in the shade. Not that there was any shade. 'Go to hell, Ms. Sullivan,' reclusive philanthropist William Whittaker Chase had said the last time Erin had pestered him for an interview. And here she freaking was.'" He glanced up. "I like the beginning. How does it end?"

"Like this." She took the book from him, placed it on the table, then climbed onto his lap. "The heroine thinks she's headed straight to hell." Smiling, she framed his face in her hands and kissed him. "But instead she finds her own little corner of heaven."

His chest tightened. "I love you," he finally managed to say past the lump in his throat.

Regan's teasing smile grew tender. She kissed him again, this time with lingering thoroughness.

Heaven, Nash thought. Sheer heaven.

And he couldn't ask for a better ending than that.

Enjoy the following excerpt from
Catherine Mulvany's
dazzling time-travel romance,

Run No More

Despite the fact Tasya wasn't a hundred percent convinced that time travel existed outside the pages of science fiction, she sat in a corner of Dona Elizabete's library, compiling lists of time-traveling pros and cons. Topping the con list was, *Aside from Father Duarte's claims, we have no proof this works.*

On the other hand, what did she have to lose by trying? If she disappeared in a puff of smoke, what would it matter? And conversely, if it worked, she could change Ian's life, fix it so he didn't spend thirty years in a wheelchair in prison.

Or was that, fix it so he fell in love with her and put her life back on track?

Okay, her determination to save Ian was not entirely selfless. She'd been cheated of her happy ending the first time around. A second chance was only fair.

Since when is life fair?

Since never, but . . .

Besides, he won't remember anything that's happened between the two of you because—surprise, surprise—it won't have happened yet. What makes you think even if you do manage to track him down that he'll fall in love with you again? What if he decides you're not his type? What if he's already in love with someone else? What will you do then?

She didn't know what she'd do then, but she wanted

the opportunity to find out. If she didn't try to save Ian, she'd never forgive herself.

On the pro side, she wrote: *I can make him happy. I can make myself happy.*

"Tasya?" Dona Elizabete poked her head into the room. "You'll never guess what I just saw."

Tasya smiled at the older woman's excitement. "What?"

"Paulinho and Vania kissing."

"Really?"

Dona Elizabete gave a giddy laugh. "I was never so surprised in my life. Is it not romantic?"

Romantic? Yes. Surprising? No. Tasya had known from that first blistering moment of eye contact in the hotel lobby that the two were meant for each other.

Suddenly, a degree of wariness and speculation tempered Dona Elizabete's enthusiasm. "But perhaps you felt something more than friendship for Paulinho? You expected—"

Tasya shook her head. "I love Paulinho, but only as a friend." She stared out the window, thinking of Ian. Not Ian in his grave, but Ian as he had been in real life and in her oh-so-vivid dreams. She smiled, remembering. Definitely a sexual component to that relationship.

"You are pleased, then?" Dona Elizabete said.

"About Paulinho and Vania? Certainly." She paused. "Dona Elizabete, I have something to ask you."

"Yes?"

"Do you believe Father Duarte's claim? Do you think it's possible to travel through time?"

"Yes, but it is not a journey to undertake lightly." Her eyes radiated compassion. "You're thinking about Ian Mac-Pherson."

"Yes—if only he had never agreed to help steal Milagre, things would have been different. He wouldn't have wasted half his life in prison. He wouldn't have lost the use of his legs."

"Nor would he have met you."

"I want to go back, Dona Elizabete. I want to interrupt the chain of events that destroyed his life. If there's the slightest chance I can rescue him, then I owe it to him to try."

"You realize the man in the past is not the same man you knew?"

"Yes."

"You loved him, didn't you?"

"Very much."

"How would you feel meeting him again as a stranger?"

Tasya clenched her hands together in her lap. "I know it won't be easy, but I want to try. The stones belong to you, however, so the choice is yours."

Dona Elizabete shook her head, a faint smile playing about the corners of her mouth.

"Don't say no. Please."

"Child, you misunderstand. I am guardian of the stones, but I don't own them. No one does. The stones choose who travels."

"What do you mean?"

A worried expression came over Dona Elizabete's face. "Not everyone is suited for time travel. Father Duarte believed only a few people have the right physiology."

"Only those who feel the heat," Tasya guessed.

Dona Elizabete gripped Tasya's hands. "The stones can't generate heat. Tourmalines aren't alive."

"But I felt it. More than once."

"What you felt was the heat produced by your own body."

"Then why doesn't everyone feel it?"

"Because there are variations in body chemistry. Yours

is atypical. The heat your body generates creates a pyro-electric charge in the tourmaline, a charge that I suspect promotes healing and enables time travel.

"Father Duarte believed there was a continuum of sensitivity, but there's no way to judge where on the continuum a person falls. With healing, it makes little difference, but with time traveling, it makes all the difference."

"You mean some people are successful and some people aren't. That's all right. I don't mind failing, but I'll never forgive myself if I don't try."

Dona Elizabete sighed. "If only it were so simple." She squeezed Tasya's hands. "Some people are successful," she said. "And some people die."

"I don't care. I have to try. Without Ian, I might as well be dead."

"According to the legend," Dona Elizabete said, "the *babalaô* predicted that a traveler would appear to reunite Milagre and Gêmeo, then use the stones to journey to the past." Dona Elizabete shot her a worried look. "But not even the *babalaô* could tell whether or not the traveler would succeed."

Tasya lay in bed in her hotel room on Copacabana Beach, unable to sleep. Some time after midnight, she'd made up her mind. She was going to try time travel.

If her gamble paid off, there was a good chance she could save Ian years of pain and frustration. If not, she'd die. Electrocuted, according to Father Duarte's eyewitness account of a failed attempt.

Shivering, she pulled the covers up to her chin.

Electrocution. A more painful way to die than the barbiturate overdose she'd planned. She tried not to think about it.

Unfortunately she could think of little else. She had

read Father Duarte's diary from cover to cover. In it, he'd described the tragedy in elaborate detail. Blackened fingers cooked onto the crystals. Smoke rising from the victim's head moments before his hair caught fire. The body jerked by involuntary spasms so violent they'd dislocated vertebrae.

Focus on something else.

Okay, given she survived the trip up the river of life, would she recognize the uncrippled, uncareworn, unembittered thirty-year-old version of Ian MacPherson? *What did you look like back then, Ian? What about you was different? And more important, what about you was the same?*

Even Paulinho had pointed out that there were no guarantees. The younger version of Ian did not know her. He might not come to feel the same way about her that the older version had. How would she feel, Paulinho had demanded, if she made this sacrifice and Ian rejected her?

How would she feel? Devastated, certainly. And worse, betrayed. But she refused to let such worries dissuade her. Her mind was made up.

Tasya spent the next few weeks preparing for her journey. Her most challenging task was obtaining an out-of-date American passport. If the forger wondered why she wanted a passport that listed her birth date as August 28, 1951, he asked no questions, any qualms he might have felt soothed by a thick stack of crisp new reais.

Clothes were no problem. Current retro styles would work, and long, straight hair had been as fashionable then as now. To transform herself into an authentic child of the seventies, all she really had to do was use a pale lip gloss and switch to liquid eyeliner. "Forget the false eyelashes, though," she told Paulinho after sitting through an old

James Bond movie—historical research—in which the heroine had worn stiff black fringes on her eyelids.

The day of her scheduled departure dawned clear and sunny. Vania took the day off work so she could be there to lend moral support. "Don't worry about anachronisms," she told Tasya. "Since no one there knows what the future looks like, they aren't apt to be suspicious if you accidentally mention Tiger Woods or DVD players."

Tasya traced the words etched into Dona Elizabete's sundial. *Tempus fugit.*

Vania squeezed her arm. "It will be all right."

"I wish I were certain of that," Paulinho said. "I wish you luck, *moça.*"

An awkward silence fell.

They had gathered in the shade of the palms on the tiled terrace behind the Sodré mansion—Tasya, Vania, and Paulinho. Dona Elizabete was inside, retrieving the tourmalines.

"It's a beautiful day," Vania said, obviously uncomfortable with the silence.

A beautiful day to die.

No, she wouldn't think that way. Tasya shifted her weight from foot to foot. *Think about Ian. Think about all the pain you can spare him.*

Paulinho touched her shoulder, and his troubled gaze snared hers. "Are you sure about this, *moça?*"

She nodded, afraid she'd cry if she tried to speak.

He gathered her in his arms and folded her close. "I will miss you."

And I you. She hugged him tight.

Vania tapped her shoulder. "My turn," she said, holding out her arms.

Paulinho released her, and she and Vania embraced.

"You are so brave," Vania whispered, "but if it were Paulinho in danger, I would do the same—whatever the cost."

Tasya held her at arm's length, smiling despite the whirlpool of emotions threatening to drag her under. She swallowed hard. "Thank you."

Dona Elizabete emerged from the house, carrying a stone in each hand. A shaft of sunlight penetrated the palm fronds to bounce off Milagre in a dazzle of refracted and reflected rays. Dona Elizabete took a step forward and the light hit Gêmeo, too. For a split second, the glare blinded Tasya.

Then Dona Elizabete moved into the shade, and the miniature fireballs changed back into tourmalines. "It is time," she said.

It began with the pain. Tasya had experienced Milagre's power firsthand. She thought she knew what to expect, but she was wrong. Not even Richard, damn his soul, had prepared her for this. Fiery bursts of agony ricocheted up her arms and down her legs. They rocketed through her torso, exploded in her brain. "Tahiti," she said. "May 1972. Tahiti, May 1972."

Her lungs burned. Her nerve endings screamed. Every hair on her body stood up. Oh, God, was this the part where she burst into flames? "Tahiti, May 1972. Tahiti, May 1972."

The humming drowned her out, growing in volume and intensity until it reached thunderous proportions, as loud as a jet engine, as loud as an avalanche, as loud as the end of the world. And she vibrated to its frequency.

Something was happening to her. Something more than the heat scorching her body, more than the fearsome cacophony assaulting her ears. Something inside.

She felt as if her internal glue had come unstuck, as

if she were no longer a sum of parts but the parts themselves, individual atoms quivering on the verge of dissolution. Maybe no one traveled through time. Maybe those who didn't burst into flames disintegrated, shattering into millions of invisible splinters.

"Tahiti, May 1972. Tahiti, May 1972."

The roar and the pain crescendoed in tandem. A brilliant blue light engulfed her for an instant. Then the sound and heat were gone, as if they'd never been. The garden rippled once, then stabilized. Solidified.

She flexed her hands. The stones had vanished, but she was still there. Still alive. Still in Brazil. She'd gazed long into the abyss, and the abyss had spit in her eye, eliminating the last hope, destroying the last dream. Disappointment leached the color from her world. She closed her eyes, weary and brokenhearted, too spent for bitterness, too sad for tears.

"*Meu Deus!*" Dona Elizabete said from behind her.

She'd forgotten the others. If only they'd forgotten her. She was too tired to deal with a postmortem of her failure; all she wanted was time alone.

"*Meu Deus,*" Dona Elizabete said, more softly this time.

Steeling herself, Tasya turned. Or tried to. She stumbled into a gardenia bush she hadn't remembered being there.

"*Bem-vinda ao Brasil. Bem-vinda, viajante.* Welcome to Brazil. Welcome, traveler."

Tasya met Dona Elizabete's gaze, and shock waves shuddered through her. She recognized Dona Elizabete's eyes, Dona Elizabete's voice, but this was not the Dona Elizabete she knew. This was the dark-haired woman of her long-ago dream.

"What year is this?" Tasya said.

Enjoy the following excerpt from
Catherine Mulvany's thrilling novel of
passion and sorcery,

Shawdows All Around Her

"Caitlin O'Shaughnessy is scheduled to arrive in Edinburgh at eleven-oh-six a.m. after a short layover at Heathrow," Janus said.

"Fascinating." Pressing the satellite phone to his ear, Dominic pried his eyelids open far enough to glance at the alarm clock on his bedside table. Bloody hell. A quarter to six? Janus had called him at a quarter to six? He'd been in bed less than four hours. "And exactly how did you come by that bit of information?"

"I have contacts, Fortune. She made hotel reservations, then canceled, saying she planned to stay with relatives."

"But the only relative she has in Edinburgh is—"

"Wallace Armstrong. Precisely. Volunteer to pick her up at the airport."

"Why?"

"I want you to get close to Caitlin O'Shaughnessy."

"When you say 'get close' . . ."

"The young woman may be in danger," Janus said.

"So that was 'close' as in bodyguard close?"

"And she may know something."

"Ah. 'Close' as in spy-on-her close."

"This is hardly a joking matter, Fortune."

"That was hardly a joke. More like mild impudence."

Janus grunted. "Any luck locating her stepfather?"

"None. He's still registered at his hotel, but no one's seen him in days." Dominic stifled a yawn. "Not at the hotel and not at the symposium. He was a no-show for his scheduled lecture yesterday."

"What do you think? Is he working with our smugglers? Against them? Is he an innocent bystander? Or is he perhaps not involved at all? Is his disappearance merely a coincidence?"

"I don't know. My guess—and I emphasize that word—is that he's an innocent who got caught up in events beyond his control," Dominic said slowly. "I spoke with a waiter who saw Armstrong with Grant."

"When?"

"Monday night."

"And Grant's body turned up. . . ?"

"Wednesday, though by the time the maid found his body, he'd been dead for approximately eighteen hours. Apparently he ingested a lethal combination of sleeping pills and whisky. Officially, the police are calling it a drug overdose, but the tabloid press—and many members of the academic community—are talking suicide."

"He left no note?"

"No note and no manuscript," Dominic said. "I don't think his death was an accident. Nor do I buy into the suicide theory."

"You suspect he was murdered."

"How else do you explain the missing manuscript?"

"But murdered by whom? Our smugglers have no motive."

"No apparent motive."

Janus didn't respond immediately. "Have you considered the possibility that Magnus Armstrong may have killed Erskine Grant?"

"It occurred to me, yes."

"Perhaps the reason no one's seen him is that he's gone into hiding."

"Perhaps," Dominic said.

"You don't sound convinced."

"If I'd just arranged a colleague's 'suicide,' the last thing I'd do is run. His disappearance is suspicious in itself. I don't think the man's that stupid."

"Nor do I," Janus admitted. "I agree. It seems likely someone's kidnapped him. Why? We don't know. What we do know is that there's a probable Calixian connection."

"You're referring to the protection charm I ripped off the thug who attacked me in Magnus's hotel suite. Funny thing about that charm. Did I tell you it was a Fraternitas?"

Janus didn't say anything for a second or two. "Interesting. I'd heard rumors they were . . . extending their membership. Apparently those rumors were true."

"Extending their membership?"

"And their focus."

"Meaning?"

"An informant—a somewhat unreliable informant, admittedly—reported months ago that an outlaw branch of Fraternitas has turned to smuggling." Janus gave him a moment to absorb this new information. "If Yuli was searching Armstrong's suite, it suggests Armstrong has something Fraternitas wants."

"The manuscript?" Dominic said.

"That would be my guess."

"But why? The *Chronicles* have been around since the seventeenth century. Why the sudden interest?"

"Every schoolchild on Calix knows the legend of Brother Hamish, the monkish recluse of the Aeternus Mountains, but how many people have read the actual manuscripts? None. They've been under lock and key for literally hundreds of years. Perhaps they hold the secret—"

"To what? Eternal life?"

"To something of value," Janus finished, unruffled by Dominic's sarcasm.

"Such as?"

"Hidden treasure, perhaps. Didn't Brother Hamish claim he'd seen a ship full of Roman gold lying at the bottom of the sea?"

"It's a legend, Janus. Granted, some people take it literally. Adventurers have been searching for the wreck for hundreds of years. But if the gold truly existed, don't you think someone would have found it by now?"

Janus considered that. "We may never know why the thieves want the manuscript back," he said at last. "Suffice it to say they do want it and badly. Your assignment is threefold. One, find Magnus Armstrong. Two, recover the manuscript. And three, identify whoever's plundering the treasures of Calix."

"Got it. Find Magnus Armstrong, recover the manuscript, and identify whoever's plundering the treasures of Calix. Plus, get close to Ms. O'Shaughnessy, and perhaps while I'm at it, leap a few tall buildings in a single bound."

Silence stretched the length of three heartbeats. "This is a serious matter of national security, Fortune. Your levity is misplaced. I could sack you on the spot for insubordination."

"You could, but you won't. I'm the most daring and resourceful agent you have."

"Daring and resourceful, yes. Also smug and disrespectful."

"Too true, Janus, but then again I'm charming as hell. Ms. O'Shaughnessy doesn't stand a chance."

Though Caitlin and Bree would be stuck at opposite ends of the plane on the short hop from Heathrow to Edinburgh, they'd been lucky enough to secure adjoining seats in first class for the long flight to London.

Unlike Caitlin, who was too wired to do anything but fret, Bree had slept for the first half of the trip and was now engrossed in the in-flight movie, a quirky action-adventure film featuring George Clooney and some blonde Caitlin didn't recognize.

Caitlin had tried to watch the film, and she might have succeeded in distracting herself if the star had been anyone but Clooney, whose dark eyes and stubborn jaw reminded her of a younger version of her stepfather.

Frustrated, she dug around in her backpack for the thriller she'd purchased at the airport. Instead her fingers latched onto the manuscript she'd slipped into her bag at the last minute, hoping against all reason that it might yet provide a clue to Magnus's disappearance.

Starting at the beginning, she began to read.

A few minutes later, she let out a muffled whoop and grabbed Bree's arm.

Her friend stared at her as if she'd lost her mind. "What is it?"

"Oh, my God! Oh, my God. Oh, my God. Oh. My. God!"

Bree removed her headset. "What?" she repeated.

"The manuscript Magnus sent me."

"What about it?"

"I think I know now why he included it with my bones. It mentions John Napier."

Bree gave her a blank stare.

"John Napier, the mathematician I wrote about for

my dissertation. Hamish MacNeill, the author of the manuscript, actually knew Napier. My God, if only I could have gotten my hands on this before I wrote my dissertation. I mean, to read a firsthand account by someone who was well acquainted with the man . . ."

"Quite a coincidence," Bree murmured, readjusting her headset.

"An amazing coincidence," Caitlin said. "See?" She shoved the pages under Bree's nose. "Right there. See?"

Frowning, Bree removed her headset a second time. "See what? Is this supposed to be English?"

"Takes a while to get used to the spelling, and some of the vocabulary's obsolete, but yes, it's English. Check out this page. Hamish mentions Napier, bemoaning the fact that his friend and mentor is dead."

" 'Called out of this transitorie lyfe.' In other words, deceased. I get that. But where does it say John Napier?"

"Right there." Caitlin pointed.

"You weren't kidding about the spelling. Jhone Neper? That's the bones guy, right?"

"Right, though Napier's logarithm tables were his greatest claim to fame. Without logarithms, there'd have been no slide rule. Without slide rules, there'd have been no space program. Napier's logarithms might not have been as life-altering as the discovery of fire or the invention of the wheel, but on a scale of one to ten, they score a solid eight and a half."

"Uh-huh." Bree glanced at the actors on the miniature screen.

"What I've always found most intriguing about Napier, though, are the rumors that he dabbled in sorcery. I mean, talk about contradictions. Here's this brilliant mathematician and inventor—did I tell you about his designs for war machines?—not to mention a theologian of some repute. And yet he's suspected of being in league with the devil."

"Fascinating," Bree said, *fascinating* in this case clearly code for "Hint, hint. You're boring my socks off."

Caitlin shot her an apologetic grin. "Not as fascinating as George Clooney, though, huh?"

"Not even close."

DESIRE LURKS
AFTER DARK..

BESTSELLING PARANORMAL ROMANCES
FROM POCKET BOOKS!

NO REST FOR THE WICKED KRESLEY COLE

He's a vampire weary of eternal life. She's a Valkyrie sworn to
destroy him. Now they must compete in a legendary contest—
and their passion is the ultimate prize.

DARK DEFENDER ALEXIS MORGAN

He is an immortal warrior born to protect mankind from ultimate
evil. But who defends the defenders?

DARK ANGEL LUCY BLUE

Brought together by an ancient power, a vampire princess and a
mortal knight discover desire is stronger than destiny...

A BABE IN GHOSTLAND LISA CACH

SINGLE MALE SEEKS FEMALE FOR GHOSTBUSTING....
and maybe more.